BLACK PELICAN

WILL GREED AND LUST UPSET THE OUTER BANKS COMMUNITY?

INTRODUCING ATTORNEY CARRIE WOODBRIDGE

SANDRA BRIGGMAN
DAVID BRIGGMAN

*Dedicated to our wonderful
children and grandchildren*

*Thanks to the Talk:House restaurant in Stuart, Florida,
where the plot was developed over a few cocktails*

She called her daughter Roanna's cell phone to find out where she was, but she didn't answer. Two more calls went unanswered. It was so unlike her.

1

Joan and Anthony Roselli lived on Sanderling Street in the city of Chesapeake, Virginia. They had three children: Roanna, fourteen, Josh, eleven, and Penny, nine. Joan worked as an administrative assistant for Johnson Travers, a financial advisor in Norfolk, and was well respected. Joan was thirty-eight years old and stood five feet eight inches tall. She was in good shape and worked hard to keep her weight down and her body fit. Her dark brown hair was long and wavy, and it bounced when she walked and was the envy of all the women she worked with- and the men, well, they just wanted to touch it. She controlled the Travers office like a dictator, demanding attention to detail, even of the boss, which worked well for him. He didn't have to be the bad guy when Joan was around. This also kept the men from hitting on her. They feared that she would either knock them flat on their ass or she would give them more projects and be especially critical, demanding excellence more than usual. Joan's office was in one of those high-rise buildings in downtown Norfolk near the MacArthur Center. Johnson Travers was considered a small company in the field, so money was a little tight, which only warranted a lower level floor of the building, the second floor. This actually worked out well because it was more convenient for the company's customers. The first floor held restaurants, a coffee shop, and boutiques available to the building's occupants and to the public. It was great for Joan - she would stop every morning and get her "skinny, grande, extra hot, soy, three pumps sugar free caramel, three shots espresso" to kick-start her work day. Joan NEVER used an elevator. No matter how bogged down she was with files and her coffee, she took the stairs. Several times a day. She also worked out at the little rinky-dink work out room she'd finagled her boss into putting together in one of the rooms they rented. It was known by all, even her boss, not to remotely think about interrupting her thirty minute lunch session each day.

Anthony was an English teacher and assistant football coach at one of the high schools in the district. He, himself, had been a football player in high school and college but his career didn't go anywhere due to a knee injury his third year in college. With a degree in education and his love for the sport, he was perfect as a high school teacher and coach. Anthony was very popular with his students and rarely had a complaint from any of the parents. He never sent students to the principal's office. His most notable classroom phrase to a student who was talking or checking a phone instead of following directions was, "You ever been hit by a Mack truck?" A smirk would follow, the student stopped doing whatever he was doing, and all was fine. Problems with girls misbehaving were an unusual experience for him. They all swooned with crushes for Mr. Roselli. Anthony was six feet two inches tall and had wavy blond hair. Though he carried a few extra pounds, he was muscular and had the physique of a football player. As a defensive coordinator for the Hornets, his teams had had the fewest points scored against them throughout southeastern Virginia for the last three years. There was talk of Anthony getting the head coaching job in the near future and he was ready to take it on. Both students and players knew exactly what he expected of them in clear concise terms. His players found a place on the bench if they didn't 'get it'.

The Roselli's attended church at St. Mark's, a relatively small Episcopal church about a mile from their home. The church was built in the 1980's and was more contemporary in architecture than you would expect. No standard pews but rather connecting chairs that could be taken apart and rearranged. The only stained glass in the building was behind the altar - a huge wide cross with vibrant-colored glass in an abstract pattern. It was beautiful and very modern which went with the overall theme of the church. All three children were in the youth group, which generally gathered on Sunday afternoons for a dinner, a Bible lesson, and games chosen by the kids. Roanna was a very pretty teenager. She had fairly long blond hair the color of her father's. She often wore it up in a ponytail. She had high cheek bones and a sharp, firm jaw. Her large blue eyes twinkled whenever she talked to anyone and she smiled easily. Roanna had a crush on a sixteen year-old boy named Bobby Lee Gillespie, who was also a member of the youth group. All the girls loved Bobby Lee. He was easy to like. He liked to have fun and goof around; he would pay attention to the girls and give them attention, and he was not afraid to embarrass himself for a laugh. Definitely a confident young man. Bobby Lee knew Roanna had a crush on him and he thought it was cute. They attended the same high school and would often cross paths in the hallway. Both flirted with each other, but they had not officially gone on a date yet.

On the night of March 3, Joan got home before Anthony who had after-school meetings. Josh and Penny were already home, but not Roanna. Roanna rode the high school bus, which was different from the one her younger siblings rode. Josh and Penny had no idea where Roanna was or could be. They were always dropped off by their bus before Roanna was. Joan was a little miffed with her daughter that she didn't call before making any plans and wanted to know why and where she was. Joan was already not looking forward to a confrontation with her daughter after a tough day at work. She called Roanna's cell phone to find out where she was, but she didn't answer. Anthony got home around five and Joan met him at the door with news that Roanna wasn't home yet. Anthony also found that odd and he himself called his daughter's phone. Two more calls went unanswered. Now Anthony was getting concerned. Where was his precious older daughter? It was so unlike her. Anthony pulled out his school directory and called Roanna's history teacher (her last class of the day), Mark Johnson, and asked if he knew where she might be. Maybe she stayed after school to finish homework or a project? But he had no clue. Another call went to her school bus driver, who said Roanna got off the bus at the usual stop. Around six o'clock, the Roselli's' concern morphed into fear. Where was Roanna? She was never this late and she always answered her phone in fear the phone would be taken away from her or restricted. Why have a phone if you don't answer when your parents call? Joan started to call every friend of Roanna's that she could think of, frantically asking if they knew where she was. Had they seen her, and when was the last time they saw her? While Roanna was making calls, Anthony couldn't just sit or stand around, so he walked to where the bus would have dropped off Roanna. There was no sign of her or her things.

2

The Seaview area of the city of Chesapeake was an older development in southeastern Virginia. Despite the name, it had no view of the sea. Homes typically had three bedrooms, a small kitchen, one and a half baths, and a combination dining room/living room. Most were built during the '80's boom with a few into the '90's. Sanderling Street, in the western part of the city, was a twisted narrow road that stretched about a mile and had little through traffic.

Donald Sprout lived at 325 Sanderling, a lower middle class section of Sea View. The homes were generally well maintained from the outside. The gardens and lawns had matured growth that was nicely taken care of. Sprout's home was typical for the neighborhood, but on the small side. In Sprout's home, the bedrooms were tiny. One had his twin bed on the floor with no frame, another had an old futon he'd picked up at the thrift store, and a third he used for some storage. There were two recliners, a table, and a TV in the living room. And nothing else. The furniture looked like '60's vintage. The kitchen had the customary appliances and a small counter top. No table or chairs. The house had been a fixer-upper when Sprout bought it but he did nothing to improve its condition. He just lived in it. The entire inside needed a lot of tender loving care. Sprout lived alone – a twenty six year-old bachelor. He had dated once or twice in high school but not since. He took Liz Gomar to the prom and a few weeks later he took her to the movies but she dumped him. She couldn't stand his hands all over her and he was a bore. Nothing fun or lively about him, she told her friends, so why waste the time. When he graduated from high school, Sprout enlisted in the Air Force and within a year, was stationed in the Middle East. Within two months, his tour of duty ended. He was aboard a C-130 Super Hercules flying a supply mission when a Taliban rocket hit and disabled the plane. All personnel were ordered to bail out, which Sprout did. He broke his leg when landing but was rescued within four hours while under heavy enemy fire. Those four hours were some of the longest in his life, never to be forgotten. After Sprout was transferred stateside, he had surgery to repair his injuries and recuperated in a VA hospital. He received a medical discharge, and after a number of months, he got a job at Home Depot and bought the house on Sanderling Street. His employment lasted less than a year due to failing a random drug test. After moving from one job to another, barely paying the bills, he was now a bottom rated carpenter working for a house builder.

Sprout saw everything in his life as unfair. It was unfair that he didn't have the brains to do well in school. It was unfair that he wasn't handsome and a babe magnet. It was unfair that he wasn't an athlete. It was unfair that he had no usable skills. It was unfair that he still had a limp from his accident. It was unfair that the government money ran out on his medical stipend. And, in his mind, he had lots of people to blame.

Sprout would usually head out for work around eight a.m., the same time that school buses were making their final rounds in the neighborhood. He hated the damn buses, stopping every few blocks. He watched the children - he guessed high schoolers - walking to the bus stops, waiting for the buses, or getting on the buses. He did like watching the girls with pony tails, short skirts, and developing breasts. He especially liked blondes.

Sprout's neighbors really didn't know him. Marsha Willis, two doors down, brought him some muffins when he moved in, but had hardly seen him since. Jack and Sally Rider, across the street, occasionally saw Sprout come and go without even a wave. Back in the summer, Jack had confronted Sprout about his overgrown yard, about it being an eye sore in the neighborhood. Sprout told him it was none of his business. When Jack offered to mow Sprout's grass, Sprout replied "Whatever. Just don't think about asking me for money!" So Jack took care of the lawn from then on.

3

The Atlantic Ocean along the coast of North Carolina is absolutely beautiful. There is something about the peacefulness of listening to the waves crashing that lures people to the coast. Cody Delaney was one of those people. Had been all of his life. Cody loved mornings, or what was left of them. Getting up around eleven a.m. meant that he had his breakfast when most were eating lunch. With his girlfriend gone to work most days, he'd usually made himself a bacon, egg (over medium), and cheese biscuit. One or two. He'd walk across the street with their pit bull, Reef, sit in the sand at the ocean's edge, and savor the meal. Reef often shared the sandwich. He'd carefully notice the waves, the direction and strength of the wind and if any surfers were in sight. Didn't matter what time of year or what the temperature was, he had to get out in the water on the best beach to try. He was a surfer dude.

Cody looked the part. He was six feet or so tall and weighed 170 pounds, with slightly long, blondish hair usually tied in a ponytail, and a strong, tanned face. Well, most of his body was tanned. Both ears were pierced, usually adorned with earrings in the shape of a lion, symbolic of his zodiac sign, Leo. He had a surf board tattoo on one arm and a Buddha tattoo on the other. When not working, he wore either baggy, maroon swimming trunks when surfing or, when not surfing, loose, untucked, frayed shirts with baggy cargo shorts which looked like rejects not suitable for sale at the local Goodwill store and flip-flops.

Cody used to drive down to the "Buck" beach, where a lot of other surfers hung out or were out on the waves. A few years ago, the beaches had been re-nourished by ships pumping thousands of cubic feet of sand onto miles of beaches, widening them. This changed where the best surf could be found. The "hot" beach before the re-nourishment, the "Buck", was nothing special now. A sand bar had developed a hundred yards out and killed the rollers. Today, for instance, there were just small shore breaks. For strange reasons, maybe nostalgia, the dudes still congregated there, would check things out, and most would decide to try surfing elsewhere. There was always someone who professed to know where the best waves were. Jack, better known as Chump Change, told everyone within listening range, which for Chump Change was quite a distance, that he'd had good rides up off of Mansion Beach, north of the town of Duck.

Cody headed back to his car and headed north. Reef rode shotgun, usually with his tan head with white markings sticking out in the breeze. Calling his vehicle a "car" was somewhat of an exaggeration. He actually had a name for the thing: Kassie, after a girl in high school that he dreamed of dating. So now, he rode around *in* Kassie. This Kassie was an old, beat up Jeep, which looked like it had bounced around on the plains of Africa on safaris after being used during World War I. Held together with Bondo, covered in various shades of Rust-Oleum, with a surfboard attached to pipes he'd mounted onto the roof, wet suit bundled in the trunk, and a bottle of Gatorade on the passenger seat, he was good to go. That is, if the thing would run. He loved Kassie, but the damn thing kept breaking down.

It took the ocean a while to catch up with the air temperature, so, in March, the water was pretty chilly. Tuesday was a sunny day and the temp was near seventy, so if Chump Change was right, Cody would have some good rides. Mansion Beach was not an official name, like most of the surfing beaches. They referred to it that way because of the huge houses built there on the beach. Ten-bedrooms, twelve-bedrooms, even eighteen-bedrooms were common. Cody often gazed up at the rental houses, wondering what it was really like inside and what it might feel like to stay in one of those places. Cody's job, his "night" job, was serving tables at the Atlantic Bistro in Kitty Hawk, close to his beach box home. One night, a guest he served, left his cell phone at the restaurant. Cody picked it up and threw it into his pocket. About half an hour later, it started ringing and Cody answered. It was the phone's owner. He was staying in one of those mansions and hoped someone had found his personal phone. Cody was dying to see the inside of one of these places so he offered to drop it off the next morning. When he did, he was invited in for a Bloody Mary, which Cody declined, but he got a quick look around the main floor. Everything was first class as far as he could tell and he was impressed by how much cash it must have taken to decorate it.

Cody turned onto Sea Spray Lane, a street accessing eight of these huge rental houses. He parked on the road side, getting all four tires off of the paved street so as not to get a ticket. Three other cars were parked there, probably other surfers. He opened the trunk, retrieved his wet suit and climbed into the back seat to undress and put on the suit. Practice had cut this ritual down to a couple of minutes. Once in his suit, he gathered his board and his Gatorade. Sea Spray Lane ended at a 'T' on Sea Oats Lane. Cody walked to the end of Sea Oats where there weren't any houses and crossed over the dune and onto the beach with Reef in close step. He sat down near the ebbing waves, placed his board on his lap, and started the mandatory waxing of the board's top surface. He would pay half attention to the waxing and half to what was going on out on the waves. Reef chased the seagulls and sanderlings. The wind was light and from the east. Four dudes and one girl were bobbing up and down, watching behind them for the ideal wave. Cody liked what he saw, stood up, and, as was his habit, took a running start and splashed into the cool Atlantic. Surging through one wave after another and paddling quickly, he reached his cohorts. Reef sat near the ocean and watched Cody intently. He would not go into the water until Cody yelled "Reef, swim."

Cody asked "Crew" (named due to his haircut), "Sup?"

Crew answered, "They're rolling today, dude. Why so late?"

"Had stuff, man. Then went to the Buck."

Crew said, "Dude, you missed some big rides."

It only took Cody a couple of minutes to catch his first wave. He chose the wrong direction and the wave broke before he had much momentum. The next effort was much more successful. Cody loved to surf, and he was very good.

By the time he was done for the day and back at the water's edge, Chump Change had arrived on the beach just to see what was going on. Chump Change had an age old habit of belittling anything. For example: "I just bought a Cadillac." "Aw, that's chump change." "I just won a hundred grand in the lottery." "Aw, that's chump change." Hence the name. Cody didn't know what Chump Change's real name was, and it didn't really matter.

Cody asked, "Hey dude, what took you so long?"

"I dunno, was hanging with a hot chick, but she left before we got friendly, ya know. Wasted my time. So, it looks good up here."

Cody said, "Yup, just like you said."

Chump Change offered Cody a drag on his joint which Cody obliged. They stood there without saying a word for a moment, just staring out at the ocean. Cody said, "Time to be sweet to the high rollers and make some coin."

"Gotcha dude, let's roll." Walking toward their parked vehicles and the last house in the row, something caught Chump Change's eye.

"Dude, check out the third floor."

Still a hundred yards or so away, Cody saw what caught Chump Change's attention. A couple was lounging on the south end of the balcony. She was naked, completely naked, had long dark hair, and she looked like she had curves in the right places. *He was older. How did he get so lucky?* they both thought to themselves, stopping to admire the scene.

"Wonder how she's staying warm."

"Must be true love!" Cody said with a laugh and shook his head, looking down.

4

Sea Dunes Concierge Realty had ventured into a new real estate market on the Outer Banks of North Carolina. The company, created eight years ago, was involved in property management renting vacation homes for their contracted owners, and home purchasing. Their unique calling card was providing owners, buyers, and sellers concierge services. At a price, of course. In the rental market, they only handled high-end properties. The homes were, without exception, directly on the beach or one lot away from the beach. Sea Dunes managed either luxury rental homes with a relatively small number of bedrooms (four to six) or the really large units that had twelve to sixteen bedrooms, with luxury amenities. The sales department only handled these types of units as well.

Sharna Curry was Sea Dunes's owner and ever-present manager. She had received a master's from Georgetown University and her doctorate from UNC Chapel Hill. She got involved in hospitality and then real estate when employment befitting her education did not pan out. Had to pay the bills. She worked as a front desk attendant at a major chain hotel and was quickly promoted to the daytime concierge. She received Employee of the Year awards for three straight years. Sharna was then, as a member of Les Clefs d'Or, designated as a Certified Hotel Concierge. She honored all of the principles of the organization and took that culture to Sea Dunes.

Sharna was single, middle-aged, brilliant, attractive but not pretty, and full of life. She kept her hair short with blond highlights. While working as a concierge at the hotel, she had taken classes to earn her real estate brokerage license. After learning the ropes as an agent in Outer Banks real estate, she bravely started her own company. At first, she sold or rented whatever came her way. Soon she saw a niche when developers started building huge houses north of the town of Duck. The niche, was concierge real estate services.

Sharna was well liked by her employees. When something was said to her that required a response, Sharna often twisted her face which gave an answer without any verbiage. The office loved the facial expressions. Sharna trained her staff thoroughly, embedding in them quality customer service, which was what the company was all about. It was rare that anyone voluntarily left Sea Dunes.

In the rental division, the concierge services were provided to both the renter and the owner. Owners paid a fixed fee for services that included white-glove cleaning and inspection of all home functions, such as appliance operation, lighting, etc. Any minor repairs were covered except for materials. Sea Dunes also paid utility bills, which were financed by each owner maintaining a fund for such costs. Turnkey at its best!

The concierge services provided to renters, or "guests" were extensive. These services included but were not limited to courier services, dinner reservations, boating trips, fishing excursions, sailboat rentals, underwater adventures, water sports equipment, golf courses, horseback riding, surfboard rentals, bar hopping, limousines, hair stylists, massages, manicures, dentists/physicians, unusual outings, and just about anything under the sun that a customer would want or need. When a potential guest inquired about a property, an agent would go to the property when it was unoccupied and conduct a personal live video tour. The advantage of this type of presentation over the more common stock video tour was that the customer could ask to see specific details of the house that might otherwise not be obvious. The agent would also conduct an in-person tour if the potential client was in town. All the rental paper work was handled via the internet with an agent on the phone to clarify any questions that might come up.

Upon check-in, there was one simple document for the client to sign. This was important, since many clients had their office or personal assistant make most or all of the rental arrangements. The agent would then escort the guest to the contracted home. Once there, the agent supplied brochures and pertinent information for anything that the guest had expressed interest in and gave the guest a tour of the facility, which included a demonstration of televisions, cable boxes, appliances, bed massage units, and the like. The refrigerator and pantries were stocked with food items that the guest and his or her staff had indicated they enjoyed. This included alcoholic beverages. For the guests that requested maid and / or butler services, the agent would personally introduce the guest to the personnel. For additional services that the guests might require, the agent would leave her (all the agents were women) contact information and business card.

The rental price for the homes, in-season, ranged from $20,000 to $80,000 per week. The concierge service added an additional $5,000 with the reservation plus $4,000 per week which did not include housekeepers, rentals, or other expenses. That fee provided an agent, known to the guest as a Concierge Service Manager, or CSM, to be available 24/7. A CSM had only one guest to take care of. This could result in a dozen calls a day to nearly none. The CSM would shop, personally provide any transportation services required in one of the company's limos, and generally wait on a guest's every whim.

Phoebe Razario was a CSM.

5

Phoebe was an Italian version of a Barbie Doll. She had long, straight, dark hair that she brushed over one shoulder. She had naturally tanned skin, even in the winter, stood five feet six and weighed 115 pounds. Her body could have qualified her to be a model. She loved pizza with pineapple and anchovies and private time with a container of Talenti mango gelato. Neither seemed to go to her waist.

Phoebe was excellent at her job. She wore upscale dresses that looked sexy and she could calm and charm the seeds out of an apple. Her face would light up when she would meet a guest in a sincere, not artificial way. Her voice had that smooth, earthy tone that men found irresistible. She didn't have to get to the office until noon today. Her client was being driven in from the Norfolk, Virginia, airport by one of Sea Dunes's chauffeurs and wouldn't arrive until around four. Her client was Preston Kerrigan who was a running back for the Chicago something-or-others. Phoebe was not a sports fan but had to study Kerrigan's career so she could be fluent in his language. Hence, she'd get to the office and check out the internet to learn as much as possible. Kerrigan wanted to have a month-long retreat to get away from the fans and press and to chill. His year had gone really well. He'd amassed over fourteen hundred yards on the ground and caught forty nine passes. His agent wanted to renegotiate his contract, but Kerrigan was uncomfortable with the appearance of being a money grabber, so he wanted to reflect on it. He liked the team and the guys he was with, liked the coach and was also worried that the chemistry would be upset if he held out for a better deal.

Kerrigan's agent, Patrice Cheger, who had made the rental arrangements, had listed a number of requirements. First, work-out equipment. Lots of work-out equipment. Phoebe had to call six house owners before she got one to agree to have the heavy equipment (with appropriate mats to preserve the floors) brought into the house. Also required were a few bottles of Four Roses

Single Barrel bourbon, boxes of Raisin Nut Bran cereal, almond milk (can't call it milk anymore), Café Bustelo espresso K-Cups, Dave's Killer Bread organic Powerseed in the red bag, cashew butter, and blueberry preserves. Phoebe had everything set.

She was looking forward to meeting the popular handsome famous Preston Kerrigan. Her research indicated that he was popular with his teammates and comfortable with the fans. He sponsored a few charities in the Chicago area and was frequently seen at the children's hospital, sitting with the sick children, giving them souvenirs and tickets to games when they were well enough to attend. Kerrigan stood six feet four inches and weighed 235 pounds, give or take.

Marco, one of Sea Dunes's limo drivers, arrived at the office at four thirty p.m. with his passenger, Preston. He was traveling alone, without his wife. Phoebe introduced herself and asked if he would like anything to drink. "Bourbon on the rocks would be nice," he said with a faint smirk. She asked Whitney, the office administrative assistant, who moved around the office like a hummingbird, to go to the office pantry. She pulled out a bottle of his requested Four Roses, put some ice in a glass, and poured him a healthy portion. As she handed the freshly poured drink to him, Preston said, "Wow, you have my drink." "Yes sir, that's what we do here." Phoebe then went over the concierge instruction sheet which included her personal phone number and a very few do's and don'ts. Kerrigan signed the document without a glance.

"I would recommend that you put my number on your phone's contact list."

He quipped, "You bet, honey."

"OK, are you ready to get to your beach home?"

"Sure, you going with me, right?"

"Yes sir!"

6

Kerrigan's luggage was still in the limo. Phoebe asked Marco to take them to 32 Sea Cove Lane. Marco already knew what the destination was, but this was Phoebe's way of showing that she was in charge. The drive from the office in Duck to the house took less than ten minutes. Marco pulled up to the front steps, shut the limo down, and got out and opened Kerrigan's door.

"Mr. Kerrigan, you have arrived." said Marco.

"Please, call me Preston, Miss Razario. I assume it's 'Miss'."

"Yes, it's 'Miss'. Please call me Phoebe. Marco will take care of your luggage. Let me give you a tour."

The main entry was a door with a beautiful stained glass window facing west with a view of the Currituck Sound on the third floor. Once in the foyer, one had to walk to either side around a wall to a sitting area with ultra-thick love seats facing a fireplace framed in solid oak beams. The master suite was located on the south side of the sitting area. The bedroom was over five hundred square feet and had a sliding glass door on the ocean side and wrap-around windows going around the south side. A sixty-five inch flat-screen was mounted in a bookcase, hidden behind a wooden door. When the TV was turned on from either of the remotes attached to both nightstands, the TV door would automatically lower. Of course, the sheets, pillows, and duvet were first class. The bathroom was actually two rooms. One held a large hot tub and a shower that a pony could fit in. It had over twenty water nozzles. The other held two sinks opposite each other and two toilet enclosures. The floor consisted of wavy teal colored tiles. Hundreds of dollars' worth of fixtures dominated both areas. There were also two walk-in closets that were bigger than most bedrooms.

On the other side of the main sitting area in the middle of the first floor was another master bedroom suite, which was significantly smaller than the first one, but still large by any standard. This suite also fronted the ocean. Behind it, on the sound side, were two smaller bedrooms with their own bath. Both of these bedrooms had their furniture removed and a variety of exercise equipment had been brought in. Just as Kerrigan requested. Kerrigan smiled when he saw the equipment.

"I'm impressed."

"Preston, it is what you asked for, yes?"

"Absolutely, but I really didn't think you would do it!"

The path upstairs was either by a wide, semi-circular staircase or an elevator. Preston and Phoebe chose the stairs, which opened to the massive living area. Its walls were entirely composed of windows overlooking the breaking surf. Two sliding glass doors, which automatically retracted when a button was pushed, opened to the wide deck that surrounded the house on all but the sound side. The balcony was outfitted with a variety of padded deck chairs and lounges, plus another hot tub, and a wet bar. The living area back inside was furnished as if it were three separate rooms. One area, facing away from the ocean, had sectional sofas that could comfortably seat ten facing a massive sixty-five inch TV with all the bells and whistles. Each of the other two areas was on the ocean side of the room, and they were separated by a gas firepit. Each had seating in roughly a circle, open on the ocean side, with a small table for every two seats. The dining area was divided from the living area by a partial three-foot-high wall, which included a wet bar and hidden desk. The room was dominated by a chestnut table that could seat two on each of its four sides. The table could be expanded to seat twelve. The kitchen was behind a large serving bar; it had two extra-large refrigerators, two double gas stoves, and every gourmet small appliance and gadget one could imagine. On the half third floor, above the kitchen and dining area was a game room with a ping pong table, foosball table, air hockey table, and a couple of video games.

Preston was impressed again. He said, "The only thing missing is a beautiful woman," with a flirty smirk.

Phoebe said, "Now, now, we don't want you to get into trouble! I'll call tomorrow to see what you'd like me to arrange. What would you like to do for dinner?"

"How about a simple seafood restaurant. Someone for company would be nice."

"I'll make a few calls. When would you like to eat?"

"I already missed happy hour, so maybe in an hour?"

"Uber, taxi, or limo?"

"Taxi, please. Unless SHE has a car."

"That is not one of the services that Sea Dunes provides. I'll see if one of my friends is available and I'll call you pronto".

7

Donald Sprout watched high schoolers get off the bus. He noticed a tall boy and a blond girl with a pony-tail get off and walk away together. The bus left and the kids dissipated in every direction, except this boy and girl. It was cloudy and beginning to get dark earlier than normal. A storm was moving in. The boy and girl walked over to a bench in a small park overlooking a little brook and sat down. Sprout watched from across the street, his car turned off in a parking lot. The couple chatted and giggled and flirted with each other. The girl then leaned over and kissed the boy on the cheek. The talking stopped as they looked at each other and started to kiss intensely. Sprout watched jealously; he wanted to be that boy.

Two days later Sprout was sitting in his ancient Chevy Impala watching again. The boy and the girl didn't waste any time getting down to kissing. Then, they went behind a tree instead of to the bench. Sort of like not wanting anyone to see them. Sprout was getting perturbed because his view was now limited. He got out of the car and slowly and carefully shut his door. He didn't want to scare those two, because then they might stop and he wouldn't be able to see. Sprout crouched down and quietly but swiftly went from tree to tree to get a better look. He found a place to squat down and he pulled out his phone. He put it on mute and started to snap photographs. He was so proud of himself for thinking of the photos because now he could look at them any time he wanted to. Yes, they were really kissing and Sprout licked his lips. Then the boy's hands started to roam all over the girl's body. The boy put his hand under her shirt and she yelped but then started to laugh. What would they do next? This was such a good show. *Next time I will record them,* Sprout thought. *That could and should be me, not that boy.* He reached down and held his erection, imagining what it would feel like inside that girl.

Sprout witnessed the pattern one more time. This time he was ready and waiting squatting in the same location with his video function ready on his phone. He knew he had to make a plan to take care of his urges. He knew it wouldn't be easy. He wasn't stupid, after all. When he was home, he checked the internet on his outdated laptop for information on the effects of chloroform as well as the date rape drug, liquid ecstasy. Ecstasy was actually gamma-hydroxybutyric acid, or GHB, a hypnotic depressant. He learned that its effects range from drowsiness, forgetfulness, and loss of muscle tone to seizure-like activity, slowed heartbeat and breathing, and coma. The coma could last one to two hours, with full recovery usually occurring by eight hours.

He worked with a guy who did dry wall and knew he could score some ecstasy, cocaine, crack, or any variety of drugs. Donald himself preferred alcohol and marijuana. It took two days for this guy to show up at the construction site. Sprout asked him about getting some ecstasy and how long it would take. The guy chuckled and asked, "Find yourself a reluctant girlfriend, huh, Sprout?"

"Naah. My girl likes the stuff."

"OK, I'll have it for you tomorrow. Bring cash."

Now Sprout was ready. He sat in his Chevy anticipating the event. He wore dark clothing and a hoodie. He felt clever because he'd thought of the hoodie at the last minute. He watched and waited. The teens got off the bus. *Oh my, that ponytail*, he thought as he licked his lips. The same boy and girl started their walk in a different direction from the rest of the kids and when everyone else was gone, they turned around and went to sit on the bench this time. *How lovely*, he thought sarcastically. When the kissing, hand-holding, and petting finally ended, the boy and the girl got up and went their separate ways as they had done every time before. The clouds made the early evening sky darker than normal. Donald got out of his car and crossed the street. He walked right up to the girl.

"Miss?"

She looked over at him and said, "Yes?"

"Do you know where the Judsons live?"

Shaking her head, she said, "No, never heard of them."

That brief exchange gave Donald a chance to get shoulder to shoulder with the girl. He quickly covered her face with a chloroform-soaked rag. She became limp, and he held her up as straight as he could. He looked around to see if anyone was watching. He saw no one so he lifted her up over his shoulder and cut through a path that led to an area between houses that was overgrown. He knew the area well. He stumbled once, half landing on the girl, then gently brushed her hair back, and got up. The girl's phone rang in her backpack and Donald had to put her down to find it. It said "Mom". He took the phone and crushed it with his boot against a large tree root and left the phone and her backpack behind. In about five minutes, he was at the rear of his house and opened the unlocked back door and carried the girl in. He laid her on the futon in the second bedroom and waited for the girl to wake up. He knew he needed to get the ecstasy into her ASAP. As she woke up, he held her head and offered her a straw to drink from. She looked at him with wide eyes and drank. The chloroform had made her mouth parched. She was scared. He laid her head back down and brushed the strands of her hair out of her face with his hand and leaned down to smell her. He took a deep breath of her scent and whispered, "You are mine now." As the girl became drowsy, he fondled her firm breasts and ran his hands down her belly to her crotch. He thought, *just like that boy was doing*. It was more than he could stand.

Donald had to have her. He had such an erection it actually hurt. He nudged her to see if she was awake and she did not respond. It wasn't the way he wanted things, but it was better than nothing. Better than no girlfriend. Better than being alone. He fumbled with the button on her jeans and deftly unzipped her. Such beautiful, soft, unmarred skin. Her panties were a goofy childish print. But lace. Oh, he loved lace. He tried to get the jeans pulled down, but they jeans were so tight-fitting he was having difficulty. He cursed out loud and managed to get them to her knees. He was so excited he couldn't wait any more. He undid his sweats and yanked them off. He would have to bypass taking her shirt off now. He just couldn't wait any longer. He laid down on top of her and exploded.

Stupid, stupid, stupid! You couldn't wait, could you? You are stupid, stupid, stupid, he thought.

8

Joan Roselli was close to hysterical not being able to find her daughter. She and Anthony talked to each other to figure out what they should do about Roanna. Anthony decided to call the police. A young officer named Johnson arrived and rang the doorbell within minutes of the 911 call. Anthony answered the door and invited the policeman in.

"According to your call, your daughter did not come home from school today. Correct?"

Joan said, "Yes" wringing her hands. "She is never this late and she always answers her phone."

"How often has this happened?"

Joan said, "She never fails to come home. Sometimes she's a little late, but not like this."

"Did you try calling her?"

Anthony said, "Of course! We've tried calling every fifteen minutes or so. At first it continued to ring and went to voicemail. Then, it went straight to voicemail, so it somehow got turned off."

"OK, does your daughter normally go anywhere after school? Any activities? Stay at any friend's house?"

"No."

"Alright, let me get some info. How tall is she, what does she weigh, what was she wearing, any photos?"

Joan said, "Anthony, get him a photo. She's five four. Probably weighs a hundred, maybe a hundred five. She has blond hair that's fairly long and she usually wears it in a ponytail. Today, she wore a greenish shirt and jeans."

"What does she like to do?"

"She played girls basketball but hurt her knee and had to miss the end of the season. Likes to listen to Ariana Grande and Dua Lipa."

"Who?"

"I don't know – you know, kids."

"Does she have any birthmarks, anything that is unique, any tattoos?"

"She has a small tattoo on the inside of her left forearm. An angel. Both her ears are pierced and she always wears earrings. She still has a slight limp from the knee injury."

"OK, I'm going back to the station to file a report. Because she is under seventeen years old, we can get an AMBER Alert out once this data is entered into the system. Time really is of the essence. One last question, does she have a boyfriend or does she like a particular boy?"

"No, none that she has told me about."

"If you think of anyone, call me immediately. Here's my card. If you think of or remember anything else, anything at all, call us."

"Oh my God. Please find her," Joan cried, wiping her eyes. Joan was now shaking.

Anthony returned with Roanna's school photo. He gave it to the officer and put his arms around his wife. He whispered, "We will find her."

To the officer he said, "What can I do? I can't just sit here, what can I do!"

"The best thing you can do is stay here in case she shows up and I will be in contact real soon. Also, if you remember anything at all that could help me, please call this number. We will be forming a search team immediately."

9

Cody got home around three in the afternoon. His girlfriend, Phoebe Razario, had left him a note. "I have to do a check-in and maybe take one of the clients to a restaurant. Will call. XOXO Phoebs." Cody knew the drill. Phoebe often had evening duty. He didn't really mind that too much since he served tables most nights at the Atlantic Bistro. He was due to start his shift at four, so he started his ritual of showering, trimming his beard so that it looked like it was only four days old, getting his hair back into a neat ponytail, and making himself smell and look like a server, not a surfer.

Cody and Phoebe became a couple three years ago and there hadn't been many issues clouding the relationship. They met at Midgett's, a fine dining restaurant where Cody worked as a bus boy. Phoebe was a waitress. They dated on and off for a while until they both changed employment. Cody was hired as a server at the Atlantic Bistro, and Phoebe took the CSM job at Sea Dunes Concierge Realty. Cody kept suggesting that they shack up, and after two years of spending nights over at each other's place, they decided it would be better financially to live together. Share expenses. They rented a small house, locally called a beach box, in Kitty Hawk. The house had a fairly large living room / dining room combination, a small kitchen, and two bedrooms. They slept in one bedroom and used the other as a large closet for Phoebe's work attire and her small workshop. Phoebe needed a wide variety of clothes for her business. She had classy short and long dresses for the meet and greets, utilitarian shirts and shorts or designer jeans for escorting clients to various activities, and a wide selection of jewelry. The workshop area was set up for Phoebe's stained glass hobby. She had taken lessons from the local stained glass guru for years and was now very good at designing and making a wide range of pieces. Her boss at Sea Dunes, Sharna Curry, liked Phoebe's work and allowed her to display and sell some of her nicer pieces. The office secretary took care of any sales to clients or home owners.

Cody had the living room decorated in classic surfer style. Which is to say that there were three boards resting against the wall - two Wave Riding Vehicles boards, the Slayer and the El Jefe, and a Jason Stephenson Monstra. And a full-sized poster from the movie *Endless Summer*. The movie embodied his bucket list – to travel around the world looking for the perfect wave. He had some money saved for such an adventure, but knew he needed a lot more. He felt certain that one day he would do it. He just didn't know if Phoebe would go with him.

Cody's other prized possession was a small replica of the Wright Brothers' first plane. He loved aviation and was fascinated by what the brothers accomplished. Every year he attended the December 17 anniversary celebration of the Wright Brothers' first flight. On a bookshelf in the dining area, Cody had two books on flying: *The Airplane Flying Handbook* and *The Student Pilot's Flight Manual*. These represented another item on Cody's bucket list: learning to fly.

Cody was ready to get to work. He threw on the Apple watch Phoebe had surprised him with last Christmas. It was a convenience, since employees couldn't have their cell phones in their possession while on the clock. Everyone was to leave their phones in a rack behind the bar. With the Apple watch, Cody could see if a call or text was coming in while he worked.

The Atlantic Bistro had a retro look about it. Half the bistro was a very popular high-end bar with comfortable bar seats with backs. The cushions were maroon colored. The liquor bottles on the shelves along the rear wall were backlit, giving the bar a cozy atmosphere. The bar itself was shaped like a shortened "U." Many locals staked out a seat, enjoyed their favorite martini or whatever, ate at the bar, and continued sipping the rest of the evening. Regulars as well as tourists.

The remainder of the room had a row of tables relatively close to one another other on one side and discreet booths with head-high padded benches on the other side. At the end was an open kitchen. Each table had a small lamp that accented the dim indirect lighting. The Atlantic Bistro was no ordinary Outer Banks restaurant.

The Bistro bragged about its unusual variety of martinis and cosmopolitans, but it also featured sixty wines from around the world. A certified sommelier was always available for recommendations.

The menu always included Wagyu steak, duck, racks of lamb, and fresh seafood brought in from the docks of Wanchese, half an hour away. Appetizers were worth the visit. A plate with Brie cheese, presented one way or another, carpaccio, and foie gras was highlighted.

Cody was the "gold" server, given the best tables. His looks and style made every customer feel comfortable and special. The ladies usually flirted. At the Bistro, the server of a table escorted the party to "his" table (there were no female servers). Cody would introduce himself and would initially address comments to the person who made the reservation. Once his people were seated, he stooped down to be at eye level with the diners. He handed out the alcoholic beverage menu with its extensive wine list, asked if anyone would like a cocktail or glass or bottle of wine (calling for the sommelier, if desired), and handed out the simple dinner menus. Being personal and gaining their trust was paramount to a good tip. When he returned with drinks, Cody, back down at eye level, would explain the selections on the menu and describe the specials of the night. Making eye contact with each patron, the appearance of not being in a rush, and listening intently to every comment or question was his method, and it worked.

When Cody initially started waiting tables at the Bistro, the dining room manager told him that he was not to write down patron's orders while at the table. He thought it was tacky and not befitting of a classy place like the Bistro. Cody did well until the second month he was there. After taking the order for a four-top, he walked back to the computer to enter the drinks and food for the bar and kitchen. However, a customer at another table got his attention and asked a number of questions. Cody thought he remembered the original order, but he made a hot mess of it. The diners at his table were not happy. One of the men was especially upset and began to raise his voice. A loud discussion ensued, and the manager had to take over to calm things down and make things right. At the end of his shift, Cody talked to the manager, who had since left the Bistro. The discussion was unpleasant. The manager made some oblique suggestions that Cody needed to do it the Bistro way or leave. Cody convinced him that he could take notes discreetly while listening to the order and not be "tacky." The manager relented and told Cody he would let him try it his way, but that Cody would be watched. Cody developed a note pad with the table seating shown and a short-hand method to record orders. S1 was for the first special, FR, for a rare filet mignon, and so forth. He would only take notes when a diner was looking at the menu, not while they were looking up at Cody. It worked and the manager gave him and the other servers his blessing to use such a system.

10

Wednesday nights in March were pretty dead for most restaurants on the Outer Banks, but not at the Atlantic Bistro. Cody had three tables by six, and he picked up another by seven. The Bistro staffed the restaurant with ample servers, so it was rare that Cody couldn't give each of his tables the attention he liked to give them. He continually scanned his tables to notice any body language that might indicate that he was needed. He was not intrusive, never making an unrequested visit asking, "How is everything?"

A little before eight, a tall, muscular man entered with a gorgeous brown-haired lady. He knew the female; it was Jessica Rigon, Phoebe's best friend. Jessica was on the short side, so she always wore five-inch heels. That helped to accentuate her beautiful legs. She was wearing a lovely flowing white sun-dress with lace, and her makeup was impeccable. Her blue eyes beamed when she smiled, and her hair was pulled back and knotted at the top of her head with strategically planned strands hanging loose, outlining her face.

Cody whispered to his buddy and fellow server Gavin, "Who's the big dude with Jess?"

"No clue. Never saw him."

It was Cody's turn in the barrel, and he got a nod from Amelia, the hostess. He walked up to the couple and introduced himself.

Jess said, "Hi, Cody."

Cody acknowledged her. "Jessica."

"This is my handsome date, Preston Kerrigan."

Cody showed the couple one of the booths and went through his usual routine.

Preston ordered a Peach Cosmo for the lady and asked if they had Four Roses Single Barrel bourbon. Cody replied, "Yes sir." Kerrigan asked for a double on the rocks and told Cody they weren't in any rush. When Cody brought them their drinks,

Preston said he would let him know when they were ready to order.

Jessica asked Kerrigan, "Have you ever been to the Outer Banks before?"

"Once when I was a kid. Maybe eight or nine. We stayed in a little motel in Kitty Hawk."

"This is Kitty Hawk!"

"Oh, it was dark and I didn't recognize the area. That was twenty years ago. My dad was in the navy and stationed up in Norfolk. My mom got sick, so we didn't travel much. Loved the beach though."

Kerrigan downed his first drink and Cody arrived at the table.

"Anything I can do for you?"

"Another round, please."

"So, Phoebe tells me you are a football player. Sorry, I'm not much into football. Where do you play?"

"Chicago."

"The Packers?"

"Sweetheart, wash your mouth!" He laughed. "We Windy City people find that team to be full of evil bastards. But we beat them once this year, so that felt good."

"And you are one of the runners?"

Again, another chuckle. "Yes, a running back, or tailback. The quarterback hands me the ball and I do the hard part. Smash into three hundred pounders and hope to live for the next play."

"Doesn't that hurt? Don't you get all bruised?"

The second round of drinks arrived. "Thanks, man. You can bring us the menus now."

Cody did as instructed.

"I'll show you my legs later. Name a color and I'll find it. We just had spring practice and some of my defensive teammates think it's really funny to beat up on the ball handlers. Our coach lets it go to a point but obviously he doesn't want anyone to get seriously hurt. Yeah, it hurts for a week but the trainers take good care of us. Give us some strong stuff - nothing illegal you know, just strong stuff."

They opened their menus.

"What's good here?"

"Everything. What are you in the mood for?"

"Other than you, honey? A big steak, I guess."

"Their New York strip is first class. Wagyu."

"Who?"

"It's a type of beef. Marbled, a really nice cut."

"Sold. You?"

"Let's see what the specials are."

Cody ascertained that Kerrigan and Jessica were ready to order and walked over, crouched down to be at eye level, and said, "Would you like to know what's on special this evening?"

"You bet."

After Cody described the specials, Preston said, "OK, sweetie, what sounds good?"

"I'd like the Bistro Mahi Mahi".

"It is especially good tonight. And you, sir?"

"I understand that the New York strip is worth a try."

"It's great."

"Good, extra large, medium rare."

"Fine. Can I get you another beverage or some wine?"

"Jessica? Red or white?"

"Better be red, I guess. I prefer red over white even if I am having fish." She gave him a shy sexy look.

"Good, get us a nice merlot?"

"Let me call over the sommelier."

Lucas joined Cody at the table. "They're having the New York strip and the Bistro Mahi Mahi. The gentleman would like a merlot."

"Good. To pair with your choices, I would like to recommend a 2015 Sonoma merlot, Thirty-Seven Reserve."

Preston glanced at Jessica, whose facial expression broadcasted, "Don't look at me."

"Sounds good to me."

After the sommelier poured them their first glass, a tall, semi-balding man in his forties approached Kerrigan and Jessica's table.

"You're Preston Kerrigan, aren't you?"

"Yep."

"You're a bastard, leaving the Skins the way you did. Just a big money-hungry prick."

Preston stood up, grabbed the man by the shirt, and said, "OK, loser, what are you going to do about it?"

Despite being in Kerrigan's hold, the man kneed Preston in the groin and Kerrigan doubled over. Cody, Gavin, and the Bistro manager, Brady, rushed to the scene. Kerrigan, down on his knees, grabbed the man's legs and Lucas got him in a bear hug. Lucas was fifty pounds and four inches bigger than the man and wrestled him to the front door where his embarrassed wife joined him. Lucas said, "Sir, you're going to have to leave now. Give me your credit card to pay for what was served and we'll call it even– which is to say that we won't call the police."

"That bastard grabbed me first!"

"Your credit card, please."

His wife dug her card out of her purse and gave it to Lucas with her hands shaking. The sideways looks she was giving to her husband meant that they were not going to have a pleasant conversation after they left the Bistro.

"What were you thinking, you jerk?!" she said as they exited out onto the street.

Lucas went back to Kerrigan's table to see if he was okay. He apologized to Preston and Jessica and said that the man would never be welcomed in his establishment again.

Preston, acting like nothing happened, shrugged his shoulders and said, "A scrawny little punk can't hurt a big macho football player, right?"

Jessica, still unsteady from the commotion, straightened from her cowering position and, shaking her head said, "I don't think I can eat a thing now."

"Aw, come on, baby. It's okay. Just talk to me and look at me. I got you."

She smiled at him, but when the food came to their table, she didn't even take one bite. She was embarrassed and shook up from the commotion. She really didn't know how far Preston would go to silence that idiot.

11

Cody woke up the next morning and snuggled with his very naked girlfriend. Phoebe always slept naked. She stirred, opened her eyes, and smiled. A killer smile any time of the day. Their mid-sized pit bull, Reef, put his paws up on the bed and licked Phoebe's cheek– not the wakeup call she expected. She brushed Reef down, saying, "Too early for kisses."

"Phoebs, your friend Jessica came by the Bistro last night. With a guy named Preston."

"Yeah, I sent them there."

"How did Jess know Preston?"

"Oh, he's a client. Just came in yesterday and wanted to have company for dinner. I thought Jess would like a free meal."

"I'm not sure Jess enjoyed the show."

"What show?"

"Some dirtbag made a scene. Jess's date didn't like it and they got physical. We threw the dirtbag out. Jessica didn't eat her dinner and I think Jess's date was a little sore. In the wrong place!"

"Oh God! Did Jess and Kerrigan leave?"

"No, they stayed and he ate. I think the alcohol helped."

"Fuck, fuck, fuck! I gotta get up and call Jess." Cody laid there in bed and admired the scene. Reef licked her bare legs.

Phoebe called Jessica and, after five rings, Jess answered.

"Jess, OH MY GOD, Cody just told me what happened in the restaurant last night. I am so, so, so sorry. Was Kerrigan a jerk?"

"No, no, no, it's all good. Um, I can't really talk now."

"Oh, okay, sorry. Just tell me if Kerrigan is okay?"

"He's fine. Mighty fine, Phoebs. Stayed the night and it was great. I mean, really great."

"So are you with him now?"

"You bet. But he's still sawing the logs."

"When he is up, have him call me. I need to check to see how he is and give him breakfast recommendations."

"Gotcha."

Cody was curious about the arrangement and figured out from the phone call that Jessica had stayed the night.

He said with a little smirk, "You operating a dating service now?"

"Whatever a client wants!"

"Okay, sign me up. I want you! Come on over here."

Walking over to Cody's outstretched arms, she said, "I can't think about sex right now!"

"Phoebs, love making, my dear, love making."

She laid next to him and snuggled into his arms and murmured, "Okay, okay. I don't have a lot of time, ya know. It can't be one of your marathon 'love making' sessions."

"I'll take whatever I can get. I can never get enough of you!"

Cody kissed the top of her head and with his hand lifted her chin up to be able to kiss her lips. He whispered as he lowered his lips to within an inch of hers and said, "Dreamy, you have such dreamy eyes. And, you have a gorgeous face and such luscious lips. Lips like candy and a body, oh you have such a wonderful body. I get lost in you." He kissed her so gently that she melted. Phoebe kissed him back and the intensity deepened. Now she wanted him.

Phoebe ran her hands up into his hair and heard him moan. She rolled him over so she was on top of him and knew he was ready for her. She teased him a little by rubbing against him but not letting him enter her. When she couldn't take it any longer, she let him in and they made slow steady love until he couldn't hold out any longer.

Cody said, "You better get what you need because I can't last much longer."

With each pulse she thought, "What I need is a ring, you idiot" but the words didn't come out. She knew better than to push that subject. With that, he was done and she was satisfied.

12

Phoebe hopped into the shower, anticipating a call from Kerrigan any minute. Cody talked to her while the water poured over her body.

"Where are Jess and the big guy staying?"

"Up north of Duck, in one of those big houses on the beach. Sea Cove Lane."

"Got lots of money then. Mister big guy?"

"Pro football player. A real good one from my research, so, yeah, he's doing okay."

"Jess, a one-night stand?"

"Guess we'll find out."

Phoebe dried her hair, put on some makeup, not that she needed any, and got dressed. She had paper-work she could do at the office until she heard from Kerrigan.

Not long after Phoebe arrived at the office, Kerrigan called.

"Hey, Phoebe, interesting restaurant you sent me to last night."

"I heard. What the heck happened? I'm so sorry. What can I do for you?"

"No worries, I'm okay. Jessica was just what the doctor ordered. Took care of my wounds. Speaking of Jessica, she's not into the cereal I like. She says she knows a good little joint that serves a great breakfast, but she says it's down in Nags Head on what she called the beach road and it will take a while to get there. Named after a guy and a gal. Sound familiar?"

"Yeah, I know the place she likes."

"Is it somewhat touristy?"

"No, mostly locals. Good place to go. She driving?"

"That's what she offered."

"What do you need me to do for you today? And ask Jessica to give me a call when it's convenient."

"I'll tell her. I'll call you after we eat."

Meanwhile, Cody got ready for another surfing day. He walked across the street with his ever-present dog to the beach to check out the waves. A gentle southeast wind was pushing in sea rollers. So Cody returned to the house, made his usual bacon, egg and cheese biscuit, and started thinking about what he'd seen up at Mansion Beach yesterday. He wondered if the undressed babe he saw on the balcony was the guy's wife, his girlfriend, or a local providing inside entertainment. Jessica's date was a rich football player. Rich men like and can afford beautiful female company. "When the cat's away, the mice will play" was running through his head. He was curious and had an inside source, Phoebe.

The following morning, Phoebe seemed in no rush to get to work. She showered as soon as she got up, just in case Kerrigan called, but then lingered over coffee and half of a bagel. She then went into the second bedroom to work on the design for a new stained glass project. Cody came in and sat down.

"Hey, Phoebs, how many of your clients are rich, single guys like the football player?"

"Well, first of all, the football player is married but came here alone. To answer your question, most are men traveling alone. Getting 'away' time. I know some of them are married, but don't know that about everyone."

"Do you normally provide dates?"

"No! What kind of business do you think I work for?! Geez, Cody. To answer your question, Kerrigan wanted a companion and I thought Jess would have a good time if she was available. Why do you ask?"

"Just curious." Half laughing he said, "I didn't know how much concierge service you all provided!"

Phoebe, also smiling said, "You being a smart ass?"

"You know me, Phoebs." And he gave her a sloppy kiss on the cheek.

Cody had errands to run and grocery shopping on his schedule. Phoebe hated to go grocery shopping, and, always being on call, she worried that she could have a car full of groceries and get a call from a client wanting something immediately.

Phoebe stopped her designing and thought about what Cody sarcastically suggested that the service would provide female companionship. She moved her head from side to side, her habit when mulling over an idea. Why not provide a service that some men want? Like an escort service. Not a raunchy escort service, but a high-class sophisticated date. Phoebe decided she was on to something but, after some thought, knew that Sharna would never go for it.

After a few days of running the idea back and forth in her mind, Phoebe decided to call Jess to ask her some careful questions about her date with Kerrigan.

"Hey, Jess. What's doing, sweetie?"

"I'm having a good time with your client."

"Yeah, I wanted to ask you about that scenario. If we had other clients come in who wanted female companionship and wanted to pay for it, do you think having some girl available would be a good idea?. I mean, would it work?"

"Phoebs, first of all, your boss would never go for it. And second, isn't that like prostitution? Like, illegal? Like, go to jail illegal?"

"I don't think it's prostitution if you just provide a date."

"Really, girl? You're not that naïve, are you?"

"Seriously, Jess, once boy meets girl, who knows what happens. You know, like what happens in Vegas stays in Vegas."

"Phoebs, you're not in Vegas."

"I know, but would you go on a date again if someone was interested?"

"Probably."

Nevertheless, Phoebe smelled an opportunity. Yes, Sharna wouldn't go for it. No question about that. But what if she offered the service herself, not as part of her job, but as a private business, so to speak? She had direct access to the clients and personal knowledge of who they were and most times a lot of information about what they liked. She thought about the details, both major and minor, that would have to be worked out. Who would she get for the "female talent"? How would she operate with them? How would she get the information to her clients? How would she work the finances? Most importantly, how would she keep the operation a secret?

13

Phoebe still hadn't heard anything from Kerrigan, so she decided it would be good to iron out some details to the idea running wildly in her head. First, where would the girls come from and how would she keep things confidential? The solution came directly from her past life. Phoebe had once aspired to become a model, eventually moving into TV, movies or whatever. She signed on with Virginia Talent, a modeling agency located in Virginia Beach, an hour and a half away but her career sputtered, and she never got anywhere in the entertainment business. Her career path led her away from modeling to the real estate business, but she still had contacts at Virginia Talent. She knew that she could request applicants for a fictitious modeling job and see if any of the girls would be interested in snuggling up with a millionaire. Then there was confidentiality. She would have to guarantee that the girls didn't leak what was going on. Her job, and maybe more, would be at stake. She didn't want paper trails but certainly had to have some sort of a contract. The "position" would be simply for a companion. She would add that the arrangement would be totally confidential and that legal action would occur if there was any breach. She would verbally warn anyone who signed on but also incentivize them by adding that if things went well, there would be future opportunities.

Phoebe decided that the smartest way to go about this would be to get a burner phone for herself and then lay a card with the burner phone number on it somewhere in each client's rental house. If she got a call, she would describe the arrangement. A one-nighter would cost $1,000. A girl 24/7 for a week would cost $5,000. Cash, up front. The client was to provide all meals and cost of entertainment for their companion as well. Phoebe would take fifty percent and the girls would take the other fifty. She would introduce the girl to the client in a little meet and greet date. If the client said it was a go, she'd collect the cash.

She figured that she'd work out any small details as they arose. She would tell no one, not even Cody.

Jessica was at work– an administrative assistant at the local hospital. Phoebe thought she could try an experiment with Jessica and Kerrigan, so she called Jess at work.

Phoebe said, "May I speak with Jessica Rigon, please?" "One moment please." Then Jessica picked up.

Phoebe said, "Hey girl, ya got a minute?"

"Sure, Phoebs."

"So, everything went alright with Kerrigan?"

"Yeah really great. Had to nurse him a little after what happened at the Bistro, but that didn't seem to affect his important functions, if ya know what I mean."

"Super. So here's what I've been thinking. He seems to want female company. What do I care? I thought of offering him a deal, a companion for a price. Would you be interested?"

"Yeah, I suppose, but I have to get to work. I can't afford to lose my job."

"Right. OK, I'll make him an offer and we'll split the cash. Do you care for how long?"

"The longer, the better, if the money's right."

"I'll let you know what he says."

Jessica hung up and thought, *what did I just agree to?? . . . . I could really use the money. I already know Kerrigan. So, what the heck?*

14

Colonel Richard Curtis Wilson had retired from the Air Force and was elected to the U. S. Congress from North Carolina three years ago. During his short time in Congress, he had aggressively pursued legislation to control immigration and a very popular bill to limit the production and distribution of narcotic medicines. One of the current senators from North Carolina, John Pritchard from Charlotte, had recently announced his intention to retire when his term was complete. Wilson was a Republican, as was Pritchard, and it seemed that if he wanted to exercise his ambitions to go further in politics, this would be his opportunity. Granted, he was pretty green at politics and had not established any state organization, but he was tall, lean, and handsome and was an excellent speaker. His reputation was good, he had no skeletons in the closet (at least, he thought), and he was a decorated veteran. He met with Pritchard to seek his endorsement in September, a year before the election. Pritchard told Wilson that if his campaign got some traction, he would give him his endorsement. Pritchard wanted to be hired on as a lobbyist when he retired and only wanted to back the person who was likely to win. He would then be a shoo-in for the job because they would "owe" him. A decent but usual strategy.

Wilson announced his candidacy a week later and met with the North Carolina Republican Committee to determine what assistance he might receive. The primary was scheduled for May, and since there were other party candidates, no aid would be available until after the election. The committee head did assure Wilson that he would be an excellent candidate. Two others had filed for the primary, Judy Lawless, mayor of Rocky Mount, and Bob Monte, a state senator. Neither had Wilson's charisma.

Donald Sprout hated Wilson. Wilson had been Sprout's commanding officer in Afghanistan when Sprout's plane was shot down. Sprout blamed all the officers involved for ruining his life, but especially Wilson. He thought that the supply mission that he was on was unnecessary, that the pilot flew into an unauthorized area, and that he wasn't rescued quickly enough. He had no basis for any of these conclusions, but why let facts get in the way?

He loathed Wilson.

Donald listened to the Norfolk talk radio station every day. During the morning newsy call-in show he heard that Wilson was running for the Senate. That really set him off. He had not been aware that Wilson was a congressman, and he dreaded the idea that this incompetent, evil (his opinion) man could be in Congress. He googled the Wilson campaign and got up to speed with the latest news. There were a few "Wilson for the Senate" photos with Wilson's toothy smile beaming delight. Sprout read all the promises that were clearly lies (to him), but when he read the biography detailing Wilson's Air Force service, he flew into a rage. Sprout printed out three photos of Wilson, took a Sharpie and drew a thick circle with a diagonal stripe through it on each, and tacked them to his bedroom wall. As he was doing this, he muttered to himself, "You won't live to see it, you motherfucker." Back on Wilson's web page, he looked at the campaign stops that were listed. In two days, on Wednesday, the next appearance was at the Crabtree Valley Mall just outside Raleigh at noon. Crabtree was approximately three and a quarter hours away. He decided that he would be there.

But what to do with Roanna, who Sprout now called Vixen? He had her hands and arms tied to her bed and her mouth sealed with duct tape. He would only remove the tape to feed her and would only untie her so she could go to the bathroom while he stood close by. He also watched to make sure she didn't run when she took the weekly shower he let her have. He decided that going to Raleigh wouldn't be unlike a normal work day. Vixen would have to remain in bed until he returned.

Sprout threw a load of his laundry in the washing machine so he could wear clean jeans and a flannel shirt for the trip. He had no real plan; he just wanted to see the evil man in person. Maybe have a few words with him, or maybe not. He didn't want any security guards noticing him.

The next day, he got up early, fed Vixen, gave her a heavy dose of OxyContin pills, took his underwear off and held his penis and told her, "I will give you a little of this when I get back." He then put on his clean jeans and flannel shirt, locked the door behind him, and got settled in his beat-up Impala.

His first stop was at a 7-Eleven down the road. He went in and poured himself a large coffee with cream and a ton of sugar. He picked out the largest apple fritter he could find and paid cash. He thought 7-Eleven's apple fritters were the bomb. Sipping his coffee and biting chunks out of the fritter did not calm him. He was seething. He both couldn't wait to see Wilson in person and was in a way dreading it. Two hours into the drive, his bladder was full, so he stopped at a gas station, filled the tank, grumbling that gas was more expensive in North Carolina, relieved his bladder, and bought more coffee. Taped to the inside window of the store was a "Wilson for Senate" flyer. He saw it and ripped it down. The clerk yelled "Hey, put that back" as Sprout left the store. Sprout threw him the bird and left. Once in his car, he crumpled up the flyer and said to himself, "Wait till you see what I do to you, you bastard."

He arrived at the mall at eleven thirty. He drove around the parking lot and saw no sign of any event, so he parked and entered through the Belk department store. He walked through the store, passing by the cosmetics section with all its smelly perfumes, and into the mall's main aisle, where he was immediately greeted with a sign announcing Wilson's appearance that day, to be held in the main court in the food court end of the facility. Once there, he found a group of people, possibly numbering close to one hundred supporters. What was wrong with these people?

He approached an older lady and asked, "You here to see Wilson?"

"Why, of course! We need a man like this in the Senate."

He mumbled, "Well you're not going to get him." The lady didn't hear what he said and didn't really care. At about ten minutes after noon, a man dressed in a suit got up on the small improvised stage and made a rousing introduction, including the ubiquitous phrase "Now, your next senator from North Carolina...." Congressman Richard Curtis Wilson stepped up onto the platform, waved with both hands, and smiled his wide smile. He was tall and handsome and looked like a candidate. The group gathered there gave him a thunderous greeting with hoots and hollers. A few started a chant, "We want Wilson, we want Wilson," and the crowd picked up the cheer. Wilson raised his arms in a gesture to quiet the crowd but was obviously enjoying the moment, and he stood there to soak it all in. He again raised his arms and more convincingly calmed the group.

One person was not cheering.

"Thank you, all of you, for coming out today. I have been honored to represent North Carolina for three years and I know I can continue to listen to you and take your message to Washington." The speech, probably used over and over, lasted ten minutes. In finishing, he said, "I'll be here for a few minutes and would love to talk to any one of you individually." From the back of the crowd, they all heard someone say, "You don't want to talk to me, motherfucker."

Everyone looked back to see who'd yelled the curse word, but Sprout turned around and walked away. The local police hired to control the event didn't waste any energy following him. Just some disgruntled jerk. Sprout sat in his car for a good thirty minutes. He turned the radio on and found a country music station but only listened for a couple of songs. Keith Urban came on and Sprout murmured to himself, "What's the Australian pussy know about country?!" He turned the radio off and stared out the windshield. What to do? He'd left his guns at home and he didn't like the prospect of a physical confrontation, so he brooded. He turned the key and pulled out of the mall's parking lot into the Raleigh traffic. Flipping the bird at two or three other drivers, he headed back to Chesapeake.

<h1 style="text-align:center">15</h1>

Detective Michael Hasbee was appointed the lead detective on the Roanna Roselli missing person case. He met with the Roselli's and went through the information that they'd given to the original police officers. His interview didn't reveal any additional facts that were very useful. They discussed all of her teachers, some of which Anthony knew, and they mentioned her basketball playing and her involvement in the church youth group. Hasbee asked if she had any close friends or boyfriends. They told him that she was tight with Ava Harper and the two got together after school at each other's homes. They also thought she liked a boy in the youth group but couldn't remember his name. Hasbee also questioned Roanna's siblings, but all he learned was that Roanna didn't talk much about her personal life. He inquired about the Rosellis' professional lives.

"Did either of you have any problems at work? Anyone who you might have irritated?"

Anthony Roselli said, "I'm a teacher and football coach. There are lots of parents that might be unhappy about something or other that I did with their kids, but I have not had an official complaint yet. You know, "Not fair, not giving them or their kid a chance." There is always some kind of small complaint and people wanting to have a conference to tell me how to do my job better. All the coaches get that treatment as well as the teachers."

"Anybody ever get physical?"

"Not recently. Couple of years ago, a guy punched me on the practice field. He was arrested, but I didn't press charges. Never saw him again. That's it really."

"Mrs. Roselli, how about you? Any trouble I should know about?"

"No, nothing. I'm an office administrator. My firm has some disgruntled clients, clients whose investments don't do as well as they wish. But they take it out on the firm's financial advisors, not me. I have very little contact with the clients."

Hasbee visited next door neighbors and got nothing of substance. He visited the Harper residence and spoke to Ava's parents. They told him that Roanna visited often and she and their daughter, Ava, were good friends. They would go up to Ava's room and stay most of the afternoon doing homework and talking like teenagers do. There was always a lot of laughter. Hasbee asked if he could interview Ava. They agreed but warned that she was still very upset.

"Hi, I'm Detective Michael Hasbee. Please just call me Mike. I'd like to ask you a few questions about Roanna. We're trying to find her. Would that be okay?"

Ava just nodded.

"You're good friends with Roanna, right?" Another nod.

"How long have you known her?"

"Since middle school, I guess."

"And she likes to come over here and you go over to her house?"

"Yeah."

"Tell me some things about her. What do you do when you're together?"

"Well, we study. Sometimes." She grinned slightly. "We talk, you know, about our friends and teachers and stuff. And we'll check out our Facebook pages and Instagram."

"Does Roanna have any other close friends?"

"Everybody likes her, but I'm her only close friend. She does kinda like a boy though."

"Who's that, Ava?"

"Ahh, that's kinda personal."

"Ava, we have to find her. Any information could help."

"But. . .her parents might get mad." She whined.

"Ava, I really need your help."

"Okay, but you didn't hear it from me! His name is Bobby Lee."

"Is Lee his last name?"

"No, sorry. It's Bobby Lee Gillespie."

"Does he go to your school?"

"Yeah, and Roanna's church group."

After leaving the Harper residence and Ava, Hasbee checked records on his car computer and found two Gillespies registered at the high school. They were apparently brothers. One was named Robert Lee. Hasbee drove to the Gillespie home. He walked up to the front door, pushed the doorbell button, and waited. No one answered. There was a car in the driveway in front of the garage, so Hasbee assumed that someone was home. He pushed the doorbell again and listened. He heard the doorbell chimes but nothing else. There were thin windows on either side of the front door, and someone pulled a curtain covering one of these windows to peek out at who was at the door. It was a teenage boy.

"Who are you?"

"Detective Hasbee. I need to come in." He held up his badge.

"My parents are asleep. They work nights. I can't let you in unless they say it's OK."

"Get them up."

"Ahh, OK. I'll be right back." Hasbee waited. In a minute or so a man, presumedly Bobby's dad, opened the door slightly. He looked very tired and not all that pleased.

"You're a detective?"

"Yes sir."

"May I see the badge?"

Hasbee showed him the badge and said, "I just need to ask a couple of questions about Roanna Roselli."

"Well, I know she's missing, but we don't have anything to do with that."

"Please, sir, let me come in."

Gillespie opened the door wider and, with a thick-armed wave, invited Hasbee in.

"Is this your son, Robert Lee?"

"Yes. We call him Bobby."

"I need to ask him a few questions. You can stay if you like. Bobby, I'm investigating the disappearance of Roanna Roselli." Hasbee observed Bobby Lee's eyes look down at the floor as he gestured that he understood.

"You know her pretty well, right?"

"Yes sir."

"Boyfriend?"

"Yes sir, you could say that."

"You go to her school and her church, correct?"

He nodded.

"Did you ever go out on a date with her?"

"No, sir."

"Ever get together with her outside of school or church?"

"Well, yeah. We'd walk together after the bus dropped us off. Maybe spend a few minutes together talking."

"She disappeared on March 3rd. After school. Did you spend time with her then?"

"Yeah."

"Tell me about it. All the details. Maybe you were the last person to see her."

Bobby Lee glanced at his father, and Hasbee could tell that he was considering what his dad might think about what he had to say.

"Well, um, we got off the bus and she hung with a couple of her friends talking. I stalled around and started walking. Finally she told them 'bye' and met up with me. We went to this bench that we like to sit on. Over in River Park. Ya know, we hung out for a while and then it started to get dark, so we walked home."

"About what time?"

"Dunno. It was pretty dark."

"You and Roanna go to that park often?"

"Yeah, sure. We liked talking to each other." Hasbee had to control a smirk.

"Same bench?"

"Yeah, pretty much."

"Ever notice anyone watching? Anybody there most of the time?"

"No, not really. I was mostly paying attention to Roanna."

"Can you take me to the bench, with dad's permission, of course?"

Dad said OK, and Hasbee took Bobby Lee to River Park to view the scene. The bench was along a pathway surrounded by azalea bushes. The park's small parking lot was across the street. There were no streetlights over by the path or at the lot. A narrow street ran between the bench, the path, and the parking lot.

"Is this the bench you were talking about?"

"Yes sir."

"You were with Roanna for quite a while that afternoon. Did you do anything else but just talk?" Bobby Lee gave the detective a blank stare and then looked down.

"The details, Bobby. Just between you and me. You won't get in trouble. It's cool, man."

"We kissed and made out a little. It was the only time we could be alone. Sometimes we would go behind one of the bigger trees so no one could see us."

"Okay, okay. Which way did she go when the making out ended?"

"She walked that way, toward her house, like always. I went this way to mine," he said, pointing in different directions.

"One more time, did you notice anyone there? Any cars over in the parking lot? Anything?"

"Not really, sir. Maybe there were cars there, but I really didn't look. I was too into Roanna."

Hasbee took the teen back home and went to the door with him. Bobby's dad opened the door. The detective gave him his card and asked if either person thought of anything that might help, to give him a call anytime, night or day.

"Damn, I can't get a break, can I?" he said out loud to himself as he walked to his car.

16

Hasbee went back to his office at the precinct headquarters. He knocked on Chief Detective Marnee Forbish's door frame and she invited him in. Forbish was the first female detective in Chesapeake and had been promoted to precinct Chief Detective four years ago. She was attractive, black, motherly to her detectives, and a pit bull to anyone else.

"Whatcha got, Mike? Make it good."

"Not much. Visited the Rosellis. Nothing new there. They said Roanna was tight with a girl named Ava Harper. Talked to her. Not much there either but she did tell me that Roanna was seeing a boy named Bobby Lee Gillespie. He was with Roanna the afternoon she went missing. Making out on a bench in River Park. He didn't notice anything unusual or was aware of anyone else there. Guess just blinded by love. It got dark and they both headed home in different directions. Did the search team find anything yet?"

"No. What was the scene like?"

"Bench by some bushes. A few large trees. The park's parking lot is across the street. No lights."

"Get CSI to check out any tire marks or surveillance cameras. Okay, what's next?"

"Going to the school this afternoon. I'll talk to the guidance counselor and her teachers. Never know. I'll check out where Mrs. Roselli works tomorrow, but I'm not expecting anything. I'll get onto CSI."

"While you're talking to them, have them scour the area again. They had to have missed something. See if there are any signs of a struggle or an abduction. Time's not on our side, Michael."

"Yes ma'am, I know."

Hasbee got to the school before the final bell. He told the receptionist that he needed to speak with the principal. He told the principal he needed to talk to the guidance counselor and to have Roanna's teachers stay until he spoke to them. The principal said no problem; he'd make the arrangements. Hasbee was directed to the guidance counselor's office. The door plaque said Dr. Deborah Pope. He entered, introduced himself, and was invited to be seated. He related to Dr. Pope that he was investigating the disappearance of Miss Roselli and wanted to know anything she could tell him about Roanna: her school work, her activities, and if she ever got into any trouble.

"I hate to disappoint you, detective, but I don't have much. Roanna is just a freshman, so she has only been here this school year. She hasn't visited my office yet, either voluntarily or involuntarily. She played on the girls' freshman basketball team; I know that she got injured but don't know anything about it. Let me check her grades for you."

Dr. Pope did and reported that she'd received A's and B's in her first semester. The detective told Pope that he wanted to meet with her teachers and asked how that would be facilitated. Dr. Pope called the front office and was told that Hasbee could visit each one in their final classroom, the dismissal bell having already been rung. She scribbled down a list of room numbers for him.

Freshmen didn't choose a curriculum pathway, so Roanna's classes were fairly general, math, language arts, social studies, science, and Spanish. None of the teachers had much to say other than Roanna was a good student and had a lively personality. She generally was a delight to have in the classroom. During the spring semester, some of the classes populated by freshmen were shared with upper classmen. Her Spanish teacher did mention that she seemed to show affection for a certain sophomore, Robert Gillespie. Hasbee queried the teacher about the relationship and about Robert. The teacher disclosed that Robert was an average student and thought he was popular; other than that, he had nothing.

The next day, Hasbee visited Johnson Travers Financial Consultants in Norfolk. The building was a fairly large two-story brick structure on a busy corner. The parking lot was in the rear of the building. Hasbee entered and, at the reception desk, identified himself and displayed his badge. He asked to see the person in charge.

"That would be Mr. Travers. He's in a meeting right now. Let me check with his secretary to see how long he'll be tied up." She buzzed the extension and learned that Travers would be available in a few minutes. Hasbee sat and waited.

Fifteen or twenty minutes later, the receptionist told him that she could take him back to meet Travers.

Travers offered a hand shake and gestured for Hasbee to have a seat.

"Hi, what can I do for you?"

"My Name is Detective Michael Hasbee. I'm investigating the disappearance of Roanna Roselli."

"Yes, Mrs. Roselli is employed here, an excellent staff member."

"That's why I'm here. Do you know if Mrs. Roselli has any enemies, anyone with a problem with her, here at your firm or outside clients?"

"God, no. She keeps the office ticking and everyone likes her. We all know we can count on Joan. She doesn't interface with the clients; our consultants and their secretaries do that."

"Was she promoted into her current job or hired into it?"

"She was promoted. I created a new position due to our needs."

"Anyone unhappy that they got passed over?"

Travers wrinkled his eyebrows and said, "Not that I'm aware of. I really don't think anyone here was bent out of shape. It is a tough job and Joan is perfect for the position. Now, there are times when she can get a little demanding of my agents, but it all works out."

17

Cody headed to the beach in his Jeep, Kassie-surfboards, wet suit, his companion Reef, and Gatorade in place. He headed up to Mansion Beach, and more specifically to the beaches in front of Sea Cove Lane where the football player was staying. Maybe curiosity kills the cat, but Cody had to check it out. Would he see the football player? With a babe? With Jess? When he got to the street that led to Sea Cove Lane, he parked Kassie off the road as usual, put on the wet suit in the back seat, and walked to the beach. He held the board between him and the houses thinking that it might be a good idea if he wasn't recognized. It was around 10 a.m., so the sun was still over the ocean, putting his face in a shadow once he was on the beach. He splashed into the nice rollers in the surf and paddled through the breakers to the float zone where he would normally watch for a good ride. Reef stood guard on the beach. But this morning, Cody was on a sightseeing mission. He paddled north past the first house which had no one outside. The second had an older couple seemingly sipping coffee and enjoying a nice April day. He hit the jackpot in front of house number three. He saw the football player and a girl out on the lower balcony. He had a small glass in his hand- bourbon so early? Cody couldn't make out who the girl was, but she was wearing a skimpy nighty that was blowing gently in the breeze. He paddled back south a little so as not to be right in front of the house, where he could watch without being obvious. The couple was bathed in sunlight and he now determined that the girl had nothing on underneath the nighty, at least on top. Nice boobs. As he studied them a little longer, the girl stood up, also holding a glass, and he got a better view. Jessica. *Wow, he thought, Jessica is a prostitute?* He paddled back to where he started from and waited for a good wave. But he really wasn't concentrating. Jessica was still with the football player and for more than just dinner, a lot more. And it seemed pretty likely that Phoebe set it up. How much of this kind of thing was going on? The football player was married. He caught some good waves, but his heart wasn't in it. A few other dudes were out on the waves now, so he came ashore and sat and pondered while watching his surfer buds. Good ole Chump Change was looking good out there, as were a few others. He enjoyed the show but was deep in thought. Chump Change finished a ride, strode out of the ocean, and jogged over to Cody. Reef gave him the obligatory licks on his shins.

"Sup, dude?"

"Just pondering."

"You OK?"

"Yeah, cool. No worries."

"Whatcha pondering?" Chump Change said, empathizing the word "pondering".

"Just thinking about what we saw the other day, you know, up on the balcony."

"Dude, you got a gorgeous piece of ass at your crib. Why you thinking about someone else's babe?"

"Nah, you don't understand. I wouldn't trade Phoebs for any babe. There's just something about a rich guy having any old bitch he wants that bothers me. Don't know why it bothers me."

"How do you know that guy's rich? And how do you know she wasn't his missus?"

"Dude, do you think some ordinary guy can rent one of those places? And, man, you saw how old that guy was. Do you really think that sweet thing was his wife? Really, get real, man." Cody didn't want to mention that he was really pondering the football player and Jessica.

"Cody, I think you ponder too much!" Chump Change said, empathizing "ponder" again. He smirked, and gave Cody a slap on the back as he charged back into the surf.

Cody stayed sitting on the beach. He unzipped his wet suit since the sun was heating it up. He had better get wet or head back to Kassie and take it off. He knew that the football player was married. Since he was, what would his wife think about him being with a live-in girlfriend? Food for thought.

Cody went back into the ocean for a few more rides. Chump Change paddled close by and yelled, "Way to get off the pondering stuff, dude." When done, Cody headed back to Kassie, changed in the back seat, and headed home. Back in his crib, he was still thinking of Jess and the football player. He remembered his name, Preston something. And he heard that he played for Chicago. He called Amelia at the Bistro and she answered although it was still early.

"Shocker hearing from you at this hour of the day. What's going on, Cody? You're not calling in sick, are you? Like 'the surf's up sick'?"

"Hey sweetie, no, I'm good. Remember last week, we had that incident with the football player?"

"Sure, hard to forget."

"Look up the reservation and see if it was in his name."

"OK." She checked. "Yeah, his name is Kerrigan."

"Cool. Gracias."

He pulled out his laptop and googled Preston Kerrigan. His photo came up (it was him) and a short football bio. He clicked on the name and more choices came up. The web-site he chose had a detailed bio, including personal information. Married to his wife, Samantha, for five years. She was a college sweetheart. Had one child, a four-year-old boy. Allegedly earned a guaranteed base salary of seven mil and change plus bonuses. He had endorsements from a major sportswear company, a tire manufacturer, and an energy drink. He lived in an exclusive, gated community about forty miles outside Chicago. He'd attended college in the Big Ten and played all four years but did not graduate. He broke every school record and some Big Ten records for rushing. The bio said he had a reputation for being an aggressive tiger on the field and a clean-living pussycat off.

So Preston Kerrigan was a clean-living married man and probably a wonderful father. Ahh, maybe not so much. Cody deepened his research and brought up every newspaper article he could find on Kerrigan. He wasn't looking for football stats or descriptions of how he performed in this game or that gam; Cody was looking for more personal information. He found little. Kerrigan was involved with a couple of local charities and made a few personal appearances, but Cody couldn't scrape up much of anything else. The picture that was painted, though, was of a model, God-loving young man committed to his family.

Cody longed to make some extra dough for his dream of an Endless Summer trip. He smelled an opportunity here. Rich family man shacking up with a knockout. Seemed like he could pick off some low-hanging fruit via a little blackmail. Why not? He had to figure out how. Careful details could get him some nice coin and, importantly, keep him out of jail. So Cody considered the task at hand. First, he had to get photos, good photos clearly showing him with a girl that was not his wife. Then, he had to communicate to Kerrigan that he had the photos and that they were for sale for a certain price. He had to provide some assurance that, once the photos were bought, they would not reappear. And he had to get the money.

18

The physical situation was well known. Cody surfed often in front of the mansions. He could take the photos from his surfboard with a waterproof camera or cell phone. He called the local water-sports company just down the beach- he often visited there- and asked if they had any floating, waterproof cell phone pouches in stock that would hold his phone. They had one made by Mpow that everyone was pleased with. Cody asked if you could take photos while the phone was in the pouch. The store salesman said, "sure." So Cody decided to try taking some photos using a pouch. He hopped into Kassie and boogied down to the water-sports store. He took a few shots with his phone in the Mpow pouch, liked the results, and bought it.

The next issue was notifying Kerrigan. Cody now knew which house he was in, so he could easily print the photos and get them to the house. But he had to provide a path for Kerrigan to communicate with him and he with Kerrigan. He thought that a simple burner phone should work. Why not? His local Walmart had them in stock and the TracFone with a simple cheap plan was all he needed. He bought both with cash. He got the phone up and running within an hour and decided that he'd leapt over that hurdle. As soon as his business with Kerrigan was finished, he would destroy the device and dispose of the parts in some dumpster, after wiping off any fingerprints.

How to get the money? Cash, of course. Cody wasn't experienced in this type of crime, or any type of crime for that matter. He was an amateur and knew it. He read that offshore accounts could be set up, but he knew nothing about that and had no idea how anonymous they were. So that was out. Mail or any commercial delivery service was clearly not workable. He had no one to consult. He didn't think there was a "How to Blackmail Someone" YouTube or book available, so this one he had to solve on his own. He thought it over for days. He would have to collect the money without being arrested and without the threat of being harmed. Also, he would have to assure Kerrigan that once he paid, the photos would not exist anymore. He anguished over the problem for a couple of days, coming close to abandoning the whole project. He had to hatch a plan that he was satisfied with. It probably would be risky, but any plan would.

The next day, Cody drove Kassie up to Mansion Beach to try his phone's camera in its waterproof pouch. He went through the routine of getting dressed and hiking to the edge of the surf, this time with the phone pouch with his normal cell phone in it tied around his wrist. The surf was rough with a strong northeast breeze churning up the foaming breakers. Not a good day for surfing, but Cody wasn't out there to catch a wave. He paddled up to the huge houses against the wind and waves. The first house had someone walking out on the balcony. That would do for a test. He typed in the password and opened the camera app. Touching the screen to focus, he popped off a few shots and zoomed in, shot a few more, and zoomed in more and shot more. The person disappeared inside the house, probably too chilly, and Cody called it a day. He required little effort to get back down to his start point and he belly surfed to the shore. He was so psyched he was shaking. He packed up, went to Kassie and changed, and headed home. Once there, he downloaded the photos onto his computer and scrolled through them. They weren't great and he didn't think he could make out the person's face with any certainty. He was deflated. He needed a better idea.

Cody googled a number of video surveillance web sites and one caught his attention: drones. Could he fly a drone close enough to a house without it being too obvious and come away with quality photos? He was energized now. He continued his research into drones, their flying capability and various characteristics. He would need a drone that could fly far enough that he couldn't be spotted flying it. He needed it to have a camera that could take quality photos with enough pixels to discern facial features, and he wanted one that was relatively stealthy, and quiet. There was a tremendous amount of information on the internet, but, again, he was an amateur and much of the technical jargon was beyond him. He found a company called Drones Virginia up in Virginia Beach, about an hour and a half north of him. He called the company and told them the basics of what he was looking for and a price range. They told him that the best thing to do was to come there and look at what they had in stock or do a demonstration, and he could get a better feel for what was available. Cody asked what time they opened tomorrow and they said ten. He'd check them out then.

The next day, Phoebe woke up around eight and Cody was already dressed. She asked where he was headed and he said that a dude up in Virginia Beach was selling a surfboard and he wanted to check it out. She shrugged as if to say "whatever" and rolled over. He gave her a silly, sloppy kiss on the back of her head and she said, "Go play with your surfboard, sweetie." Cody headed to Virginia, making a stop at Hardees for a large coffee, three sugars, and a bacon, egg, and cheese biscuit. There was always the adventure of not knowing if Kassie would make it all the way. He arrived right at ten, when Drones Virginia opened. They had a small window with numerous drone brand decals on it and a few drones on display.

"Hi, my name is Brandon. What can I help you with today?"

"Cody here. I'm looking for a drone. One with certain capabilities."

"Cool, man. Are you the dude that called late yesterday?"

"Yep."

"OK. How about you go through your requirements again. You ever fly one before?"

"No, think I'll need some lessons. Don't want to auger in on the first try." Cody continued, "Looking at five hundred dollars or less. Need a quiet machine. Good quality camera for stills and videos. Need it to go a mile or so. Good in the wind. And black if possible."

"Mind if I ask what your main use will be?"

"Taking some shots of surfers on the waves and on the beach for a promotion that I volunteered to do," he lied.

"How portable? Do you need a bird that can be folded up for transportation?"

"Yeah, that would be cool."

"OK, here's the deal. I think you should think about the DJI Mavic Air. You have semi-professional needs and the Mavic is a first-class bird. It folds up for easy travel and storage. It has a three-axis gimbaled camera with vibration dampers and automatic exposure control. It features eight gigabytes of internal storage, a micro SD card slot, and has a USB port. It can actively track a subject, like a surfer. It can fly for twenty minutes or so, can easily get you your mile range. And it's a quiet unit."

"I'm new at this, but that sounds great. How much?"

"More than your five hundred, but we have it on sale for seven ninety-nine plus tax."

"Ouch! How much are a few lessons?"

"Cody, not only do we sell and repair drones, but we provide any service you'll need. We give you all the training you'll need to be confident. But the Mavic is easy to use. It has a good remote-control unit and you can use your smart phone if you want. I'll throw in a case to sweeten the deal."

"OK, sold. When can I get my first lesson?"

"I'm the only one here now. We have another staff member due to get here at one. Do you want your training then?"

"OK, let's take care of the deal and I'll be back at one."

Cody took care of business and headed to Doc Taylor's for lunch. He loved the joint. It once was a motel, more like an old inn, and then an office and residence for Dr. Taylor, right on Twenty-Third Street a couple of blocks from the ocean. Cody also loved Tautog's, a sister restaurant next door only open for dinner. Cody ordered a bowl of She Crab Soup, a Catfish Po-Boy, and their famous Bloody Mary. He was in a good mood. His phone camera experiment hadn't worked out as he hoped, but he was excited by the idea of flying the drone. He was enamored with the idea of learning to fly some day and was a big fan of the Wright Brothers, who'd flown their gliders, first airplane, and subsequent models just a few miles from where he lived. He occasionally would drive to the Kitty Hawk Airport off of Colington Road in Kill Devil Hills to see if there was a plane sitting there. From there, it was an easy walk to the Wright Brothers National Memorial, where they did their flying over a hundred years ago. So Cody would get his first chance at flying, so to speak, after lunch. The Bloody Mary arrived and he sipped it lovingly– definitely a good version!

He drove back to Drones Virginia and Brandon. His new Mavic was ready to go. Drones Virginia was across the street from a large park, which was why they'd purchased the building. Brandon and Cody crossed the street and Cody was stoked to try out the bird. Brandon went through all the flying information first and then flew a demonstration flight to show Cody what the Mavic could do and how the remote control worked. Now it was Cody's turn. Brandon cautioned him on how to maneuver the device slowly at first so as not to crash. Some drones don't survive their first flight. Cody cautiously lifted the Mavic off the ground and, as instructed, once about five feet up, performed some basic turns and guided the vehicle to travel a short distance in all four directions. Then, with Brandon studiously observing, he brought the bird back to terra firma.

Cody yelped, "Yes! Good job, Black Pelican!"

"Dude, what do you mean 'Black Pelican'?"

"It needs a name, doesn't it? I thought Black Pelican was a winner since it would be skimming across the tops of the waves– like pelicans do."

"Gotcha. Let's try another couple of flights before I tell you how to operate the camera and store your photos and videos."

The lessons continued for fifteen more minutes until the Black Pelican's battery got low. Brandon thought that Cody understood how to operate the drone and told Cody to go home and practice a number of times before getting too adventurous. He reminded Cody to get FAA certified, which Cody had no intention of doing. He also gave Cody his business card and told him to call anytime with questions.

19

Phoebe was in the office sipping the last drops of her morning coffee when Kerrigan called her around ten. He had two questions. How could he have money wired to him, and could she propose some activities, price not being a major concern. As for the first question, Sea Dunes Concierge Realty routinely handled receipt and disbursement of cash transfers for their clients through their local bank, so she told Kerrigan that getting cash would not be a problem. She added that Sea Dunes typically escrowed money in a client's account to pay for activities, entertainment, or any other needs. She said she would get the wiring information to him. He told her that he would take care of that later and that she should withdraw the amount that he owed her for Jessica. Phoebe told him that he would have to withdraw cash himself for payment to her for Jess, that she was acting as a private contractor, not for Sea Dunes.

As far as activities, the Outer Banks was known for a variety of water sports and golfing, as well as sight-seeing. Birding was popular, as well as taking four-wheeler tours to observe the Corolla wild horses and visiting lighthouses, the Wright Brothers site of the first flight, the Lost Colony of the first English settlers, and so forth. She also mentioned that the Tidewater area of nearby Virginia featured shows, concerts, an excellent museum, and other cultural events. He asked Phoebe what water sports were available considering the time of year. She told him that deep-sea and sound fishing could easily be arranged, and surfing, wind surfing, kayaking, kite-boarding, paddle boarding, and parasailing could be available if he had or wanted to buy a wet or dry suit. Kerrigan told Phoebe that he liked the idea of deep-sea fishing.

"Do you want to join a fishing party or charter a boat by yourself? They can be pretty pricey."

"Let's do a solo, maybe I'll find someone to keep me company."

"OK, cool. I'll check when the boats think a good day will be. They don't like to go out when there's strong winds. Does it matter to you when you go?"

"Nope. Will I need anything?"

"Just some warm clothing. I'll order food and beverages. You'll have to let me know how many people will be going. What do you want to eat and drink?"

"Let's say two people. I think beer would be the ticket. Kinda like Yuengling. Could they grill steaks on board?"

"They can do anything for a price."

"A couple of rib eyes with the fixings."

"You got it."

Phoebe called the charter boat she liked the best for her clients. The boat was the Tuna Xpress, captained by Jock Sanders. The boat came out of the Oregon Inlet Fishing Center, which had quick access through the inlet to the ocean and wasn't that far relatively from Kerrigan's house. Jock's boat could comfortably carry eight guests in addition to Jock and his mate, Casey Evans. Jock was young for a boat owner and captain and was still paying off a loan for the boat. He was deeply tanned, a good-looking guy, with a personality that kept guests entertained throughout a trip. Phoebe liked that Jock was very flexible– he was willing to do just about anything. His mate, Casey Evans, was also a live wire and got along with anyone. They knew their fishing and where to find the best spots. The Tuna Xpress always got good tips. Phoebe told Jock the client was a professional football player and a guest, and that was it. She told him what Kerrigan had requested for food and drinks and she also added Kerrigan's bourbon to the order.

"When do you think you could go?"

"Casey and I will have to clean up the boat a little, get the food, and get my grill secured. The forecast is good for the next few days, supposed to be pretty calm, so any time after tomorrow. Do you want me to splurge?"

"Yes! Aim for the day after tomorrow, then."

Phoebe called Kerrigan back and told him that the trip would be in two days. They would have to leave early; she proposed picking him up at five in the morning. He had no problem with that. She asked about his guest and he said it would be Jessica. She cautioned him to not drink much the night before and to lay off greasy foods. Kerrigan told her that, since the next day was open, he'd like to get in a round of golf but didn't bring his clubs. His agent could overnight his clubs, but he didn't know what time they'd arrive. Phoebe told him to give it a try and to let her know. Otherwise, Sea Dunes had a few sets of clubs he could use if his couldn't get there.

Kerrigan called Patrice Cheger, his agent, and made the request. Cheger said he would get it done and would call back with the delivery information. Kerrigan told him to ship them to Sea Dunes Concierge Realty. Thirty minutes later, Cheger called Kerrigan back and said that the clubs were being picked up and would arrive by ten the next morning. Kerrigan thanked him and called Phoebe with the news. She told him she'd reserve a tee time at Duck Woods Country Club, a beautiful course in the town of Southern Shores, for one. That she'd pick him up at twelve thirty with his clubs ready to go.

The next day, the clubs arrived as planned and Phoebe picked up Kerrigan and took him to the golf club. Sea Dunes was a corporate member and benefactor of the club.

"We have really nice courses down here, so you should have a good round. The grass is still a little brown, but in good shape. Did you want to walk it or use a cart?"

"I need the exercise. I'll walk it if they allow."

Kerrigan loved golfing almost as much as football. Maybe more. He'd taken a number of lessons from different pros since leaving college and shot a six handicap. The course was uncrowded, and he finished the picturesque eighteen with a 79. He got back to the clubhouse to find the bar and catch a double on the rocks of his favorite, Four Roses Single Barrel bourbon. The next day he'd be out at sea.

20

Donald Sprout continually monitored the Wilson campaign. He targeted a scheduled campaign appearance in Rocky Mount, North Carolina, the following day. He checked on MapQuest and the travel time was two and a half hours. He would follow the same routine that he used when he traveled to the last campaign stop. He gave Vixen another dose of oxy, duck-taped her mouth and tied her to the bed. Looking at her, he started getting hard, but that had to wait, he had business to take care of. Once again, he had clean jeans and a flannel shirt to wear, but there was one difference from the last trip.

This time, he would pack his Glock 17. Sprout had purchased the small hand gun a couple of years ago. The purchase was illegal with no paperwork. No one knew that he possessed a firearm. The firearm used nine-millimeter bullets and was reputed to be easy to use. Sprout had visited a farm out past Suffolk, Virginia, where the owner had set up a private firing range complete with rudimentary moving targets. The owner didn't ask questions and only charged five dollars for use of the range, plus any ammunition purchased. Sprout had mastered the Glock and was confident he could use it whenever he had to. This trip might be one of those times.

Sprout left Chesapeake and made his common stop at 7-Eleven. Large coffee, cream and lots of sugar. A cinnamon coffee roll was his choice of the day. Back in the Impala, he turned on the local country music station, the Eagle. *Why do radio stations need to call themselves a name?* he thought. The station played a nice mix of new country and older top hits. Sprout didn't know many of the words, but he la la la'd his way to Rocky Mount. *Congressman Colonel Richard Curtis Wilson, I'm coming to get you.*

He read that Wilson was to speak at the Senior Center in Rocky Mount. He had no clue where that was and hadn't done his internet homework. When he arrived in the city, he pulled into a gas station, went in to see the clerk at the cash register, and asked where the Center was. The clerk didn't know. Sprout rippled his hand over the snacks in front of the check-out area, dumping most of them on the floor, threw the attendant the bird, and yelled, "Useless cocksucker!"

"Wait, come back here. Look at this mess."

He drove into the main part of town and stopped at another station and got the directions. The event was scheduled for eleven and it was already five of. He found the Senior Center and parked on the grass since all the marked spaces were used. He saw a crowd outside near what looked like a gazebo. He bumped into an older, obese lady and asked her, "Is that where Wilson is speaking?" She quizzically stared at him and said, "Of course it is." Sprout marched over a little bridge and shouldered through the small crowd to get close. A portable speaker system had been set up, and some ancient guy was extolling the concern that Congressman Wilson showed for the senior community.

"Congressman Wilson has sponsored or cosponsored more legislation for us senior citizens than any other congressman in North Carolina history. And yet, he is a strong advocate to limit government spending and has refused to accept frivolous pork-barrel projects in his district. There is no better man for senator for our great state than Congressman Colonel Richard Curtis Wilson." Wilson stepped up onto the platform and held his hands up high to recognize and ease the light but genuine applause. Then Wilson cupped his hands over his heart and began his speech.

"I am delighted to be with you good people from Rocky Mount, Edgecombe, and Nash Counties. I am here to tell you why I am running to be your next senator in Washington and to answer any questions you might have. I hope I can count on your support in the upcoming primary election." The speech continued with the usual platitudes and promises, emphasizing his record for seniors and what he'd do in the future. When the questioning started, Sprout listened to Wilson's feeble, ignorant supporters stepping up to the microphone asking their feeble, ignorant questions. After Wilson delivered one overly lengthy response, Sprout hollered out, "What about the men you killed in Afghanistan?" The crowd noticeably hushed and most turned back to see who had yelled such a poor remark. Wilson also peered into the crowd to see who it was.

"I don't have any idea of what you're asking. Why don't you step up to the microphone and we can all find out." The congressman was a little shaken but was willing to see who the heckler was. Sprout instantly starting sweating but felt pressured to confront this demon. It seemed like it was too public a place to use his weapon, but would he have a better chance again? Sprout went to the microphone and said, "I'm one of the airmen that you sent into a suicide mission. I survived, but my buddies didn't, you bastard."

"I have no idea what this man is talking about." Sprout stared at Wilson and lowered his right hand under his jacket. Then, one of Wilson's security details came to the microphone, put his arm firmly around Sprout's shoulder, and whispered, "That'll be enough." And he dragged Sprout away from the gazebo. The crowd was so quiet that the frogs in the nearby pond could be heard. Sprout was pushed back to the parking area and told that he should leave before anything bad happened to him. Sprout spat at the nearest guard, turned and began to walk away. Over his shoulder, he mumbled, "I'll be back and you won't stop me." Sprout got back into his car and the guards watched him pull out, noting his license plate number. Sprout pushed heavily on the steering wheel and blasted his car horn for a good minute. About a mile away, he pulled over, sweating profusely, and wet his pants. So much for the clean jeans! Now, for an uncomfortable ride home.

His brain was crowded with a riot of thoughts. Why did he have the guts to step up to the microphone and confront his Satan? Why didn't he muscle away from those so-called security guards? Why didn't he pull out the Glock and pop a few rounds into Wilson? *You dumb fuck, only fifteen or twenty feet away and you blew it? Why?* Was he a pussy? Wasn't he man enough to do what he wanted to do? He swore to himself that there would be a next time and he wouldn't chicken out.

He arrived home and changed his embarrassingly wet pants. He went down to Vixen to relieve his sexual anxiety. He pulled her panties down and stared at her, but he couldn't get it up. He still had the prick Wilson on his mind. He was still mad at himself.

"Maybe we can have some fun later, little one."

21

Detective Hasbee was in his office when he got a call from CSI investigator Jordan Speed. Speed brought Hasbee up to date on his findings and wanted to know how to proceed. The investigator was a little over six feet tall, medium build, and fashioned a well-trimmed short beard and a mustache. He had dark brown hair and was handsome. He also was loud and very talkative, unusual in the CSI group, and every detective liked working with him. Speed had found vegetation that showed signs of being matted leading away from the bench where Roanna was last seen. Matting that looked like something had been dragged through the brush. He had not discovered any other clues. Hasbee suggested that they both go to the scene and look around some more. "Roanna must be somewhere. Let's hope alive." Speed got into Hasbee's service vehicle, a dark blue, unmarked Dodge Charger. Hasbee drove to the park area where Roanna was last seen. Hasbee parked and they both got out of the vehicle, determined to find some sort of clue that was missed. They headed straight for the area that Speed had noted and photographed the matted vegetation. It was hard to detect now where the exact area was, but Speed remembered the general direction the short path must have taken. They spread out a bit and continued in the general direction of Speed's memory, carefully checking under every bush or weed to see if they could find a clue as to what happened to that sweet girl. Anything. They were desperate for any indication or clue. After a short time, Hasbee's eye caught a shining object on the ground about ten feet away. "What's over there? I saw something reflecting the sun." They walked over to the general area of the reflection and found a smashed electronic device deep in the soil. A cell phone. It was somewhat intact but had been severely damaged, as if it had been stepped on and ground into the grass. Speed put his thin gloves on and placed the parts in an evidence bag. Talking to the device more than to Hasbee, Speed said, "Let's pray you are our girl's phone."

"There has to be more. Let's continue searching before we run that phone off to the lab. Let's continue around this area."

They decided to split up a little to cover more ground. Speed turned to the left and Hasbee to the right of where the phone was discovered. About twenty feet into his search, Speed yelled, "I got something, Mike." Hasbee strutted through the brush toward Speed, once cursing a small branch that snapped back at him and raked his face. He found Speed standing over a backpack on the ground. "What have we got here?" They didn't have an evidence bag big enough for the whole backpack, so with his gloves still on, Speed unzipped the bag and looked inside. Some notebooks and school text books, three of them. He carefully pulled out one of the notebooks. On the front cover, the name Roanna Roselli was written in fancy, broad, purple letters. Speed glanced at Hasbee with his eyebrows squeezed upward. Hasbee closed his eyes, shook his head, and said, "At least we found something connected to her." Speed then removed one of the text books, a math book. Speed opened the book and inside the back cover was a sheet with a list of names on it, obviously a list of students that had possessed the book. Roanna's was the last name on the list. He put the book back into the backpack and looked at Hasbee.

"We might be on to something. Let's continue. I'll give headquarters a call to be sure a lab tech is available when we get back."

After the phone call, they continued in the same general direction, pushing aside limbs and branches in order to pass through. Soon they came to a clearing at the rear of a row of houses. They were behind Sanderling Street, the street that Roanna lived on, but several blocks away. They walked around one of the houses to check the address and then headed back the way they came to get to their vehicle all the while checking to see if they could find even more clues.

Speed put the backpack and cell phone in the trunk of the car and said, "Take me back to the lab. I have to check this stuff in for analysis. I'll let you know if we find anything, maybe prints if we get really lucky. What's next for you?"

"I'm going back to the Rosellis' to see if they know anybody over where we were. Then it's door to door. You know, look under every rock."

Hasbee knew that the Roselli's would probably be at work that time of the day. Neither Anthony nor Joan wanted to continue their lives until their daughter was home safe and sound, but they had to survive, and they had two other children who also needed them. Anthony went back to work with the idea that the staff there would support him and get him the minute there was any news concerning his daughter. Joan went back to work but could not function. Knowing that Joan was a complete mess emotionally, Hasbee headed to the school where Anthony Roselli taught. At the reception desk, he displayed his badge and asked for Roselli. The receptionist checked the schedule and told Hasbee that Roselli was in class but that she had strict orders by the principal to interrupt Anthony at any time if an officer needed to speak to him. While she buzzed Anthony and spoke to him, Hasbee sat down and tapped on the Candy Crush icon on his phone, a good way to kill a few minutes. It was a large high school and he wasn't sure how long it would take for Anthony to reach the front office.

Roselli appeared and noticed Hasbee right away. "Detective, hi. Do you have any news?"

"Is there a place we can talk privately?"

Anthony looked at the secretary and she pointed to the principal's office. It was vacant at the moment.

"Mr. Hasbee, please."

"Yes, we found Roanna's backpack. It's being processed now at the lab. I don't have any results yet, but it is a great team and they are working on it. Do you or Mrs. Roselli know anyone in the three- to-five hundred block of Sanderling?"

"Ahh, no. No one that I can think of. Maybe Joan does. Why do you ask?"

"That may be an area of interest, not sure."

"Let me call Joan. You can ask her."

Roselli called the Johnson Travers number and asked to speak with Joan.

"Hey, honey, I'm with Detective- ahh, I'm sorry…"

"Hasbee."

"Detective Hasbee. He has a question for you. Here he is."

"Hi, Mrs. Roselli. Just a quick one: do you know anyone in the area around the three- to five-hundred block of Sanderling?"

"Humm. Not anyone that comes to mind. That's not really very close to our house. Do you think Ro might be there? Anthony, I am leaving work right now so we can go there!"

"No, hold on a minute, Mrs. Roselli. It's just an area we're looking at. If you think of anything, give me a call. Going to that area is not going to help us. We are on this, Joan. Let us do our jobs." He gave Roselli his card and said, "Stay in touch if anything comes to mind."

It was way past lunch-time and his stomach was growling, so Hasbee made a quick stop at Arby's to pick up a Chicken Cordon Bleu sandwich. He drove back to Sanderling ready to start his canvasing of those homes. Starting with the two-hundred block, he went door-to-door showing Roanna's photo to anyone that answered. He would introduce himself and typically ask if the person had ever seen the girl in the picture or if they knew anyone who might look like the girl in the picture. Most people had heard of the missing girl but did not know her. He would continue the conversation by asking if they had witnessed anyone who acted strange or suspicious recently. He noted which homes answered his approach and which ones did not. More than half the homes did not answer, and for those that did, he wasn't able to get any useful information. He got to the three-hundred block. He found Marsha Willis at home. She told the detective no, she hadn't seen the girl. However, when discussing unusual neighbors, she mentioned the man in 325 as an unfriendly loner who she saw coming and going, but never outside other than that. She had tried to strike up a conversation a few times but just received grunts in return and never a facial recognition that he wanted her to say anything else. She didn't remember his name. He scribbled the information in his notebook. He also caught Sally Rider at home. Sally was gregarious and welcomed Hasbee inside, offering him a cup of coffee. He graciously declined. She also described the odd behavior of the man in 325. She told Hasbee that her husband had decided to occasionally mow 325's lawn. She described the man to be like a hermit, never doing anything outside. The place was becoming an eyesore, and her husband, Jack, had gone over to the house a few times and suggested that the man get his grass cut. She reported that he would just sneer at her husband and ask him to get off his property. She also did not know his name. Hasbee's interest in 325 piqued and he was beginning to smell a rat, but there are a lot of strange people in the world. A couple of other neighbors made the same observations but had nothing specific to add. No unusual behavior at 325, not that they kept a close watch. The man was weird.

22

Hasbee rang the doorbell several times at 325 but nobody answered. There was a car, a Chevy Impala, in the driveway. Hasbee felt the hood; it was cold. He looked inside the car and saw a mess, including a few cups from Dunkin' Donuts. But no smoking gun. He wrote down the license plate number and walked around the side of the house, dodging overgrown weeds and bushes. *I guess the neighbor didn't cut the grass in the front,* he thought. The house, once tan in color, was in grave need of a paint job. The back-yard was worse than the side if that was at all possible. The grass (weeds) looked like they hadn't been mowed in years. A short set of wooden steps led up to the back door. The wood looked rotted and ready to fall apart. He did notice that the grass had been matted down leading from the back door. He was startled when he heard, "What the fuck are you doing in my back-yard?"

"Hi. Sorry. I'm Detective Hasbee. I saw a car in the driveway and nobody answered the door, so I thought someone may be outside back here."

"Whatever you want, git out!"

"I'd just like to ask you a couple of questions."

The man had a pistol in his right hand that was pointed to the ground, and he said, "You are trespassing! I know my rights! Now get off my property."

Hasbee waved, said, "no problem," and fought his way past the side of the house. The neighbors were right– an unpleasant sort.

Hasbee continued his canvass up the three-hundred, four-hundred, and five-hundred blocks and got nothing. He would have to return after the evening rush hour to see if he could catch anyone else at home.

Sprout was shaken by the visit. Did they know about Vixen? Did they know about his hate for Wilson? He went to the living room, darkened by heavy shades, and sat down on one of the recliners, stooping over his knees. "Why a detective? Why was a detective here? What was he looking for? Vixen is mine now, he can't take her away. That's not what the detective should be doing. She needs to be here. She's mine and this is her new home. She'll have my babies. She'll learn to love me. That's no crime. This is what's best for her. She loves me. She is so much in love with me. No one will take her away from me. My Vixen is my forever! I will never be alone again! " He stared at the floor. But what if the detective came back? Could he defend his property? Would he defend his property? He had no right to come here. He heard that detectives could go to some corrupt judge and get a piece of paper that would allow them to trespass. He wouldn't let that happen. He'd get a lawyer. No, he'd use his trusty pistol. The government had no right to be on his property. No right. Sprout walked to his back door and opened it. He walked out onto the tiny porch.

To no one there, he shouted as he paced back and forth, "This is my property! Stay away! You are not welcome here! You are trespassing! Git out or I'll blow you away! You have no right to bother me! Get off of my property! I know my rights! I have the right to bear arms and protect what is mine! This is my property! This is mine! You stay away, you piece of crap! Don't come back here! I will shoot trespassers! I can do that and you can't tell me I can't! Stay away!" The rant continued for ten more minutes. Sprout was so wound up he was almost foaming at the mouth. He went inside to the kitchen and downed one of his little happy pills. He sat down again on his recliner and was shaking with fury. He'd wait for the pill to kick in and then go visit Vixen.

23

Cody followed his morning habits. Attach the board to Kassie, nuke a breakfast sandwich, feed Reef and take him for a run on the beach, and pour hot coffee into his Yeti. This time he took one more thing with him, the Black Pelican. The surf-board and his wet suit would be a rouse. Today he would be fishing– fishing for money. He drove back up to Mansion Beach but didn't park at his usual place. He drove north to Ocean Mist Lane, just beyond Sea Spray Lane, the access road to Kerrigan's house. Ocean Mist Lane headed to another strip of a dozen huge houses on High Dunes Lane. As usual, he parked Kassie off the road and walked to the beach. He was about a quarter of a mile from Kerrigan's house. He sat at the base of the dune, somewhat out of view from the adjacent houses. All the other surfers were south of him, beyond Kerrigan. Cody took the Black Pelican out of its travel pouch and got it ready for flight. There was a gentle land breeze, so he didn't think he'd have trouble controlling the machine. He placed it on level sand and in a second, it was airborne. He wisely wanted to get a feel for its performance before sending it on a mission. Up, down, left, right, everything was a "go", in NASA speech. The camera was also operating fine, so Cody directed the Black Pelican southward and viewed the houses as they went by. He flew over the ocean, only fifteen to twenty feet high. When it was in front of Kerrigan's house, he saw nobody outside despite it being a warm April day. Shit! He brought the bird back to the launch site and landed somewhat hard but didn't damage anything. He decided that he'd wait fifteen minute– everybody needs a potty break, or a coffee break- maybe Kerrigan would reappear. He waited but it seemed like forever. He launched the drone again and flew it back down the beach, but there still wasn't anyone outside. Did he have the right house? Yes, he was sure. He had no choice but to wait for another day.

Little did Cody know that Kerrigan was on the high seas, deep-sea fishing. Phoebe had hit the road very early and left Cody a note that a client had an early appointment. He hadn't given it much thought that the client might have been Kerrigan and that Kerrigan might not be home in the morning. Phoebe picked up Kerrigan, and Jessica, who apparently was taking the day off, at five thirty. She stopped at a great local coffee shop at what was designated milepost six for everyone to tank up on caffeine and tasty treats. Back on the fairly empty road, they arrived at the Oregon Inlet Fishing Center around twenty after six. Jock Sanders hopped out of his boat and walked over to the three arrivals.

"I'm Captain Jock Sanders. You don't have to salute," he said with a broad smile. "I understand you're the best player in the NFL." Holding his hand out he said, "Just promise me you won't tackle me."

Kerrigan laughed and said, "Naah. I'm a half back. I just bowl people over."

"Well, I have a full back and would like to keep it that way. This is my ace crew, Casey Evans. Your job is to catch a lot of fish to keep him busy." Evans shook hands with Kerrigan and nodded toward Jessica. "Haven't had the pleasure, pretty lady."

"Jessica."

Jock waved them aboard. "Okay, some simple rules. Number one: have fun. It's gonna be a beautiful day out there. Number two: don't fall overboard, I won't come back to get you, it's a waste of gas! If we take on water and it gets up to your knees, put one of these life jackets on." A bright, toothy smile sent a message that Sanders was kidding. "Casey will help you with the tackle. Mr. Football Player, you should know about tackles! But first, Casey is offering you all a Bonine pill for sea-sickness. Even if you don't think that'll be a problem, take the pill. You get seasick and your day is ruined. So is mine because I have to clean up the boat. We'll be out most of the day. Got sunscreen up here in the cabin, highly recommended. Casey surely will volunteer to apply it to the pretty lady! Or not. For breakfast, we have coffee, tea, pastries, OJ, and Bloody Marys. We have plenty of beer and maybe some special bourbon and some great steaks for lunch. I can't serve you alcohol, but if you happen to find my stash, what can I do– throw you off the boat? Just remember, this will be a great experience and too much alcohol may blur your memory.

"OK, Case, cast off!" The Tuna Xpress chugged to a higher pitch and it pulled out of its slip. Jock bore west to avoid the shoals nearby and had to cruise about a mile to get to a safe passage under the Bonner Bridge and the new bridge under construction, through the inlet, to the open ocean. Jock pushed the throttle down to a nice cruising speed of twenty-five knots. The chop was minimal near shore with a land breeze blowing but got a little heavier when they were a couple of miles out. Jock turned toward his passengers and said, "Casey is now serving breakfast." Kerrigan asked Jessica what she'd like, and she asked for OJ and a chocolate croissant. Casey poured Jessica her juice and handed it and the croissant to her, saying, "Here ya are, pretty lady." Jessica didn't mind Casey's cute appellation. Kerrigan lifted the cooler lid looking for the self-serve Bloody Marys. Casey handed him a plastic glass full of ice for him to fill, a lime slice, and a celery stalk. Kerrigan asked Casey if they had anything other than pastries aboard for breakfast. Jock had ordered some steak, eggs, and cheese bagels. Casey told Kerrigan to give him a couple of minutes to warm the sandwich and he could chow down. They continued to the Gulf Stream, miles offshore.

Jock turned to his little group and explained, "Okay, we're out here where we want to be. We'll be going for tuna and dolphin today."

Jessica said, "I'm not catching Flipper!"

"No, that's a bottlenose dolphin, ya know, a porpoise, a mammal. A dolphin is the slang word often used for it. We'll be looking for the dolphin fish, also called mahi mahi, which sounds better than Flipper. The fish won't find us, we have to find them. We have a fairly sophisticated sonar aboard and will be talking to the other boats out here, although there aren't many today. We'll motor back and forth and up and down the Gulf

Stream to find them. Meanwhile, Casey will get the fishing tackle ready for you. We're here to help you catch fish, so ask for assistance if you need to and any questions that come to mind."

Jock kept hunting for nearly an hour, seeing some blips on his fish finder, but nothing to get excited about. April was not prime time for tuna. Then he saw what he was looking for off to the east. "Okay, here we go. Casey, you're the man!"

The Tuna Xpress meandered in every compass direction following the school. Kerrigan was the first to get a bite. A big bite. Casey showed the proper techniques to keep the beast on the line and to slowly reel it in. Kerrigan had his first prize, a nice yellow-fin tuna about five feet in length. The fish fought once reeled, in as much as it did in the water. Casey gave it what looked like a bear hug, slipped, and flopped flat onto the deck. The scene looked strange and both Kerrigan and Jessica started laughing. Jock yelled to Casey, "If you're wrestling Mr. Tuna, I'm betting on the tuna!" Casey got back up on his feet and got the struggling fish into the hold, which was full of ice.

The trip continued. Casey and Jock served up delicious medium-rare rib eyes, beer, and bourbon. All four aboard ate like they hadn't for a week. Kerrigan complimented, "You guys could fall back in the restaurant business." Jock smiled and nodded his appreciation of the thought. The return trip was highlighted by Kerrigan consuming bourbon. A lot of bourbon. Jock spotted a pod of dolphins (the Flipper type) off the starboard bow and turned the boat toward them, shouting, "Dolphins off the bow."

Kerrigan, somewhat inebriated, said, "I've never swam with dolphins!" He looked at Jessica, followed his liquored-up urge and courage and dove in.

Casey immediately yelled, "Man overboard!" He couldn't believe what he had seen. They'd had passengers fall off before, but no one had ever jumped off intentionally in the middle of the ocean. He quickly threw Kerrigan a life ring but Kerrigan didn't reach for it. Jock winked at Casey; they had a solution. Casey smirked and bellowed, "Shark! Shark!" and pointed to a spot out beyond Kerrigan. Kerrigan frantically swam to the life ring and Casey started to pull him in.

Jock said, "Always works like a charm." They chuckled to themselves.

Casey bent over to help Kerrigan back into the boat. Why was it that an inebriated person was so uncoordinated? Jessica didn't say much, but when she saw Kerrigan back on the boat safe and sound, she just couldn't control her chuckling. "Very funny, Casey. Ha ha. Shark, my ass!" Kerrigan grumbled. "Hey, we didn't leave you there, isn't that something?" Casey replied. Jessica handed a towel to Kerrigan and wrapped it around his shoulders and kissed his pouting face on the cheek. She patted him on the shoulder and with a smile and a teasing sparkle in her eyes she said, "Like those dolphins, huh?"

The haul wasn't great– two tuna and four dolphin fish. Back at the slip with the adventure over, Casey filleted the catch, Kerrigan handed out generous tips, and Phoebe was there to take them back to Duck. Kerrigan and Jessica were exhausted. They showered, Jess ordered pizza, and, a couple of beers later, they called it an early night.

24

Cody was up early and anxious to try a Black Pelican flight again. Phoebe rolled over and, noticing that the sun had just crested the dune, said, "My, we're the early bird today. Lookin' to catch a worm?"

"This bird ain't catching no worms. Maybe a couple of waves though. I have to do a little maintenance on my boards and couldn't sleep, so I thought I'd get going. Gotta catch some eats first."

"Well, whatever you're cooking, cook one for me."

"You bet, sweet ass."

"Sweet ass? Really?" Phoebe said and rolled over.

Cody served her breakfast in bed: sausage links, scrambled eggs, and muffins. He sat on the edge of the bed enjoying his food and watched Phoebe wolf down hers.

Meanwhile, farther up the beach, Kerrigan and Jessica were struggling to recuperate from their whiskey-drowned day on the open sea. Kerrigan in particular was hurting.

"Hey, Jess, got any solutions for a wicked hangover? Anything for the sunburn on my arms? I feel like shit!"

"Excedrin is the only thing that works for my hangovers. I have a bottle in my purse, but don't take it on an empty stomach. We'll have to get something for the sunburn unless there's something here. Let me check." Jessica started investigating the bathroom cabinets; the house was well stocked, and she found some aloe lotion. She gave it to Kerrigan and said, "Try this."

Kerrigan called to her, "Aww, sugar lips, don't you want to help me out with this burn stuff? I need some TLC over here."

"Well, you big stud, you should have let me do this yesterday. The sun is not picky as to who it burns!"

She started to rub on the lotion and Kerrigan winced. "Easy now, doll."

After eating his favorite cereal with almond milk, Kerrigan wanted to enjoy the morning breezes and play backgammon with Jessica out on the ocean front balcony. It was Saturday and Jessica didn't have to go to work, but she warned him about added sun exposure. He told her he'd put on a long-sleeve shirt to cover up his aloe-soaked arms.

"But Jess, you didn't get burnt yesterday, so maybe your hot body needs some vitamin D."

Jessica took the suggestion and put on a skimpy bikini.

Cody loaded up Kassie and headed up to Mansion Beach. He was storing the drone under his bed where he didn't think Phoebe would find it. If she did, he was going to tell her that a friend lent it to him so he could see if he liked playing with it. He again passed Sea Spray Lane and turned off on Ocean Mist Lane and parked off the road. The residents in the houses on High Dunes Lane, where Ocean Mist Lane led, weren't excited about surfer dudes parking there and heading to the beach–THEIR beach- but there was no law against it. Yet. This time, he didn't bother with the surfboard or wet suit. It was a nice warm April morning with little wind and clear skies. He unbagged the Black Pelican, visually checked it out. The bird was ready to fly. As he slowly flew it south, he spotted Kerrigan and Jessica out on their balcony. Bingo! He decided to fly past the house so as not to be too obvious but then thought, *Why do I care if they see it?* He could tell from the fly by that Jessica didn't have a lot of clothes on, but the drone was too low to get a full view. He increased the drone's altitude in front of the house next to Kerrigan's to get the right angle and then flew back past Kerrigan's. The extra time couldn't have worked out better. Kerrigan was sitting on a lounge chair and Jessica was sitting on him, now topless. Cody snapped a few shots while they were kissing and the drone apparently hadn't been noticed. At least, neither lover wanted to be bothered. He flew the drone back to the south so that the sun would make it difficult to see, reversed direction, and flew it back again. This time, both their faces were clearly visible, and Cody snapped some more shots. Then he hit the jackpot! Kerrigan lifted her up slightly and sucked on one of her nipples. The drone snapped away. Cody flew it back to his beach and landed it softly on the sand. His heart was beating wildly. He would send the photos to his phone. He packed up the drone and headed home to see what he had. Once home, he sent the photos to his laptop. They were gold! Kerrigan was easily recognizable, Jessica was clearly not his wife, and they weren't playing gin rummy. He cropped three shots: one in which you could tell who they were, one of them kissing, and one with her breast in his mouth. He printed them, holding them with a towel so as not to leave fingerprints. He put them in an envelope with a computer printer message that read, "These could stay buried. Call 252-260-0678." The number was Cody's burner phone. As a little personal touch, he drew a silhouette of a pelican on the note, his idea of a signature.

He finished serving tables and all the clean up a little after midnight and drove up to Kerrigan's house. He left the envelope by the front door with a rock on it. He then went home and turned the ringer on his burner off so that Phoebe didn't answer it. The next morning, he checked it frequently, but no call. Phoebe did get a phone call, seemed instantly upset, and said, "I'll get dressed and be right there."

"Whatsup, Phoebs?"

"Got a client with a problem. A big problem. I'll call you later."

She put on her underwear, threw on a sun-dress, gave herself a quick coating of make-up, and flew out the door. Cody contemplated what had just happened. Had Kerrigan found the note and called Phoebe? He waited by the burner, but it stayed silent.

Phoebe shot up to Sea Cove Lane, dove out of her car, and hammered the doorbell. Jessica opened the door and, with a wave fit for a princess, directed Phoebe inside. Kerrigan was sitting on one of the sofas facing the ocean with a glass filled with a golden-tannish liquid and some ice. Bourbon this early?

Phoebe asked, "What happened, Preston?"

"Here, take a look." He handed Phoebe the envelope with the photos and the note.

Phoebe was stunned. "Fuck, fuck, fuck." She glanced at both Kerrigan and Jessica, neither of whom were happy campers.

Kerrigan growled, "Did you know anything about this?"

"My God, no. Of course not. No. No. No."

"Has this happened to any of your clients before?"

"No, not that I know about, and I think I'd know. What are you going to do?"

"I don't know. I just don't know. I think I'll call my lawyer back in Chicago first. See what he thinks I should do. I don't want to call the cops. I don't want this getting out. Jess, I think we need to end this. Oh my God, my career? Fuck my career, my wife is going to rake me over the coals!"

Jessica was pacing back and forth in a robe with her arms crossed, shaking her head. "Phoebs, this is not good. I can't lose my job! You know how hard I've worked to get that job!"

"I know, I know, Jess."

"Preston, I'm so sorry. I just don't know how to handle this. What, if anything, can I do?"

"I don't really know either. I guess, use your local contacts and ask around; see if anyone knows anything. But please don't let my name out. Please. And no cops."

The town of Duck is in Dare County, but Kerrigan's house was in Currituck. Phoebe didn't have a lot of contacts in Currituck, but she knew lots of business owners and policemen in Dare. She called a Dare County detective that she knew named Clint Heaton. Clint's parents were big Clint Eastwood fans, hence the name. Clint stood about six feet high, was slightly burly but not fat, had a mustache, combed his hair straight back, and was famous for his sarcastic wit. Phoebe had gone to school with his little sister, and once in a while, he flirted with Phoebe when she was a teenager.

"Hey, Phoebe, haven't seen you in a long time. How's tricks?"

"Everything's good, except for one little problem. Really, one big problem."

"Okay, what's the problem?"

"I have a client who's in a house on the beach up past the Sanderling Resort. He found an envelope at his front door this morning with some photos in it and a note with a number to call. Um, these are photos are head shots, if you know what I mean."

"Did he call the number yet?"

"No. He doesn't know what to do. He doesn't want any publicity and doesn't want this to get out under any circumstances. He was going to call his lawyer for advice. He asked me to check around, see if anyone knew what was going on. He said no cops."

"And you came to a cop. Well, this is a first, at least since I've been with the county. I'll check around, make a few calls. Can I see the pics?"

"I probably can take you there, but you'd have to say you're just a friend or something."

Phoebe called Kerrigan and he agreed to let her have the photos for a short time. She told him that she knew a PI that was a photo expert. He also told her that his lawyer told him to go to the cops, but he said absolutely not. Phoebe got the envelope with the photos and called Clint. They chose to meet at a little deli in Duck.

Phoebe got to the deli before Clint, found a seat in the back of the room, and ordered coffee. Clint arrived ten minutes later, turned down coffee, but requested a glass of ice water.

"Just as beautiful as ever, I see. Let me see what you've got."

"Hey, Clint, thanks for coming to see me."

She looked around and then handed him the envelope. He put a pair of gloves on and removed the photos from the envelope. "Probably any prints have been smeared, but I thought I'd be careful. Anyway, he doesn't want the police to get involved. The photos show them on a balcony. What floor is it on? Looks high."

"The second floor, but the first floor is elevated, so sorta the third."

"And the camera view is looking down. It was pretty high. Must have been a drone. I can check with the FAA to see who has registered a drone down here. Where's the house?"

"Thirty-two Sea Cove Lane, north of here."

"Is that in Dare? Doesn't ring a bell. Let me look it up." He did a search through his phone. "Nope, in Currituck. I'll call a detective up there and ask him if we can canvass the area together. I'll tell him to keep it quiet for now. Anything else?"

"Not that I can think of. Thanks, Clint."

"You got it, hon."

25

Heaton returned to his office couple of hours later and checked an FAA data base for drone registration. The number was daunting. Within the last four years, sixty-eight drones had been registered to residents in Dare and Currituck counties. That would require a lot of snooping for a crime that hadn't been reported. He decided to call a man he knew that owned a drone company in Durham. Heaton had talked to him previously on a couple of cases, one when a drone crashed into someone's house, and another few when a property owner complained about a drone flying over their homes. The guy knew everything there was to know about drones.

"Hey, Josh, Clint Heaton over in Dare here. Got a question, buddy. Can you tell from a drone photo what type of drone it came from?"

"That would be a needle in a haystack, Clint. You could tell whether the camera was HD, but that's about all. And one can install a separate camera on many drones, so it would be really hard to tell. Gotta photo problem?"

"Yeah. I'm just sniffing around. Nothing official yet. OK, thanks Josh."

"Any time. Give me a yell if I can help."

Lots of drones and no way to tell one from the other from what he had. Heaton called Dimitrios Nickolopoulos, a detective up in Currituck. Everyone called Dimitrios "Nicky" mainly because of the length of his very Greek name. Nicky's grandfather had arrived from Greece just before World War II and settled in Norfolk, Virginia. There he opened a Greek restaurant in the Ghent neighborhood that became a big success. One of his sons, Nicky's father, moved to Nags Head on the Outer Banks and also opened a Greek restaurant. He soon opened up the menu to be more "Mediterranean", which is to say, he added Italian choices. It was a hit. Nicky, having grown up working in the kitchen and as a bus boy, wanted nothing to do with the family business. Instead, he attended East Carolina University and received a degree in Criminal Justice. His parents weren't overjoyed with Nicky's career path.

"Yo, Nicky. Got a problem I need help with."

"Go for it, Clint."

"Got a guy in one of those mega houses on Sea Cove Lane that had some nasty photos taken. He doesn't want any PR or cops."

"So how did you get involved?"

"A favor. Pretty lady. You know how it goes. You must have a lot of them!"

"Never too many pretty ladies, is there?"

"Looks like the photos were taken from a drone. I wanted to canvass the houses all around there to see if anyone saw anything. Can we do it? Your turf."

"Yeah, no worries. When did this happen?"

"Yesterday, I believe."

"Wow, you're on it. OK, I'm open tomorrow a.m."

"Great, see you at Sea Cove at nine."

Clint never liked going door-to-door, fishing for any information he could get. The genius was figuring out what question to ask that may lead to more information. A tricky business, to be sure.

Heaton met Nicky in front of 22 Sea Cove Lane, the first house at the north end of the road. Odd that the addresses started at twenty-two. There were no cars visible in front of any of the houses on Sea Cove, but most had garages. Only one person answered their approach, not counting Kerrigan's house, which they avoided, and the person had not seen any drones two days ago. The two detectives drove up to the nearby High Dunes Lane. Going from one house to another, they finally found one person, a woman, who had seen a drone. But she thought it was three days ago, not two, but wasn't sure. What she was sure of was that it came from the beach just north of her and flew down the beach twice. She told the detectives it was low, lower than her second-floor balcony that she was sitting on. She got a distant view of who she thought was controlling it. It was a guy who had his arms outstretched, as if he was reaching for something.

"Could you see what he looked like?"

"He looked like a surfer. They come here, you know. Had what looked like a wet suit on and I saw a surfboard."

"Can you tell us anything about his appearance? Age? Anything?"

"Not much. Not sure about his age, I'd guess young. Had a blond ponytail. Don't they all have ponytails?"

"Guess many of them do, ma'am. How far up the beach was he standing?"

She took them out on her balcony and pointed to where she saw him, noting that it was just beyond the house farthest to the north.

"Thanks. Here are our cards if you remember anything else."

Heaton told Nickolopoulos that he appreciated the hospitality and the ride along. Heaton's aim was to head to some of the known surfer beaches and see if anyone fit the description that the lady had given him. His first stop was just down the road at the so-called Mansion Beach. There were only a few cars parked off the paved road in a slapdash manner, so his expectations weren't high. The surf wasn't up, and the word gets around in a surfer community. He crested the dune and observed three active surfers and two sitting on the beach, smoking something. As he approached the two, the emanation of an illegal substance filled the air. The dudes, sitting there enjoying some deep inhalations, turned to see the approaching detective. Their eyes widened bigger than a tennis ball; they knew the jig was up. Heaton flashed his badge.

"No worries, gentlemen. I just have a few questions. Sit tight. Either of you know a surfer dude with a blond ponytail? Young, like you guys?"

They glanced at each other, surely not wanting to rat out a comrade.

"There's some, not too many though."

"Know any names?"

"Naa. Don't hang with any of them."

"Here's my card in case you start hanging with them or once your haze wears off and you can answer my question."

Heaton headed down to the "Buck" beach and parked in the motel parking lot across the street. He went to the front desk and told them what his business was, as a courtesy. While there, he asked the same questions about a surfer. They had seen a few that crossed over the dune on the way to the beach. Heaton climbed the steps going over the large dune and surveyed the scene. Again, there were only two surfers sitting out beyond where there were any waves, not that there were many waves, and none on the beach. He decided that it would be more fruitful to return when the surfing was better.

26

Kerrigan's lawyer gave him the simple, anticipated advice: call the police ASAP. Kerrigan told him he didn't want to do that because if this got out, his career and marriage would be over. His lawyer told him that he had no control over whether it got out or not. If the person was a blackmailer, which was quite likely, what guarantee would Kerrigan have that the photos would go away if he paid up?

Kerrigan hung up the phone abruptly on his lawyer and cursed. "Fuck, fuck, fuck me! What the fuck! What do I pay that fucker for?!" he yelled to no one.

Kerrigan called the number on the note. The person accepted the call but said nothing.

"Anybody there? I'm calling you, speak up."

"Smart move to call. Are you ready to make a deal, one that would profit both of us?"

"Yeah, what's the deal?"

"Ten grand, all in cash, unmarked, untraceable hundreds"

"And what do I get for ten grand?"

"The photos get buried."

"How can you assure me that they will never surface?"

"As long as the cash isn't traced, they will never surface. If I get ID'd or anything else, my partner publishes the photos. You have no guarantees. But, be assured, if this goes well, I won't want to risk nailing you again." Cody did not have a partner.

"OK, it'll take time to get the cash."

"No, brother. Time is of the essence here. You can get it overnighted or wired or something. Get it tomorrow. I'll call you in the afternoon and you better answer. I'll give you delivery instructions then. So get busy."

Cody hung up. He was shaking so badly he almost couldn't push the correct button. He calmed himself and noted the phone number Kerrigan had called from. He was smirking now, a little delighted with himself. He decided to run out to buy another burner phone. He would keep the first one, just in case, but would not answer another call. He would use the second burner for phase two. While he was out, he opened savings accounts at three local banks. His thinking was that there would be less suspicion with deposits that weren't as large as ten grand.

Kerrigan called his agent, Patrice Cheger; she handled lots of Kerrigan's affairs. She- yes, a lady in the sports business- was a college friend who had gone to law school and found her niche in sports. He told her to wire ten grand more (lots had already been sent) to his Sea Dunes account. She thought he must be really having a great time, little did she know. The money appeared in the account in a matter of minutes. He then called Phoebe and told her to get ten grand out of the account in hundreds. Nothing traceable. Phoebe knew why and complied. Phoebe took the cash up to Kerrigan's house. He answered the door bell and invited her in.

Kerrigan looked like hell. He hadn't shaved, his clothes were in disarray and his hair was standing straight up like he'd been pulling on it or something.

"He wanted ten grand. I decided to pay it and hope it goes away. Have you learned anything?"

"No, but the feelers are out. I think we'll find out something, Preston. I'll keep working on it."

"I really want to find the son of a bitch. Really like him to pay for this, you know what I mean."

"Me too, Preston, me too. More than you could ever know." Phoebe was beginning to get a little scared herself. What if Sharna found out about Jessica being a companion for Preston, all arranged by her? Nothing was illegal, but Sharna would be pissed. Her job could be terminated if Sharna thought anything was done that was illegal.

After Phoebe left, Kerrigan sat down on the sofa facing the Atlantic and brooded. What a mess. He decided to call the number on the note, but no one answered. Cody heard the first burner phone buzz and looked at the caller ID; it was Kerrigan's number. He got a rush of adrenaline- did Kerrigan get the cash? Or was there bad news? Or did Kerrigan give the number to the cops? Cody would wait an hour to call back, thinking that if the cops were there, they'd leave by then. Kerrigan was getting more fidgety by the minute and decided it would be best to take his favorite calming syrup– bourbon on the rocks. He returned to the padded couch, sipped his tannish elixir, and waited. He just stared out at the ocean and waited. His cell phone rang and Kerrigan answered it, not recognizing the number.

"Did you get the cash?"

"Yep."

"Hang loose, I'll call with instructions."

Cody hung a heavy duty envelope attached to ropes that dangled from the bottom of the Black Pelican. It was thick enough to be sure to hold a hundred of one hundred-dollar bills. Cody drove to Ocean Mist Lane but parked Kassie across the main road in a parking lot in front of a small strip mall. He was dressed in in a beige shirt and khaki cut-offs. He carried the Black Pelican in its storage pouch, crossed the street, and walked on Ocean Mist Lane toward the beach. He crossed the dune and huddled in a small nook in the dune and got the drone ready for flight. He called Kerrigan using his second burner. Kerrigan answered.

"In one minute, a drone will land on the beach in front of your house. It has an envelope attached below it. Put the cash in the envelope and seal it and lay the drone back on the beach. Do this correctly and your worries will fly away with the drone. Got it, dude!"

Cody hung up before Kerrigan could reply. The worst that could happen would be for the guy to smash his drone. Then he would be out the $700 plus, what it cost, but Cody was willing to risk it.

Cody revved up the motor and the drone streaked southward. When in front of Kerrigan's house, Cody gently lowered the bird for a soft landing on the sand. Kerrigan saw it coming and walked out onto the beach. When the drone landed, the propellers stopped, and Kerrigan did as he was instructed. He backed away and the drone started up and lifted straight up. Kerrigan watched as the drone lifted and started to run in the direction the drone was flying only to realize, he could never keep track of it. Cody had considered a flight path which Kerrigan, from the beach, could not follow just in case the stupid jock tried to catch it. Instead of returning in the direction that the drone had flown from, Cody flew farther south and then turned west away from the beach. Cody had by now left the beach and was walking back on Ocean Mist Lane. He flew the Black Pelican close and parallel to the main street, U.S. Route 12, until it approached him. He slowly brought it down onto the paved lane, turned it off and quickly, stowed it in its pouch, and, with his heart beating fast and perspiration beginning to soak his shirt, walked back to Kassie. He drove north, in the opposite direction from going home. He thought if anyone saw him, driving in the opposite direction might send cops on a wild goose chase. He drove into the parking lot of a golf course and pulled into a space. He unpackaged the drone and, with butterflies in his stomach and shaking hands, opened the envelope. Hundred-dollar bills, lots of them. He looked around and, with nobody in sight near him, he counted. Ten thousand dollars as demanded. He smiled, fist pumped, and yelped, "Damn! It worked." He had already thought out the next steps. He would hide the money under the bed and deposit some in each of his three bank accounts every week, no deposit over a thousand bucks.

27

Donald Sprout was more deeply obsessed with Wilson than ever. He looked at news releases every hour that he wasn't working or sleeping. He read the campaign speeches as reported and followed his itinerary. He even ignored Vixen. The Colonel was touring the western portion of the state, too far for Sprout to comfortably travel to and return. The primaries were only a couple of weeks away. Sprout simmered; he had to do something to stop Wilson. He found the campaign schedule and noticed a stop in two days at the College of The Albemarle in Elizabeth City, which was less than an hour away. Sprout was now totally preoccupied with the thought of driving to the college. What would he do? He wanted to stop Wilson's drive to higher office- hell, he wanted Wilson dead- but he didn't want to get arrested and go to jail. He paced around his living room, mumbling to himself, sitting down and getting up again. Frantic and inconsolable– what could he do? He could try to smear Wilson. Tell the press what an evil soldier he was. He could make up some dirt and get the press to print it. He was so entrenched in his thoughts that he forgot to eat, forgot Vixen. Elizabeth City was waiting.

He decided on Plan C first; he would make up lies, print them out, and try to hand them out to the press, or to anybody else he could. What lie could he make up? He decided on sexual misconduct, surely a killer for a candidate that was promoting a squeaky-clean image. He only had the two days and, not being a rocket scientist when it came to computers- or anything else- he decided on producing a flyer with the accusation. He got busy on the internet. He found a photo of a very attractive lady in her twenties. The woman had long, brown, flowing hair and a low-cut dress revealing substantial cleavage. He pasted the photo onto a Word document and led with the headline "Congressman Wilson's Latest Girlfriend." The text below the photo identified (falsely) the girl as Angela Myers, a backroom campaign volunteer for Wilson. It claimed that she was seen with the congressman in numerous restaurants and that she was pregnant, the innuendo being with Wilson's baby. At the bottom, it listed "Center for Morality in Government." a fictional organization. Sprout liked his creation. He printed fifty copies.

The two days passed. The speech was scheduled for ten in the morning. Sprout followed his routine when leaving the house, giving Vixen another dose of oxy, duct-taping her mouth, and tying her to the bed. He placed his flyers in a large envelope, got dressed in decent clothes, shaved, and combed his hair for a change (since he wanted to look authentic) and set out for Elizabeth City at eight thirty, allotting time for his coffee and pastry stop. When he got to the college on Route 17, a sign was posted that the event had been delayed to start at eleven instead of ten. If there had been a crowd of any size there before he arrived, there was only a handful of people milling around now. He decided to head down Route 17 to the nearest gas station that looked like it had a bathroom and small store. He didn't need gas, North Carolina's gas prices being higher than Virginia's, but needed to get rid of his first coffee and buy another. After relieving himself, he purchased the large coffee and a pack of Grandma's cookies. The coffee wasn't great, but he just wanted it to wash down the cookies. After reviving his blood sugar, he drove back to the college. He asked a few pedestrians where the speech was to be made. They directed him to the Performing Arts Center. There he found a small group of people and some "Wilson for Senate" signs. He was approached by a young man with a "Wilson for Senate" button on and was asked if he'd like any campaign literature. Sprout nodded and held out his hands to accept Wilson's propaganda. Eleven finally rolled along and the doors opened, and in came an entourage of Wilson stalwarts and the man himself. The congressman stepped up onto the stage and the college president provided a warm welcome for the aspiring politician. Wilson stepped behind the podium and started his canned speech. Sprout had heard what he thought were Wilson's lies and nonsense before. Near the end of the speech, before the applause ended the affair, Sprout yelled, "He cheats on his wife!" and started handing out his flyers. A college security guard reacted to Sprout's utterance and grabbed him roughly by the arm before many of the flyers were handed out. Sprout wrestled his arm free and yelled at the guard, "I didn't do anything illegal– just getting the truth out. Touch me again and I'll sue your ass!" Another guard arrived and, despite the threat, Sprout was viciously ushered out. He continued to make a disturbance on the way out, yelling, "The man is a fraud. He cheats. He's a killer. . ."

Sprout was shoved out of the auditorium but thought he had made a statement. He couldn't wait to get home and see the news coverage of his allegations. He hoped that maybe his rough treatment might even make the evening news. He was stoked. He now looked forward to returning to Vixen and fucking her. Finally doing it because now she loved him and he loved her.

Sprout had made a huge mistake before leaving that morning. In his frenzy to spread his anti-Wilson flyers to the world, he'd grabbed the wrong bottle, and instead of cramming the normal oxy pill down Vixen's throat, he had mistakenly picked up and given her a generic ibuprofen pill. Vixen had not gone into a hazy sleep for the day. She was alert; the most alert she had been since the day she was abducted. Realizing her situation and with her heart beating fast, she squirmed and wiggled and pulled with as much strength as she could muster to try and free herself. To her relief, she was able to pull one hand out of the restraint Sprout had tied. She slowly pulled off the tape from her mouth and untied her other hand, then her feet. She had freed herself. She frantically looked around not knowing what to do. She had barely enough strength to walk since she had nearly been starved and her muscles had atrophied from a month of non-use. She listened for any sound of that crazy little man. She looked down at herself and realized that she couldn't outrun him, but she heard nothing and didn't know where he was. Where was he? What would he do if he found her untied? All she knew was that she had to get out of there. Then she remembered that he was dressed better than normal and had shaved before making her swallow the pill that morning.

Roanna was shaking and weak and wobbly. She found her way to the living room, clinging to the walls to steady her. Her legs were so weak. Just that short distance of walking caused her to collapse onto the bare floor. Not sure she could stand up, she crawled toward the front door desperate to escape from this hell. Suddenly she heard a sound– a car door shutting. She whimpered, "No, no, no, no." She froze and listened, silence. Then she heard a man talking, barely audible. She couldn't make out any words. Then she heard a woman's voice and finally made out "Don't forget the bag in the back seat." She listened. Another car door shutting and then nothing. Tears of terror rolled down her cheeks. She bravely squirmed to the front door and pulled herself up by grabbing the door-knob. Still no sound. She had to go for it. If that horrible man was outside, she would scream as loud as her weakened body would allow and hope someone would hear her. The door opened and she peeked outside. It was a sunny day and the bright light blurred her vision. She blinked and squinted her eyes until she adjusted to the brightness. She looked back and forth across the front lawn and saw no one there. She climbed down the three steps and out to the ancient, weed-infested sidewalk. She saw houses all around her and decided to head to one to her right, a nicely maintained red brick edifice. She stumbled and wobbled but her determination to get to that house overtook her physical ability. It took her a while to get to the front door; she pushed the doorbell button repeatedly, and finally someone opened the door. She collapsed.

A middle-aged woman, gray-haired and a little on the plump side, opened the door just as Roanna was falling to the ground.

"Can I help you? Oh dear, oh my dear, oh my."

The woman grabbed ahold of Roanna's arms and helped to steady her back to her feet.

"Oh my dear, goodness, you look awful, my child. Let's get inside and sit, my dear. Oh my."

Roanna just nodded and barely looked at the woman. Once Roanna was settled in a chair and a glass of water put into her hand, the woman sat next to her at the edge of the chair and tried to assess the situation to see how she could help this wounded bird.

"Dear, what is your name? What has happened to you?"

"Roanna, or Vixen."

The lady turned around and yelled, "George, come here. There's a girl here named Roanna. Isn't that the name of the missing girl?"

They questioned Roanna and learned little other than that she had been abducted and tortured. They called 911.

The police and paramedics arrived almost simultaneously. An EMT gestured to the officer to leave him alone with the teenager until he could evaluate her. He noted bruising everywhere. Her wrists and ankles were raw. Her hair was cut oddly and was greasy. She smelled to high heaven. They questioned Roanna where she was in pain and asked her, on a scale of one to ten, to evaluate the pain. She reported more than a few high numbers. It was apparent that she had been severely attacked or beaten. They rolled in the stretcher to load her into the ambulance and transport her to the nearest hospital, Chesapeake Regional Medical Center. One of the policemen that had arrived asked the EMT, "May I please ask her a couple of questions before you get her into the ambulance?"

"Sure, but don't get in our way."

"What is your name?"

"Roanna but I'm called Vixen."

"Roanna, what is your last name?"

"Ahhh, I, I don't really know. Maybe Roselli. Yes, Roselli."

The cop stared at his partner. "This is our missing girl. Get on the horn to a detective."

His partner, a woman in her thirties, stepped outside and contacted the detective branch and told them the limited information that she had. She was told that the assigned detective was Michael Hasbee. They asked her the address and said that they would contact him. She let the communications officer know that the girl would soon be headed to the hospital. She was told to go to the hospital with the girl for her protection. Hasbee would question the couple who found the girl and then meet them all at the hospital.

Hasbee, temporary lights flashing, roared to the residence where the officers had been. The police and the ambulance were gone. Hasbee asked the couple who resided there a few questions, but they didn't know much. They informed Hasbee that the girl rang the doorbell, could barely walk or talk, looked terrible, and they called 911. Pretty much end of story. He asked if they had any idea where she came from. They told him they did not, but thought that she couldn't have walked far. Hasbee called the precinct and asked for a few squad cars to position themselves on the street nearby and conduct a door-to-door canvass while he headed to the hospital.

When Hasbee finally got to the hospital, Roanna was in the emergency room. He went up to the registration desk and showed his badge. He was immediately escorted to the room where Roanna was being evaluated. A nurse had Roanna hooked up to a myriad of wires and tubes. He asked the nurse to step outside for a moment to bring him up to date on Roanna's condition. The nurse called for the attending physician, and in the hall-way they detailed Roanna's condition– she had contusions on both arms, both legs, her back, and her abdomen, abrasions on her wrists and ankles, and strange marks on her breasts. "We'll get a rape kit done on her as soon as we can. CT scans had been ordered of her head and back. Nothing appeared to be life threatening from the initial evaluation, but she's in bad shape. She was close to ninety-three pounds now and extremely dehydrated and malnourished."

"May I ask her a few questions?"

"Yes, but please don't traumatize her any more than what she's obviously been exposed to."

"Roger."

Hasbee entered the room again aware that this child was traumatized but so glad she was alive.

"Hi, Roanna. My name is Michael Hasbee. I am a detective with the City of Chesapeake police. You've been missing for some time now. Can you remember what happened?"

Roanna rolled her head back and forth, signaling that she didn't remember.

"Did some man capture you?"

Roanna nodded yes.

"Did he take you to his house?"

Another nod.

"Is he the one who hurt you?"

Roanna nodded and started to cry.

"I'm sorry, Roanna. Very, very sorry. Do you know who it was, where his house was, can you describe him?"

Roanna finally spoke, "He was thin, not tall. He had a pony tail. He walked funny, like he had a hurt leg. He smelled bad."

"Any idea where he lived?"

"It was close."

"Close to what, Roanna?"

"Close to where the police came. Real close."

"OK. Would you recognize him if you saw him?"

"Yes." Tears were pouring out of her eyes down to the pillow her head was lying on.

"OK, good. I'll let the doctors take care of you and I'll be back. We've notified your parents and they're on their way here."

More tears rolled out of her eyes and she moaned. "He said he owned me."

Hasbee left the hospital as the Rosellis were rushing to the emergency entrance doors. He stopped to acknowledge them.

"She's had a real rough time, but they say she'll be OK."

"Oh my baby, my baby!" Joan cried. Anthony held onto his wife and they continued inside.

Hasbee called into the precinct and requested a canvass of the neighborhood concentrated within a few houses of where Roanna was found.

Every house that the police visited was occupied, except for one. Those who answered the knock on their doors were curious about what all the fuss was about and were willing to answer all questions. There was nothing that the police found suspicious at all during the interviews and they got no information to help them figure out where Roanna had come from. No one answered at one house. A quick computer check indicated that it was owned by Donald Sprout. Records disclosed that he'd had numerous traffic violations and was once arrested for disturbing the peace, but the charges were dropped. The officers returned to the neighbors on both sides of the house and inquired about the occupant or occupants. The picture the officers got of the owner of the house was that of a loner, a person that had no social skills, an unpleasant and raggedy looking short man. They thought that he lived alone because they never saw anyone else coming or going. They observed that he was thin, short, had brown hair often in a ponytail, and was unshaven most of the time. He drove a beat-up gray Impala.

One officer radioed back requesting guidance on how to proceed. They were told to stake out the property until they were relieved by a second crew. If they saw anyone who looked like Sprout, they were to question him and request to be allowed to inspect the home. If he resisted, they were to bring him in.

The officers waited for four hours. No sightings. They brought their relief crew up to speed and the stake out continued. Nothing.

<h1 style="text-align:center">29</h1>

Sprout rounded a curve on Sanderling Street and saw a police car parked in front of his house. He pulled over, anxiously wondering why they were there. He sat and watched. He didn't see any cop walking around, just the car parked there. He anguished over what to do, mumbling to himself. "What do the fucking cops want?" He decided to head to a bar he occasionally hung out at in the Greenbriar section of town. He entered and sat at the bar and ordered a scotch and soda. A number of TVs hung on the wall in the darkened room. One, tuned to one of the local network channels, had a crawler running. Sprout was stunned when seeing the message; "Missing Roselli girl found. Police report that they are investigating the circumstances of her disappearance. . ." Sprout nearly shit his pants. That explained the cop car. He sipped his scotch, placed it back on the bar, and watched the TV. The crawler ran again. He downed his drink and made the hand signal for the bartender to pour another. As he sipped away, he stared at the TV and a cold sweat trickled down his chest and back. He needed a plan. He knew that, while the cops were watching, he couldn't go home. How long would they stay there? Would they dare to trespass on his property? Would they dare to break in? Fucking cops. Did they find his Vixen? How did they suspect him? He had flown under the radar. Fucking cops. He needed a plan. First, he needed cash. He had to go to the ATM and withdraw as much as he could. He didn't have much in his checking account; he lived mostly on cash. He realized that he couldn't use his debit or credit cards because he would be traced. He had to get home sooner or later, but when? When would the coast be clear? They couldn't watch his place forever. And how could he find Wilson without his laptop? Would the cops take his laptop? He stood up and walked out of the bar without paying. "Hey, buster, get back in here and pay your tab!"

Sprout headed for an ATM at one of his bank's branches. He withdrew three hundred dollars and decided he'd come back the next day for more. He drove back to Sanderling Street. He pulled over and saw that the cop car was still there. It was getting dark and he wouldn't be able to watch from a safe distance much longer, so he headed to the shopping mall nearby. He parked in the middle of the parking lot, not too close to the mall where there would be lots of people coming and going, and not on the outskirts where his car could be easily identified. He walked into the mall, headed to the restroom, and relieved himself. He'd sleep in his car tonight and see what was going on tomorrow. A little after midnight, his car lit up with flashing blue lights. What the fuck. He peeked out and witnessed a police car winding through the lot. How did they know he was there? They didn't and soon they were gone. But now, sleep would be elusive.

As the sun rose, Sprout headed back to Sanderling. As he rounded the curve a few blocks north of his house, he pulled over. The cop car was still there, lights flashing, and other cars were in his driveway and parked on the street. Bastard cops! He watched. Though he was a distance away, he could see people, cops he assumed, coming and going into his house. They had no right. He so wanted to drive up and fire a couple of shots into their chests. Yes, he had his firearm (his Glock 17) in the car. But he had to be patient. What would they take? They would have to know that Roanna was there by now. What would they do? He decided that he would make one more stop at the ATM and head to North Carolina. Surely they wouldn't follow him there. And he could somehow find out what Congressman Wilson was up to. Three hundred dollars later, he drove back to Sanderling one more time. The bastards were still there! He summoned his courage and actually drove past his house, cops cars and all, and headed toward Route 17, south to Carolina.

He headed toward Elizabeth City, for no particular reason, found a bar, and decided to resume his mission to derail Congressman Wilson. He motioned to the barkeep for a scotch and soda. He chatted up the keeper, who had no other customers at the time. This bar, like most bars these days, had flat screens all over the place. Most were showing various sports events, some of which Sprout had no clue what the objective was. A guy standing there with a flat bat– what the hell was that? A couple of others had cable news channels rolling. He didn't pay much attention to any of it. Brooding and fear used a lot of energy and Sprout was doing quite a bit of both. He missed Vixen too.

"Where ya from, don't mind me asking?"

Sprout looked up at the proprietor, not sure that he wanted to answer. Finally, "Virginia."

"Just traveling through or got business down here?"

"Personal business."

The bartender walked away, sensing that the man didn't want to be bothered. Bartenders are good at that.

"You pay any attention to local politics?" Sprout questioned.

"Some. Bartenders need to know a little about everything."

"Know anything about Congressman Wilson's campaign?"

"Sure. Won the primary two days ago. Pretty easily. He's got a good shot at the Senate. You know him?"

"Served in the Air Force with him. Just an admirer."

"Heard he's headed to the Outer Banks for some down time before the election fires up. Maybe you can catch up with him over there. You're not far away."

"Yeah, maybe."

Sprout had left his laptop at home, but he wanted to check the internet to get an update on Wilson's whereabouts. "Any place around here with access to a computer and the internet?"

"I'm pretty sure the library has computers."

"Where's the library?"

"Right on Colonial Avenue, right in downtown."

Sprout got directions to the library, gave a thumbs-up, left cash on the bar to cover his drink, and waved goodbye. It was only a few blocks from the bar, so Sprout walked there. Once in the building, he asked the receptionist where public computers were. He was directed to go upstairs and quickly found them. He picked the computer at the far end, wanting to be alone and not have anyone looking over his shoulder. He pecked away on the keyboard, found the campaign website, and brought up photos of the delighted candidate reveling in the primary victory. Bastard! The story depicted a sizeable win and optimism for the same results in the November election. There wasn't any information about his future itinerary or schedule. He then googled Congressman Richard Curtis Wilson and scanned information on the bills he'd introduced in Congress, a number of bios, a story about his primary acceptance speech, photos of Wilson in his military uniform, and lots more. A popular fellow! He finally found an article about the primary election and the rumor that he was to rent a house on the Outer Banks for a couple of weeks of rest and relaxation and to hold a summit with his advisors on campaign strategy for the general election. His opponent would be Mercer Harris, a former mayor of Raleigh. Harris had won his primary also with ease though he was not seriously challenged.

Sprout didn't have a clue about how to find Wilson, so he decided to make the short drive there and keep his ear to the ground. Someone somewhere would surely know. On the way, through a swampy area, he concocted a game plan. First, he would drive up and down the beaches looking for any cars with Wilson signs plastered all over them, or any other sign of Wilson's presence. If that failed, he'd go to the nicer restaurants and ask if they were expecting to serve Wilson's party. He would pretend to be a journalist from the western part of the state. If that became strike two, he thought he'd go to real estate offices, but he wasn't clear on what story to use.

So first, Plan A. He wasn't very familiar with the Outer Banks and really didn't know where to look. He decided to find a real estate company, not to enact Plan C, but just to find where the primo houses to rent were. He guessed that it would be a large house if Wilson was going to hold strategy meetings. He stopped at Carolina Banks Realty. Their outside electronic information board described a variety of types of homes for sale or for rent. It also advertised that it was an MLS realtor. Sprout figured that they would have the area covered, so he went to the reception desk. His shirt and jeans were wrinkled, dirty, and somewhat smelly.

"Good afternoon, sir. How may I help you?"

Find Wilson for me, bitch. "Excuse how I'm dressed; just finished work and drove down here. I want to rent a large house this summer and wondered if you had information on such accommodations?" He smirked, proud of himself for using such a sophisticated word.

"Do you know how many bedrooms?"

Sprout hadn't thought that such a question would be asked. "Not sure, really. A lot."

"Then I'll give you our premier rental brochure. It lists larger homes that we rent as well as the more luxurious ones. Would that be useful?"

"Ahh, let me take a look. I want to drive by them to see where they are and what they look like. Is there a map or anything?"

"Sure, let me show you. It's in the back."

Sprout took a look and decided that it would do for now and thanked the lady. She offered her card, which he took and stuck into the brochure. Could always use a book marker.

30

Joan and Anthony Roselli arrived at the hospital while the hospital was preparing to move Roanna out of the emergency room to a regular patient room. Tears flooded both their faces as they laid eyes on the daughter that they'd feared they would never see again. Their joyful emotions could not be controlled. The nurse warned them not to touch her unless very lightly due to the severity of her injuries. They walked up to the bed and wailed, seeing what injuries that they could see. Roanna wasn't herself and was confused by the crying.

"Mom, Dad? What's wrong? It's me. I'm here, I am really here. Don't cry, it's me, Momma."

"I know, angel, I know. We are here and you are safe love."

The Rosellis were unsure how to respond. They didn't really know what else to say, so they gently touched her. Joan garbled, "We love you so much, baby. We will always love you." Roanna blinked her eyes and a small smile lit up her battered face. They stood there until hospital personnel came in to move her- IVs, monitors and the works. The Rosellis walked with them, entered the oversized elevator, and ascended up to the floor where she'd be staying for a while. Once Roanna was in her room and moved to the bed, a nurse told the Rosellis to leave the room and she'd have the physician attending to Roanna brief them on their daughter's status. The nurse sensed how scared they were and caringly put a hand on Joan's arm and said, "She is going to be alright. It is going to take time, but she will be okay." Roanna's physician walked up to the couple and asked them to follow him into a private room off of the waiting room to address Roanna's situation and treatment plan. They believed that Roanna would fully recover from her injuries physically but that they needed a treatment plan for her psychologically. She had been beaten and malnourished. The X-rays uncovered no broken bones; however, they hadn't performed the CT scan of her head and badly bruised back. That would be performed within a couple of hours. There was no way to fully evaluate Roanna's psychological damage until a psychiatrist visited her and did an examination, which was scheduled for tomorrow. The Rosellis asked how this happened, how had she been found? Was she truly safe now? The physician did not have that information but felt certain that the police department and detectives on Roanna's case could answer all their questions.

There was still no sign of life at Sprout's house. The police were getting antsy. The longer they waited, the more time the guy would have to get rid of evidence or run away, if he was the right guy. At seven in the evening, while it was still light out, the chief gave the order to enter the house forcefully if necessary. Hasbee had returned to the scene by then and three squad cars were in position. One policeman positioned himself just to the right side of the front door, rang the doorbell, and knocked hard, announcing again that it was the police. Another officer remained in place at the rear entrance. After a few more hard knocks, an officer yelled, "Open the door or we're breaking it down." They waited. Nothing. An officer with a ram walked up to the door and, on the count of three, smashed the door open. It splintered and the damage rendered it worthless. As they carefully entered, shouts of "Police" could be heard a couple of houses away. The entire neighborhood was now outside watching the show.

"Nobody needs to get hurt, identify where you are." No response. They slowly crept into all the rooms and then the basement. "All clear!" was sounded as every room was checked out. They turned the lights on and beckoned Hasbee to come in and see what was found. What caught the eye initially, other than the sparse furnishings, were the walls in the living room. They were plastered with photos and news articles of what was obviously Congressman Wilson. All of the photos were smudged with ragged X's and words like "Die, fucker" and "Killer" and "Loser." Hasbee said, "I think we have a problem here!" The kitchen was a slovenly mess. Dirty dishes, pots and pans, food, and trash were everywhere. The pungent odor was horrific.

"How many months has this stuff been here?!" One officer told Hasbee, "Some of it hasn't been out too long." The main bathroom and half bathroom were equally disgusting, if that was possible. Clothes had been left piled knee high on the floors; the sinks, toilets, and bathtub were stained almost beyond recognition. The smell there was not too pleasant either. The rear bedroom, the largest of the three, was clearly the occupant's room. It was furnished with a twin-sized bed with no head board or foot board. The filthy sheet and stained blanket were pushed to one side. The room had a nightstand, a simple wooden chair, and a small dresser. Hasbee saw a laptop on the dresser and requested that it be tagged. Hasbee's hands were already gloved, so he opened the computer up and pressed the enter button. The screen came to life. Hasbee pulled the chair close and sat down. He wasn't going to perform an exhaustive search, but he wanted to see if there were any clues that tied the owner, identified as Sprout, to the Roselli girl. The recent internet searches disclosed lots of research on Congressman Wilson. Then an officer called Hasbee. "I hit the mother lode, detective. Come on in here!" Hasbee found him in a bedroom that was to the rear of the living room. Again, the furnishings were sparse. The bed - an opened futon, at first glance- was probably all the evidence that he needed. There were pieces of duct tape lying on the floor. Frayed pieces of rope were tied to the iron bed frame, hanging down near the middle of the bed and at the heel of the bed. The locations could easily correspond to where Roanna's wrists and ankles would have been secured. There were substances on all four pieces of rope that had the general appearance of dried blood. The sheet that partly covered the mattress was stained and dirty and also had indications of dried blood. Hasbee had everything bagged and told the attending patrolman to get them to the lab to determine if the substance was blood and to run a DNA check. Hasbee also found girl's clothing lying on the floor of the room's closet. He held the clothes up and guessed that they would have fit Roanna. Those also would be sent to the lab.

31

The Wilson campaign rented one of the houses on Mansion Beach. It featured most aspects that these houses had– oceanfront, multiple living areas, eight bedrooms, ten baths or half baths, all the bells and whistles. Wilson's campaign manager, Sid Freeze, made the rental arrangements, of course through the campaign. Of Wilson's central campaign staff, Sid was the only gay individual. That had nothing to do with Sid's position. Sid had worked for Wilson's campaigns since day one and was completely trusted by Wilson. He was efficient. Everybody knew he was the boss. He understood what it took to win. Freeze was of medium height and build, clean-shaven, with short dark hair parted from the left, and good-looking. Wilson, being a conservative, was somewhat brave to have a gay person in charge. He didn't care; he had no quarrel with gay people, and Freeze was top drawer. Freeze wanted Wilson in the Senate for personal as well as professional reasons. He loved the Georgetown nightlife scene, including both the straight bars and the gay bars. He loved the museums and all the cultural trappings that D. C. had to offer. He rented an apartment in Arlington, across the Potomac, near a Metro station. Not cheap, but it was situated in an active area where he could hop down to an espresso bar, chic shops, and little cafés of numerous nationalities. And Freeze loved being someone special– assistant chief of staff for a U.S. congressman, which morphed into campaign chairman most of the time. Congressmen seemed to be always running for the next election. Hoping to move over to the more elite Senate side of Congress, Freeze hoped that Wilson would offer him the Chief of Staff position. As such, he envisioned rubbing elbows with everyone who was someone in Washington.

Freeze wanted to get started on the main campaign, but first, he wanted to give Wilson a chance to chill out. He advised Wilson that he should host a party for the campaign staff that was closest to him and asked if some of the committee heads could be housed at Wilson's rental. Others would be domiciled in suites in a nearby motel. Wilson agreed to all of the plans, telling Freeze to make the arrangements and let him know what to do and when to do it, normally what Freeze did anyway. He arranged the affair in Wilson's honor to celebrate what had been accomplished, the primary win, and quickly got the word out. Freeze had his administrative assistant, Julie Massey, send emailed invitations. Six chairmen were invited to stay at Wilson's, eighteen others off-site. The party would start Friday night and end Sunday night. Those staying in the main house would then meet Monday morning to develop the strategy to proceed on to November.

First things first, planning the party. This would be somewhat Chappaquiddick-style but, hopefully, not with the dramatic headlines. Julie Massey was in charge. With her bubbly personality, cute looks, and boundless energy, she could arrange anything. A bartender would be hired for Friday night and all day Saturday and Sunday. She arranged a highly reputed caterer who was available for the weekend (after being told there would be a bonus payment) to provide and serve all the meals. She personally would shop for snacks and some decorations, which she would bring from Raleigh, and had another worker buy a corn-hole set, a ladder golf set, and volleyball equipment. The event would have to include meetings and planning events so that the campaign funds could be used. The meetings, except the ones on Monday, would be a sham. Wilson or Freeze would open a session, ask if there were any comments (which there wouldn't be), and close the meeting. Dot the I's and cross the T's!

For Friday night, Julie arranged with the caterer a simple cookout. The meal would feature ribs, hamburgers, barbequed chicken, corn on the cob, a crab dip and other appetizers, and apple pie. The Saturday and Sunday breakfasts would include an omelet bar with any imaginable ingredient including a rich seafood topping, pancakes, bagels, gourmet coffee and a variety of fresh squeezed juices. Monday's meal would be a brunch with eggs, bacon, sausage, ham, pastries, the Outer Banks' famous Duck Donuts, and open-face meat and dolphin Reuben sandwiches. Saturday's lunch would feature gourmet pizzas and salads. Sunday's lunch was highlighted by local seafood, fried, blackened, or broiled. Saturday evening's menu starred champagne, shrimp cocktail, and surf and turf- that is, Maine lobster tails and filet mignons. Sunday's events would conclude the weekend for most with a New England-style clam-bake. Julie arranged a highly recommended quartet to entertain the group both Saturday and Sunday nights. She had to offer an extra fee because the short notice required them to cancel their previously scheduled gig.

Sprout drove north from the real estate office toward the town of Duck. It was Thursday afternoon. From the brochure, he thought that the-higher end houses were concentrated from Duck to Corolla. The road, not paved until the 1980s, was a winding two-lane path that passed wild dunes, a golf course, and large houses, mostly rentals, that locals called "mini-hotel". The speed limit varied from twenty-five to forty-five, and it didn't take much traffic to bring the flow to a crawl. During the summer tourist season and popular holidays, it was a crawl most of the day. Sprout continued his search pulling off of the main drag, Route 12, to drive past all the clusters of houses, looking for any sign of Wilson. He found it somewhat tedious, as he was easily bored, but he was motivated. Find Wilson. Having found no sign, he entered the Corolla area. Sparsely populated just forty years ago, Corolla now consisted of over five thousand houses and a summertime population of over fifty thousand. It was no longer that little village that no one had ever heard of. Sprout was confused as to where to go and how to surveil the houses. He turned at the first road to the right going toward the ocean. He was assuming, based on nothing, that Wilson would be at an oceanfront house. He meandered around the southern part of town, driving back to Route 12 and then departing from it with no luck. This seemed like an impossible mission. He pulled into a parking lot in front of what looked like a sports bar. It was getting close to most happy hours and Sprout sat at the bar.

Although this was an informal, laid-back town, Sprout was scruffier than the usual visitor. Flat screens were everywhere.

"What can I do for you?"

"Got any happy hour specials?"

"Sure. Well, drinks and certain beers are half price."

"Good. Good. Make it scotch and soda."

"You bet."

Sprout enjoyed the upscale bar seat and swiveled around to check if there was anything on the early news about Wilson. His scotch was served and he continued to scan the TV's. The bar was fairly empty. After he downed drink number one, the bartender asked if he would like a refill and Sprout pushed the glass toward him and gave a thumbs-up. When his drink returned, Sprout asked, "Hear Congressman Wilson is holing up around here. Like to meet him. Any idea where he might be?"

"No. Heard the same, but this is a big area. Maybe you should email his campaign. Sure he'd like to meet a supporter."

"Yep, I bet he would."

A few more customers trickled in. Sprout caught a headline on the screen tuned to the Norfolk news: "Police search for Donald Sprout, suspected kidnapper of Roanna Roselli."

Under his breath he said, "Fuck, fuck, fuck." He was dazed. Could they find him down here? Why would they even look for him down here? Better lie low. He asked the bartender where the bathroom was, and he was directed to go around the right side of the bar. When the mixologist was busy with an order from one of the tables, Sprout headed toward the rest-room, entered and peed, then slowly came out, saw that the barkeep was still busy, and quietly walked out of the pub. He was in his car and pulling out before the tender realized he had been stiffed. He hurriedly walked out from behind the bar, hoping at least to glimpse the jerk's license plate, but it was too late; Sprout was gone.

Plan A wasn't fruitful and it seemed like it would be insurmountable to find Wilson by driving up and down the beach towns. He actually started Plan B, asking around, but on the first try, that provided nothing more than a few free scotches. Sprout thought that the email idea was a good one, but he'd have to find a computer, send the email, and wait for an answer. Also, he wouldn't want to use his email address since, maybe, the cops could track him down. He also was spooked to go to an ATM for more cash. The damn cops probably could find out where he withdrew money. He decided to get a fast-food burger, find a quiet, off-the-beaten-path spot, and spend the night snoozing on the back seat. Tomorrow, he'd think of some way, somehow, to get information about where Wilson was. He closed his eyes and his Vixen flashed before him. He was so sad and he missed her. Did she miss him?

32

Cody Delaney was elated with his success at his first blackmail attempt. As far as he knew, nobody had sniffed him out or even suspected him. He was slightly worried that Phoebe might catch on, but, then, why would she think he would do anything like that? To be a little safer, he decided to keep the drone in its pouch in a small suitcase that he locked. He asked the general manager to allow him to store the suitcase at the Atlantic Bistro, where he worked. He fabricated a story that it held important papers and he was worried that his house wasn't safe. He also kept any of the cash that he hadn't deposited in the case.

Getting out of bed, he staggered to the kitchen and started the drip coffee maker. He sat on one of the two kitchen chairs and waited for his first shot of caffeine. Years ago, he'd had some digestive issues and finally went to a doctor. Before doing (and paying for) extensive tests, the doctor suggested that Cody try an elimination diet. He liked the idea and after two months or so determined that the culprit was dairy products. He was lactose intolerant. Big time. So, he started drinking coffee black with sugar and, although he could have tried lactose-free milk or substitutes like almond milk, he got used to his joe without whiteners.

He poured himself a mug, added sugar, and noticed that Phoebe was stirring. He walked over to the bed, stooped down, and whispered, "Hey, buttercup, are we finally awake?"

"Uhuh."

"Ready for some java?"

"Yeah, in a minute."

Cody went back to the kitchen, pulled out her favorite mug from the cabinet, one she'd purchased from a local potter, and placed it next to the coffee maker, ready for use. He opened his laptop and browsed the local news websites and found nothing about his stunt. He didn't want to go back to any site that had to do with Chicago football or Kerrigan himself. He obviously knew that Kerrigan was one of Phoebe's clients, but she hadn't said anything to him about what had happened. Cody was ready to try again, but he wanted to be careful and fly under the radar. He didn't want Phoebe or anyone else to know what he was up to. Phoebe got up out of bed and went into the bathroom. She liked to look somewhat decent for Cody before sitting down with him. He poured her the first mug, lots of half and half. When she reappeared, he said, "Good morning, beautiful. Here's your wake-up drink."

"Thanks, hon."

"What's happening today?"

"Got a new client coming in. Some big movie hotshot, Harrison Shane."

"Oh boy. What do you know about him?" he asked, trying to be casual.

"Quite a bit. You know we try to research the clients to get some insight as to what they'd like. We got a nine-page document from some studio wheel telling us what Shane liked and didn't like. That's a lot of detail, in my experience."

"Is he going to be a pain in that sweet little ass of yours? What's so important on his list?"

"Booze, of course. Single malt scotch. Something called The Macallan Twelve Years Old. We found it was hard to get. Ever hear of it?"

"No, but I'll check with Willow at the Bistro. There's nothing she doesn't know about whiskey. Where are you putting this dude up at?"

"Up in one of our places on Mansion Beach."

"Traveling alone, just curious?"

"Yeah. Momma doesn't get to come. Heard he likes the ladies. He's a big guy– six five, three hundred pounds probably."

"Hope the house is well built!"

Phoebe showered, spent some time getting made up, and put on one of her sexiest dresses.

"Whoa– you're gonna be his lady of the night, are you babe?"

Phoebe gave him a playful slap on the face and said, "He's got more dough than you, hon."

"But I got other attributes."

She smiled, "Yes, you do! So don't get too tired at work tonight."

Phoebe smiled wickedly, waved, and headed to the office. When she arrived, she checked in with her boss, Sharna. She assured Sharna that everything was in place for the movie guy's arrival later that day. The "movie guy", Harrison Shane, had directed a whole lot of movies and had two Oscars on his mantle. A delivery of a case of Shane's favorite beverage, The Macallan Twelve Years Old scotch, had just been delivered yesterday. Shane liked Cuban cigars so, after days of research and phone calls, Phoebe found a store in Miami's Little Havana that bragged that they sold authentic Cubans. Shane's favorite was the Bolivar Libertador, at roughly thirty dollars a pop, an extravagance for most people. Not for Academy Award winners. Phoebe ordered five boxes filled with ten cigars each. The house he was renting was non-smoking, so Phoebe was loud and clear to the studio administrator who made all of the arrangements that Shane could not smoke in the house, but he could on the balconies. The director was a golfaholic and the document Phoebe had received asked for tee times, preferably at ten, be set up for the best courses on or around the Outer Banks. It also stated that Shane liked to play in twosomes or foursomes, so they needed to find partners. They would have to pay their own greens fees; Shane was notoriously cheap. Phoebe knew it would be easy to find golfers, on and off the Banks. Most guys would love to play a round with a famous movie director. No ladies need apply. Shane liked a locker-room atmosphere on the course. He was banal, even disgusting with everyone he dealt with but on the golf course, no holds were barred! The studio's information sheet listed that Shane needed a private cook and daily maid service (per Shane's reputation, a French maid would likely be preferred). He preferred the best steaks money could buy and would like to try local seafood. Caviar and champagne were prominent on the list. Also included were gallons of coffee-flavored ice cream, homemade peach pies- never mind that it wasn't peach season yet- and gourmet peanuts. Yes, there is such a thing. He also requested a large number of movie DVDs, some of which were movies he'd directed. Presumably, he appreciated his own fine work.

Phoebe had everything in place. The weather for the next couple of days was predicted to be ideal for golfing: temperatures in the low seventies, slight breezes, partly cloudy. She called Jorge at the Currituck Club, set up a tee time at ten a.m., and asked if he knew any high rollers to partner up with her Hollywood director. Jorge said they had a twosome scheduled to tee up at nine; He was sure he could get another club member; how important was the ten o'clock request? Phoebe told him it was cast in stone. Jorge said he'd do what he could and get back to her. She made further arrangements for some of the other courses nearby. So tomorrow it would be the Currituck Club; Saturday, The Point; Sunday, Nags Head Golf Links; and then Duck Woods Country Club, Kilmarlic, and Sea Scape. She knew they had their own personalities and Shane could tell her which one best fit his style. She had excellent rapport with each club's starters-- money and charm works-wonders- so she was assured that each course could find three other golfers to team up with Phoebe's guest.

Whitney, Sea Dune's receptionist, buzzed Phoebe and told her that Marco was on the line for her. Marco, the limo driver, was waiting at the general aviation terminal at Norfolk for Shane's private jet to land.

"Hey, cutie, they pulled up and found their parking space. The jet jock knows where to find me."

"OK, Marco. Text me when you land the big fish. I'll meet you at the house with his paperwork. Remember, eighteen High Dunes Lane."

"I know where I'm going, darling. At least today!"

Harrison Shane never flew commercially. He owned a Gulfstream G100. The plane was finished with luxurious appointments. Shane had it modified to seat five with space for a kitchen and bar. The plane was powered by two Honeywell turbofan engines and could cruise at 470 knots and at 41,000 feet. The jet's range could take him from L.A. to the east coast in typically five hours, depending on the jet stream, without refueling. It required an airport with a runway over a mile long, meaning Shane could not use the closer airport in Manteo, North Carolina. Shane was flying alone this day, and as soon as he was whisked away, the pilot and co-pilot would take a cab to a nearby motel and return to L.A. the next day.

Shane, somewhat anesthetized from the contents of the plane's bar, carefully climbed down the planes steps and spotted Marco holding a sign with "Mr. Shane" printed on it. Marco, of course, knew what Shane looked like and waved at his soon-to-be rider. An airport jockey retrieved Shane's bags from the plane, and when he was near Marco, Marco said, "Got them from here."

"Mr. Shane, welcome to the east coast. My name is Marco. How was your flight?"

"Fine. Fine. Never been to the Outer Banks. I'm told it's a great place to relax."

"Yes sir, we've got aces in the relax suit!"

"Got any hot babes?"

"Oh, you'll have to talk to Miss Razario about that. I stay close to home with the missus."

Marco loaded up the limo. He texted Phoebe that they were on the way and that Shane was feeling no pain. Shane asked about babes.

"How long are we going to be driving?"

"About an hour and a half, maybe a little more depending on traffic."

"Got any sauce in this beast?"

"Yes sir. In the console in front of you, you'll find some ice, a bottle of Macallan scotch, soda, and water, sir."

"Ahh, Marco, you da man!"

Later during the ride he asked, "Marco, you got good restaurants down there?"

"Yes sir, by my standards, anyway. I don't know how they compare to L.A. Never been there."

"We'll have to get you there. Any dominant food specialties?"

"Fresh seafood, sir. We're known for that. I'm sure Miss Razario will point you in whatever direction you're interested."

"What do you know about the golf courses, Marco?"

"Sir, I don't play, so I can only tell you what other clients tell me. They say the courses are super, hidden gems on the east coast. I know Miss Razario has you scheduled tomorrow."

"Fine. Fine."

33

Hasbee drove to the CSI division and found Jordan Speed, the investigator on the Roselli case. Speed had invited Hasbee to come talk over the lab results that he'd received. Hasbee was depressed somewhat. He thought that if he and Speed had only searched more thoroughly for Roanna when they found her phone and book bag, they might have found her. They were not far from Sprout's house. Then, he actually caught Sprout at home, but with Sprout's belligerent attitude, Hasbee had decided to pack up and leave. So close!

"Detective, you don't look too spunky this morning. What's up?"

"Just thinking how this case could have come off better."

"Mike, would have, could have, should have. You know what hindsight is, right? The girl is alive, so we have that going for us."

Speed had gotten prints and DNA from the book bag and smashed cell phone that they'd discovered early in the investigation. He got the results from the blood, hair, saliva, and prints, among other things, from the samples taken from Sprout's house.

"The Roselli girl was the one in the bed. The ropes and duct tape were on her. Sprout's DNA was everywhere. Got some other findings, but we couldn't identify them. Might have been old, don't know. Mike, no question what he was doing with the girl. Lots of male secretion on both bed sheets."

"Good job, Jordan."

"Where are you at on finding the bastard? Got the dragnet out?"

"You been watching some vintage cop shows, Jordan?"

"Just the facts, Mike, just the facts." They both chuckled.

"The dragnet" Hasbee drew out the word "hasn't found a trace yet. We're going to alert the North Carolina Staties. Having seen all of the hate messages about Congressman Wilson down there, we're thinking he may be hunting him down. We did set alarms at his house and notified neighbors to call us if they see him. Nobody has, yet. We're thinking that he knows we busted the house and he may not come back. Did you get anything useful from his computer?"

"Oh yeah, forgot about that. No password, so it was easy. Had photos of the Roselli girl sitting on a park bench with some kid. Probably the bench we started at. Photos of her tied to the bed, no shirt, sick perv. Also, googled lots of porn. He had lots of internet searches for Wilson. He searched his background, personal life, congressional record, the whole nine yards. Lots of checks on the campaign site and his itinerary. He googled looking for information on some of Wilson's scheduled stops. Did a few MapQuest direction searches. Didn't find any email. Apparently he didn't email for whatever reason. Nothing about any friends. That should bring you up to speed, pun intended!"

"Thanks, Jordan. Keep me up to 'Speed' if you get anything else significant."

"You got it."

Hasbee grabbed a coffee that Speed always had ready and returned to his office and knocked on the doorframe of Chief Marnee Forbish.

"Hey Chief, ya got a minute?"

"For you, detective, of course!" she said with a whimsical smile.

"Been over with Speed at CSI. No question that the Roselli girl was being held there at Sprout's. No question that the prick was doing some nasty things to her."

"Yep, falls into place. We got the rape kit results back while you were partying with Speed. She was raped numerous times. The samples were sent over to CSI. Check back with Speed in a couple of days, but we all know what the answer will be, don't we?"

"Yes ma'am, we do."

"What's next on tracking him down?"

"I'm thinking he figured out that we're on to him and he won't come home. With his obsession with Wilson, I want to alert Carolina. Sprout may be hunting the congressman down. Heard he just won the primary."

"OK, do it. Have you figured out what he's got against Wilson?"

"Not really. They were in the Air Force together in Afghanistan. Wilson was the commanding officer of the unit that Sprout was in. Sprout was injured when a plane he was traveling in was shot down by a rocket. Believed to be from the Taliban. I couldn't find any connection between Wilson and the crash."

"Then find some of the other airmen involved and see what comes up. Meanwhile, get onto Carolina Staties. Have you brought the Rosellis up to speed?"

"Will do on the first two. No, just got back from CSI, so I haven't shared anything with them."

"Call Carolina, then get your ass over to the Rosellis and be gentle."

"Aye, aye, Madame Capitan." Hasbee smiled and saluted. Chief Forbish just shook her head.

Hasbee called the North Carolina State Police headquarters, identified himself, and was connected to an officer at the intake desk. He told him about the suspicion that Sprout was on the hunt for Wilson and that he was going to email them the entire scoop he had on Sprout, including a photo from his military file. The officer thanked Hasbee, got Hasbee's contact information, and promised to stay in touch.

Hasbee left the office, got into the carpool vehicle and drove to the Roselli home. On the way, he passed Sprout's house and decided to stop and walk around. He wasn't sure what he was looking for, but, what the hell, he was there. It was a beneficial visit. Under the stoop by the rear door he saw something reflecting in the sun. He put on a pair of gloves and reached under the stoop and pulled out a cell phone. He mumbled to himself, "What have we got here?" He pressed the home button but nothing happened. He walked back to the car and dug out an evidence bag and placed the phone with an information tag in the bag. "Another present for Jordan Speed."

He got back into the car and arrived at the Roselli residence. He rang the doorbell and waited, but apparently no one was home. It was a weekday. He called Joan at her office and told her he would like to meet with her and her husband at their convenience to bring them up to date on the investigation. She told Hasbee that any time after six would be fine. He agreed to return at six.

Hasbee dropped the phone off at CSI and told the receptionist that it was a present for Speed. Jordan would understand what to do with it. He returned to his office and called the military information office. To get data on Sprout's unit, they required a letter from him, on police letterhead, stating the reason for the request. Hasbee told the bureaucrat it was a matter of urgency and the woman gave him a fax number that he could send it to. She said that once they received the fax, it would have to be staffed, might take a couple of days, and for him to call back then. Hasbee thanked her, insincerely, and drafted the letter and fired it off to the number she had given him.

Hasbee arrived at the Roselli home at six. They welcomed him in and invited him into their living room. Joan offered him coffee, which he accepted, cream, and sweetener, and he sat in a large comfortable chair near the fireplace. Anthony asked the two younger children to go upstairs to play. Roanna was still in rehabilitation. Anthony sat on the love seat facing the fireplace and waited for Joan to bring the coffees. She brought in a tray with three cups of coffee and some petit fours. Each picked up a cup and added cream, sugar, or sweetener as desired.

Joan said, "Thanks for coming by, Detective."

"Please, call me Mike."

"OK, thanks, Mike. I assume you're busy and this is after hours, so we appreciate it."

Anthony added, "Yes, thanks."

"I wanted to brief you on where the investigation stands. We've done an analysis on various samples, and your daughter was definitely at the house of a man named Donald Sprout. The evidence strongly points to her being held captive there. We believe that Sprout abducted her the afternoon that she went missing and kept her there at his house. We think he planned it. We believe he may have been watching her, waiting for an opportunity."

Joan said, "Why Roanna? Why?"

"We don't know, ma'am. He appears to be a twisted individual. We don't know his exact motivation to take her."

"What do you know about how she was treated?"

"The hospital has given us the preliminary report summarizing her injuries. They were extensive, as I'm sure you know. We can only conclude that Sprout inflicted those on her. Your daughter hasn't told us much and we haven't pushed it. The psychiatrist warned us that she's very fragile right now and may be for some time. She was terribly traumatized."

Anthony questioned, "What do you know about this Sprout guy?"

"Not much yet. We believe that he's on the lam, possibly in North Carolina. He could very well have found out that we know what he did to your daughter. We have them watching out for him. We know what kind of car he's driving. We're also investigating things, like his laptop, that we found in his house."

Joan asked, "Are we safe? Is Roanna safe?"

"We have an officer stationed at your daughter's rehab center at the hospital as a precaution, but we have no reason to believe that he knows where she is or that he'll get anywhere close to her or to you. Or to his house, for that matter. Just keep your eyes open; you never can predict the future."

"Thanks, Detective- er, I mean, Mike."

Mike stood and headed for the door. "Thanks for the coffee and we will keep you posted. I *will* get this guy."

34

After Phoebe left for the office, Cody pulled out his laptop to google Harrison Shane. Knowledge is power! He thought even if Phoebe found the search, he could explain that it was idle curiosity. Cody viewed a number of photos of Shane, including one of him holding an Oscar. He read some mini-bios and newspaper articles. He was reputed as being an excellent director, but was ruthless with production staff and actors, and there were plentiful stories of confrontations. Actors would work for him knowing that the end result would be a plus for their careers, but they dreaded the filmmaking journey. To his credit, seven actors and actresses had received Academy Awards under his direction. Cody also read copious articles about his suspected womanizing. Shane didn't invent the "director's couch", but he was depicted as having mastered it. He was married to his fifth wife, the stunning actress Natalie Shields, and, in interviews, he claimed to be monogamous since the marriage. Cody thought, yeah right. Old habits die hard! His profile in the media was of an arrogant, narcissistic prick who would screw anyone to get what he wanted. One story in Hollywood lore was that during a movie he was directing, which was released as *The Big Lucky*, he yearned to bed the leading actress. However, she was romantically tied to a minor actor in the same flick. Shane fired the actor, blackballed him by making up a salacious story about him and ruined his career. The story went that he never got to drag the actress into bed. She never did another film with him.

Cody decided to head up to Mansion Beach the next day and do a little spying. This guy had to be loaded. With his reputation, he might not be worried about being seen with a woman that wasn't his wife, but with the Me Too movement still strong, such a revelation might hurt his career and standing in Hollywood, one of the liberal capitals of the world.

Clint Heaton was getting nowhere fast investigating the incident with Kerrigan. He called Phoebe and asked if he could stop by and talk. This being Shane's first full day on her watch, she told Heaton that she would be in her office but might have to leave at a moment's notice if her client called. Heaton arrived about half an hour later and Phoebe invited her old friend into her private office.

"We tapped a dry well. I reached out to Currituck County and we couldn't find anything. We think the blackmailer used a drone. Very clever, actually. We've asked all the local police departments to tell us if they saw anyone using a drone on the beach. We've gotten a few leads, but they didn't pan out. The pilots were either visitors, which we couldn't do much about if they were the perpetrators, or a local or two that just didn't meet our profile, which is pretty wide open. We're watching though. What did your client do?"

"He paid and hoped it would go away. The guy did use a drone. He picked up the cash with it."

"How much cash?"

"Ten big ones."

"OK, I'll check with the local banks to see if they can tell me about any large deposits. Not hopeful, though they're pretty tight-lipped about their customers' business. Do you know if there were any more threats?"

"Not by the time Kerrigan left. I haven't talked to him since. I don't think he's sure that I didn't have anything to do with it. But it certainly wasn't good for me or for our company."

"Nor the Outer Banks, for that matter. We'll keep on watching, Phoebe. I'll stay in touch."

After Heaton left Phoebe's office, Sharna, her boss, came to the doorway.

"Wasn't that a detective?"

"Yeah. Clint Heaton with Dare County."

"Anything I should know about?"

"No, just old friends catching up," she lied.

Sharna scrunched her face and said, "OK, if you're sure."

Heaton decided to take his tour of the local banks to see if there had been any large deposits made. He knew he was looking for ten thousand dollars. He hoped that the blackmailer wasn't too smart and had dropped all of it in a local bank. There were a lot of banks on the Outer Banks. The real estate market was huge, and the mortgage business ranged from vibrant to lethargic depending on interest rates and the general economy. He decided to start in the north, in Corolla, where the banks were almost absent. No luck there, the bank's vice president citing confidentiality. Heaton continued south to Duck, then Southern Shores. He was stonewalled at each stop, even using his story that this was a matter of high importance. Visit after visit all the way down to Nags Head, same story– Sorry, detective, that's confidential customer information unless it passes federal limit. We can't help you unless you have a subpoena.

Heaton still had the water bottle that he and Nicky had found on the beach where a lady had seen a dude with a drone. He could have a DNA test performed, but he would have to file a crime first and he had nothing to match any DNA with, so he kept the bottle in its evidence bag in a drawer in his office desk.

The next day, Cody drove Kassie up to Mansion Beach. He turned off of NC 12 onto Ocean Mist Lane, where he pulled off onto the grass to park. He went through the ritual of putting his wet suit on and carrying his surfboard to the beach, but he wasn't there to surf. He was there to do reconnaissance. He walked to the north end of High Dunes Lane and crossed over the dune. There was a well-traveled path there, as in other places, through the sea oats and various other dune vegetation. This was the area that he had launched his drone when he perpetrated the Kerrigan caper. He liked to start there because the other surfers usually hung out farther south by Sea Cove Lane. There was a slight breeze from the north and the waves weren't robust, so Cody decided to do his spying from out beyond the breakers, where he wouldn't be too obvious, and let the wind take him past the large houses. He didn't observe anyone outside along High Dunes Lane that fit the scanty description that he had for Shane, and he drifted toward the houses on Sea Cove Lane. He struck out there also. There were other stretches of large houses elsewhere along the beach, but it would take forever to check them all out. He'd chosen this area because he knew that Phoebe's real estate company listed a number of homes there. Cody ended his nautical moseying where a clump of surfers were bobbing up and down waiting for the right wave. Not many good ones were rolling in. Cody waited for his wave, hooked one that only took him about twenty yards, and paddled in to the shore and walked back up to where he'd parked. After he emerged out of the wet suit, he threw it onto the back seat, secured the surfboard onto his pipe contraption, and headed for home. Once there, after a quick stop for a burger at a locally owned shack, he opened his laptop and googled Sea Dunes Concierge Realty. He clicked on the homes to rent button and narrowed the search by specifying oceanfront and six bedrooms or more. He had to declare a time frame, so he picked October 16, thinking that all the units would be available by then. Nineteen homes resulted from the search. As he expected, four were on High Dunes Lane and five more were on Sea Cove Lane, almost half of the nineteen. He wrote down the addresses of all of them; he didn't want to email the information to his phone because he didn't take his phone into the water when he surfed, and he didn't want the list to be accidently discovered by Phoebe. He brought up Google Maps to find where the others were. To make the search mission easier, he printed a couple of maps that covered the entire area where the houses were located. He drew dots on the maps for each house with their address.

Since it was early afternoon, he decided to go on a sightseeing trip to familiarize himself with the locations and perhaps take a short walk in front of a few. He would have his antenna up, watching for any evidence of Harrison Shane. He left his house and drove north again, no longer with surfboard and wet suit. Kassie clunked and hissed but as always got him where he wanted to go. After two hundred and ten or so miles, Kassie was getting tired. Two of the rentals were about three miles north of Mansion Beach, an area he wasn't acquainted with. He pulled off onto the access road and wandered past a patch of oceanfront that had no houses. He found the rentals he was looking for. Cars were parked in front of both places. Cody walked past them and crossed over to the beach between the homes. He hoped to look like a vacationer out for a nice walk. In front of the first suspect house, there were a gaggle of kids playing in the sand and a few adults in attendance, five of them sitting on the balcony enjoying the breeze. Definitely not Shane's house. A couple of houses down was the next candidate. The scene was somewhat similar– fewer on the beach, but more on either of the two decks. Strike two. Cody casually turned around and crossed over the same path that he'd entered the beach from, and he plunked down in the driver's seat of Kassie. He crossed those two off the list. It was getting close to when he had to get to the restaurant, so he pointed Kassie southward and headed home.

35

S id Freeze arranged for a golf outing for Wilson Friday morning, before the festivities started. Wilson was a natural athlete and enjoyed hitting the links but rarely made time for a casual game. He shot a six handicap. Lobby golf was more common, but Wilson didn't enjoy the company of most lobbyists. Today, it would be just for fun. He was placed in a foursome, set to tee off at the Currituck Club at ten. One member of the club, a very successful local real estate agent, and two well-off vacationers filled out the group. Harrison Shane was one of the guests. All four arrived around nine thirty, signed in, and went to the locker room to change into their spikes. The pro came down and introduced himself and each of the foursome to one another. This was a Currituck Club tradition. He welcomed them and covered some of the local rules, which, of course, the club member knew. No alcoholic drinks, wink, wink. A potpourri of bets were agreed to at ten bucks a bet. Sometimes, it seemed that the bets were more fun than the golf. The club member was somber by golfing standards. He was intimidated by the company and didn't want to play like a duffer. The vacationer was talkative and a hoot when around those that appreciated humor. He partnered with the club member. Shane and Wilson were the other partners. Shane had met and played with many politicians, so he wasn't all that impressed with playing with Wilson. Seen one congressman, seen them all.

The foursome enjoyed the breeze and the temperature in the high seventies. When they turned to the back nine, Shane and Wilson, individually and as partners, were ahead in the betting, which was kept on a separate score card. With each shooter pretty familiar with each other's strengths and weaknesses by then, it was time for Shane to shine. It was gravy time. He cheated. He didn't have a bad lie the rest of the course. A few shots that apparently traveled into the pampas or dune grass on the fringes magically appeared just on the rough. He ended up on the plus side of two hundred dollars, with Wilson up fifty. It was a good thing when Shane lost a betting pool, he promised payment later and often welched.

They changed back to their street wear and met in the clubhouse bar. The club member, wanting to be a gracious host, offered to buy the first round. Wilson chose a gin (Bombay) and tonic, Shane asked for his Macallan scotch, on the rocks. The bartender apologized, he had no Macallan. He offered Glenfiddich and Shane reluctantly accepted. The conversation started about the day's round and all of the great (relatively), lucky, and bad shots. Shane, accustomed to being in charge, took charge of the conversation. Though he was gruff and his language banal, he also had more charm than a room full of babies. In this setting, he was the star. They discussed the financial world and the local scene, with the local pointing out attractions, things to do, and places to get a good meal. Politics was next on the agenda. The club member, being from North Carolina, was most interested in hearing Wilson's views and inside stories. All offered unsolicited advice of what Wilson should do to get elected and what he should do if elected. None of it was heavy-handed, so Wilson rolled with it. Another round was ordered and Shane was elected to cover the charges since he was the day's big winner. And everyone knew Shane had cheated. Shane, being cheap, wasn't happy with the decision but pretended to be delighted to fork over some of his winnings.

As they were leaving, Wilson sequestered Shane in the lobby while they were each waiting for their ride and invited Shane to the weekend party. Shane thought he wouldn't be available either that night or Saturday, but would love to drop in on Sunday, after a round of golf, that is.

Sid Freeze arrived and drove Wilson back to the beach house. Wilson told Sid of the invite and Sid was none too happy after all, this was an official campaign-planning session. Michael Wilson told Freeze to be cool; the campaign staff would see Shane's visit as a plus. He added that Julie, his administrative assistant, should order Macallan scotch for Shane. The first get-together, which was an official campaign meeting, was actually a quick orientation as to what was on the menu and what festivities would take place over the weekend. It wasn't scheduled for an hour, so Wilson had time to shower, get dressed, and get the gin off his breath. Sid had arranged Christmas parties and post-election staff parties, but nothing as grand as this one. By "arrange", he really meant telling Julie Massey what he wanted to have done and cutting her loose to do it.

Julie was one of the most organized people you could ever meet; with her boundless energy, she could get anything done. She was attractive, though not what many would say was pretty. She had short, dirty-blond hair, not her natural color, and was trim. She was a force to be reckoned with. Sid was very confident this would be a memorable event.

The congressman was fresh and ready for an evening of fun. He promised himself to sip his drinks and circulate amongst all the guests. The aforementioned kickoff meeting, with all gathered in the huge living area, was opened by Freeze welcoming everyone and introducing Julie to explain the agenda and what was available throughout the weekend. She assured all that she would be available to answer any questions or to resolve any issues. The mike was passed back to Sid, who introduced the congressman.

"Good evening. First I want, and need, to thank everyone in this room. What we accomplished together has been outstanding. We did it, together! Now it is time to regroup and set our sights on November. That starts here. Get to know each other; you'll be spending a lot of time together for the next six months, so you need to like each other." Some chuckled throughout the room. "We'll need to add some staff, but let me assure you that you are the core; you are the engine that is going to power and steer this bus. God bless you all and have a great weekend."

Wilson handed the mike back to Freeze, who added, "Have fun. Julie arranged a feast. And the bar is officially open!"

This was not a paper plate-and-plastic-fork affair. Beautiful ceramic plates and silverware were the order for the weekend. The caterer had arrived at noon to start the grills and smokers. Julie badgered them to make sure there would be enough to eat for everyone. The appetizers, headlined by homemade, fresh crab dip, were outstanding and were washed down with nearly anything you could order from a bar, including champagne, of course. The smoked ribs and grilled meats were gobbled up by everyone.

On Saturday, after a scrumptious all-you-can-eat breakfast, Julie organized activities that she hoped would be team-building and bonding experiences. First up was a photographic scavenger hunt. The group was broken up in teams of four and given a list of things to take a photo of. One phone per team could be used to take the photos. Julie listed various items in the house, on the house grounds, and on the beach in front of the house. The clues were in most cases imprecise, requiring each team to use their imagination. Julie allowed two hours to complete the hunt. Each member of the winning team would be awarded a bottle of Piper-Heidsieck champagne. The teams finished their searches; Julie presented the champagne to the winners, and all gathered to chow down on a wide variety of homemade pizzas and an extensive salad bar. Oh, beer, wine, and cocktails to revive spirits!

The remainder of the afternoon was a laid-back assortment of board and lawn games with beach chairs and umbrellas in place for those who just wanted to relax and enjoy the surf. Paddleboards and surfboards had been rented but there were only a few takers. To the amusement of the beach loungers, the inevitable wipeouts were cheered lustily. The staffers excitedly looked forward to the Saturday evening meal. After fresh shrimp cocktail was devoured with champagne, the outside candlelit dinner of filet mignon and Maine lobster tails served with appropriate wine pairings was the weekend's star attraction. Wilson was to occupy a table with Freeze and a couple of long-term staff heads, but instead, he chose to roam, folding chair in hand, to join every table at some point during the repast, listening to stories and idle chatting. He would dine when most were ready for dessert.

Sunday's meals included breakfast similar to Saturday's, a seafood buffet for lunch, and a New England clam bake for dinner. Julie arranged for a half-day off shore fishing trip for any brave mariners. The trip was popular, and to accommodate those that signed up, Julie chartered three boats out of the Oregon Inlet Fishing Center. In addition to any fish hooked, Julie had a prize waiting for the anglers of the boat that caught the most, by weight: dinner for two for each member of the winning crew at the Saint Jacques French Cuisine in Raleigh. A highly spirited competition resulted. After the sailors returned and had time to clean up, the clambake and reggae music finished a perfect day.

Before the bulk of the staffers departed on Monday, brunch was served. The core staff stayed on for a real strategy meeting. The agenda was authored by Sid Freeze in coordination with Wilson. Sid led the meeting, first having everyone identify Wilson's strengths and weaknesses (no holds barred) and the strengths and weaknesses of his opponent, Mercer Harris. Next, Sid asked each person what could be done to accentuate the positives and eliminate the negatives, as the famous song goes. Julie compiled the lists. Then, each contributed to the discussion as to how this could be achieved. PR and advertising, especially TV ads, were paramount in this session. Then Sid opened up discussion on what to schedule for the congressman in the near term. Finally, fundraising– how much was needed, how best to tap the general public, and which political action committees could be counted on and could any new ones be encouraged to form. They reviewed the history of Richard Curtis Wilson's previous campaigns.

When the meeting concluded, each person was given action items and, except for Wilson, Freeze, and Julie Massey, they packed up and headed home. The three remaining walked out onto the oceanfront deck to review the results of the meeting and the weekend and to have one more adult beverage before they also departed. That was when the reports of two gun shots were heard.

36

Michael Hasbee was summoned to the office of his boss, Chief Detective Marnee Forbish.

"Bring me up to speed with the Roselli case, Detective. Have you been ducking me?"

"Nobody could duck such a lovely lady, boss."

"OK, cut the bullshit, where are we?"

"Got the results of the rape kit back. DNA was solid for Sprout. I visited the Rosellis and gave them an update without any gory details. Their anguish is evolving into cold anger. Can't say that's a surprise. Can't blame them either."

"What about Sprout's service records?"

"Had to go through some hoops. He was in a transport plane that got hit by rocket fire. Thirty-eight were aboard, thirty-six bailed out, and thirty-four survived with a variety of injuries, some severe. They came under fire before being rescued. Their commanding officer was one Colonel Richard Curtis Wilson. I talked to six of the survivors. The picture they drew was pretty consistent. The mission was a simple troop movement. Nobody expected any trouble, as they were flying in relatively safe airspace. They were rescued as quickly as they thought was possible, under the conditions. The enemy was nearby and was approaching the site where most landed. The rescue choppers came under fire also, and some Apaches put an end to that. Those that had significant injuries were evacuated to Germany and then to Reed. Sprout was obviously one of them. The guys I talked to had no ill will against anyone in our military, and were actually pretty grateful for the rescue efforts. Except Sprout. One man that I reached rehabbed with Sprout. Sprout ranted that Wilson never should have sent them on a "suicide" mission. It was Wilson's fault that they got killed or injured. The guy said that the complaining was so constant and unpalatable that he requested to be moved away from him."

"So now we know what's driving him. What kind of injury did Sprout incur?"

"He broke his right femur in a couple of places. It healed pretty well, but he apparently still walks with a limp."

"And where might our boy be hiding?"

"I thought you'd never ask," he said with a smirk. "Don't have much news there. As far as we can tell, he hasn't stopped by his house. He hasn't used a credit card or an ATM. Really hiding in shadows. We notified the boys down in Carolina, gave them whatever we have, and warned them to watch Wilson's campaign stops. He won his primary but his schedule hasn't been published. I contacted the campaign manager, let me see, a guy named Freeze. He is aware of the potential threat and the state police are in contact with him."

"Where is Wilson now?"

"Freeze said they were holding campaign meetings somewhere on the Outer Banks."

"Stay on it. If you need to go down there, go. Not very far away."

"Aye, aye." Hasbee saluted as he left Forbish's office. She could only shake her head and offer a sarcastic salute back.

Roanna was still not back in school. She probably would not go back for some time. Her friends asked to come visit, but she told her parents she wanted to be alone. She stayed in her room for much of the day and at random times, she cried. She would not talk to her siblings. Her parents pushed sessions with a therapist, which Roanna finally, reluctantly agreed to. She did not give the therapist permission to discuss their meetings with anyone else, including her parents. Her therapists simply told them that she was severely psychologically damaged and it would take a while, perhaps a long while, for Roanna to deal with what had happened.

Anthony and Joan were able to get Roanna to mention a detail or two of what had happened every few days. Late one night, Roanna went into her parents' bedroom crying. Joan reached for her to crawl next to her in bed and pulled her to her side and snuggled with her. Stroking her hair Joan softly said, "Talk to me, honey."

"I shouldn't have been there, Mom."

Joan waited.

"It was my fault. I was bad." And she cried some more. Joan glanced at Anthony with eyebrows raised. He raised his shoulders as if to say "don't ask me." They laid there for a while and Joan had to speak.

"Honey, none of this was your fault." Joan dabbed Roanna's cheeks with her sheet.

Roanna, still weeping, said, "No, Mom, you don't know. I was there."

"Where, honey?"

"On the park bench. With Bobby Lee."

"OK, honey, how was that a problem?"

"We hung out there. We got up and headed home in different directions. I was walking alone. He grabbed me out of nowhere."

"The bad man?"

"Yes, of course, Mom."

They were both quiet. So now Roanna's parents had an inkling of how the abduction had occurred and why she thought it was her fault.

A few days later, when Anthony and Joan arrived home after work, Roanna was sitting in the living room staring at the TV, kind of in a trance. Joan offered, "What can I do for you, honey?"

"Can I talk to you?" Anthony was nearby, and both parents sat down, Joan on the sofa with Roanna and Anthony in the chair next to them. Her siblings, Josh and Penny, were in their bedrooms, supposedly doing homework.

"He was mean. He hurt me and seemed to like it. He was disgusting, dirty, smelled awful. I was so scared. He tied me to the bed all day while he was gone. I just wanted something to eat or drink." She stopped and leaned against her mother. She got teary but didn't cry.

"He hit me. He touched me everywhere. It hurt. I hate him. But he's not going to make me cry anymore."

Anthony said, "OK, honey, OK."

"Did they get him?"

Anthony said, "No, they're looking everywhere. We don't have to worry; the cops drive by frequently, watching for him. The police think he may have gone to North Carolina. He's mad at someone down there."

"Dad, he's crazy. He gave me Cheerios and water both before he left and when he came home. Hardly anything else. He called me Vixen. He told me that I was his, like his possession. I was so scared. Sometimes I thought he'd kill me, sometimes I wanted him to kill me." Once again, she put her head against her mother and sobbed.

Joan knew a little more than she told Roanna. As perhaps any mother would, she was obsessed with finding out anything that could help the police find Sprout. At times at work, she researched whatever she could find out about Sprout on the internet, which wasn't much, and followed Wilson's progress in the election. She occasionally talked to Hasbee, getting updates. With her permission, Hasbee had the lead North Carolina detective assigned on the case, Max Ramsey, call her to learn anything that would be helpful. He invited Joan to call him anytime, and she did. Ramsey didn't have much information except that they were on the lookout for his vehicle, which they hoped he was still driving. He also notified the state police to surveil the Wilson campaign. But, so far, nothing had developed. Joan found a reference to the Wilson campaign staff meeting somewhere on the Outer Banks. She couldn't uncover anything else, so she called the campaign headquarters. They confirmed that meetings were being held but wouldn't disclose where. She called several restaurants down there but found not a sniff of Wilson. She even tried watching traffic cams to find Sprout's gray Impala, but the resolution wasn't good enough for her to determine if any were his car.

She wanted to find him and cause him as much pain as he'd caused her daughter. She knew that wouldn't help Roanna, but it would help her. She was crazed at trying to find this animal. She confided in her rector at Saint Mark's. He told her what she already knew, that what happened, happened, and couldn't be changed. When he got caught, fine, he'd be punished. But whatever was his fate, it wouldn't help Roanna. That job was for her and her family and professionals.

37

Cody arrived at the Atlantic Bistro at three fifteen, a little late for the chef's meeting. Jamie Hooper was the head chef, who everyone called "Hoops." Hoops was a big guy, hair in a ponytail, loud, an extrovert, and in command in his kitchen and here with the staff. If Hoops said to do it, whatever "it" was, you did it. Often, all he had to do was give you a look and you got the message. He was respected but did have a great sense of humor and was well liked. He was the highest-paid chef on the Outer Banks. He said to Cody as he sat down, "Glad you could make it. Don't like my cooking anymore?"

"Thought I'd stop at McDonald's on the way here."

"You want McDonald's, I'll make McDonald's!" Hoops said with a smile. "Okay, let's size up the specials for tonight. The regular menu is available as it stands. I wasn't in my creative zone this morning, I apologize." This was like da Vinci apologizing for the *Mona Lisa*. "First, we did salmon with a sherry cheese sauce, over a bed of capers and spinach, asparagus tips finishing it. I recommend medium rare. Take a taste." Hoops placed a platter in front of the staff. The four servers, Willow, the head barkeeper, Lucas, the sommelier, and Amelia, the hostess, sampled the dish. Thumbs-up all around. The sommelier suggested a few sauvignon blancs to pair with the entrée.

The second special was a rack of lamb with a raspberry reduction glaze, laid over a cake made of risotto, feta, and spinach. Again, Hoops placed the platter on the middle of the table and, as it passed, he described the meal, mentioning that it had been featured a week ago and was a big hit. "I'll only do it rare to medium. If anyone asks for well, make a face and tell them that I won't do it. I won't!"

Willow volunteered, "Just as great as last week!" Again, all-thumbs-up.

Lucas added, "Everybody was happy with our better merlots when we served this last."

Hoops concluded, "Same instructions as always. Tell me what works and what doesn't. You all know which entrées take longer to prepare, so keep your table busy if one is ordered. Go get'em."

Those at the table finished both samples and prepared for business. The Bistro didn't open for dinner until five, but the doors were opened earlier if a customer wanted to enjoy a cocktail, beer, or a glass of wine at the bar. Martinis of every concoction were the calling card here. There were evenings that the bar would be full with standing room by five.

Jayden, one of the new servers at the Bistro, cornered Cody when the others were double-checking their tables. "You got the dead presidents you owe me, bro?"

"Not on me, dude."

"Look, bro, I got bills to pay and I'm getting pressed. You owe me. They'll touch me and if they do, I'll be ratting you out. Do I make myself clear?"

"Dude, I'll have it tomorrow."

"I'll empty my pockets for you. Tomorrow, bro, not a day later."

Cody was a little shaken by the not-so-veiled threat. Cody was buying recreational quantities for himself and Phoebe and sort of forgetting to pay Jayden, his source. The evening was uneventful, however; with every tip that Cody pocketed he looked to see if Jayden was watching. He was.

The next morning Cody woke late as usual; Phoebe was gone. He prepared his favorite breakfast sandwich, wolfed it down and readied himself for the next recon mission. He decided that the odds were that Shane was housed in one of the rentals at Mansion Beach. He decided, to be efficient time-wise, to fly his Black Pelican. It would be good to get more practice. He was a little apprehensive that if someone reported the drone, it might lead back to him and the Kerrigan caper. However, he'd heard nothing in the local scuttlebutt about anything that happened, so he felt somewhat confident that Kerrigan licked his wounds and kept his mouth shut.

He again headed to the north end of the section, pulled off on Ocean Mist Lane, and parked on the sandy side. He decided not to bother with the disguise, the wet suit and surfboard, and just head on the path over the dune to the beach. The dunes were high here. He bunkered in an inward curve in the dune where he thought he would be somewhat hidden. He took the drone out of its bag and prepared it for flight. Up it went with its relatively quiet buzz. He practiced some maneuvers first then aimed it down the beach, observing the decks and beach scene in front of every building. The drone passed one house with a number of people, no children, scattered around its two decks. Plates of food were precariously perched on the railing tops and everyone seemed to be holding a beverage. Looked like a party. From the railings hung red, white, and blue buntings. It was clear to him that something was being celebrated, but he didn't know what. The drone flew adjacent to a short gap of beach where there weren't any houses. He noticed a person on the beach looking through binoculars toward the houses that the Black Pelican had just passed. He zoomed in and watched. The guy was scruffy-looking, with dirty clothes, unshaven– he looked like a homeless person. Cody thought it was odd that someone like that had binoculars and was looking toward houses, not at something in the ocean. The drone meandered southward, continuing its recon mission. He found no evidence of Shane. As the drone flew back to its launch site, Cody observed the man still on the beach, still aiming the glasses at the house. A peeping Tom? Cody chuckled to himself; after all, that's what he was.

The bird landed on the soft sand and Cody packaged the drone up and walked over the dune back to Kassie. He headed to a little bar he liked not far up the road. It was rustic and tried to fit the Tiki motif. He sat at the bar and ordered a Yuengling long neck and a cheeseburger with pickles, fried onions, mayo, and catsup, with a side of onion rings. He asked for A.1. to dip the rings in. The joint had one small flat screen over the liquor shelf behind the bar. It continuously showed surfing videos which

Cody enjoyed. His "Endless Summer" was waiting for him. Lunch consumed, he headed back to his hollowed-out spot in the dune. He unpackaged the drone and mounted a fresh battery for a second flight. Launch was perfect, and the bird stealthily flew over the waves. The house that appeared to be party central now had three people on the lower deck and the bunting was gone. Guess the party was over. He then observed the mystery man walking on the beach, binoculars strapped around his neck. The drone's journey continued to the end of both rows of houses, still with no sighting of Harrison Shane. On the return trip, the mystery man was standing still near the party house. Cody brought the drone back to the launch site and prepared to leave, frustrated that he'd wasted the day getting nowhere. He then heard two loud pops down by one of the houses and then some voices that sounded like screams. Being familiar with guns, he knew what he'd heard was gunfire. He wanted to hightail it out of there as fast as he could. Back in Kassie, he got out onto Route 12 and shortly, down the road, a police car and ambulance passed him going in the opposite direction. He thought they were headed to the site where he'd heard the gun shots.

Cody got home and turned on the TV to see if anything was on the local news yet, but there wasn't. He thought maybe he should download the day's flight videos to see what he had, if anything. Before doing that and before deleting anything, he decided to review the video on the drone's camera first, focusing on the movements of the mystery man. Frustrated with the small screen, Cody pulled the micro SD card out of the drone and inserted it into his laptop for a clearer view. He looked at the stills he had taken of the man and thought that the resolution was good enough that he could recognize him if he ever encountered him. One shot in particular had the man looking straight at the drone, apparently having heard it and wondered what it was. As it was time to suit up for work, he closed the photo app on the laptop and shoved the drone case under his bed where he usually kept it. Cody walked out of the house and got in Kassie and headed to work.

After the staff dinner specials orientation was given at the Bistro, Cody glanced at Jayden and Jayden motioned with his head to step outside.

"Got my money, dude?"

"Look, I am thinking you owe me, dude!"

"Ha ha, too funny. Where's my fucking twenty-two hundred?"

Jayden quickly closed the distance between them and was now inches away from Cody, nose to nose, his fists clenched, his eyebrows narrowed, and his jaw set with gritted teeth.

"Where is my money? If I don't have something by tonight, you won't be riding the waves tomorrow!"

"Whoa, back off, dude. That last batch you sold me was *crap*! I AIN'T PAYING FOR BAD DRUGS!"

"Shut the fuck up. I did not give you any bad shit."

"The hell you didn't. Everybody, including me, that used that batch didn't get high, man. It sucked, so whoever you got it from fucked you up, man. I'm not-."

Before Cody could say another word, Jayden punched him in the stomach. Cody fell backward against the dumpster and slid down to a sitting position, holding his stomach. With shock all over his face and his eyes wide in surprise, he said, "What the fuck did you do that for, asshole?"

"Look, I am getting pressed for money and I want to keep my kneecaps, so get me the FUCKING MONEY. I mean it, man. If I don't have something after shift tonight, and the rest tomorrow, it will be *them* coming after you, not me."

Jayden turned and went back into the building and Cody sat there for a minute before he got up, brushed off his pants and apron, and headed back into the Bistro. Amelia, the cute fortyish hostess, gave Cody an "Is everything alright?" look and said, "You good?"

"Yep, good. Thanks, Amelia." He gave her a thumbs-up.

Cody spruced up his tables and visited Willow at the bar. "Got any super concoctions tonight?"

Willow really liked Cody and would often flirt with him. He enjoyed all of it. Willow had the perfect personality for a bartender. Spunky and outgoing, she was someone you would like in about five seconds. She was, as they say, out there. And she was easy on the eyes. She had long auburn hair, stunning blue eyes set in a lovely round face with prominent cheekbones, and a body often showcased by a revealing shirt that kept male patrons' minds off their tab.

"You know everything I have is super, Cody! I'm always open for business."

"I was talking about the drinks for tonight, sweetie."

"Oh, damn! OK, got some fresh peaches, so push Peach Cosmos. They'll be great. Maybe we should call it the 'Congressman Martini.'"

"Huh?"

"Didn't ya hear the news? Some congressman staying up in Duck was shot."

"Wow, no, didn't hear, is he dead?"

"No, but I didn't catch how badly he was hurt."

Cody nodded and waved as he walked around the half wall that divided the bar from the dining area. Now Cody knew what the *pop, pop* was that he'd heard. Was it possible that he had a photo of the assailant? *Damn*, he thought, *it probably was what he heard.*

Now there were two things bearing on Cody's mind: the money he owed Jayden, which he had but didn't want to part with- plus the drugs really were weak- and the evidence he might have from his drone. It affected the service that he provided the diners that night. Thankfully, there weren't many to worry about. His tips were not sensational. After the last customer left the dining area (the bar was still open), the servers and bussers cleared the tables. The full deep clean wouldn't be until the morning. Jayden moseyed close to Cody and said, "How much did you make for me, bro?"

"Don't know. I'll count it in a few."

"Don't leave without seeing me."

Cody checked to see what his credit card take in tips for the night was and then went to the men's room and pulled out all of his cash tips and counted it. The take for the night in total added up to be two hundred and forty bucks, not a good night, but it was something to give to Jayden. The whole business with Jayden was pissing him off but he knew if he wanted to easily get more drugs in the future, he'd better dig into his own till at home and pay him. *Damn*, he thought, *I really hate to dig into my savings!* A broad smile on his face was what Jayden saw when he entered the men's room.

"What are you smiling about? Did you get all my money in tips tonight?"

"Nah, but don't worry, here is two forty. Meet me tomorrow at my place after Phoebs goes to work and I will give you the rest."

"*Really*? You are screwing with me, aren't you?"

"Don't be an idiot. I will text you when she leaves so you can stop by."

As Jayden walked away, Cody said mockingly, "That is, if you still want to keep your knee caps intact?"

The bar stayed occupied until midnight, Monday night's closing time. Cody went to Willow for the credit card cash-out of his tips. She was surprised that he wanted his cut now. The usual practice at the Bistro was to get your earnings the next day you worked. Willow questioned, "You really need it, Cody?"

"Yeah, I got pressing debts."

"Jayden?"

"Yeah, how did you know?" he asked with a quizzical look on his face.

"I know everything going on, hon. There's a lot of talking at my bar. I'm a very good listener."

"I bet you're good at a lot of things."

She gave him a flirty, sexy smile. "Maybe sometime you should find out what I'm really, really good at."

38

Cody was awakened by Phoebe's morning ritual. Phoebe went over to the bed and sat down.

"What time did you get in, babe?

"Too late. It was a long night. Hey, did you hear about the shooting up at Mansion Beach? Don't you have a client staying up there?"

"Yeah, didn't hear much. The news said some congressman got shot. Apparently he'll live. I have Harrison Shane staying a few houses away. He was still out on the golf course when it happened. He called me, pretty irritated, and asked if the area was safe. I told him that I couldn't remember the last time we had a shooting on the Outer Banks. I told him that this must have something to do with politics because it was an isolated occurrence and probably not a random thing. Or a robbery or something like that."

"Guess I'll check the internet to see what it says." Trying to get the scoop on Shane, he casually asked, "So, your client is a golfer?"

"Oh yes, and a lot more!"

"I've heard that dyed-in-the-wool golfers like to play at certain times. Shane?"

"Yeah, he wants ten every morning. Keeps him out of my hair, at least."

When Phoebe was ready to leave for work, she gave Cody a peck on the cheek and gently grabbed his crotch. "Maybe you should try to get home earlier, tonight."

"Don't have to get asked twice, babe." He reached out and gave her a playful slap on the ass. Phoebe gave Reef a few good-bye scratches behind his ears and left.

Cody sent a text to Jayden and sat down to see what he could learn about the shooting.

Once on the internet, Cody read the reports of yesterday's event. Two shots were fired (he knew that). The shots were apparently fired from the beach. One shot hit Congressman Wilson in the left thigh. The other bullet hit one of the congressman's staffers in the arm. Both were taken to Chesapeake Regional Medical Center. Surgery was performed to remove the bullet from Wilson's leg. The staffer had more serious surgery as the bullet that struck her splintered her Humerus, the bone in her upper right arm. The report stated that both surgeries were successful and both patients were expected to make complete recoveries. The police had recovered some evidence and the investigation was beginning.

"Oh my God, oh my God, oh my God! What if I have a photo of the guy who did this?"

Cody was consumed with the moral conundrum, not that morality was his long suit. He had photos, probably of the shooter. But if he gave the cops his photos, they'd probably figure out that they were taken from a drone. Then, with the cops knowing that he used his drone in that area, he might not be able to pull off another scam. Also, he had no idea if Kerrigan had gone to the cops. If he did, his drone photos could lead the cops to him for that too. He thought that he could drop off the photos anonymously, but he was worried that it could somehow lead back to him. Why risk his ten thousand in the bank, any future gains, and possibly jail time? The scales were getting strongly tipped in the direction of not disclosing what he knew.

There was a loud rap on the door and Cody jumped about a mile. The noise really spooked him. Reef ran to the door and barked and growled. Cody's first thought was, *Oh my God, they are here for me.* He quickly realized that was stupid when Jayden yelled, "Open up, shithead!"

Cody opened up the door, hanging onto Reef's collar, and Jayden looked at him and said, "What happened to you, did you see a ghost?"

"Jayden, you are delusional. Here's your money, now get outta here. See ya at the Bistro, dude."

Jayden left and Cody calmed down and thought, *Damn it, let the police figure the congressman thing out for themselves! Hell, it might not be the guy I got on camera anyway.*

Detective Clint Heaton, who had done the unofficial investigation of the Kerrigan blackmailing, was put in charge of the Wilson shooting. With a candidate for the U.S. Senate involved, Heaton was concerned that he could be in over his head. The evidence that they had wasn't much. He found nobody who saw the shooter. Of the three people on the deck, Wilson and Julie Massey were hit by gunfire and went down immediately. Sid Freeze, who was not hit, had his entire attention diverted to his two fallen friends and coworkers. They weren't aware of anybody on the beach before the incident, being consumed in campaign conversations. No one in any of the nearby houses noticed anybody on the beach or saw anybody rushing away from the scene in a car. Heaton found footprints and had casts taken of them, which could be useful evidence should there ever be a trial, if they found a suspect. They did not find any shell casings but would come back to search the beach with a metal detector. Heaton checked in with the sheriff. After he described what he had and what he didn't have, the sheriff decided it was time to get more man power. He called the North Carolina State Bureau of Investigation, or SBI, and requested assistance. About half an hour later, he received a call from Max Ramsey.

Max Ramsey was a veteran of the SBI and very popular with his coworkers. He had already been assigned to the Sprout case; the Wilson shooting seemed like it could be connected. Max was a cool guy. Tall and handsome with a pleasant smile, he was divorced; his wife had wanted kids, but Max was married to the job and he thought he wouldn't have time for them. He was still friendly with his ex-wife. He was a fan of the Olive Garden restaurants and looked forward to his Friday night poker game with four or five friends, one of whom was a female coworker. The stakes had low limits, but the cocktails and beer had no limits. When Max hosted the event, his mixology expertise was eagerly awaited by his guests, a variety of cosmopolitans being his prime call to fame.

Ramsey lived in a two-bedroom condo in Cary, just outside of Raleigh. He had little time or inclination to do much decorating, but the unit was comfortable, organized, and clean. He was somewhat OCD and it showed. His current squeeze was an attractive once-divorced nurse at a nearby hospital. Max's schedule and her schedule didn't always fit well, but they loved spending whatever time together that they could and loved doing simple things together.

On the phone, Max asked, "Hey, Sheriff, this is Max Ramsey, SBI. What can we do for you?"

"My detective is knee-deep in nothing. Evidence, that is. We had a nasty shooting. Did you catch the news of Congressman Wilson?"

"Yeah, but I don't have anything official."

"Well, we'd like to get some help here. We think we're nearing a dead end. Can you get over here, and, if so, when?"

"That's why I called. I can be there tomorrow morning, around nine. Who do I hook up with?"

"Come to my office. Detective Clint Heaton will be your man."

39

Phoebe was taking care of Harrison Shane's needs, except one: he wanted a female guest. Phoebe had left a card on the credenza near the entrance to Shane's rental that advertised, "Female Escorts and Companions Call 252-260-6769." After his round of golf on Saturday, he called the number. It was to Phoebe's burner phone that she'd decided to set up for her little unofficial business.

"Hello, Mr. Shane, what can I do for you?"

"Phoebe?"

"Yes, this is Phoebe."

"I was calling about the card left in the house. Is it your card?"

"Yes. I run a private side business to provide services that Sea Dunes doesn't."

"Well then, I'm lonely, ya know what I mean. What can you offer?"

"I can find you someone as a companion for a day or a week. I need to get paid with cash, up front." She provided the details.

"Can I define the type of woman I would like?"

"Certainly."

"What if I don't like her when we get together?"

"I arrange a 'meet and greet,' kind of a quick date. If you are not happy, I give you a full refund."

"Okay. Let's give it a go. Tall, nice trim body, really pretty, great legs, long hair, color is not important, outgoing but not a blabbermouth."

"Okay, when is a good time to meet tomorrow?"

"After I shower after my eighteen holes. Let's say three. Where?"

"She'll be at the Village Table and Tavern, a super restaurant on the sound near your place. I'll pick you up at three."

"Phoebe, what's 'the sound'?"

"That big body of water on the opposite side of your house from the ocean."

"Oh."

Phoebe got to work. She called Virginia Talent and asked them to text a list of the girls available and a detailed description of each. The agency was well organized and asked Phoebe if there were specific requirements. Phoebe gave them Shane's list of requirements. They told her that they had six girls that met the criteria currently available at this time, not sure about the blabbermouth issue. In fifteen minutes, Phoebe received bios of the girls with photos. She chose one named Veronica and called the agency back. She asked to speak to Veronica for a one night modeling job. The agency charged a fee for any referral. They told Phoebe that they would have the girl call as soon as they could get in touch with her.

"Hi, I understand you have a modeling job for me?"

"Yes. My name is Phoebe. It's not quite like modeling. I have a guest, an executive from Hollywood, who would like some female companionship. If you are both compatible, he would like to hire you for a week, maybe more. This is not something that the agency needs to know. Interested?"

"So you're like an escort service?"

"Sorta."

Phoebe went through the details, including the financial end, and confidentiality. She added that the first meeting would be a getting-to-know-you meeting and either party could opt out. Veronica liked what she heard. Phoebe asked if she could be at the restaurant at two thirty the next day. She wanted to make sure she'd be on time, and, more importantly, she wanted to meet the girl before bringing Shane there.

The next morning, Phoebe slept in. Cody got up from bed at his usual late hour and started making his breakfast, surprised that his girlfriend was still in the sack. When she finally rolled over and mumbled something that was incoherent to Cody, he went over and sat on the bed next to her.

"Good morning, sweetie."

Phoebe reached out and pulled Cody down to her and kissed him hard.

He was instantly turned on. It amazed him how quickly she could get him going. Even after all this time together. He pulled away from the kiss and smiled at her.

"Hey, you promised me something yesterday. Are you up for the challenge?"

"Well, stud muffin, I can be if you are interested."

Smiling at her, he touched her hair and smoothed it away from her eyes. Her hair always got tangled in her sleep when she tossed and turned, and last night she'd tossed and turned a lot!

"I am always interested when it comes to you."

She smiled and he rolled onto the bed next to her. She rolled to her side and ran her finger tips over his eyebrows and down his cheek.

"I miss us. I miss us not doing stuff like we used to."

"I know. With your crazy schedule and mine, we need to get back to us. Let's start right now!"

Cody kissed the tip of Phoebe's nose and then her right eye and then her cheek and continued putting little kisses down to her cheekbone and neck. His hands were already roaming down her shoulder to her nipple and he squeezed it slightly, finding it perky like always. He began to whisper into her ear.

"You are beautiful. You are magnificent. Your hair, your eyes, your luscious body. I love the way you move. I love watching you move. You are all I want. You are all I will ever want."

Phoebe's eyes were closed, and with the words whispered into her ear, her sense of touch and arousal was heightened. Cody continued to gently trail kisses down her body to her belly button all the while whispering words of need and compliments. He touched her and she was ready. He was ready and hard as a rock the moment he'd kissed the tip of her nose. He rolled over on top of her and they made slow, comfortable, passionate love filled with a deep need to connect.

Phoebe laid still, basking in the endorphin release she just experienced, breathing heavy and holding Cody's hand.

Cody's eyes were closed and his breathing was finally back to a normal rhythm. Cody took her hand and, with it still linked in his, kissed her knuckles.

"No work today?"

"Ugh, I have to go out to meet my client this afternoon. I probably won't be too long. What are you doing today?"

"I'm going to run some errands and then see what the surf is doing. When are you leaving?"

"Around two."

Cody wasn't planning on doing any of what he told Phoebe. He was going to screw around until two and then try to secretly follow her to Shane's house, hoping that was where she was meeting him. He wanted to see where Shane was staying. He knew following her in Kassie and not being seen wouldn't be easy, but he could just say he was heading up that way to check the surf. At one thirty, he parked a block down the street in the opposite direction that she would be going. He hid Kassie behind another car where he didn't think he'd be seen. Right at two, Phoebe rolled out of the driveway. She drove a rich red Camry that was easy to pick out. She turned onto a side street and then onto what was called by locals the Bypass. She turned right to go north which was what Cody expected. He followed her, making sure there were a few cars between them. It was a tricky business. He didn't want to fall too far behind and have a traffic light separate them. He was lucky, although once he had to put the pedal to the metal to make the light. They caravanned along the curving road to and through the town of Duck. Just past the main section of the town, Phoebe turned on her left turn signal and pulled into a restaurant parking lot. He thought, *shit* and drove past. Now what? He pulled into a parking lot next to the restaurant, parked where he could see her car, and waited. At about ten of three, Phoebe left and turned north. He wasn't scheduled to work, so he didn't have to worry about getting back. Phoebe pulled onto Ocean Mist Lane. Cody drove past her and turned onto the next street. He pulled off the road and onto the weeds and got out quickly so as not to lose sight of Phoebe. He walked to where he could see her car. She was climbing up the steps to the third house on High Dunes Lane, number eighteen. She rang the doorbell and waited. The door finally opened and she went in. After what seemed to be only a minute, she came out followed by a tall, heavy man. Shane, he was sure. Bingo! Phoebe motored out and Cody waited. He smiled, knowing he'd gotten the info he was hoping to get.

<h1 style="text-align:center">40</h1>

Cody went home. He would head up to High Dunes Lane first thing in the morning with the Black Pelican and hope to catch Mister Shane with a lady.

He got up early, took Reef out, and made himself a breakfast sandwich to go and headed north. He didn't want to get to Mansion Beach late because he thought Shane might leave for his golf outing. He was in his surfer disguise: board strapped to the pipes on top of Kassie's roof, wet suit on the back seat. He didn't want to launch too close to the target house, so he chose to pull off onto Sea Spray Lane, where the other surfers hung out. But, now, another decision. He really didn't want the other surfers to observe what he was doing. Word gets out. He walked down the dune line, opposite the beach, and found a little hollow in the dunes and nestled in with the drone. He removed it from its case and found a sandy spot to launch from. He navigated it away from the beach until it was adjacent to the row of houses where Shane had rented. He turned it toward the beach and slowly flew it over the ocean. When in front of the targeted house, he saw nobody outside. He kept flying it to the end of the row, thinking it wouldn't be obvious that he was looking for Shane. On the return trip, he struck gold. Bright, shiny gold! It was easy to recognize Shane: he was a big fellow and Cody had studied the internet photos. Shane was only wearing his skivvies and was carrying a young woman who was scantily clad- in fact, topless. Cody thought she was a ten from what he could see. He had enough time left on the drone's battery to fly it well past the house and then back for one more look. Shane now sat down on one of the deck chairs, babe on his lap, and one hand clearly over her breast. His head was back as if he was laughing and his mouth open. Perfect shot. Blackmail magic.

Cody flew the bird back down the beach to his spot behind the dune and brought it in for a landing. It had been noticed with curiosity by some of the surfers who were hanging on the beach. One surfer in particular had more curiosity than the others: Chump Change. He followed the flight and homed in on where it came down over the dune. He left his board and climbed over the dune on a path through the vegetation. Behold, he saw Cody packaging up the drone.

"'Sup, Cody? See you got a new toy."

"Hey, Chump Change. Yep, it's pretty cool. Just learning to fly it."

"Really? Like, what does it do?"

"Mainly takes photos and videos."

"So, like, what are you shooting shots of?"

"Nothing in particular, just practicing for now. Getting some scenes of the beach and surf, and, of course, you surfers."

"Dude, that's not what I heard."

"What do you mean by that?"

"Dude, the cops were checking up on a surfer dude taking some illegal videos. The description fit you to a T. Sounded like some nasty stuff. Don't know any other surfers that are flying drones down here."

"Sounds like it's none of your business, man."

"Sounds like it's a lot of my business, Cody. I think you might want to make it my business. I think I have some valuable information about your cute little moneymaking scheme. Looks to me like you're shaking down another victim."

"Whaaaaat! What do you want? I thought we were buddies."

"Thick as thieves! Just a cut, man, just a cut to forget everything. I wouldn't want to obstruct justice, would I?"

"You are a first-class prick. OK, how much will amnesia cost me, dude?"

"Twenty five percent would be cool. Of each one you shake down, past and present."

"Umm, pretty stiff. I do all the work and have all of the risk and you have neither. You can't be serious."

"Wanna bet? The cops are sniffing around, Cody. It would be easy to do the right thing and help them. So let's make this work. How many capers have you pulled off?"

"One, so far. Working on number two."

"What did you rake in on number one?"

He lied, "Five grand."

"Cool. So let me do the math. Twenty-five percent and five big ones is, hmm, twelve hundred and fifty, right? Not that much."

"Look, I had to buy the drone and get lessons. Not cheap. How 'bout an even thou and you get twenty-five percent from here on out?"

"OK, dude. Make sure you're straight with me, or else. Anything I can do to help the process? Like, to actually earn my keep?"

"Maybe. Let me think about it."

Chump Change climbed back over the dune with a happy skip in his step, feeling pretty good about what had just transpired. A quick thousand– cha ching!

Cody was miffed- no, down right pissed. He'd thought that Chump Change was a buddy. Now he knew that he was a buddy fucker. Cody really couldn't celebrate his successful spying on Shane. His thoughts centered on whether he was achieving secrecy. If Chump Change had heard about what he did to Kerrigan, who else knew? Had Kerrigan gotten the cops involved, and were they looking for him? They must have talked to Chump Change; who else had they talked to? What evidence could they possibly find? Yes, they would know that a drone was involved, but there were a lot of drones out there. He would erase all the photos and videos of Kerrigan and make sure that they didn't find their way to the cloud. Had anyone identified him? He was pretty sure that he hadn't been close to anyone while he was launching or retrieving the Black Pelican, except for his former buddy, so he was comfortable thinking that he was undetected.

What about the money? His large deposits made right after he pulled off the Kerrigan deal would smell funny. But he had already made the deposits and the record was there. The cops could follow the money. He could make excuses, like he was hoarding cash from his tips and decided to deposit it in a safe place. It might be plausible, but the timing. The timing.

He got home and downloaded his videos onto his computer. He had hit the nail on the head. Both faces were easily identifiable. Better than he'd observed during the flight, one shot clearly showed Shane kissing or sucking one of the girl's nipples, and the shot of him laughing was *perfect*. With recent disclosures and accusations brought out in the media, this was a big deal.

Shane had been a target of the Me Too movement and other women's rights groups. He was a professional womanizer and was unrepentant about his conduct until publicity made his actions public. His career was taking a hit, and producers were shying away from hiring him due to possible liability by association downstream. He was the defendant in three lawsuits to date, with more expected to come. A current investigation involved an actress in a movie that he'd directed five years ago. The actress became pregnant, claimed Shane had raped her, and wanted to keep the baby. Shane had gone into a full-throttle rage and claimed that there was no way for the child to be his, denying the entire affair. The actress was paid off to have an abortion and DNA tests were done on the fetus. Shane was bound and determined to prove to himself, and especially to the actress, that he was not the father. The results were not in Shane's favor so the production company was alerted, and they paid to cover up the affair and scandal with the intent to keep Shane out of the news. One big problem arose. The abortion procedure didn't go well with some of the woman's organs being damaged. She recovered after a three-week stay in the hospital, but the doctors advised that she shouldn't try to get pregnant again. The actress was distraught and wanted more money for her pain and suffering, both physical and emotional. Shane refused. The former actress was now violating the non-disclosure agreement. She was pressured by the Me Too movement to make the whole mess public with the belief that Shane's lawyers wouldn't do anything because it would shine more light onto his conduct. Another case against Shane was brewing.   Twenty-some years ago, an actress was beaten so badly- allegedly by Shane during a drunken jealous rage- that she barely survived. She too was paid greatly for silence, but photos of her battered body, bruises, lacerations, and bloodied hair, were now being printed coast to coast with Shane cited as the assailant. His lawyers advised him to deny, deny, deny– her word against yours. And they told him to stay away from women for a while until things cooled off. One more incident and not only would his Hollywood life end as he knew it, he might be watching life from behind bars.

Cody had read all of the comments and rumors on the internet. When he saw a story about Shane highlighted on the front page of one of the tabloids in the grocery store, he bought it and devoured the article before trashing the paper. He knew what Shane was up against and thought that he would be particularly vulnerable right now. Despite his sinking feeling after his confrontation with Chump Change, a new payday was his aphrodisiac. This guy was probably worth more than ten grand. The first time around, the entire operation went flawlessly. So how easy would a second hit be? The only thing he would have to figure out was how to hide the money.

<h1 style="text-align:center">41</h1>

Max Ramsey arrived at the sheriff's office and was introduced to Detective Clint Heaton. Heaton was anxious to get more manpower for the Wilson case since he was getting nowhere fast.

"Agent Ramsey, would you care for a cup of coffee?"

"Sure, cream and some sort of sweetener. So, what have you got here, Detective?"

"Here's your cup-a-joe. So, we don't have much of anything on this case. It was a clever hit. The suspect wasn't a great shot, though. Fired from about forty yards away, no doubt using a hand gun. Hit Wilson in the thigh and a staffer in the arm. A third person on the deck wasn't hit but didn't see the assailant. We found some recent footprints, prints of shoes, which are somewhat unusual for the beach. Lots of other footprints as well. We ran a metal detector over the entire area; found some jewelry, a cell phone, and about a buck fifty in change, but no shell casings. The phone had been reported lost by a fifteen-year-old female visitor. The bullets came from a .38 special."

"Anything helpful from Wilson or the other victim?"

"No. You're welcome to talk to them and the other guy on the deck, but . . .

I didn't get anything useful."

"We've been trying to track down a character named Donald Sprout. He's wanted for another unrelated crime in Virginia and they lost track of him up there. He had some vile stuff against Wilson in his house and on his computer, so the locals up there asked for us to look out for him down here. We haven't found him, but we're watching. I'll get you his photo, and I think it's time we post him on our most wanted list."

"Sounds good. When do you want to interview the vics?"

"ASAP."

Heaton made some calls. Both Wilson and Julie Massey were out of the hospital and recuperating at home. Heaton contacted

Wilson, who lived outside of Durham. He told Heaton that he had nothing on his schedule for the next few days due to doctor's orders. After that, he would resume the campaign. Heaton also caught Massey at home. She told him that her recuperation would take longer, perhaps another month, and she would stay at home most of the time. She lived alone. She would rejoin the campaign when the doctors gave her a green light. Sid Freeze did not answer his phone. Heaton left a voicemail and then called Wilson's campaign headquarters. Freeze was there. He could be available tomorrow afternoon. Heaton told Ramsey to be ready for a road trip the next day. They would try to kill three interviews in one trip. Ramsey, booked temporarily in an oceanfront motel, asked Heaton for some inexpensive restaurant recommendations and things to do that afternoon.

A car trip down to Cape Hatteras appealed to Ramsey the most. He headed to his motel, a nice place named after the Wright Brothers, checked in, and then headed south to the Cape. He passed the Bodie Island Lighthouse (which was no longer on an island) and crossed over a body of water named the Oregon Inlet. He thought that name was odd, considering the state of Oregon was across the country. Driving through the Cape Hatteras National Seashore, he traveled through the small, touristy towns of Rodanthe, Waves, Salvo, and Avon. Surrounded by dunes covered with majestic sea oats and the wide waters of the sound, he was in a natural heaven. He pulled off the road a few times to walk over to the ocean. There, he found a broad beach that had one or two people within sight, with waves gently breaking on the shore. It was a calming, mesmerizing slice of heaven. At the Cape, he drove to the famous lighthouse, a national monument that had been moved a number of years ago to save it from the encroaching, stormy Atlantic. He was able to purchase a ticket to climb to the top, a strenuous endeavor. He paused twice to catch his breath. The effort was worth it to all who tried the climb. The view of that part of the island, the ocean, and the sound was spectacular. Back in the car, the first order of business was finding a bottle of water. He headed south as far as the road went, to the departure point for the ferry to Ocracoke Island. He pulled into a parking lot at a small shopping area there and roamed in and around the shops, picking up a sweatshirt for his girlfriend. Back on the road, he decided to look for a restaurant for dinner and a beer. He checked the internet and decided to try the Pangea Tavern. He ordered an IPA draft (passing on his normal cosmopolitan), a cup of crab bisque and the Cape Crab Cakes. He told the waitress that he was in no hurry and enjoyed the atmosphere, including the fish hanging from the ceiling. The food met the internet's high praise. *Nice little day vacation*, he thought.

Ramsey and Heaton agreed to meet at Heaton's office at eight sharp. They would use Heaton's official car, but Max chose to drive, since he lived there and knew his way around the capital area and Durham. They would go to Wilson's residence outside Durham first. Then they would go to Julie Massey's, and finally to Wilson's campaign headquarters to interview Freeze. Both officials had their morning coffee to sip on and after some small talk, mainly about Ramsey's sightseeing trip the previous day, they started talking business.

Heaton started, "So, what do you know about the guy you told me about yesterday?"

"Donald Sprout." Ramsey voiced a long narrative starting with Sprout being under Wilson's command in Afghanistan, Sprout being shot down, and how he hated Wilson and blamed his injury and his poor lot in life on Wilson, thanks to the information Ramsey had received from the detectives in Chesapeake.

"Is he still injured?"

"The report is that he has a noticeable limp. Not sure about psychological damage. He is a nasty guy, maybe has a mental disorder. He abducted a fourteen-year old girl, which is how the cops got involved in the first place, and really roughed her up. There are a number of warrants out for his arrest."

"Firearms?"

"Nothing registered. The girl he kidnapped didn't report seeing any. So who knows? He drives an old gray Impala. We have the plate number. We posted him last night, so we'll all be watching. Oh, by the way, I brought a copy of his photo for you– it's in the tan envelope in my briefcase."

"Did he make any threats against Wilson?"

"Not publicly. The walls of his living room were nicely decorated with articles about Wilson with some pretty hateful messages scribbled all over them. He had lots of searches on his computer, seemed to be following the campaign closely."

"The girl he kidnapped– did she know anything about his fixation on Wilson?"

"I don't know if they questioned her about that. I think she was extremely fragile and they probably wanted to hold off on that discussion for now."

Heaton called Wilson and said they should arrive around noon and asked if that was all right. Wilson said that would be fine and that his wife would have a light lunch ready, no worries. They arrived and Wilson's wife, Dawn, opened their front door before they started up the walk way. She had an elegant, simple beauty about her and a stunning smile. She was dressed in brightly colored leggings, which highlighted her shapely legs, and a low-cut blouse that hung loosely over her hips. The Wilsons' home wasn't a mansion but wasn't a double-wide either; it was a two-story, beige brick colonial. The neighborhood had similar homes with well-manicured landscaping.

"Gentlemen, welcome to our home. My name is Dawn and I am the congressman's wife."

From behind her, a man appeared and said, "And best friend, I might add. Please come in."

The home had a formal foyer and split off to a living room on one side, a dining room on the other, and stairs down the hall.

Introductions were made. Ramsey and Heaton asked the congressman to address them by their first names and Wilson did likewise. They asked how the leg was healing, having noticed a slight limp, and Wilson said that he still had pain, which the doctors told him would last a little bit longer. Other than that, he was OK; he felt very lucky. They entered the living room and found their places on over-stuffed chairs.

Max said, "Do you have any idea who would have done this? Have any threats been made?"

"Well, maybe you should check the alibis of my opponents." He chuckled and they all laughed. "Seriously, I've heard a few threats shouted at a couple of rallies. My staff confirmed the disturbances. At a rally in Rocky Mount, some man was shouting that I was a killer or something like that, and I invited him to the microphone to have his say. He accused me of sending him on a suicide mission, and the guards grabbed him before he said much of anything else."

Max and Clint looked at each other knowingly. Heaton asked Wilson if he'd gotten a good look at the man and he said he had. Max retrieved Sprout's picture from his briefcase and showed it to Wilson. "Look like the guy?"

"Maybe, could be, I'm not sure. I know my staff took photos and a video. You need to check with them."

Max said, "We're scheduled to meet Sid Freeze there this afternoon. Any other threats?"

"Two other incidents come to mind. At the Crabtree Valley Mall in Raleigh, some man in the rear of the small group was yelling something, creating a disturbance. At another rally at a college in Elizabeth City, some guy was distributing some derogatory literature claiming that I cheated on my wife. A flyer had a photo of a girl and claimed that she was working on the campaign. None of us have ever met the girl pictured. We saved a copy of the handout."

"Did you or any of your staff see the man?"

"I don't know. Ask Freeze when you meet him. We did get that copy of the flyer."

Dawn poked her head into the room and asked, "Anyone hungry?"

Wilson stood up and said, "It's not polite to keep a lady waiting."

The lunch consisted of a spinach salad with a homemade bacon-based dressing, oyster stew, and a roll. Both visitors thought that this was as good as any restaurant, and especially better than the fast-food restaurant that they probably would have ended up at. Dawn joined them, saying, "Would it be alright if I accompanied you, or is this all super secret, hush hush?"

They all chuckled and Richard said to his wife, "A pretty lady is always welcome."

The investigators directed the conversation to Dawn, wondering how she liked the campaign.

"It's stressful, and Richard is away too much. He goes to Washington to do his job and then rushes back here for some campaign event. So I get to kiss him hello and goodbye. One of my friends suggested that I was the one who shot him just to keep him home for a few days."

They all had a good laugh. "She's wanted to shoot me for less than that," Wilson joked.

"Seriously, the campaign is tiring for Richard. It's a lot of work. His staff is great, but it's still exhausting. The good news is that if he gets elected to the Senate, it's a six-year term, so we won't be campaigning for a while."

Max questioned, "What's life in Washington like?"

"It's OK, it has pluses and minuses. There are lots of things to do, culturally especially. We have an apartment in Alexandria in the main part of that city. Seems a lot more crowded than we are here. The Carolina delegation has been very nice to us, which helped us adapt. I would like to rent a house up there if he gets elected, just a small home or a townhouse or something like that, near a Metro station."

Wilson added, "She doesn't know it yet, but I'm going to put her to work if we get through."

"You are? Guess I know it now!" She chuckled.

Max Ramsey and Clint Heaton left the Wilson residence and headed to visit Julie Massey. Julie was convalescing at home and was expecting them. She was single and lived in a nice one-bedroom, third-floor apartment in Cary, just outside of Raleigh, near where Ramsey lived. She welcomed her guests and had them sit in her living room. They offered the obligatory questions about her wounds and the prognosis, and then inquired about her experience when the shooting occurred. Unfortunately, she'd had her back to the beach and the shooter and didn't see anyone. She'd felt a very sharp pain in her arm and almost simultaneously heard two bangs, the gun shots. She went down on her knees and watched the congressman collapse. Blood was splattered everywhere. She remembered being scared that more shots would follow and that she was yelling "help me." She also remembered that Wilson was moaning.

They asked her about previous campaign events and if there was any indication that something like this would happen. She related the incidents that Wilson had told them about and opined that the security guards looked at it as typical campaign mischief. No one envisioned a shooting. They each gave her their cards and thanked her for her hospitality, inquiring if she was going back to the campaign. She said enthusiastically, "You bet. Hope to be back in a couple of weeks regardless of what the doctors say!"

Ramsey and Heaton had a short drive to the campaign headquarters. It was located in a twelve-story office building in downtown Raleigh. The office occupied half of the fourth floor and the campaign had just rented space on the fifth floor. Ramsey and Heaton introduced themselves, displaying their badges to the receptionist, and expressed their wish to meet Sid Freeze. She asked if this was about the shootings and they confirmed that it was. She pushed an intercom button and said, "Sid, there are two detectives here to see you."

"Yes, I was expecting them. Send them back." She escorted them to Freeze's office.

Ramsey introduced himself and Heaton and said, "Man, this place is humming."

"These campaigns are big business. Now that the congressman has won the primary, we're staffing up even more."

Heaton asked, "How hard is it to find the people you need?"

"We have an excellent HR person, she knows how to recruit the right people, so with her, not hard at all. We look at the budget and give her the staff needs. A lot of people get excited about campaigns and want to work on them. Some I'm sure are hoping to be hired if our guy gets elected, but I think some just do it for the adrenaline. This is a high-stress environment, so everyone has to fit in."

They casually made some small talk about how many workers there were and what the structure of personnel was, then got down to the main issue.

Ramsey asked, "What can you tell us about the shooting?"

"Julie Massey and I were leaning on the deck railing with our backs to the beach and ocean, Richard was standing sideways facing north toward us. It was sunny and breezy. I heard a 'pop' and then another 'pop' and at the same time I was splattered with blood and watched both Julie and Richard go down. I knelt down by Julie because I thought she was hit in the chest or abdomen, helped her lie down and called 9 1 1. I could then tell that she was hit in the arm, not her trunk, and looked at Richard, who had his eyes closed, was grimacing and moaning. I ran inside to get a few towels and came back and wrapped one around Richard's leg where he was hit. I tried to do the same for Julie's arm, but she was in too much pain, so I went back inside to get some blankets to cover her. Sometime during the whole incident, I glanced out at the beach but didn't see anyone. Sorry."

"We understand. You had two people with significant injuries. We were with the congressman earlier today and asked about any disturbances during any campaign events. He told us about a few. Did anyone on your staff see whoever was creating the trouble?"

There were a few, shall I say, incidents. We had a heckler here in Raleigh at a shopping mall, but nobody reported seeing him. We had another in Rocky Mount and Richard invited the jerk to come onstage. The coward continued from the crowd and our guards escorted him away. They took his photo. And then in Elizabeth City, a heckler was handing out defaming flyers. Again the guards silenced him. It was the same guy."

"May we see the photos?"

"Sure." Freeze called the receptionist on the intercom and asked her to send in Peter Chek. "Peter is our security chief.

He's known Richard for years; served with him in the Air Force."

Chek came in and introductions were made. Peter was tall, about six five, and trim but muscular. He sported a dark Don Johnson- style beard and looked like he could be a professional athlete. Regardless of what job he was attending to, he was well dressed, today in a navy-blue collared shirt and khaki pants. Freeze explained why they were there.

"Peter, would you bring the photos you have of the heckler?"

"Roger that. Be right back."

Chek was only gone for a moment and re-entered Freeze's office and handed the photos to Freeze, who handed them to Ramsey.

"Sprout!" Heaton said.

Chek jerked as if surprised. "What do you mean by 'sprout'?"

Ramsey said, "There's a guy named Donald Sprout from up in Virginia. He's done some nasty things up there. When the investigators entered his home, it was plastered with anti-Wilson material. He has a beef with Wilson that goes back to his time in Afghanistan. Virginia just clued us in a week ago. He drives a gray Impala. I'll get you the plate number."

"What do you know about him?"

"Not a lot. You actually have better photos than we have."

"Do you like him for the shooting?"

"We don't know if he has a firearm. None were registered to him. Right now, we don't have anyone else to look at."

Ramsey directed the conversation back to Freeze. "We'll need Wilson's schedule so we can alert the local police and get them involved. We'll also get an extra detail of the state police on board. If you see or hear anything, let us know immediately."

Ramsey and Heaton left to return to the Outer Banks. Ramsey said, "Hungry?"

Heaton replied, "Born hungry."

"I love Olive Garden. I'll head to one I know."

42

Donald Sprout sat in a bar in Plymouth, North Carolina, about an hour and a half from where he shot Wilson, sipping his scotch and soda. He watched news coverage of the shooting. The report was that Wilson was hit but would recover completely, and some woman was also hit. The early coverage indicated that there were no suspects yet; Sprout smiled to himself about the report that the cops had no clue. Typical for cops, he thought; they were usually clueless. But he was irritated that he'd missed his target. How stupid. He showed his hand and didn't win the pot. Now he would have to try again. He had other issues. He missed Vixen. He missed the sex and the control. A lot. More importantly, he was running out of cash. He sipped his drink and put his head between his hands. The bartender noticed and traipsed over to the end of the bar where Sprout sat and said, "You OK, buddy?"

"Just have to figure things out."

His monthly phone payment was due in a few days; it was his only link to the rest of the world and he couldn't afford to let it lapse. So he decided to gamble and go to an ATM in town, withdraw what he could, get a money order, and send it to the cell phone company. But he still needed more cash. He took care of the bill and headed to the Raleigh area.

During the car trip, he brooded over the money issue. There were certainly places that he could rob, but that was a dangerous business and obviously a crime. It wasn't the criminal side that bothered him; that ship had already sailed. He decided he would hit up some churches. He thought they would hand out some dough to a poor homeless soul. He would use a false name, telling them, if they asked, that his wallet with identification was robbed. He drove into the city and started stopping at every church he encountered. His best stop that day was a visit with Pastor Francis Karney. The pastor had a huge heart and, being in charge of a large church, had full pockets. Sprout made the story sound good. He was a veteran, wounded in Afghanistan (true), his wife left him (false), he lost his job due to painkillers (once true), was robbed while sleeping in his car (false), but always attended some church when he could get there (false). The pastor forked out five hundred dollars, rented a room at a motel for him, and told him where to find the food bank.

Sprout was giddy about his acting ability. In his first day in the city, he collected eight hundred dollars, found a source for food, and had a bed to sleep in. He had to create more stories at the food bank, but he looked the part of a homeless man (which he was). At the motel, he again explained how he was robbed and had no ID. They didn't seem to care since the pastor made the reservation, which he had done before. Sprout asked for a razor and a comb and got to his room. It was clean and typical of chain motels, but certainly not the Waldorf Astoria. He took a long, hot shower, the first in almost a month, and shaved. His hair was getting too long, he thought, and it might make him recognizable. Tomorrow, he would hit up a few more churches and get a haircut. He laid down on the bed, a real bed, and turned on the TV. He surfed the channels until he found a station broadcasting the local evening news. He watched for a while but nothing was said about Wilson or the shooting. Bored waiting for some news, he opened a can of pork and beans, placed some in one of the cups in the room, and heated it in the microwave. Two cans and four slices of bread later, he was full. This might be the last hot meal in a while. He laid back down, turned the TV off, and started planning the next day. He hugged his pillow and yearned for Vixen. He yearned to be in her. He loved her and she loved him. He fell asleep, wishing he could go back and get her.

The next morning, he was awake at six and went down to the lobby to check out what kind of breakfast they had. There was the ubiquitous waffle maker, fruit, cereals, juices, yogurt, and hot scrambled eggs and sausage patties. He filled his plate and ate slowly watching the morning news. The announcer briefly touched on the Senate race, showing Wilson and his opponent, Mercer Harris. He thought Harris looked like a fuddy-duddy. He couldn't hear much of what the announcer said, but he read the closed captioning. Wilson had recovered and was ready to start the campaign. Sprout would have to check Wilson's schedule on his phone to see when another opportunity would present itself. He pocketed some fruit, a cup of Cheerios, and a bagel and went back to his room. The breakfast lasted until nine. So he took another hot shower. He found a laundry bag in the closet and packed towels, a pillow, and his bagel and fruit. Before nine, he went down to eat another large breakfast and help himself to more food for the rest of the day.

Once back in his car, Sprout decided to call the Wilson campaign headquarters, blocking his number by first dialing star sixty-seven. He asked when and where Wilson would be making speeches over the next few weeks. The first event, in a week, was at the Museum of the Albemarle in Elizabeth City. Sprout was somewhat familiar with the city but thought it was too close to home and the Outer Banks, where he'd made his first attempt. The campaign worker rattled on about a few more future appearances. One that appealed to him was on the grounds of Duke University Hospital, where Wilson was scheduled to speak about his position on health care. Sprout wasn't knowledgeable of the physical conditions there but was informed that the speech would be outside. Duke is in Durham, not far from Raleigh, where Sprout was, so he decided to head to the hospital and scope it out.

Both Detective Hasbee in Virginia and Max Ramsey were furnished with the information that someone had used Sprout's debit card at an ATM in Plymouth. The natural assumption was that it was Sprout. Since he was the only suspect for the shooting on the Outer Banks, they individually deduced that he was headed west. Ramsey alerted the Durham police, where Wilson lived, to maintain surveillance on Wilson's residence and to be on the lookout for Sprout's vehicle. Ramsey called the campaign headquarters just as Sprout had and requested an updated detailed itinerary of all of Wilson's movements. Within the next month, Wilson had fourteen scheduled events, speeches, interviews, and fund-raisers. Ramsey talked to Peter Chek, the campaign's head of security that he'd met previously, and gave him the latest on Sprout. Chek had added more security guards, some of whom would be uniformed and others in plain clothes, due to the threat.

"Peter, Max Ramsey, SBI, here. I wanted to bring you up to speed. We think Sprout is headed your way. He used an ATM in Plymouth. We're thinking that using the ATM means he's desperate for cash. We've notified the network that he may try a burglary or similar crime to get money."

Sprout, using his GPS, found Duke Hospital. He parked in the huge parking garage across the street from the hospital and walked through a long tunnel to get to the building. He found a receptionist and asked if there was a public relations office or some such thing. The lady looked at him quizzically and asked, "Yes, we have one. But is there something I can do for you?"

"NO. Just need to talk to your public relations people."

She directed him to where the office was and he walked in that direction. There were three people in the PR office that he could see. He went up to what looked like the oldest person, a lady, and said, "I need some information."

"Yes sir, what do you need to know?"

"The congressman is giving a speech here soon. I want to know where on the property that will be."

"Congressman Wilson?"

"Yes, of course, who did you think I meant?"

She gave him a disapproving look. "Mr. Wilson will be presenting his speech on health care on the lawn outside the main entrance. Is there anything else I can do for you, sir?"

"How do I get there?"

She pointed "Go down this hall and you'll see the signs for the main lobby."

He turned and walked away. When he got there, he walked outside and looked all around. It was obvious which lawn she was talking about. It was located on Erwin Road, at the end of Fulton Street. He walked around, observing everything he thought was noteworthy. He took a few photos from different vantage points. There were trees at either end of the lawn.

Toward the west, there was a copse of trees that he thought would be a good hiding place, but he wouldn't know until the day of the event where Wilson would stand. He walked back to the garage building and drove away.

The people in the PR office talked about the unusual man who asked unusual questions. He looked like a homeless person with a disagreeable aura about him. They mutually decided to call the hospital security office, just in case. The guard that answered the phone thanked them for the information. He asked when the man was there and had the security camera videos checked to see if they caught a good shot of the person. Based on the timing and the PR office description, they isolated one person leaving the main entrance. They had a good view of his face. The guard went to his chief and filled him in and inquired about what he should do with the information. The chief said he would call the Durham police with what they had as a precaution.

The Durham police had been notified by Ramsey's office to watch for Sprout. They compared the photos they were provided by the Wilson campaign and the hospital. They were a match. Durham immediately notified the state police and the SBI. Ramsey received the message and phoned both Heaton and Michael Hasbee.

Hasbee knocked on his boss's door. Chief Forbish waved him in. "What' ya got, detective?"

"Just an update from Carolina."

"You know there's two Carolinas, don't you? Which one?"

Hasbee smirked. "The nearest one, ma'am. They traced Sprout in Plymouth, which is between the Outer Banks and Raleigh, and then in Durham. In Durham, he went to Duke University Hospital."

"Whatever for?"

"Getting to that. He wanted information on a scheduled campaign event there for Congressman Wilson. He wanted to know where it would be held."

Forbish scowled and said, "Sounds like our boy is looking for trouble. I take it that Carolina, you know, the one nearest us, is on it?"

"Like flies on shit!"

"Good. Keep me up to speed. And let the Roselli's know where he is."

"Aye, aye, El Capitàn."

Hasbee recorded the information and called both Joan Roselli and Anthony Roselli at work and gave them the update. They both thanked the detective.

Max Ramsey met with Heaton at a small seafood restaurant in Nags Head on the road along the beach. The famous eatery was rustic and looked like a good place to eat fish. Ramsey had been leaning toward a Subway tuna salad with jalapeños, but Heaton told him he needed to soak up some of the local culture.

"Clint, how long has this place been here?"

"I think longer than your and my ages put together!"

"They had roads here back then?"

"Just the 'Beach Road.' Wasn't much around, according to the pictures I've seen."

"I just wanted to follow up with you. I'm heading back to Raleigh tomorrow. With Sprout on the run around Durham, and since we don't have any evidence that points to anyone else, there's nothing I can do here. Kinda a nice vacation, though."

"Yeah, agreed. If anything comes up, I'll be in touch. Really looks like that Sprout guy is our man."

Ramsey ordered a flounder sandwich with coleslaw and Heaton went for a tuna Reuben. While dining, they talked about some old cases and odd things that they'd seen. They split their bill, shook hands and departed. They would meet again.

43

As he'd done with Kerrigan, Cody printed a select few photos, again holding them with a towel so as not to leave fingerprints. He put them in an envelope with a computer-printed message that read, "These could stay buried. Call 252-301-9752. Remember, the Me Too movement lurks." The number was Cody's new burner phone. Cody added his sketch of a pelican, his signature. He decided to make the delivery after his shift as he had done before. If it ain't broke, don't fix it.

At the Bistro, he finished serving tables and all the clean-up a little after midnight and was getting ready to drive up to Shane's house when Willow called him over to the bar. They were closing up and were the only two left.

"Hey, Cody, you in any hurry?"

Cody didn't want to say yes so he answered, "No, sweetie, what's up?"

"Come here, behind the bar. I have something to show you."

Cody did as requested, and when he got there, Willow unbuttoned her shirt to display her firm, full breasts, no bra. She pulled him to her and kissed him hard on the lips and he kissed her back. She pulled one of his hands onto her breast and said, "I don't want to stop here."

"Willow! We can't be doing this here!"

"Okay, then where?"

Cody grabbed her arm and led her back to the manager's office. It was a small room but at least they would have some privacy if they needed it. During the short walk to the office, Willow was grabbing Cody on the ass and squeezing and sighing.

"What a nice ass you have, surfer boy!"

They entered the office and shut the door. Cody swung Willow around so that she was pushed up against the door with his mouth on hers and the full length of his body pressing against hers. They kissed hurriedly and Cody pulled away.

"God, what are we doing?"

"Cody, come here. Come on. I want you. I want that sexy body of yours NOW!"

She pulled him to her and she began to rub her hands under his shirt and up to his chest. He moaned and said, "No fair," with a smile on his face. She then reached down and unzipped his pants to find him already hard.

"But your body says yes, mister."

Before he knew it, they were wrapped in a fierce embrace and rolling around on the floor, each trying to get clothes off each other. The need to feel skin-to-skin contact was overpowering. Her desire was so obvious and her body so giving. He couldn't stand it anymore and gave in to her. Their passion took his breath away. Comfort was not an issue, nor needed. Each other was what was desired. Breathing heavy and out of breath, they lay on the floor staring at the ceiling.

"What was that?"

"Something I have wanted for a long, long time, surfer boy, and you did not disappoint. Get over here."

Cody finally left the Bistro, and he wasn't sure he had enough energy to drive the envelope up to Duck. He couldn't remember having better sex.

Harrison Shane lounged on his balcony sipping Macallan scotch on the rocks- yes, at nine-in-the morning, with his bikini-clad live-in date, Veronica. They breakfasted on a couple of English muffins and bacon with a dessert of passionate sex. Shane was very happy with his hired companion and she was delighted with the job except when the sex got a little too rough. The wind was light and the surf was fairly calm and quiet. Shane got up, kissed her, took a quick shower, and got dressed for another day on the links. The Duck Woods Country Club, which he had already played once, was the scheduled course.

Phoebe provided transportation that day. Marco, Sea Dunes's usual driver, was committed to another guest and Phoebe hadn't talked to Shane for a few days and wanted to make sure that things were going well. She had his clubs in her trunk. Shane saw her cruise up the driveway as he stepped out of the front door. He glanced down and saw an envelope lying there, picked it up, and tossed it onto an accent table in the foyer. It was a perfect day for golf, or anything outside. The temperature was in the mid-seventies, with a forecasted high around eighty, with white puffy clouds and a gentle breeze predicted to stay that way all day.

"Good morning, Mr. Shane. You're looking sprightly this morning!"

"Good as ever, Phoebe. You know me well enough to address me by my first name. But no Harrys. So where's Marco?"

"He thought you'd rather have me pick you up! Seriously, he had a commitment and I wanted to see how your vacation was going anyway. How is it going?" Phoebe turned left onto Route 12 toward the country club.

"Super. I'm enjoying everything, especially your friend Veronica. I needed to get out of Hollywood for a while to let some simmering pots cool down. Seems like no one will find me here."

"Yes, it can be pretty quiet and private here. For today's round, I have you paired with Bob Hones. He's one of the richest bankers here, maybe the richest for all I know. I'm told he shoots a seven handicap. I'm also told he cheats."

"No problem, so do I!" He chuckled, an evil smirk on his face. "How about a really nice place to eat tonight?"

"OK, I'll see if I can get you a reservation at Kimball's Kitchen. It's first-rate, at the Sanderling Resort. What time is good for you?"

"How about seven, seven thirty. Table for Veronica and me."

"Good. I'm on it."

She pulled into the country club and popped the trunk open. Shane said, "I'll get the bag."

"Great. Call me when you want to head back. Give me fifteen minutes or so."

"Probably mid-afternoon, depending on how much I win from Bob and how many drinks he buys me."

Phoebe escorted Shane into the clubhouse and found Hones. She introduced him to Shane and wished them luck. Shane said, "Phoebe, I don't need luck, and I don't want Bob here to have any." He laughed, and Bob and Phoebe politely joined in. Phoebe took off and the two golfers made the preliminary bets. Shane showed Hones a card stating that his handicap was nine. It was really three. The cheating started.

Hones asked, "Ever play Duck Woods before?"

"No, Phoebe tells me it's a nice course. You'll have to help me with the course nuances." Shane lied; he'd played the course a week earlier. They went to the putting green and made small talk. Shane made sure that he looked weak on the green to increase Hones's interest in betting larger sums. On hole number one, a par five, Hones said, "How about we add a hundred per hole, straight up, no handicaps?"

"That's fucking tilted your way, with your better handicap and knowledge of the course. But, what the hell, you're on. I'd better have one of my better days!" He would have a good day on the course, but not when he returned home.

They got to the seventeenth hole with Shane up two holes and ahead on the side bets. Shane offered, "Five hundred bucks for closest to the hole."

Hones, trying to recoup some of his loses, said, "You're on."

Shane was up and lofted a beauty that settled five feet from the hole.

"Fucking lucky bastard," Hones said with a smile.

"Better to be lucky than good!"

Hones, unnerved now, had his tee shot hit the green and roll off. Shane won the eighteenth as well and pocketed well over a thousand for the day's work.

Hones shook his hand, had a laugh or two, and said, "I think you won enough to be the host at the bar." They stowed their bags in the clubhouse, removed their cleats, washed up a little, and strode up to the bar. The room was inviting since the building had been renovated. They chose a small table rather than barstools. Shane ordered a single malt scotch on the rocks (they didn't stock Macallan) and Hones requested a Cosmopolitan.

"What kind of sissy drink is a Cosmopolitan?"

"It's one that you can drink until you can't stand up!"

They'd taken some snacks out on the course, but they were starved by now and both ordered cheeseburgers with the works. Shane asked how the banking business was, pretending to be interested, while eyeing a very attractive, curvy young waitress. Hones said that the Outer Banks had some red hot days in the past but things had cooled down a little. Some banks were sold and some went greasy side up. Shane had never heard that term and said, "Think I'll use 'greasy side up' in my next flick. As long as it doesn't go 'greasy side up'." They ordered a second round with their burgers.

"When do you head back to the glitz and glamour?"

"In about two weeks. I actually have to start working on a new venture while I'm here. Might cut into my golfing, but one has to make a living." He was still glancing at the young lady.

"Well, with days like you had today, you could make a living hustling golf opponents."

"Every dog has his day!"

Shane texted Phoebe. When she arrived, she collected his clubs, spikes, and the like and came up to the bar. Shane said, "Pretty nice chauffeur, isn't she?" Then he shook Hones's hand and bid him a nice day. Phoebe reminded him of the reservation at Kimball's Kitchen for seven thirty.

"Do you want me to send Marco?"

"No, I think we'll take a taxi. Would you order one?"

"Sure. Be at your house at seven twenty?"

"No, let's leave some room for time in the bar. How about six forty-five?"

"Got it."

Phoebe dropped Shane off and said, "Remember, call me if you need anything."

<h1 style="text-align:center">44</h1>

Shane picked up the envelope as he made his way up the stairs. He instinctively glanced around the huge living room and saw Veronica, stunning in a string bikini, out on the balcony. He pulled the sliding glass door open and said, "Hey cutie, want to come inside to get some exercise? We're dining at a classy place tonight and you don't want to get fat."

He opened the envelope and stared at the photos and the comment about Me Too. The movement had started a campaign to bring women out of hiding who had been sexually abused. They'd targeted Shane due to his reputation in Hollywood as a brute, a womanizer, and a narcissistic prick. Five women, to date, had told their stories to the press. His face was plastered on all the tabloids with damning headlines.

One actress, Sienna Wood, who'd auditioned for a part in one of Harrison Shane's movies, claimed to be raped by him twice in the same afternoon. She got the part but was never the same. Three years later. Sienna went to the police and reported the crime against her. They told her they would file a report, but without collaborating evidence, it was a he said, she said type of case. She went to the press and the scandal broke. She decided to go to one of the most famous attorneys in Los Angeles, a man who handled many legal issues for celebrities, to represent her. He told Sienna that a suit would be hard to win or even settle. The damage in the press was already done and couldn't be made much worse with a trial. She shopped around and finally found a somewhat sleazy lawyer, John Steele, who took the case for a fifty percent contingency. He made up facts and got them into the press. He put out that Sienna went to a hospital and got a rape kit. He claimed that the examination proved that she was raped and the DNA matched Shane's. Now Steele's and Shane's photos were montaged together on all the national tabloids, Steele looking angry and Shane looking surprised. Sienna, through Steele, sued Shane for one million dollars.

At the time, Shane's lawyer, Noah Jacobowicz, called him in the middle of a production to let him know about the suit. He asked when they could meet and Shane, on location in Georgia, said he needed the lawyer to come to him. Jacobowicz told him he couldn't get away until the weekend.

"Just get your ass here, Noah."

"OK, remember that it's on the tab."

The lawyer's administrative assistant made the flight reservations- first class, of course- to Atlanta and booked the Renaissance Gateway Hotel near the airport for two nights. She also arranged for a Mercedes to be dropped off at the hotel for Jacobowicz's use. Noah flew on a Friday after his assistant cleared his schedule. At the airport, he called Shane and left the message, "Flying today. Will arrive around six thirty p.m. When can we meet tomorrow?" He did not receive a reply by the time his flight left. When he landed, Shane suggested nine a.m. and gave an address. The location was a house Shane had rented for the filming and was about forty-five minutes from Jacobowicz's hotel. The lawyer texted, "I'll be there."

When he arrived the next morning, Shane had a variety of pastries available as well as coffee and anything from the kitchen; his chef was standing by. Jacobowicz said coffee and a Danish would be fine. He brought Shane up to speed on the lawsuit. The complaint alleged that he raped Sienna Wood. The supposed evidence plastered across the media was not specified. The counselor asked Shane to deny that he raped her; he didn't want to know if he did, only wanted to hear a negative. Shane said, "I think what happened is a matter of perspective, Noah."

"Well, maybe, but juries have unpredictable perspectives. I think we should get whatever they have through discovery and dispose Ms. Wood. The problem is the PR. The longer we drag it out, the more fun the media will have. They already hate you and are feeding into the Me Too movement."

"Yes. Yes, you are right. What do you think the chances are that they have something?"

"I can get one of my investigators to try to find where she got examined, if she really did, but if he comes up with nothing, it won't mean that she wasn't. Discovery is the only sure way. Even if they don't have anything, they can still go for a trial."

"Then it's just a he said, she said thing, right?"

"Yes. And with preponderance of evidence being the criteria, who knows how it would end. Juries favor crying women."

"OK, see how much they really want. I had my assistant reserve you a table at South City Kitchen tonight, if you want to wander away from your hotel. The hotel also has some fine dining."

"I'll try South City. What time is the reservation for?"

"Eight."

"That works. I'll get back to you when I talk to her lawyer. His name is John Steele. Don't know much about him, but I will before I talk to him."

Shane invited Noah to hang around the set, and since he had nothing else to do, he accepted the invitation.

When Jacobowicz returned back to work, he had his girl friday check into Steele. She reported back that he was a small-timer with the reputation that he would sue a ham sandwich. He had cases that the judge threw out. Word in the courthouse was that Steele was the worst kind of ambulance chaser. Jacobowicz called Steele but had to leave a message. Steele returned the call and Jacobowicz told him he was preparing a countersuit alleging defamation. Steele told him his client had not done anything that would result in a judgement against her; she was stating facts. Jacobowicz asked him, just for the record, what she really wanted, that a million was ridiculous. Steele told him he'd get back to him. He did, the next day and asked if Shane would issue a public apology. Jacobowicz answered, "Not a snowball's chance in hell." Steele told him to prepare for trial.

The trial was sensational in that every network and large paper covered it. Near the end, with no evidence of any substance being offered to substantiate the allegation, Jacobowicz offered a settlement of fifty grand, take it or leave it. Wood took it. However, the PR damage to Shane's reputation had been done. There were others. None sued but they did come out of the woodwork and air the details.

The studios weren't happy and independently notified Shane that their association with him might come to an end if he didn't change. To show that he was contrite, Shane went to a sexual abuse rehabilitation center for two weeks and exited claiming that such things were all in the past. Few bought it. During the last movie he had directed, after the rehabilitation, organizers picketed the sets for three days. The producers weren't happy. Shane's name was getting to be synonymous with trouble, and that would and could hurt the box office numbers.

45

Shane called the number Cody had given him. "What do you want, you little prick?"

"Now, now, let's not get testy. This can go away for just fifty grand. Cash. Cheap at twice the price."

"What if I say no?"

"The shots might just find their way to the Me Too movement and to a tabloid or two. Actually, they may pay more. Make it easy on yourself and get this over with."

"I'll think it over, you bastard."

"You've got until five tomorrow afternoon. And if I smell a cop, you're done."

"Can't get cash that fast. You must certainly know that."

"All I know is that you're a big shot. I'm sure you can get anything done that you want. You probably should send your bimbo home."

Shane hung up. He was irate and started to throw things around the rental house, not a good move. Veronica heard the commotion and came up to the living room and said, "What the fuck, Harrison?"

"What the fuck, yourself!" He grabbed her and threw her onto one of the sofas, hard.

"You put some guy up to blackmail me, bitch?" He slapped her across the face.

She fell sideways from the impact. "What the fuck are you talking about?"

He threw the photos at her. "He wants fifty for this to go away."

"Fifty dollars?"

"No you stupid bitch, fifty THOUSAND dollars."

"Shit, Harrison. I'm so sorry. What can I do?"

"First you can tell me what you had to do with this."

"Nothing. I'm having a good time. Why would I shit on you?"

"Maybe because I'm rich? What about the real estate woman that contracted you? What about her?"

"I actually never met her until our meeting. She hired me through a talent agency." Still fuming, he picked up a TV remote and threw it at her. He missed.

"I'm calling her. And your story better check out."

He dialed Phoebe's number on his phone. "Phoebe, get your ass up to my house now."

"Mr. Shane, what's the problem?"

"I said NOW. Don't make me come to your office. There will be hell to pay."

"OK, be there in a few."

Phoebe rang the doorbell and Shane opened the door, yanked her inside by grabbing her arm and said, "Come upstairs, we gotta talk."

"Please let go of my arm, you're hurting me."

"Shut up and get upstairs."

Phoebe sensed that maybe Shane was having an issue with Veronica but that wasn't it. When they got to the second floor, Phoebe saw the mess and knew something was radically wrong. "What happened here?"

Shane went to the coffee table and grabbed the photos and shoved them at Phoebe. "A nasty note came with these. What did you or this bimbo know about it? A nice setup, I'd say!"

"Mr. Shane, I had nothing to do with this. We run a first-class operation here. I'm personally offended at your accusation and your tone."

"Well, how would you sound if someone was blackmailing you? Huh? Pretty pissed off, I'd say. This babe says she doesn't know you. Is that true?" He was right in her face.

Phoebe didn't back off. "I never met her until I had her meet you. I booked her from a reputable talent agency."

"Well, somebody knows who I am. The note here refers to the Me Too movement. They've been hassling me for years. Somebody knows I'm here. Who, Phoebe?"

"Mr. Shane, you are famous. Everyone knows what you look like. You really can't hide, not even here. What does this person want?"

"He wants fifty grand, hon."

"Shit! I have police friends, do you want me to get them involved? I heard of another case like this but don't know what happened. They would probably need to get involved soon if they can resolve this mess."

"Not yet. The bastard gave me one day to shell out. I need to talk to my lawyer first. In the meantime, get Veronica out of here."

"I assume dinner is off for tonight."

"You're another Einstein."

He looked at Veronica. "Sorry honey, duty calls. It's been fun." She was crying and wouldn't look at him.

"I'm not a bimbo."

Phoebe escorted Veronica out of the house and discussed what had happened. She had no idea how the photos were taken, but she did remember hearing and seeing a drone. She asked Phoebe, "Could they've been taken by a drone?"

"Looks that way."

Phoebe took her back to where she had parked her car and said that she felt bad that it had to end this way. Veronica agreed and told her it wasn't her fault. Once again, Phoebe resorted to calling her friend, Detective Clint Heaton. He was back in the office.

"Hi Clint, it's Phoebe."

"Hi Phoebe. Are you checking on the Kerrigan matter?"

"No. I got another one, same circumstances. Like Kerrigan, the guy wants no cops."

"Who's the victim this time?"

"Harrison Shane, movie director."

"You mean the guy that the tabloids are flogging?"

"One and the same."

"So what do you know about this second incident?"

"From what I saw in the photos, it looks like they weren't taken from beach level. I didn't get to study them, so I could be wrong. The lady involved told me she heard and saw a drone at some point. The blackmailer wants fifty grand."

"Phew, the stakes have been raised. Sounds like the same guy. Maybe Kerrigan was his test case; now he has confidence in the shakedown. Since the guy wants no cops, I can quietly snoop around and check out the scene as we did last time, but, as you know, that didn't get us anywhere. What's the address this time?"

"Eighteen High Dunes Lane."

"OK, I'll be in touch."

46

Shane decided to call two people: his lawyer, Noah Jacobowicz, and his Hollywood agent, Herb Gellar. The lawyer took the call on his cell despite being in the courthouse with a client. He knew that it wasn't wise to let Harrison Shane wait.

"Hi Harrison. I'm over at the courthouse. What's up?"

"Noah, I don't care where the fuck you are. I got a problem."

"Listening."

"Some clown is blackmailing me. Got photos of me and a girl, let's say R-rated photos. Wants fifty grand. Got some legal advice for me?"

"Jesus, Harrison, you were supposed to lay low. Who's the babe?"

"Some girl from some talent agency. The real estate lady arranged it."

"That's what I call a service real estate agency! As far as advice, yeah, call the cops. Have them monitor any communications you have with him. Where were you and the lady when the photos were taken?"

"Out on our balcony. It's pretty secluded. I don't remember seeing anyone next door or on the beach."

"OK, call the cops."

Shane called Gellar next. "Herb, Harrison here. Need some advice." He went through what had happened again.

"What the fuck, Harrison. Keep your fucking nose clean, man. What are you going to do?"

"Jacobowicz says to call the cops. What do you say?"

"Man, this is tough. I'd stay away from the cops. It'll get out and you'll be crucified in the media again! Can you neutralize him somehow?"

"Herb, I'm not in the mafia. What do you mean 'neutralize'?"

"You know, grab him by the neck and tell him that the next time you'll squeeze hard."

"I don't think that's a great idea."

"No. Just thought I'd throw it out there. Why not pay him and tell him the cops will be watching if anything comes out."

"That plan is a little better than your first one. Get my office to call Phoebe at Sea Dunes Concierge Realty to wire the fifty. ASAP. I'll figure out what to do after that."

Heaton drove up to High Dunes Lane. He checked with the occupants on either side of number eighteen, asking if they'd seen anyone on the beach taking pictures of the houses (as opposed to family or beach scenes), any unusual behavior, or a drone. The families occupying the house on the south side were no help; however, nothing seemed strange. However one of the occupants on the north side did see a drone on a couple of occasions. The last incident was a couple of days ago. The drone came from the north, slowed down near their rentals, flew farther south, and then sped back to the north. It was as high as the rooftops. Heaton continued visiting the houses on the row but didn't learn anything new. So he took his shoes off and walked on the beach, going north from Shane's house. He got to the end and noticed something lying in the dune. He walked over to the area, a recess in the dune line. He found a discarded empty Bai Molokai Coconut bottle and a towel there. He put on a pair of plastic gloves and placed the items in an evidence bag that he'd brought. The sand was too soft to make out footprints or any other discernable marks, so Heaton hiked over the dune and walked down High Dunes Lane to its access road, Ocean Mist Lane, just on a hunch that he might find something, anything. He did notice tire tracks in the sand off the road and thought they were good enough to get an imprint. He called his office and requested CSI to come to make the impressions. They told him they couldn't get there for an hour, so he gave them directions and got some yellow crime scene tape and laid it on the ground around the tire tracks. He took the evidence bag back to the office and signed it in with a tag labeled Case TBD. He called Phoebe and told her what the neighbor reported about the drone and what he found.

"You said there was a Bai bottle? Do you know what flavor?"

"Yeah, I recorded it. It was Molokai Coconut, whatever that is. Why did you ask?"

"Just a curiosity, I guess. Thanks. I'll tell the victim that the photos might have come from a drone. Let me know if you hear anything."

"You bet."

Phoebe sat in her office, somewhat stunned, somewhat confused. Cody's favorite drink was Bai Molokai Coconut. He probably had a number of bottles in the fridge.

The next day, fifty grand was wired to the realty's bank and placed into Shane's account. Whitney at Sea Dunes was notified of the deposit and thought that the size of the deposit was extremely unusual. Extremely unusual. She went to Sharna's office and said, "Hey boss, got a minute?"

"Sure Whitney, you look concerned. Everything okay?"

"Not really, just a little stunned. We just received fifty thousand to be put into Harrison Shane's account. Fifty thousand. At this point in his stay, that's enormous."

"Sounds substantial. Check with Phoebe to see what it's all about. Maybe someone made a mistake."

"Maybe he wants to buy the house he's in."

"Take a lot more than fifty K to put a down payment on that baby!"

Whitney went to Phoebe's desk in her open office. She told her about the transfer.

"I have no idea what that's all about. I'll check with him."

She called Shane, not to check with him, but to let him know about the bank activity.

Shane called the number that Cody listed on the sheet.

"Hello, Harrison. Ya got something for me?"

"Look, you bastard, how do I know that the photos get buried? You're a crook; I don't think crooks can be trusted."

"But Harrison, I'm a good crook. All I need is fifty. Pay and it's over. No cops, no problem, you'll never hear from me again."

"My lawyer says I should go to the cops."

"Harrison, they'll never catch me. And besides, your lawyer has nothing to lose; you do. So what'll it be?"

"OK, how do you want it?"

"I guess Franklins will have to do."

"How do I get it to you?"

"Call me after you get the cash." Cody hung up, did a fist pump, and bellowed, "Yes. Getting close to that Endless Summer." Cody stayed seated on his threadbare living room chair with a smile from ear to ear.

Shane called Phoebe back and asked her to withdraw the fifty K in hundreds. She told him that the rental agreement only allowed her to sign for up to one thousand. He would have to accompany her to the bank for anything over that. She said she would drive up to his place now to pick him up. She called the bank and let them know about the huge withdrawal. They were used to large withdrawals from the realty company, but this one was high. The bank vice president told her that she would have to check to see if they could cover that much. She put Phoebe on hold. After about a minute, she picked up and said that they could do it, but not until noon.

When she arrived at the rental, Shane was waiting outside.

"Good morning, Mr. Shane."

"Fuck this morning. I'm about to split with fifty grand. Doesn't sound good to me."

"The bank can't have the cash ready until noon."

"Fine, let's go there and sit."

The rest of the trip to the bank was in silence. They signed the necessary paperwork and waited for the teller to alert them that the cash was ready. At around eleven thirty, they were directed into the vice president's office, who took over the transaction. When everything was in order, she handed Shane a large envelope with the money inside. She thanked them for their business and Phoebe and Shane returned to his house.

"Anything else, Mr. Shane?"

"May need a lot more scotch."

"I'll get Marco to bring you some."

Shane called Cody's burner when he got settled with a glass of scotch in his hand.

"OK, I got the cash. How do I get it to you?"

"Are you at the house?"

"Of course, where else would I be?"

"OK, stay there. I'll call soon with instructions."

Cody hopped into Kassie and headed north toward Shane's house. It was lunchtime and he was hungry, so he pulled off into a strip mall that had a bagel shop and ordered a baked ham, Swiss cheese, tomato, and mayonnaise sandwich on an asiago bagel to go. He added a Bai drink and a small bag of salt and vinegar chips and started chowing down when he was back on the road. He turned off onto Ocean Mist Lane but there were a number of cars there parked in the sand. Surfers or just ordinary beachgoers, probably. He didn't think he could launch his drone secretly if there were a mess of people on the beach. So he turned around and headed to the next turnoff, Dolphin Loop. No cars were parked off the road there, so he pulled over and took the Black Pelican in its case with him. He didn't bring the surfboard this time. He found a suitable recess in the dunes behind an unoccupied beach and unpacked the bird. As before, he hung a heavy-duty envelope attached to ropes that dangled from the bottom of the Black Pelican. He'd researched how thick it had to be. It had to be thick enough to be sure to hold five hundred, one hundred dollar bills. In preparation, he went to the back and got a hundred one-dollar bills. He measured and weighed them and checked the Mavic's specifications to make sure it could carry the load. He was a little concerned that the breeze, moderate off the ocean, might be a problem, so he would visually observe the flight for the first hundred yards. He was also concerned with the distance to Shane's house, and if the battery would hold out, but he thought there was some margin of error. He launched the drone and had it head south toward Shane's rental. He watched it and the flight did not seem problematic, so he kept flying it down the beach. He landed it right next to the pool in front of Shane's house and called him.

"Mr. Shane, there is a drone out on your pool patio with an envelope strapped to it. Put the money in the envelope and seal it and watch your troubles fly away."

"This better be the last I hear from you or anything about the pictures."

"Get the money in the envelope and you'll forget I ever existed. Call me when you have completed your little task."

Shane went down the stairs, money in hand, to the pool. Sure enough, there was a drone sitting there. He saw the envelope, crouched down, opened it, and placed the cash in it, and then sealed it. He stood over the drone and took several photos of it with his cell phone. He stepped back from the thing and called the number.

"Your present is gift wrapped. Get it out of here."

The drone hummed and took off, nearly straight up. Cody could see Shane on the concrete and said, out loud, "Adios, sucker."

Cody took a few steps out of the little dune recess to wait for the appearance of the drone. He picked it up soon and went back in the recess and waited for the rest of the flight. He heard the drone approaching and smiled, thinking it had made the distance and he would be fifty grand richer in a few moments. It finally came into view and Cody looked at it quizzically. He didn't see the envelope. He brought it down near where he was standing and, sure enough, no envelope. He peed his pants. He had flown it back over the beach because it was the most direct route. He placed the drone in the dune nook and started to run down the beach. Did Shane mess with the ropes holding the envelope, intentionally or accidently? Or did he take it off there at his house?

Cody kept running down the beach, past a family or two spread out enjoying the ocean, noticing a few surfers. He got to the nearest house on High Dunes Lane and saw something, tan-colored, stuck in the dune grass. He scampered to it and what a relief– the envelope. It was sealed. He didn't see anyone close or within easy sight, so he opened it up. The cash, in neatly wrapped bundles was there. Cody did a quick count– fifty grand. His heart was beating out of his chest, it was pumping so hard.

47

Chump Change was one of the surfers out on the ocean waiting for the perfect wave. He was close to where Cody discovered the fallen envelope and recognized him. He saw Cody retrieve something from the dune and decided to catch a wave, any wave, and propel in to see what was going on. Perhaps Cody had another jackpot. He reached shore just as Cody opened the envelope. Chump Change stuck his surfboard into the sand and jogged toward Cody, who hadn't noticed him.

"Hey, bro, whatcha got there? Is it something wonderful for you and me?"

Cody jumped when he heard Chump Change's voice and fumbled with the envelope. "Just a piece of mail, dude."

"Out here in the dune? Strange place to have your mail delivered. Maybe I can help you check out your 'mail.'"

"Bug off, man, this isn't any of your business."

"Oh, I have a feeling it is some of my business. Remember, we have a deal. You don't want it to blow up on you, do you? What's in the envelope, Cody? Let's look together."

"OK, dude, you win. But not here. Follow me and we'll check it out where I launched the drone."

They walked together without saying a word until they arrived at Cody's little launch pad. The drone sat there where he'd left it. Cody opened the envelope for Chump Change to see.

"Wow how much is in there?"

"Should be fifty grand."

"What did you say? Fifty?"

"Yep, let's count the bundles." They did and indeed they counted fifty big ones.

"OK, man, I want my cut."

"I don't want you to get caught with all this dough on the beach. Let's do this. I'll meet you in an hour behind the grocery store in Southern Shores". Chump Change knew the place.

"Nobody but delivery trucks go there. You know where I live, so I'm not going to hide from you. And I don't want to go there because my girlfriend might be there. So I'll meet you. We'll celebrate; I bought some really good stuff last week."

Chump Change started walking back to where he'd parked his board, trying to do the math in his head. What was twenty-five percent of fifty grand? Math was not his strong suit. Cody headed back to his house. He had a stash of heroin in a bag hidden in a sock and a small container of fentanyl. He retrieved two ziplock snack bags and poured a little heroin in one and a mixture of heroin and fentanyl in the other. Heavy on the fentanyl. He marked the bag without the fentanyl with a Sharpie and put both in his pocket. He counted out the twenty-five percent, twelve thousand five hundred, and put it back into the envelope. The remainder he buried underneath his mattress. He waited there until the hour was almost up and drove to the agreed-to meeting spot. He pulled behind a delivery truck parked there. The truck was just idling with no one unloading it, the driver apparently asleep in the cab. He waited for Chump Change to arrive. He watched in his rearview mirror and saw a rusting tan Toyota Camry drive in, Chump's car. Cody got out of Kassie and got in the passenger side of the Camry.

"Here's your cut: twelve and a half grand. I want you to count it so there won't be any hard feelings. And I brought us a little celebration powder. If we're going to be partners in crime, we need to enjoy it." He kept the marked bag for himself and gave the other to Chump Change. They both placed some powder on a credit card and snorted it.

"We'll feel good in a second. First-class heroin."

Both snorted again. Cody waited. "Whatcha gonna do with your share, dude?"

Chump Change's eyes rolled, and he grasped his chest, struggled for breath, vomited, and became limp. All very quickly. Cody looked around and there were no obvious cameras where he was, so he felt safe. He took the envelope with the cash and the bag of drugs out of the dead man's hands, wiped the inside and outside door handles clean, and went back to Kassie and drove off. On his way home, he saw a dumpster behind a breakfast restaurant, now with no cars in the parking lot, and opened the lid and threw the drug bag with the fentanyl in. Some quick thinking had just retrieved his twelve and a half and at the same time he'd disposed of future trouble.

Shane called Phoebe and said, "Whoever is blackmailing me made the pickup. He flew a drone in and had an empty envelope attached to it. He told me to put the cash in the envelope, which I did, and off it flew."

"Which way did it go, out of curiosity?"

"North. It flew north as far as I could see."

"OK, I'm going to check around. I know a lot of people here, so we'll see what anyone knows."

She hung up and immediately called Heaton. "Hey Clint, got some info on my blackmailed client."

"What do you have, Phoebe?"

"The blackmailer, a man, sent a drone in to pick up the loot. He had an envelope attached somehow and instructed Shane to put the cash in it. It flew north from Shane's rental house."

"Hmmm. Sounds like he may have launched from where we found some items last week. I'll check it out again, Phoebe. Has this happened to anyone other than your two clients that you know of?"

"No, just these two, as far as I know."

"Who knows who's staying at these houses? Who has access to whatever files you keep but nobody else in your office uses? Seems like this is more than a coincidence. There seems to be a beginning of a pattern here."

"The people in my office know where clients are or, at least, have access to the files. We do lock the file cabinets at night, but all of the CSM's have keys, as does Sharna, our boss, and Whitney, our receptionist and secretary."

"What's a CSM?"

"A concierge service manager, like me."

"OK, give me their full names and I'll see if I can find anything. I'll go back up to Duck and ask around again."

Phoebe gave Heaton the information. He checked with the local banks and, although they wouldn't tell him much, there didn't seem to be any unusually large deposits made by any of the realty staff. The next day, he visited all of the houses on High Dunes Lane. Two vacationers had noticed a drone flying past their houses, but they saw no one. However, one person, thinking that the drone was a curiosity, took a video of one of the flights. Heaton asked the vacationer to message the video to him, which he did. Back in his car, Heaton studied the video. The quality was good. He could make out that an envelope was tied to it. He wondered if the clarity was good enough to identify what kind of drone it was. Once again, he called his friend who owned the drone retail shop in Durham.

"Hey Josh, this is Detective Heaton over in Dare. Got a minute?"

"Sure, Clint, what's up?"

"I have a video of a drone flying over the ocean. It looks pretty clear. I'd like to send it to you to see if you can identify what kind of drone it is."

"Sure. Send it to this number. I'll check it out and call you back."

Heaton put the video in a text and sent it. About fifteen minutes later, Josh called him back.

"Clint, I'm almost certain that the drone is a DJI Mavic. Maybe ninety percent sure."

"Who sells whatever you just said?"

"Everybody. It's pretty popular."

"OK, would you spell it for me?"

Josh did.

"You have a record of who you sold any of them to?"

"Sure, want me to check?"

"Yep. See if you had any customers in Dare or Currituck Counties."

"Well, Clint, I don't know what towns are in which county, so let me rattle off the towns and see if any strike your fancy."

"Thanks, Josh."

Josh had sold two drones to people that lived in towns in Dare and Currituck Counties, one in the town of Southern Shores and the other in Nags Head. Heaton headed to the address in Southern Shores first. A fifty-something man answered the door. Heaton asked him if he owned a drone and he said he did. It was registered, so he wondered if there was a problem. Heaton told him that there was no issue with the paperwork and asked if he could see the drone. The man was cooperative and took the drone out of its case. Heaton tried to see if there was any sign of an envelope being attached; there was none.

"Where do you fly it?" Heaton asked.

"Nowhere in particular. It's fun to fly. I've flown it over the beach and down at the sand dunes. We went down to Hatteras Island a couple of times. I love the view it gives you."

"Ever fly it up over the beaches north of Duck?"

"No, the beach accesses up there aren't good. I like to keep eye contact with it, so I never fly it far from where I'm standing."

"OK, thanks for your cooperation."

"Is there some trouble, detective?"

"Maybe, we're just crossing T's and dotting I's."

Heaton went to the address in Nags Head, but no one answered the door.

48

Richard Curtis Wilson was feeling one hundred percent and was beginning to get into full campaign mode. He liked his congressional staff and had chosen some favorites to be on his campaign staff. He liked rubbing elbows with the voters. He liked taking questions in a social atmosphere and asking questions of the voters as well. He liked giving speeches and was particularly good at doing them extemporaneously. He liked all of it.

He hosted another strategy meeting and wanted it to be in a relaxed atmosphere. His wife, Dawn, suggested that he hold it in their home, considering that there would only be about ten staffers attending. She geared up to make it a pleasant event. The meeting was to begin at ten, so she welcomed attendees with coffee, lattes, and an assortment of teas, plus homemade cookies. The working lunch would be her gourmet grilled cheese sandwiches filled with either ham, spinach, portobello mushrooms, turkey, or flounder, or any combination of these that they requested. She used her home-baked sourdough bread, which was delicious. A mixed fruit salad complemented the sandwiches.

Wilson welcomed each arrival personally and invited them into the large living room. The room usually seated eight, so he brought in a few folding chairs and mini-tables for the session. He opened up the meeting asking Sid Freeze to update him and the group on the latest polls. Though early, they were encouraging. Wilson was polling at forty-six percent, up from forty-two percent, and his opponent, Mercer Harris, was at thirty-six percent. The rest said they were undecided. Freeze opined that they needed to keep the momentum going and analyze Harris's speeches and literature to find weaknesses. He pointed out that Harris was campaigning for lots of new entitlements and government programs, all of which cost the taxpayer a bundle. Harris was previously a mayor, and the city's budgets, and therefore its taxes, had increased by forty percent over the eight years of his reign. Freeze said that this was the big soft spot that they would have to exploit. Wilson agreed, and Freeze appointed a young, energetic woman, Marcia Seagate, to spearhead the Harris research. Wilson took over the conversation saying that he'd like to empathize what he'd accomplished in Congress so far and how he could represent the state better than Harris. He told the gathering that he knew they had to work on some of Harris's failings, but he wanted to show the voters what he could offer. Freeze added that this basic strategy generally energized the party base and was the right way to proceed, as long as the polls held.

Julie Massey, now mostly recovered from being shot but still having pain in her arm, spoke up and suggested that they come up with a set of plans for Wilson to present and campaign on, with some proposal that would really get the voter's attention. Freeze applauded the tactic, having already been working on that, and thought whatever the big proposal would be, Wilson should wait until late in the campaign to make an announcement. That way, they would be giving Harris little opportunity to attack it. The rest of the meeting would center on maturing and fleshing out Wilson's platform and how and when to present it.

Dawn, efficient as ever, had given blank cards to everyone with spaces for their names and what type of sandwich they wished for lunch. She retired to the kitchen and got the assembly line going. Cooking for ten or so was a piece of cake; she'd handled over forty in the house all by herself. She entered the living room and stood there waiting for a pause in the discussions. She then announced that drinks would be self-serve from the wet bar while she served lunch. The meeting was temporarily interrupted by everyone getting up to get their drinks and Dawn handing them their plates and silverware. The powwow had been spirited but usually only one person spoke at a time. Now, while chowing down on delicious sandwiches, multiple conversations were occurring throughout the room. Freeze brought the session back in order. He reviewed the campaign's finances and said that the subcommittee in charge of fund raising was in high gear and providing what was needed to date. He then went up to a dry-erase board that he'd brought to record ideas about which issues Wilson should stress. Lots of suggestions had been brought up during the earlier lively period, so Freeze wanted to establish a consensus on what should be the main thrusts. On top of everyone's mental list were taxes and government spending, so details about what could be done to get the federal spending under control were batted around. They covered areas that they thought Mercer Harris's time in office was weak on. The usual social issues were added to the dry board, and, of course, homeland security and defense were there. There was not a general agreement on an October blockbuster, so Wilson asked the group to keep that on their mind and take notes for the next campaign summit.

PR and advertising were next on the agenda. Freeze had hired a company that specialized in political web pages to create Wilson's internet presence. He asked everyone to review the web and Facebook pages and email him suggested additions, deletions, and comments. He stressed that these were vital in fund raising in the internet culture.

Then they went on to review campaign events that Wilson would attend. North Carolina consisted of one hundred counties. Freeze stated that he didn't think there was a need to go to each county; Wilson, after all, had a day job, and certain areas were strongholds for his party. The assembly nominated those areas they considered a must to visit through September. After that, Freeze said the polls would dictate where he should go. Raleigh, Durham, Winston-Salem, Greensboro, Charlotte, and Fayetteville, all with populations over two hundred thousand, were obvious choices for multiple visits. Wilmington, High Point, Jacksonville, and Ashville were also strongly supported for multiple stops.

Freeze directed, "OK, let's find events happening in these areas that we listed, or make up events, and come up with a schedule. I will email you the congressman's availability so we can fit in appearances. Remember, we don't want to break him, so bigger events are better." Everyone chuckled as Wilson gave a thumbs-up. Julie Massey asked if anyone else had any pressing issues and Peter Chek spoke up. "What are we going to do to neutralize this Sprout guy?"

Freeze elaborated, "For those that aren't up to speed, a guy named Donald Sprout has heckled the congressman at a few events and handed out some salacious flyers. The SBI suspects that he may have been the one who shot the congressman and Julie. I'm going to email his photos to all of you so you can be watchful. Peter, I assume you are in contact with all the relevant authorities?"

"Roger that, Sid. I probably need to hire a few more guards for the events."

"Whatever you need. The money is coming in."

49

Donald Sprout pulled off at a rest stop on Interstate 40. He used the rest room, wiped his face and upper body off with some paper towels, disgusting some other travelers, and returned to his car. He drank a Coke and ate a pastry that he purchased from the snack machines, crawled into the back seat, cracked the window, and went to sleep for the night. Sunrise woke him up, getting earlier this time of the year. After returning to the restroom, he walked around the facility for a few minutes. Once again, he was low on cash and hungry. He was a mess and his clothes were a mess. He needed a new plan. Back in the car, he pondered ideas on what to do. The Wilson event at Duke University Hospital was still a week away and he wanted to be ready. He wanted to eat also. He returned to the highway and headed to Greensboro, just west of where he was. Since he'd been successful at the beg-at-a-church gig, he pulled into the parking lot of the first large church he passed. He walked into the church's office, looking appalling and smelling worse, and asked the secretary if he could meet with the pastor. She got up, tried to control her facial expression, and said, "Let me see if he's available."

She returned and said, "He can see you for a few minutes right now. Just head down the hallway, the last door on the left." Sprout apologized for dropping in and explained that he didn't have a nickel to his name, was hungry, and was hoping that the pastor, in the name of the Lord, could help him. They discussed his situation, which Sprout completely made up. The pastor wanted to know what skills he had, and Sprout said he had been in sales and carpentry but hadn't been able to work due to an injury to his arm. The pastor asked if he had a phone and he pulled it out of his pocket. He gave Sprout the names of two builders that attended the church and their phone numbers and told him to contact them and use the pastor's name. He stood up and told Sprout to follow him out to the secretary's office.

"Carole, would you get this gentleman a room at the local Motel Six and a couple of meal vouchers?" He shook Sprout's hand and said, "She'll take care of that for you. Good luck and God be with you." Sprout had hoped to receive cash, not vouchers, but something was better than nothing.

The Motel 6 was just down the road, off of the interstate. He went to check in, but the desk clerk told him it was too early and for him to come back in two hours. The church visit had not solved his financial situation. Nothing bad had happened when he withdrew money in Plymouth, so he decided to try again. He asked where the nearest ATM was and was given directions. He hoped his account wasn't locked, and it wasn't. The police wanted to see if he kept on trying to get cash to trace his location. He withdrew three hundred and was satisfied with himself. The cops weren't very smart, he thought. He used one of the meal vouchers at a Golden Corral, also not far from the interstate. He loved it there. No one hurried him along and he ate everything from soup to nuts over a three-hour visit. Way overfull, he headed back to the motel and checked in. He told the clerk that his wallet had been stolen and he had no ID. He gave her a false name. His room was fine. He called the desk and asked where the nearest Walmart or Kmart was. He headed to the nearest one and bought two shirts, two pairs of jeans, some underwear and socks, and some toiletries. He returned to the motel and saw a police car with its lights flashing parked in front of the office. He drove away, sweating profusely, and wondered if his visit to the ATM had tipped them off. He pulled into a gas station nearby where he could watch the motel. After a minute, he heard the siren of another emergency vehicle. An ambulance came into view and pulled into the motel. He watched and waited until both vehicles left. He drove back to the motel and, curiosity killing him, stopped at the office and asked what was going on. The clerk told him a guest had fallen and apparently broken his arm. He said that was a shame and headed to his room feeling a lot better. He took a shower, tried on some of his new clothes, turned the TV on, and laid down on the bed and relaxed. With his full belly and the excitement over, he quickly dozed off.

Again, the police got wind of the ATM withdrawal and emailed Hasbee in Chesapeake as well as Chek in the Wilson campaign. Wilson wasn't scheduled to visit Greensboro for a couple of weeks, so he wasn't sure what to make of the latest sighting. One more intriguing piece of evidence popped up. The Duck town police had found an envelope on the ground up against the information board at the entrance to the police and fire department parking lot. Inside were two photographs, both of a man on the beach in front of the house that the Wilson campaign had rented when Wilson and Massey were shot. The photo appeared to have been taken from over the ocean, about two stories up. Apparently taken from a drone. They understood the possible value of the shots and notified the SBI. The information was given to Max Ramsey. Max called his supervisor and told him that he would be traveling to Duck immediately to view the photos and hopefully get a copy of them or the originals. He made two other calls once on the road. He called his girlfriend, Summer, to break their dinner date that night. They had planned to visit a restaurant that was highly rated and that neither had been to, an intimate, private spot, so Summer was very disappointed. Max told her his trip would probably be a short one and asked when her next evening off was so he could make it up to her. He then placed a call to Bart Dozier, who was hosting the poker game the next night. Max loved these evenings and wouldn't miss them for love (ask his ex-wife) or money, but he had to tell Bart that duty called and he might not make it back in time for the game. Bart said to let him know for sure and was somewhat delighted that Ramsey would be a no-show, as he might finish the night ahead for a change.

Cody Delaney's conscience, what little he had left, was eating at him. While floating on his surfboard up near Mansion Beach, he had flashbacks of the photos he'd captured of the man lurking in front of the Wilson party rental house. He had no way of knowing if that was the gunman, but it might have been. When he returned home, he flicked on the TV while getting ready for his shift at the Bistro. He caught a news feature that updated the Senate race between Wilson and Harris. The reporter, on-site somewhere to make it look like he was doing boots-on-the-ground investigating, talked about the Wilson campaign and how the cops were out in numbers protecting Wilson. The reporter mentioned that this was required because the person who'd attempted to murder Wilson had not been found. So, impulsively, Cody reversed his previous decision and printed the photos, making sure not to leave fingerprints, slid them into one of his envelopes, and dropped them off at the sign in front of the combination police/fire station. He was pretty sure that he had not been seen.

Ramsey arrived in the afternoon at the Duck town police station. He was shown in and greeted by the sergeant on duty. The sergeant retrieved the photos and laid them on the table where Ramsey was seated.

"This is what we found, left outside by the road. We verified that the house in the photo was where the congressman and a staffer were shot. We have no idea if this was taken on the day of the shooting, but you can see a bunch of people on the deck in front of the house."

Ramsey looked at them closely.

"I'd like to take them back to the lab and have the photos blown up using our computer. We can use facial recognition software to see if we can identify anyone. We can also show them to the Wilson campaign staff to see if they can verify that this was taken when they were there."

"Sure, no problem. I'll make photo copies for us to keep and bring you some paperwork for transferal of evidence."

Since there was no reason to hang around, Ramsey headed back to his apartment in Cary. Once on the road, he called Summer and told her he'd be back home, but a little late. He asked her if she'd still like to go out. She leaped at the offer and asked when he thought he'd be back. He told her it would probably be after seven, depending on traffic. He would mostly be heading in the opposite direction of rush hour, so he said he hoped not to get delayed. He told her that he'd call to try to renew their reservation and get right back to her. He had a table reserved at a place named Vivace, an upscale Italian eatery in Raleigh. He got through and apologized for having to cancel earlier in the day- work issues you know- but now could get there, albeit later. They told him a table would be available at eight fifteen and he said he'd take it. He called Summer back and gave her the news. She asked if she could meet him at his flat and he agreed. Max also called Bart Dozier and told him to count him in for tomorrow night's poker game.

Max got through the late Raleigh rush hour and arrived at his apartment complex at a quarter of seven. He keyed his door and, entering the living room, didn't see Summer.

"Sweetie, are you here?"

From out of the bedroom came, "I'm in here."

Max walked in and laid eyes on a completely naked lady that he was in love with.

She said, "I thought you'd like an appetizer before we went out."

Max smiled and said, "I am a little hungry, for sure. What is on the menu?"

With eyes twinkling, Summer said, "Come here, big guy, and I will whisper the menu in your ear."

With that, Max stripped as fast as he could and hopped into the bed next to Summer.

"How much time do we have? How quickly can you get ready?"

"You get thirty minutes, so set that timer on your phone and let's get to it!"

Oh my, she was exquisite. Summer had that athletic firm muscular build and the longest legs you had ever seen. He was one lucky guy and he knew it. He wasn't going to mess up this relationship. He continued to make love to her with tender care, making sure she was satisfied first before his needs were met. The excitement of her surprising him like that made that effort very hard to pull off.

The phone quacked- Max liked the duck ringtone for alarms- and they both groaned. Not ready to end their love making, they reluctantly climbed out of bed and showered together as quickly as possible to make their dinner date. Once back in Max's car, Summer said, "Max, I know you love Applebee's, but please tell me we're headed to some other place."

"Vivace, my dear. I know you love Italian. Only the best for my love."

"Ohhh" she said with a broad smile.

They entered the restaurant, and he identified himself and explained that he had a reservation. A server was waiting at the desk and said, "Signor Ramsey, please follow me." Once seated and presented with menus, Max ordered a bottle of Monferrato sauvignon and calamari fritti for them to share. Summer ordered the Sicilian fish stew and Max decided on the roasted chicken for his entrée. They relaxed and chatted throughout the wonderful meal and finished it with a flute of homemade limoncello.

Hasbee updated the Rosellis with the latest whereabouts of Sprout. Joan asked if they knew why he'd be in Greensboro– was that where Wilson was campaigning? Hasbee told her that they didn't know why he was there and, no, the Carolina SBI said that Wilson wasn't due to appear in Greensboro for a few weeks.

Joan followed up, "Do they still think that he's after Wilson?"

"Yes. They know he visited some events and made disturbances. What's more, they were just furnished photographs that they think might show Sprout at the scene of the Wilson shooting. They're analyzing the photos now. On your home front, how is Roanna doing?"

Joan said, "Not really well. She's missed a lot of school; she never skipped before. She's not sleeping well and has nightmares. She picks at her food and has lost ten pounds. She didn't have that much to lose by the time she got away."

"Is she getting therapy?"

"Oh my, yes. She likes her therapist, a lady in her late twenties, who Roanna seems to have good rapport with. Her therapist thinks she has a long road to recovery ahead of her. She's so precious, my precious girl, and now she's so broken. Detective, I cry every night. One of my worst fears has materialized, and I can't help her and take her pain away. I should have protected her!" Joan was sobbing at this point.

Anthony chipped in. "Joan, love, come here. Mr. Hasbee, the only thing we can ask you to do is to get this sub-human beast. Get him off the streets!"

"Sir, that's what we intend to do."

50

An eighteen-wheeler from the grocery store chain, loaded with product to be delivered, pulled into the alley behind the store. A car was parked there in a location that made unloading the truck difficult. *Damn it* thought the driver, *I don't have time for this!* He got out to see if the car was occupied and to get it moved, pronto. Instead, he found a man who looked like he was asleep– Chump Change. He reached through the open car window and wiggled the man's arm and said, "Buddy? You asleep?" It became clear in seconds that he'd discovered a corpse. He turned around and vomited for a good minute. He went back to his truck, wiped his face, and dialed 911. Police cars and an EMT ambulance arrived, sirens echoing off the concrete wall in the rear of the store. It was way too late for the EMTs. They found his identification and significantly, his phone. They checked the contact list; there were many listed, so they would have to comb through them for a next of kin. His driver's license was from Virginia and listed his address in the town of Midlothian, just outside of Richmond. His name on the license was John Farrell. The authorities would order an autopsy, but their initial guess was an overdose.

Word spread throughout the surfer community that Chump Change was dead. He was a pretty popular dude; all of the die-hard surfers knew him. Cody caught wind of the news and various rumors. He started to have that acidic feeling in his gut. What if Chump Change had told somebody about the scam? What if he told someone that he muscled in on it? That would certainly point a finger at Cody. Cody knew that he roomed with three other guys, didn't have a girlfriend, and worked as a painter for one of the many house painting companies on the Banks.

Cody decided he'd lay low for a while and, when not working, would concentrate on his first love: surfing. He took Kassie up to Mansion Beach and followed his normal routine, with the exception that the ocean was warm enough that he didn't wear his wet suit. He trotted over the dunes and onto the beach, gave the board a final waxing, and plunged into the surf. It wasn't cold anymore, but it was cool at first and the initial plunge would get you awake. Paddling out through the breakers, he reached the area where waves were forming and waved to his surfing peers. He daydreamed about his trip– the Endless Summer– and thought he needed to make one more hit before he could afford to leave for a year and go where the good waves are. He was still keeping the drone in its case in a small suitcase at the Bistro. That suitcase now held fifty grand in cash, and he was worried about the whole thing walking away someday. In between a few good rides, he decided to rent a safe deposit box at least for the cash. Occasionally he, like the other surfers, would hang out on the beach for a while, having a drink, eating an orange or energy bar, or just enjoying watching the others. Cody engaged in idle talk with whoever was there, and the issue of Chump Change's death wasn't discussed. It was old news. Cody was somewhat relieved.

The police received the autopsy results; John Farrell had overdosed on heroin and significant amounts of fentanyl. Since he'd had some surfing artifacts in his car, the cops decided to interview some surfers to see if they could find out where he lived and who he knew, who his best buds were. Checking his address had turned up nothing. A couple of detectives from the town of Southern Shores hung out on the beaches where they found groups of surfers. They wore shorts and Tee shirts so they wouldn't stand out. They interviewed over twenty surfers. At first, they got nowhere. No one recognized the name John Farrell. Then they caught a muscular young lady, taking a break from the waves.

"Are you asking about the dude that OD'd?"

"Yes ma'am, John Farrell."

"Well, honey, I don't know John whatever his name is, but the guy that we heard OD'd was Chump Change."

The two detectives frowned at each other and one said, "Chump Change?"

"Yep, Chump Change. Is that the guy you're asking about?"

"We only know him by Farrell. We found him in his car six days ago."

"Yep, that would be Chump Change. He was out here every day, but we haven't seen him for a week. Nice guy, we all liked him."

"Any idea if he would OD intentionally or even accidentally?"

"Fuck no. He'd never do that. He was happy-go-lucky, you know what I mean. Fuck no, he wouldn't kill himself. Musta gotten hold of some bad shit."

"Do you know where he lived or where he worked, or know of anyone who might have that information?"

"Yep. See that dude out there in the red-and-blue bathing suit? That's Luke. Luke knew Chump really well. They were tight. Think they hung together a lot, you know what I mean, like socially. Not like the sex stuff."

"Got it. Socially."

"You want me to tell him to boogie on in? He won't hear you call him from here, I don't think. The surf is pounding."

"That would be great. We'll wait."

She paddled out to the guy named Luke and apparently told him what the stiffs on the beach were asking about. He caught the next decent wave.

"Yo, brothers, name's Luke. Yours?"

"Detectives Austin and Fleming. Heard you were tight with a guy named Chump Change?"

"Yeah, man, sad story. Was a really cool dude."

They showed Luke a photo of the dead John Farrell. "This him?"

"Man, put that away, that's gross, man. Yeah, that's him."

"What can you tell us about him? Where he lived? Where he worked? Where he hung out? Anything."

"Yeah, cool. He lived with some other dudes in Kitty Hawk. Part of a duplex, I think it's called. On the street between the highways, Lindbergh. Worked for a painting company, DCM Painting."

"Where did he hang out at?"

"When he wasn't on the waves, every bar in town. He liked Mama's the best. I spent lots of time there with him."

"On Lindbergh, do you know which house?"

"Never went there."

"Do you think he OD'd intentionally?"

"Yo, you mean suicide? No fucking way, man. Some bad stuff did him in, probably. Gotta be careful."

"Know anyone who would give him some bad stuff?"

"Don't know. He did talk about coming into some money recently. I don't know. Maybe he was selling. Just don't know, man."

The detective thanked Luke and gave him their cards. He shoved them into a pocket in his damp swimming trunks. They would probably disintegrate before the day was over.

Detectives Austin and Fleming walked back to their unmarked car and googled DCM Painting, found the address, and headed that way. They entered the small, white concrete block building and asked for the boss. One of the painters, obviously a painter from his now multicolored white painter's pants and shirt, saw the detectives and said, "Can I help you gentlemen?"

"We're looking for the boss."

"Look no further; you're looking at him. Seth Thomas. Need a house painted?"

They displayed their badges. "No thanks. Detectives from Southern Shores. Did you have a John Farrell working for you?"

"Ahh, man, tragic. Yeah, we called him Chump Change. Don't know how he got the name. Good guy, everybody liked him. Good worker unless the surf was up."

"Have any idea if he was using?"

"I think everyone here is using one thing or another. I operate on the 'what you don't know won't hurt you' principle."

"Do you think he had reason to OD intentionally?"

"Naah, no way. He must have gotten some nasty stuff."

"Any idea where he would have gotten his drugs?"

"Nope. I don't mess with that stuff. Don't want anything to do with it."

"Know where he lived?"

"Yeah, I'll write down his address."

"Thanks."

The detectives waved and headed to the apartment on Lindbergh. When they arrived, they knocked on the door several times. Finally, a man in his twenties opened the door. He looked like he'd had a long night, maybe a number of long nights. His odor spread outside quickly, his hair was a mess– long and scraggly- and his face was covered with a three-day old beard.

"Yeah?"

"We're here to ask about John Farrell."

"You mean Chump Change? Man, you're a little late. He's a goner, man."

The badge came out. "Yo, be cool. I didn't do nothin'."

"We didn't say you did. How about we come inside?"

"Sure, yeah, come on in."

"Who else lives here?"

"Just J R and me now. We got to recruit another dude to help pay the rent."

"What's your name? And does J R have a real name?"

"I'm Monti Michaels. They call me M&M. JR's name is Jeremy Rojas. He hates being called Jeremy."

"Good to know. Do you or J R have any idea how Farrell OD'd?"

"No, man. A real bad deal."

"Where'd he get his stuff? We don't want anyone else getting hurt if there's some bad stuff floating around."

"No idea, man."

"Mind if we look in his bedroom?"

"No, go ahead. I haven't been able to go in yet. If you find any cash, he owed me three hundred."

"We'll keep that in mind."

His room was as bad as the rest of the apartment. Fleming murmured, "Looks like a third-world country." They didn't find anything of significant interest except a magazine under his bed with seven fresh one- hundred-dollar bills in it. They bagged the cash and didn't alert M&M about their find. They came back out into the living room.

"You know if he had any relatives or a girlfriend?"

"No steady girl. He just hung at the bars. He never talked about any relatives. He came from somewhere up near Richmond."

Dispensing their cards, Austin said, "Get in touch with us if you think of anything."

They left. Fleming grumbled, "That was useless."

Austin said, "Let's check the serial numbers on the cash. Maybe something will turn up."

One more stop was to Mama's, a small restaurant that had a very active bar scene for a few hours after the workday. It was a good time to visit. The bar only had a few seats open and a few people were standing behind the seated drinkers. The crowd was pretty much half male and half female. The décor was tropical–fake palm trees and flamingos and the like. The detectives first called one of the barkeeps over and showed him the photo they had of Chump Change. "You see this man here?"

"Sure, that's Chump Change. Came here a lot. Poor son of a bitch."

"Did he hang with anyone in particular?"

"Not that I saw. He'd grab a beer and hit on one of the babes. Different one each night. I don't think he got too far, though. I never saw him leave with a girl."

"Mind if we show his photo around?"

"No, but don't spoil the happy hour mood."

"Wouldn't think of it!"

They individually went from one drinker to another. Many recognized the photo, often saying they felt sorry, but none had anything useful to say.

The detective signaled thanks to the bartender and left.

51

Cody's relationship with Phoebe was beginning to cool. They were not home together often; the sex was still great when they got to it, but other than that, they didn't have much in common. She would awaken early, shower, put on makeup, and get dressed for work often before Cody was out of bed. He would leave for work usually before she got home and finish long after she went to sleep. On days off, Phoebe loved to get in the car and go somewhere, anywhere-visit friends, sunbathe at someone's pool, or just read a book. Cody was tied to his iPad when not surfing and Phoebe's activities held no interest for him. Another factor was Willow. A big factor. Willow and Cody were with each other every night that they worked. She was completely infatuated with him and he loved the attention and the flirting. They were like magnets, a magnetic pull to each other. He would find time every night to visit the bar when it wasn't slammed and have a short conversation or just look at Willow.

On Tuesday night, Cody was busy for most of the night until things slowed down just before ten. He headed to the bar with an order for two Baileys on the rocks. Willow said to him while handing him the Baileys, "Is that all you want, handsome?" She gave him an air kiss.

"You know I'll take anything you're offering, anytime!"

"I'll be waiting for you. How about my place for a change? We'll be all alone."

"I can't wait."

This wasn't the first after-work tryst, but it was the first one away from the Bistro. It would become a habit.

Phoebe tuned in to Cody's distant coolness but brushed it off as a phase he was going through. Their small talk became very small; she asked him on occasion if everything was OK and he'd say, "Yeah, no worries." She of course had her own issues. The money she was collecting from her side business was beginning to be not insignificant. She had the same quandary that Cody had with the cash– what to do with it. She decided to buy a small safe and put it in her office. She explained to Sharna that she had a few expensive pieces of jewelry that she didn't want to keep at the house. Sharna told her that would be fine.

The next day, when Cody arrived at the Bistro, Willow was already behind the bar. It wasn't time for the daily staff meeting, so when Willow saw Cody come in, she waved him to come over to the bar.

She whispered, "So on a scale of one to ten, how was last night for you?"

"I put it at an eleven, sweetie! Best night I've had in, ahh. . . ahh. . ., like maybe ever. How about you?"

"I would like to make it a habit. What do you think? I have plenty of space. I don't think my roommate is going to stay after the end of the month."

"I can only do the visits right now. That's stupid, calling last night a visit. You know what I mean."

"Dump Phoebe. You never see her anyway. You know what I can do for you, and it can be on a daily basis, you know, night or day!"

"I have to stay another month or so, then I'll be free." Willow formed pouty lips and rubbed her eyes as if crying. He added, "Look, I want 'visits' like last night all the time. Don't worry, just give me a little time." Cody was thinking that he wanted to make one more hit and he needed information from Phoebe to pull it off. The Endless Summer was still beckoning. Since Willow surfed a little, he pumped her, "How much do you like to surf?"

She looked confused, especially at the change of subject. "You know I like to surf. Just not great at it."

"Well maybe I can take your bikini'd, tanned body where there are real waves." She gave him a look that said, "What are you talking about?" and let it drop.

After the cleanup and prep for the next day, Willow made it known that Cody was a welcomed guest again. He didn't need to be asked twice. The rendezvous resulted in Cody not getting home until early in the morning, around three, way later than normal. He slowly opened the door, trying to be as quiet as possible, but bumped into a chair and knocked it over. The noise startled Phoebe. "Cody, is that you?"

"Yeah, Phoebs, just me. Sorry, didn't mean to wake you."

"What time is it?" She squinted at the digital clock on the dresser and garbled, "Why are getting in so late?"

"Ahh, we had a problem in the kitchen. Hoops, the head chef, asked me to stay and help clean up. You know how it is; a server has to keep the chef happy."

Phoebe grunted and rolled back over. Cody knew that his late-night dates with Willow would have to end for now. How many times could he help in the kitchen?

52

Phoebe called Detective Heaton to ask if he had anything new about the two blackmail situations. He explained that without an official complaint, he couldn't do much. He did have one big piece of news, though. "The detectives up in Southern Shores ran serial numbers of some money that they recovered from a guy that OD'd. They didn't uncover anything, but they gave me the data. It turns out that when the first victim, Preston Kerrigan, paid the blackmail, he had the serial numbers recorded. He apparently decided not to do anything about it, but he gave me the list of serial numbers in case any of it showed up. The money that Southern Shores checked matched some of the numbers that Kerrigan had recorded. The dead guy was a surfer and a local painter. Southern Shores doesn't know how he got the cash. I ask if they found a drone in his apartment and they said that they did not. They didn't ask his fellow renters about a drone, they had no idea why I was asking about a drone, but I will ask when I question them. Also, if he was our guy, they should have found more than fifty grand."

"So, do you think he was the blackmailer? You said he was a surfer."

"We don't know enough yet. I checked all the local banks again and his name didn't get any attention. He obviously used narcotics and that can eat up a lot of money, but we're talking about sixty grand here in a relatively short time. The boys up in Southern Shores didn't smell anything funny. I'm going to head back out to the beach and ask around; I'll also check with his roommates."

"What was the guy's name?"

"John Farrell. I'm told that apparently everybody knew him as Chump Change."

The next morning, Phoebe asked Cody if he knew a dude who'd OD'd known as Chump Change.

"Yeah, one of the surfers out there. Nice guy. Sad what happened. Why do you ask?"

"I just heard that the guy was a surfer, that's all. Thought if you knew him, you would have said something."

"Yeah, we never hung together. Didn't know him very well. Just knew him out on the waves."

"Was he close to any of the other surfers?"

Cody got a little defensive. "Don't know. Why so inquisitive?"

"Don't bark. I was just curious."

Cody didn't want to appear concerned, but he was. Why would Phoebe be asking about him? What did she know? Did she suspect something?

Heaton headed to Chump Change's former residence and Monti Michaels (M&M) answered the door. Heaton right away showed his badge and asked to enter.

"What's all the concern, man? We just had a visit from some other cop dudes the other day."

"Well, dude, I'm a special cop dude. When somebody dies under suspicious circumstances, we start looking under every rock."

"Well, there ain't no, like, rocks here, man."

"I'll decide that. This Chump Change guy, rumor has it he came into a bunch of dough recently. Know anything about that?" Heaton made up the supposition, hoping to get the guy talking.

"Don't know anything about that." M&M elevated his voice. "Hey JR, this cop dude says Chump came into some big-time cash. You know anything about that?"

From the kitchen, JR bellowed back, "He didn't lay any of it on me, if he had any."

Heaton said, "I'll take that as a no. You boys know if this Chump Change played with a drone?"

JR joined them now and said, "Like a toy?"

"Yeah, something like a toy."

They both chuckled. M&M said, "I don't think he played with toys! He did like to play with the girls, whenever he found one that liked him. Not often, though." He chuckled.

"So no flying machines?"

"Nope."

The next day, Heaton headed back out to the popular surfing beaches, including Mansion Beach. He asked everyone who came onshore whether they knew Chump Change and if they saw anyone flying a drone. Many knew Chump Change, bowing and shaking their heads, muttering one thing or another. A few thought they'd seen a drone, but had no idea who was flying it. No one thought that the deceased had any significant amount of money, one guy offering, "If he did, he wouldn't be drinking PBRs."

So once again, Heaton was at a dead end. He decided to call Max Ramsey, since he knew the SBI man pretty well, to see if he had any suggestions.

"Max, this is Clint Heaton over in Dare. How ya been?"

"Great, Clint. What can I do for you?"

"I have an unofficial report of a crime, actually two crimes. I can't make it official; I don't have a complaint, just inside information. And I'm at a dead end."

"OK, in a nutshell, what is the issue?"

"Two blackmails. Both victims were high rollers vacationing here. Alone. Both picked up a sweetie somewhere and neither wanted it to be known. Somehow somebody found out who they were and flew a drone past their rental house and snapped some revealing photos. Then he or she used the drone to pick up the blackmail payment."

"How do you know all of this if there isn't a formal complaint? Neither victim filed a report?"

"I know the real estate agent who made both rentals. She called me about them, asked me to sniff around. She said that neither guy wanted the cops to get involved or wanted any publicity."

"Sounds like some cutie's got you tied around her little finger! Just kidding. But don't you think it's a strange coincidence that both crimes happened on her watch? How many rental agents do you have down there, after all?"

"Yeah, I've given that some thought. I've known her for quite a while, though never very well, just police business, nothing social."

"Sounds like she's the link, intentionally or otherwise. What do you know about her?"

"Not much, I guess. But she was the one who brought me into this, so I wouldn't think that she's involved."

"Maybe she is but doesn't know it. I think you need to start with her. Loose lips sink ships. Who else knows about her clients, Clint? And, I would dig into her social media to see if there is any link there."

"I checked with her once, I'll go back to talk to her again. Thanks for the advice."

"No worries. If I come across anything, I'll let you know. By the way, who were the marks?"

"Preston Kerrigan, a pro football player, and Harrison Shane, a movie. . ."

"Shane! Wow! With a tootsie, who would have thought?!" Max laughed out loud.

Heaton decided it would be smart to visit Phoebe again. He called her. "Hey Phoebe, this is Clint. Can we meet off-site sometime?"

"Sure, how about lunch tomorrow? Where at?"

"Brewing Station? Eleven thirty?"

"See you there."

Phoebe wondered if Heaton had found some information on her two cases. She had a new client arriving in the afternoon, so lunch fit into her schedule. The next day, she arrived at the restaurant early and Heaton pulled in right on time. She waited for him outside and waved when he arrived. They were seated at a small table next to the beer brewing equipment. Both knew the menu and didn't even look at it before ordering. She ordered the portobello salad and he ordered his usual, the fish and chips, which featured a huge piece of beer battered flounder. They made some small talk and Clint finally got to the point.

"I conferred with a friend of mine in the SBI. He didn't have any information, but he helped me refocus on your blackmailer. He highlighted the unlikelihood that it was a coincidence that both of the guys that got blackmailed were your clients. His thought, which was mine originally, was that someone is getting your clients' information and then blackmailing them. And, to be specific, only your clients, not clients from any other agent in your office. I need you to think of who might have access to just your clients but not to anybody else's. Think outside the box as they say."

"Off the record?"

"This whole investigation is off the record, Phoebe."

"Okay. I provided the girls that these two men were with, but they came from different places. They were escorts. This was not part of my Sea Dunes job. A side job, if you will. The football player's girl was Jessica Rigon, a good friend of mine. She works at the hospital. Kerrigan paid me for her services, and I paid Jess. Shane's girl came from an agency that I was associated with up in Virginia."

"Phoebe, this all really sounds like prostitution."

"Clint, they're hired to be escorts. I can't help it if one thing leads to another."

"Did Jessica and this other girl have any connection? In any way that they would know each other?"

"No, I can't imagine."

"What about Jessica? Did you mention to her that you provided girl number two?"

"No, we haven't talked much since the Kerrigan problem. That really spooked her. Kerrigan blamed both me and her. He got pretty nasty."

"I think I need to talk to both ladies. You have to give me contact information for girl number two; I can find your friend down at the hospital. We have two blackmails and an OD. I may not be able to keep this unofficial much longer. Who else would you have talked to?"

"Nobody, Clint. I wanted to keep this really quiet. I don't want to and can't afford to lose my job."

They finished their lunch with little conversation after the discussion. Phoebe felt too guilty and embarrassed to confide in Heaton about her little side business, and Heaton was thinking about the next interview. She treated for the lunch. Heaton left the restaurant and headed to the hospital. He went to the information booth and asked for Jessica Rigon. The older lady, a volunteer, directed him to the administrative offices. Once in the administration's outer office, he asked the first person he saw to point out Jessica. He went to her desk. "Jessica Rigon?"

"Yes. Can I help you?"

"I have a couple of quick questions to ask you." He discreetly displayed his badge. "Anywhere that's more private?"

"Sure, follow me. What's the problem?"

"Ever know a pro football player?" She snapped her head around to him, turned white, and almost fainted.

They sat at a table in the waiting area outside of the emergency room, which only had one lady waiting to be seen. "I talked to Phoebe and she told me about the deal with Kerrigan."

"Yeah, he was really pissed when he got blackmailed. Can't blame him. He came down really hard on me."

"Who else, other than Phoebe, would have known about your little, ahh, shall I say, job?"

"A lot of people. He liked to be active and we went to dinner just about every night. Lots of people would have seen us."

"But who would know that you were his escort and not his wife?"

"Gee, I don't know. Guess anyone could look up what his wife looked like. I don't know."

"I need you to give it some serious thought. I got a guy who dropped dead with some of Kerrigan's blackmail payment money in his possession."

"Oh God!"

"Get back to me. You don't want to be involved in this any more than you are."

He stood up, handed her his card, and left. She sat there crying.

He contacted Veronica at Virginia Talent. He got nothing useful from her either.

53

Donald Sprout checked out of his one-night motel. He decided to get a haircut, which he hoped would make him look more presentable and perhaps less recognizable. He found a local Supercuts and got a buzz cut. Losing a foot of hair definitely made him less recognizable. He devised a strategy for the following week and beyond. He would finish off Wilson and make an escape. His plan was to shower at a popular chain of gas stations along the interstates that had showers. In the mornings, he would sneak into side entrances of various motels and help himself to their free breakfasts. After all, their ads never mentioned that you had to stay there to get a free breakfast. Then he would only have to worry about an afternoon meal, which he could afford for a few weeks.

He went back to Duke University Hospital to case the area again. He wanted to be able to make a fast getaway. He walked around the circle outside the hospital and stood in the group of trees where he thought he might be able to take a good shot. He noticed an area next to the trees that was an extra lane– like a drop off-lane. Perfect! He would arrive right when Wilson's address was scheduled to begin, park in the pull-off lane, get out, hop over the stone wall there, take a few shots, and floor it out of the area. He drove around the area and found a quick escape route, to get to Elba Street, a block away, and he could merge right onto the Durham Freeway and get off at the first exit and hide for the rest of the day. But, damn it, he spotted a security car. Hoping not to be noticed, he decided at that moment that he needed a new license plate. His next breakfast adventure would provide quite the array of opportunities!

The hospital was equipped with security cameras and had recorded Sprout walking around, seemingly aimlessly. He caught the eye of a security guard reviewing the recording. The security guard made a note in the computer record but didn't think much of it. The person disappeared and did not enter the hospital after he was noticed.

Sprout needed to think through his plan of action. What to do if he nailed Wilson. If he missed, he would find an event to try again. This wasn't to be a suicide mission. He still needed to get back home to find his Vixen. He missed her so much and this plan had to succeed! If he got Wilson this time, his strategy would be to sneak out of town at night and head south on rural roads. He'd find a neighborhood where there were a lot of cars parked in driveways or on the street. He would go from one car to another to find one that had the keys left in it. *There is always someone who does that,* he thought. He felt like he needed to ditch his car in case someone saw him at the event. The new license plate wouldn't be enough, so he'd switch cars and get out of the state. If finding a car with the keys in it didn't work, he'd carjack some woman's vehicle at a shopping center.

In the meantime, he needed to lie low. He drove back to Raleigh and tried his church begging routine again. He drove past a large modernistic church with a number of equally large attached buildings. It looked like a rich parish from the outside. He parked and explored to find the office, the directions to which were well marked. He walked into the office labeled Administration and asked to see the pastor. The gentleman seated behind a computer told him that the pastor was not present but the assistant pastor was. Sprout said that would be fine. The man took Sprout to the clergyman's office, which was decorated with light green wallpaper with small crosses on it.

"Pastor Huth, you have a visitor."

The assistant pastor stood up, moved to the side of his desk, held out his hand, and said, "Hi, I'm Jonathan Huth."

"Jeremiah Smith. Nice to meet you."

"Jeremiah is a nice biblical name. Please have a seat and make yourself comfortable. How can I be of assistance?"

"Just got into town and lost my wallet. Don't know where. I got nothing. No cash, no credit cards, no ID, no nothing. Can you help me out?"

"We have rooms for guests or people who have a temporary traumatic issue. If you fill out a form, Jeremiah, and don't have any weapons or contagious illnesses, you can stay for up to three days. We have a kitchen that's stocked with food for breakfast. Have you reported the lost wallet?"

"No, not yet."

"OK, let me look up the address of the nearest police department for you to make a report. I'll also find the Department of Motor Vehicles office for you to apply for another driver's license. You do have a phone and a car, don't you?"

"Yes and yes."

"Good, give me a minute and I'll get that information for you."

He handed Sprout a piece of paper with the addresses and phone numbers and walked him back to the administrative office.

"Mr. Smith here needs a room for a few nights. Would you take care of his application?"

"Sure, Jonathan."

The man pulled out a two-page form and handed it to Sprout with a pen. Sprout's hand was shaking as he started to fill it out. He wasn't sure about staying in a church; he was a little nervous, but what the hell. He finished the form, leaving some blanks. The man took it back and directed him to bring in any belongings that he had and he would check them. Sprout went back to his car and grabbed a small duffel bag with his newly purchased items and came back into the church. The man in the office apologized for searching his bag; he said it was required by insurance rules. When the search was completed, he asked Sprout to follow him. They passed the kitchen and the man took Sprout in to show him where everything was for his use. He told Sprout that he could buy food and store it on the counter or in the refrigerator but to put his name on anything that he brought in.

Sprout mentioned, "I ain't got any money. I lost my wallet."

"No worries, the pastor authorized that I give you an allowance. I'll bring it to you once I get you to your room."

He stopped at a small room and handed Sprout a key and told him that if he needed anything, there would be someone in the office all night. The room was painted in bright colors in an abstract pattern and had a bunk bed, a small desk with a desk chair, a dresser with a TV and clock radio on it, a padded living room-style chair, and a bathroom that was shared with an adjacent room, which was vacant. The man came back and handed Sprout thirty dollars. "This is for today. If you stay with us another day, come see me for another allowance."

Sprout settled into his new digs. This would keep him out of sight for part of the time before Wilson's appearance in Durham. He left his room and explored the hallways and came to the main sanctuary. It was a huge space with very modern architecture. It was, in his mind, impersonal. He sat in one of the pews in the rear and daydreamed about the last time he'd been in a church. He was eighteen then and had never gotten anything out of the few services that he attended. His parents had visited a variety of nondenominational churches but didn't stay with any congregation for a long time. He looked around. No stained glass windows or statutes of Jesus or Mary or any other religious figure. There were a couple of podiums in the front of the cavernous room in front of a wall painted in a brightly colored pattern. This was not like any other church that he'd ever attended. He wondered about the amount of money that would be needed to maintain such a building but was thankful that they had some left for him. Uninspired, he left to purchase something for dinner.

He drove to the first grocery store that he encountered, a Food Lion. He chose a frozen pizza, a six-pack of Pepsi, a bag of Fritos, a jar of spicy salsa, some sliced salami, and English muffins. He really wanted to buy a six pack of beer, but wasn't sure if alcohol was allowed. Since it might be confiscated, he bought one beer for the road and headed to the ABC (Alcoholic Beverage Control) store. He was sure he could hide a small bottle of rum in his clothing, so that was his final purchase of the day.

He stored his food in the refrigerator or on the kitchen counter as was appropriate and placed a Post-it note with his name on the items. There was very little food there, which he guessed was for the office staff. He retired to his Spartan accommodations after taking a glass full of ice and a bottle of Pepsi. He closed his door and poured rum and Pepsi over the ice, heavy on the rum, and pulled up the padded chair. He studied the TV remote and figured out how to turn the TV on. He was only interested in getting a campaign update. He surfed the channels and found a local news broadcast. He settled back, sipping his drink, and patiently waited for the latest on Wilson. He dozed off briefly and decided he'd lie down in the bed for a while with the TV on. Somewhat in a foggy daze, he heard Wilson's name and sat up like an alarm clock had just gone off. The well-manicured, handsome face of a young announcer spoke with enthusiasm that Wilson was to make an appearance at a fundraising dinner in Raleigh and in two days he would participate in a town hall type of gathering in Cary. They did not mention anything about Durham.

The next day, Sprout called Wilson's campaign headquarters, after dialing star sixty-seven, and asked when Wilson would be appearing in Durham. He was told it would be the following Tuesday at one p.m. He would be waiting.

<h1 style="text-align:center">54</h1>

Clint Heaton had clues that he couldn't piece together. He called Phoebe again.

"Hey Phoebe, Clint here. I visited Jessica at the hospital and called that Veronica lady up at the agency. I didn't get much out of either one of them, but I didn't sense either was the leaker or was involved in either blackmail. Still could be a coincidence, but I really don't believe in coincidences. Could I ask you some personal questions?"

"Sure, Clint."

"Do you socialize with anyone on a regular basis? Do you belong to any organizations that you frequent, like a club, a church, or a charity?"

"No, I only belong to the Chamber of Commerce and don't meet with anyone. I go to church maybe two or three times a year. Don't really go out with anyone except the girls in the office and my boyfriend."

"Who's your boyfriend?"

"Cody. Cody Delaney. We live together. He works at the Atlantic Bistro. He's a server."

"How long have you been an item with Cody?"

"We've been living together for about a year. But we don't see much of each other. He works nights and I work days mostly."

"What does he do when he's not waiting tables?"

"Surfing. He loves to surf."

"Remember the guy who OD'd, the guy that had some of Kerrigan's blackmail payment? He was a surfer. Do you know if your boyfriend knew him?"

"He knows most of the local surfers. They're pretty tight, I think."

"Any chance you told your boyfriend any of the names of your clients, or any details?"

"Well, he was involved in an incident with the first guy, the football player. My client was dining at the Bistro and another patron started to give him a hard time. It got physical. Cody was the football player's server but didn't get involved in the commotion."

"What about the Shane guy?"

"I might have told Cody who was coming in, I really can't say I remember."

"Mind if I question Cody? Maybe he mentioned something to the other surfer."

"No, that's fine, but let me tell Cody that you're coming so he doesn't get spooked."

They hung up and she called Cody right away and told him to expect a visit from Detective Heaton. Cody almost shit his pants, but he told Phoebe that a visit would be fine and he would be expecting the detective. He had all of the incriminating physical evidence at the Bistro. He checked his laptop and wiped out anything that had to do with Kerrigan, Shane, or drones. In half an hour, there was a knock on the door. Cody opened the door and laid eyes on what looked like a professional.

"You must be the detective that my girlfriend told me was coming."

Heaton displayed his badge. "Clint Heaton with Dare County. You Cody?"

"Yes sir, Cody Delaney. Come on in and have a seat."

"Thanks. This shouldn't take long, just a few questions."

Heaton's detective antennae were up; he looked all around to see if anything was out of the ordinary. "I like the *Endless Summer* poster. I hear you're a surfer."

"Yeah, I love it. Always kinda wanted to do an Endless Summer thing, but, like, that's not happening anytime soon."

"Aren't you doing well at the Bistro? A server, right? You must get good tips, the place is pretty pricey."

"I do OK. I've put some money in the bank, but it's a long way off from a trip like that."

"You heard about the surfer who OD'd last week? Know him?"

"Yeah, everybody knew him. Went by the nickname Chump Change. A real good guy, lots of fun. Real bad what happened."

"Any idea what happened?"

"Just what the word out on the waves is. Heard he was in his car somewhere. Did he get some bad shit? He didn't seem like the hard-core drug type."

This was not information that was published.

"We had a case recently where a vacationer was blackmailed. Have any idea if Chump Change was involved?"

This was getting a little too close to home. "Nah, I wouldn't think so. I don't see him blackmailing anyone. How was the guy blackmailed?"

"Apparently by using a drone. Taking embarrassing photos with a drone. You know anyone who has a drone?"

"Aren't those like toys?"

"They can be pretty sophisticated."

"No, I don't know anyone who has one. Like, I've seen a few flying around. Looks pretty cool."

"Where was that?"

"While we were surfing. Flying them over the beach."

"Know if Chump Change owned a drone?"

"Maybe. He did like things that used, ya know, like, advanced technologies."

Cody thought he saw an opportunity to deflect suspicion for the blackmail crimes to Chump Change, since he was dead. Heaton, on the other hand, thought that Cody's comment was strange. Heaton had not seen any evidence of anything more technical at Chump Change's apartment than a toaster. And Cody's knowledge that the OD had occurred in a car bothered him. Heaton thanked Cody for his time and, handing him his card, told him the usual request that if he thought of anything that would be helpful, to give him a call. Cody said goodbye, wiping the sweat from his face.

Phoebe's next client who was traveling alone was Pierce Rockford, known as "Rocky" in very small, higher-level circles. He was the CEO of a large pharmaceutical company named Armondson Inc. The corporate offices were in Delaware.

Rockford had been a client of Phoebe's for the last two years. He loved the beach. Although he lived and worked closer to the fine beaches in Delaware and Maryland, not to mention New Jersey, the quiet serenity of the Outer Banks appealed to him. For the last two years, he'd rented a large house in the town of Rodanthe, the town made famous by Nicholas Spark's book and movie *Nights in Rodanthe*. The town was definitely off the beaten path. It is located on Hatteras Island, most of which is occupied by the Cape Hatteras National Seashore. As far as occupied goes, the National Seashore isn't, unless you count all sorts of varieties of birds and sea turtles. Towns like Rodanthe are embedded in the Seashore, which otherwise comprises miles of nearly empty beaches and dunes. The wild, natural beauty is the biggest attraction to the island. The town itself is about fifteen miles from the Carolina mainland, a true ocean island.

Rockford, unlike most of the other high rollers that Sea Dunes rented to, drove down himself, alone, in his Maserati Ghibli. He, as was true for most of Sea Dune's clients, wanted time to unwind. He was a hunting and fishing aficionado and traveled with a number of firearms. His fishing tackle wouldn't fit in his vehicle, so that was provided by the realty company. Rockford had dark wavy hair, graying a little in the sides, was six feet tall, ruggedly handsome, and had a cutting wit that could bring anyone down to size. He had a down-to earth personality that was somewhat uncommon at his level at a large company. He succeeded professionally by his competence, not by back stabbing. He liked fine wines, no whiskey, and Phoebe had his rental unit filled with the wines he preferred. His favorites generally were merlots and Gewürztraminers. Before his visit, Phoebe researched the latest wine ratings and emailed a suggested list to Rockford. He would email back with a few of his own choice vintages and would agree on some of Phoebe's suggestions.

Rockford leased the house for a month but arrived two days into the rental period. He had already wired payment and a bundle of money to be used as desired. He sent in all the required paperwork and, as a previous client, didn't require the usual welcome briefing. He walked into Sea Dune's office at four. Whitney escorted Rockford to Phoebe's office.

"Miss Razario, I presume."

"My, so formal. I thought we were friends."

"I treat all of the lovely ladies in my life with respect."

"I know you do. I stocked your house with the wines you requested and some food items to get you started. Last year, you chose to supply most of what you wanted to eat and which restaurants to go to. Do you want to operate that way this year?"

"Pretty much. You'll still be on call as in the past?"

"Yes, of course. You have the number. Is there anything special that you want me to arrange?"

"Fishing, again. I want to do some ocean fishing, like out in the Gulf Stream. I'd like to fish in the sound also. Can I rent a boat to operate by myself?"

"Absolutely. When would you like me to reserve your excursions and a boat?"

"For the offshore trip, give me a week to get settled, then maybe book a trip and I'll see if I like it. I don't have a problem with joining a party scheduled to go out, might be more fun with other people."

"OK, a makeup charter."

"And the private boat, I'd like to have it in the water all the time. Let's try to start in two or three days."

"I'll get you a boat. Maybe a twenty to twenty-five-footer. I know a place right in Rodanthe, a water-sports place that I think you could tie up at. It would be just a few blocks away."

"Sounds great. Other than that, I'll just call you when I need you."

"Good. I'll drive down behind you. I have to make sure everything is to your liking."

"OK, see you there."

Rockford knew the way. The house had very unique architecture, not an unusual feature of the older homes in Rodanthe. It had, shall we say, charm, lots of charm. Everything was renovated and in first-class condition, though. It was about forty-five minutes south of the Sea Dunes office, if traffic wasn't bad. When they arrived, Rockford got out of the Maserati and stood there, eyes closed, bathing in the ocean breezes. Phoebe got out of her car and stood there and watched, not saying a word. She knew that she shouldn't kill the scene. No reason to hurry. After a few minutes of silent immersion into the oceanfront atmosphere, Rockford said, "Phoebe, I look forward to this for months. Maybe it's time for me to think about buying a house down here. They sell houses down south, don't they?" He gave Phoebe a teasing smirk.

She smiled back and kidded, "I think we only rent down here." They both chuckled. "Our agency does sell properties also. Do you want me to line up a sales agent? With the homes rented most of the time this time of year, it's tough to get in to see them."

"No, probably I'll wait until the off-season because of what you said. Let me think about it."

This was not like the mansions that Phoebe usually handled. It was a reasonably sized building, but not huge. Rockford felt comfortable with what it offered, so this was it. Phoebe led Rockford up the steps to the front door; most houses here had little or nothing on the ground floor due to occasional storms. She unlocked the door and handed her client the keys. She directed, "Let's walk around and make sure everything is in order." Sea Dune's complimentary bottle of champagne was in a table top wine chiller. It was one that Rockford liked. Phoebe had had the wine chiller brought in and it was fully stocked with his preferred selections. They stood at the sliding glass door overlooking the beach and ocean. Phoebe tried not to be noticed inspecting that the windows had been washed– they had- while Rockford enjoyed the view.

"Like last year, I have a housekeeper scheduled to be here every morning at nine. Do you still want a cook to come in for breakfast?"

"Not yet. I don't want to be tied down to a schedule. Let's see how well Rocky can fix his own bacon and eggs, and we'll go from there. Let's have the housekeeper come at ten; I have a telephone meeting every morning at nine."

They finished the inspection tour and everything was in place. The house had a reverse floor layout from most rentals on the Outer Banks. The bedrooms were on the first floor and the living room, dining room, recreation room, and kitchen were on the second floor. Phoebe stealthily left her card for her private business. She asked Rockford if he would like help emptying his car. He thanked her for the offer and added that he traveled light and it would only take him a few minutes to unpack. They walked together down to the driveway and Phoebe said, "I'll call you about the boat and the fishing trip. I should be able to get the boat by tomorrow, or the next day if not tomorrow. Somebody will come by to drop off the boating gear, life jackets, and the like, and your fishing tackle. Do you want them to leave it under the house or bring it upstairs?"

"They can just leave it."

Phoebe gave him a thumbs-up and said, "Call me if you need anything." She got into her car and noticed that the first item he removed from the trunk was a medium-sized pistol. He held it up and waved to her, saying, "Just in case I need protection from my pharmaceutical enemies." Phoebe rolled down her window and yelled, "Hey, wanna give me some lessons? I have always wanted to go target shooting!"

Pierce Rockford loved pizza but he rarely indulged. But this was his vacation, and some comfort food would be a good start. He checked the internet and decided to try the Dough Shack, which he hadn't ordered from during his previous trips. He ordered a small pizza with bacon and pineapple for pickup. He unpacked, organized a little, and then drove out to buy some provisions, especially beer. Although he drank wine nearly every evening, beer always seemed to be the right complement to pizza. The pizza restaurant had a wonderful aroma even before entering. He found that the restaurant, true to its name, also made donuts. He decided to buy a couple for the morning and headed back to his house to kick-start his month. He placed a slice on a plate, poured himself a beer, and headed out to the balcony to enjoy the view and the food. Sunset was still an hour away, and the yellowish hue lit up the breaking waves. He was always mesmerized by the sanderlings running back and forth, avoiding the remnants of the waves, digging for food. Seagulls camped out on the beach a few houses down, just standing there facing the breeze. They seemed to be enjoying the evening as he was. Out over the ocean, a small flock of pelicans glided so close to the waves that he thought they must feel the spray once in a while. Perfect. He took a long sip of his first beer and then started devouring his first slice. The internet reviews were right on, he loved it. Three beers and half of a pizza later, he was a happy camper.

He often enjoyed sherry after dinner as well as the liqueur RumChata. He could only get RumChata at an ABC store, North Carolina's attempt to throttle the sale of alcoholic beverages. The nearest ABC store was in the town of Buxton, a little more than half an hour away. It could wait until tomorrow; Phoebe had stocked a fine sherry for him.

He walked back into the kitchen to deposit his plate and glass and noticed the card that Phoebe had left. "Female Escorts and Companions, Call 252-260-6769." He hadn't seen Phoebe drop the card, so he didn't know where it came from. He put the card back on the counter, looked at it again, and then got his glass of sherry and went back out to the balcony. He loved novels written by John Grisham and had brought three of them with him. He didn't make much time for pleasure reading during the year, so this represented his dive into a book activity.

The next morning he arose in time for sunrise, made a cup of coffee with the Keurig, added a little half and half, microwaved his first donut (purchased the night before) for five seconds, and headed out to the balcony to start his day out right and enjoy the scenery. The donuts, even though a day old, were great. There were a couple of early-bird surfers out and a boat way off shore, barely in sight under the rising sun. It was a beautiful, breezy morning and he felt that the stresses of his office life were lifting.

55

Rocky's company had recently run into a headwind over some sticky issues. Legal cases and suits were nothing new in the pharmaceutical business, and Armondson was far from immune to such difficulties. The trend seemed to be for these companies to hire more lawyers and fewer scientists.

Armondson had one huge case settled out of court and Rockford received high praise for how it was handled. Armondson had sued Laurel Pharmaceutical for stealing their patented formula for a highly effective skin cream. Intracompany documents from Laurel had been discovered and they were dynamite for Armondson's case. Legal discovery, affidavits, and disposing witnesses had lasted well over a year. The amount of the final settlement, leaked to the press, boosted Armondson's stock by over twenty percent.

Armondson also survived a class action suit that alleged that their manufacturing and promotional practices stifled competition from generic drug manufacturers. The facts brought out during negotiations supported the allegations, but the legalities were somewhat gray. Didn't all the drug companies want to stifle competition? That seemed like a normal course of doing business.

The final large suit of the year resulted in fines that, though financially damaging to a degree, could have been far worse. Three states independently sued the company for overcharging. Armondson's position was that it followed normal accepted business practices and was simply responding to supply and demand. That was frowned on in the pharmaceutical business because of the optics that you were depriving a person that was ill and in need of a potential cure. The court verdict actually cost Armondson less than the profits it made for the alleged overcharging. So it wasn't a business disaster, just a public relations mess.

Rockford was front and center in all of these legal battles. The media ripped him apart for being an uncaring bastard who had nothing on his mind but the money in his pocket. Not that they couldn't have accused most CEOs of that. Lawyers had deposed him; he had testified, and spent countless hours in meetings with the legal staff and upper-level managers. And, in the meantime, he had a business to run. He set aside Tuesday mornings for closed-door meetings with the corporate lawyers and some managers, depending on the latest issues, to plot the direction the company should go in according to whatever matter was brewing. The meeting was not to be disturbed unless one of the facilities exploded.

Rocky wasn't completely divorced from his work duties while in Rodanthe. The house was wired, with the house owner's blessing, to receive high-speed internet. Two phone lines were added as well as video lines. He brought his sophisticated company-provided laptop computer that could hook up to the TV screens in the house. At nine each morning, he connected with his office and had personnel that he'd requested to be present in a conference to review any important issues of the day. Also, the following Monday, a number of managers would attend a meeting in his house in Rodanthe for a major review on the progress of the testing of a new anti-aging skin cream. He'd had Phoebe reserve nine rooms in a motel in Buxton for a couple of nights to accommodate the attendees.

A little after ten, right after Rockford finished his morning staff call, Phoebe called her client. "Good morning, Mr. Rockford. How was your first night?"

"Phoebe, we have been dealing with each other for over two years. I would be delighted if you dropped the 'Mr.' and called me by my nickname, Rocky. To answer your question, great. It was great."

"Great- Rocky! I was able to arrange a boat for you. It's a Grady-White Fisherman 257, about twenty-five feet long. I'm told it's a real nice boat for the sound and you can take it out into the ocean most days. A solid boat to fish from. There's a water-sports business in the town of Waves, just south of

Rodanthe, that's allowing you to dock there. If it's convenient, I'll bring down the keys and the items you need for the boat. Any time better than another?"

"Anytime is good. I'm here. Give me an idea when."

"The boat's on the way and should get there in a few minutes. Why don't I leave now? Should get there in forty-five minutes or so. I'll pick you up and take you down to the boat and introduce you to the guys at the facility."

"I'll be ready."

Phoebe arrived around eleven, climbed up the stairs, and rang the doorbell. It played a few seconds of a song she wasn't familiar with. Rocky opened the door and invited Phoebe in. She told him that the boat was tied up only about a mile way.

"Good. Let me follow you there. I'll check out the boat, grab a lunch, and head out into the vast unknown."

Phoebe drove to the water-sports pier and parked. Rockford was right behind her.

Phoebe yelled, "I'll be right back," and went into the office. They knew her well there. Rockford came in anyway and poked around the store portion of the business. Phoebe made sure that the arrangements with the facility were complete, got the keys, and waved to Rockford to follow her.

"Here are the boat keys. Let me give you a quick tour of the boat. The gas tank is full, and any day after you use it, let the shop know and they will fill it up for the next trip. You can be out all day and then some on a tank. Your fishing tackle has been delivered to your house. The necessary safety equipment, an anchor, ropes, and so forth, are on board. The gentlemen here can instruct you as to where it's not safe to go and where the places are that are reported to be good fishing spots. Any questions?"

"Just one, and it's got nothing to do with boating. I found a card left in my house that said something about lady escorts; do you know anything about that?"

"Well, yes. It's a private business that I operate. I leave the card in all the houses that I service. I hope you're not offended."

"Oh no, Phoebe, not at all. I was thinking that it would be nice to go boating with a companion. Let's talk about it."

"OK. Would you have any criteria? Anything special that you like in a lady?"

"Well, I'm not a spring chicken, Phoebe, so a cute twenty-year old would not work, would she. A lady who likes outdoorsy stuff. You know, like spending a day on that boat or swimming in the ocean. And she has to like wine."

"OK. Let me check it out." She explained the financial considerations and Rocky agreed, but only on a trial basis. He asked her three times how confidential the arrangement would be. He specified that he wanted a few days of alone time and then would welcome a companion.

Phoebe drove back to her office and Rockford got back in his car and he headed to a sandwich shop he was familiar with and purchased lunch provisions. He also visited a small tourist shop to pick up some sunblock. Better to be careful and not ruin a vacation with a bad sunburn. He went back to his house to pick up the fishing tackle that had been delivered and headed to the boat. He loaded everything onto the boat and went back into the office to get advice as to where to go and where not to go. He was interested in heading to the inlet, that is Oregon Inlet, which connects the sound to the Atlantic Ocean. The manager of the facility warned that the currents through the inlet were tricky and that he should be vigilant. Rockford jumped onto the boat, started the engines, and was off. There was a southwest breeze that made the sound choppy, but the twenty-five-footer handled it well. He headed north with the breeze behind him and sped toward the inlet, some fourteen to fifteen miles away. From fishing charters and private boats to commercial fishing boats, the inlet was active. The whitecaps he'd initially encountered turned into a seemingly random maze of swirling foam. He slowed the boat down to size up where the channel was. The passage to the ocean was beckoning him, so he headed to the course taken by other vessels and navigated the unpredictable currents. Just as he entered what visually appeared to be the ocean, his boat swerved sharply to the starboard and he caught a large wave directly on the beam, heaving the boat sideways at a forty-five-degree angle. Rockford lost his footing and fell heavily against the boat's side. The boat rocked heavily to the opposite side and he slid over the soaked deck to the other side. He pulled himself up and realized that his right shoulder was in agony and his right arm dangled by his side, painfully useless. He managed to get himself back to the steering wheel and brought the boat into calmer waters and throttled down. He dug out a beach towel and fashioned a makeshift splint. He easily decided that this fishing and sightseeing trip was over and headed back through the tumbling surf to the more comfortable waters of the sound. He kept the boat speed low. The bouncing and pounding through each wave inflicted additional stabbing pain to his shoulder. The fifteen-mile return trip would take a lot longer at the slower speed. On the way, once he was as comfortable as he could possibly be, he called Phoebe and told her what had happened and asked where it would be best to receive medical treatment. Phoebe told him she'd make a few calls and get right back to him. Since money was no object, she called an orthopedic practice that she had used for past clients and asked if a doctor could meet Rockford at the hospital. After being put on hold and consulting with the physicians there, Phoebe was told that a doctor could get there in one to two hours. Phoebe called Rockford back, who was still five miles from tying up to the pier, and gave him the information.

"Can you drive, or do you want me to come down to take you to the hospital?"

"I think I can drive, but not knowing what they might do, perhaps a lift would be great. This hurts like a mother!"

"Okay, I'll leave now and should be at your house in forty-five or so. I will call and get the guys at the facility to look out for you and tie up the boat."

Rockford maneuvered the boat into the slip without any difficulty and was glad he had help securing the boat. The whole process wasn't pleasant at all. He made it to his car and got back to the house. He popped four Advils, wishing he had something stronger, but thought it wouldn't be a good idea especially because he would be heading for the hospital as soon as Phoebe got to him. Phoebe arrived right after he took the Advils. He thanked her for getting there so quickly and told her to give him a few minutes to change and get some dry shorts on. There was no way he was changing his shirt!

While driving on the bridge over the inlet, Rockford pointed out, almost to himself, "There's where the trouble started! Maybe I'll wait for better conditions to try that again." He laughed, then added, "Did you arrange for my visitor yet?"

"I'm working on it. I should have somebody lined up by the end of the day."

They checked into the emergency room and Phoebe mentioned that she'd arranged for a certain doctor to meet them there. The receptionist told them that he was already there and they could be seen in a moment. After a thorough, but painful, examination including X-rays, the doctor determined that he had sprained his shoulder, fairly severely, and that nothing was broken or permanently damaged. He offered to prescribe narcotic medicine, but Rockford declined. The physician wrote the script anyway, saying Rockford could fill it or save it if the pain became intolerable. Phoebe drove the patient back to Rodanthe and empathetically told him how sorry she was. She left saying that she would call him with the arrangements to meet his companion when she had someone lined up.

Rocky popped a couple more Advils, pulled a bottle of merlot off the wine rack and a glass, grabbed a new novel, and headed to the hot tub on the oceanfront balcony to heal some of his wounds.

56

Sprout was able to stay at the church through Monday. He departed, thanking the staff member present for the charity and kindness, and headed to Durham, not far away. Tuesday would be his big day, he thought. Just to be diligent and wanting to leave no stone unturned, he visited the area outside the hospital again. A platform had been erected in the middle of the drop-off circle where he thought the speech might be made. It had not been there a week ago. He walked to the grove of bushes, to the side of the circle where he thought would be the best place for him to take a shot. He liked the line of sight; that's where he would try to be tomorrow. A security guard noticed him, Sprout, walking around the bushes and yelled, "Hey, what are you doing there?" Sprout just waved at him, turned, and walked away. The guard, weighing in at over three hundred pounds, did not pursue him.

Sprout got back in his car and drove to one of the ubiquitous Waffle Houses in the area. It was around noon, but he ordered waffles, eggs, and sausage anyway despite lunch items being on the menu. That's what you do at the Waffle House. He took his time, downed four cups of coffee, and checked his phone for the latest update on Congressman Wilson's appearances. The website listed the speech at the hospital at eleven with a meet and greet at noon at some restaurant. He smiled to himself, a devilish smile, thinking that if his plan worked, Wilson wouldn't be meeting and greeting anyone after the speech. He cleaned his plate, paid the check, leaving a dollar for a tip, made a stop in the men's room, and got back into his car. There was a large shopping mall just off the interstate that he had learned about and he decided to head there to consume the day. He planned to sleep in the back seat of his car but wasn't sure where he could do that and not attract attention. He got bored walking around the mall, adrenaline being part of the problem. He headed to the food court on the second level, purchased a chocolate milkshake, sat down, and sipped it slowly. He was in no hurry. He stayed until the mall closed and went back out to his car. There were still a lot of cars in the parking lot. He thought it might be a safe place to sleep until he saw a security car patrolling the lot. So much for staying there. He drove back to downtown Durham and found a quiet residential street that looked like a place where no one would bother him. He parked on the street and got out, looked around, saw nobody outside, and crawled into the back seat, moving some of his clothes to make space. He lowered the windows slightly, locked the car doors, and laid down to get some shut-eye. Sleep did not come to him quickly; he was anxious and reviewed the plan in his mind over and over.

The sun rose early and woke Sprout up. He sat up and tried to look around, but his car windows were fogged up, apparently from his breathing all night. He lowered one of the rear windows and poked his head out to see if anyone was outside. It was still early and he didn't see anyone. He opened the door and got into the driver's seat, wiped off the inside of the windshield, and left the neighborhood. He hadn't passed any of his beloved 7-Eleven eleven stores but found a Dunkin Donuts. A large coffee and an apple fritter later, he found a parking space in the downtown Durham area and pulled in. The coffee and pastry tasted good, but he was nervous. He wanted to be mentally prepared; he didn't want to screw up this chance like he did the one on the Outer Banks. He pulled his Glock 17 out from under the passenger seat, made sure that the magazine was empty, and practiced some firings to reacquaint himself with the feel of the trigger pull. He looked around to make sure that he wasn't seen. He loaded the weapon's magazine and stashed it underneath the passenger seat again. It was still three hours before the speech was scheduled and he didn't want to arrive too early, but he decided to do a dry run to be sure of the timing. He drove to the hospital and onto Erwin Road, past the circle where the platform was erected. He saw police barricades along the side of the road and wondered if the cops were going to close the road. That would mean he would have to alter his plan. He muttered "shit" to himself and drove back downtown and found a place to park again.

Sweat beaded across his forehead as his nervousness peaked. What if they blocked the road? What if the pull-off lane was blocked? Shit! He still had over two hours to figure it out so he decided to drive by again. There were a few cops milling around the area; he decided he needed a Plan B. Across the street from the hospital he saw the hospital parking garage. Parking there would make a getaway difficult. Across from the garage was a health care building of some sort with an outside parking lot. It was actually right across the road from where he wanted to be, so it was somewhat ideal. He could get to it without driving on Erwin, so he thought that it could work. It had to work. More relaxed now, Sprout pulled into a residential neighborhood that was two or three blocks away and parked. He decided he would drive back out to the chosen parking lot around ten thirty, walk across the street, and bide his time until Wilson's performance. His day of reckoning was here.

Sprout wore tan-colored cargo pants that he had purchased at a thrift store while he was staying at the church. The thigh pockets were large enough to conceal the Glock. The weapon was loaded; he slipped it into the pocket and drove to the parking lot. There were a number of spaces available and he chose one that he could pull straight out of and make a quick exit. It was ten thirty. Indeed, police barricades were erected everywhere and his original plan would not have been possible. Plan B was looking better and better. He sat in the Impala for a few minutes to collect his thoughts. Yes, empty the magazine, if necessary, just hit the target where it counts.

He crossed the street near another drop-off circle, no simple task with the traffic still flowing. He looked at the main circle (actually an oval) as he was crossing and noticed a number of people gathering. He still had fifteen minutes to kill, so he walked away from the site, meandering until five minutes before eleven. As he circled back, he heard the loud speakers playing the Star-Spangled Banner. *How absolutely patriotic,* he thought. *Maybe that would be more appropriate if Wilson wasn't responsible for the deaths of his fellow soldiers and airmen.* He heard the introductory speech but was still too far away to make out the words. He crept closer to the bushes that he had staked out that would afford him a good shot. As he approached, he saw, to his horror, a policeman stationed right where he wanted to be. He was alone. Sprout hesitated and listened. He did not hear Wilson yet. He hid from the cop behind a hedge. Shit, what to do?

Finally, a loud round of applause and Wilson stepped up to the microphone. Sprout could barely see him from his vantage point and knew he had to make a decision. What would he have done when confronting the enemy in Afghanistan? He moved closer to the cop, walking in a deep knee-bend posture so as not to be seen. He got to within ten feet of the officer. He could clearly see Wilson from there but the rent-a-cop was in the fucking way. Sprout raised the Glock and pumped a round into the policeman's head. He fell forward in a heap. Sprout then stood up and had a perfect bull's eye target and opportunity to aim and hit Wilson dead on. But everyone in attendance had heard the first pop and there were shouts of "shooter" throughout the crowd. Sprout raised the weapon and took aim. With his finger ready to pull the trigger, a woman behind him screeched, "Sprout!" He spun around, startled, eyes wide open with shock and anger and adrenaline. When he turned at the mention of his name, he tripped on an exposed tree root, and clumsily fell down flat on his face with a thud. The hit to the ground took his breath away. His gun was jarred from his grip and the Glock bounded out of his hand toward the lady. She quickly picked up the gun and shakily aimed it at Sprout and sneered in a low voice even she didn't recognize, "You soulless fucking bastard."

"Give me my gun, bitch. You are ruining everything!"

He crawled and scrambled to try to get to his feet and lurched forward toward the woman. He grabbed her leg. Totally frightened, the woman instinctively pulled the trigger of the gun she had aimed at Sprout and fired twice. People all around her were screaming and she was frozen, stunned.

Peter Chek, Wilson's head of security, was standing about ten feet directly behind Wilson. He rushed forward, sensing the danger, to tackle the congressman. Before he got there, two more loud pops were heard from the bushes, the area from which the first sound had emanated. Chek landed on Wilson, who was already stooping down. Nice take down.

"Richard, are you hit?"

Wilson looked up, smiled, and said, "Only by you, Pete." The speaking engagement was over.

The police rushed in every direction. The gunshot sounds had echoed off the building, making it difficult to determine exactly where the shots were fired from. Two policemen reached the bushy area where Sprout had fired. They saw two bodies, one of large man wearing a security uniform, motionless on the ground. The officer had been killed instantly. The other body, a male, was prostrate and motionless with blood bubbling out of his back. Standing behind the fallen bodies was a woman, shaking, holding a gun with two hands, straight out, like she was frozen. Tears were streaming down her face. She was silently crying.

"Ma'am, drop the gun, please."

She didn't move. There was no obvious sign that she'd heard a word. She continued to cry.

"Ma'am, the gun, please." There were now a number of police in the area around her. The officer who had spoken raised his left hand, signaling for no one to do anything yet. The others slowly unholstered their weapons.

The woman remained in the pose but was now wailing out loud.

"Ma'am, it'll be alright. Please drop the gun."

Her crying began to ebb. She was shaking her head back and forth, mumbling, "He won't ever do that again, never again, never again." She stared at the dead bodies: then she lifted her head and glanced toward the officer, who was talking to her. She was in shock. In a meditative movement, she took her left hand off the weapon and pointed the gun at herself.

"Ma'am, no! No!" At that moment an officer who had positioned himself behind the woman dove at her, as if he was a linebacker tackling a running back. He landed on her awkwardly and the gun flew out of her hand. The policemen rushed in and secured both the woman's and Sprout's weapons on the ground. By now, the shootings had been reported and sirens were screaming from every direction. The officer, who had flattened the woman, rolled off of her, was somewhat dazed, and just looked at her.

She looked him in the eyes and said, "I'm so sorry, Officer. I am so sorry."

"Are you OK?"

She nodded in the affirmative. "If you're OK, please stand up with me. I need to cuff you and arrest you. Ma'am, what's your name?"

"Joan Roselli."

<h1 style="text-align:center">57</h1>

The scene was complete chaos. People screaming, running, not knowing what to do or where a safe place would be. Some people just laid down on the ground. Once the shooter was detained and it was determined that there were no more shooters, the police announced over the loud speaker system that it was now safe and to please remain in the area for interviews. It was easy for the cops on the scene to determine that both men who were lying face down were in fact dead. The officer had been shot in the back of the head, probably at fairly close range. He never had a chance. The police had no way to determine who the other deceased man was. He had no wallet or any type of identification on him. They had a gun, which they presumed was the man's, and they could run it through the federal data base to determine its owner, but that wouldn't necessarily be the man on the ground. The officers strung yellow crime scene tape around the area. Ballistics tests would later determine that the weapon on the ground was indeed used to murder the security man.

Everyone in the Wilson party was shaken. The police began their canvass and questioned those who were there to determine if they saw anything that would help in their investigation. Some attendees had slowly left the area, but most stood around comparing their observations and rehashing their trauma. Sid Freeze, who was on the makeshift platform with Wilson and others, helped Wilson up and asked if he was alright. They both looked around the stand and concluded that no one had been hit. Peter Chek had been standing behind the platform when all hell broke loose and scrambled up to the group in a New York minute. Once he also ascertained that everyone was physically unharmed, he told Freeze he would walk over to where the shots were fired. He got there and identified himself. The officer temporarily in charge of the crime scene asked Chek if he had any idea who the dead man might be. "Could you turn his head so I can see if it is who I think it might be?" he asked. Chek was told he would have to wait for the crime scene investigators to get there before they could get permission to move the body in a different position and asked Chek to hang around, which he agreed he would do. The investigators got there within thirty minutes, made their initial evaluation, and turned the body over. Chek had gone to his car and retrieved his photos of Sprout, and he held them in view for the officer. His hunch was right, it was Sprout. The Durham police called the SBI, and Max Ramsey was summoned to the scene. His office was only a twenty-minute ride away, on a good day. He pulled up into the access lane, the one that Sprout had wanted to use, with his lights flashing. Ramsey introduced himself and was briefed on what was known so far. He went over to Chek, shook his hand, and asked if he thought it was Sprout. Ramsey compared Chek's photos with the body and said, "Pretty clear. Guess he won't be stalking Wilson anymore."

"Who shot him?"

Chek didn't know or really care, so Ramsey approached one of the policemen on the scene.

"Do you know who the shooter is?"

"She said Joan something. Check with Harrell over there."

Ramsey went over as directed and asked again who the shooter was.

"She said her name was Joan Roselli. We took her in to the station for questioning and, I assume, to book her. She didn't have a purse or anything on her."

Ramsey thought that sounded familiar. Was that the name of the girl that Sprout kidnapped? He called his office to get the number of the detective in Virginia that was working the Sprout case.

"May I speak with Detective Hasbee, please?" In a few seconds Hasbee was on the line.

"Hasbee here. May I help you?"

"Hey Mike, Max Ramsey. I think we got your boy Sprout."

"Do tell. Where is he?"

"On his way to the morgue."

"Wow! What happened?"

"He was at a function for Congressman Wilson, apparently there to shoot him. A lady was behind Sprout and shot him. Her name sounded familiar, but I wasn't sure. Said she was Joan Roselli."

"Holy shit, no!"

"Is that the girl that Sprout kidnapped?"

"No, her mother. Shit! Shit! Shit! Has anyone called her husband?"

"Don't know. I just got to the scene. The locals took her in to the station."

"Local being where?"

"Durham."

"OK, is there someone I can talk to down there?"

"Sure, I'll get you a name. I'll get back to you as soon as I have something."

Hasbee went to his boss's office and said, "Permission to come aboard?"

Chief Marnee Forbish said, "Come on in, Mike. What do you have?"

"Remember Donald Sprout? He was shot down in Durham, North Carolina. The shooter identified herself as Joan Roselli, mother of Roanna Roselli."

"Oh my God! That's awful- that is, the part about Mrs. Roselli. Wow!"

"Just happened. They're questioning her now. Should I do anything?"

"Well, if it was definitely Sprout, looks like your case is over! Wow! This is some news. Call the husband. Find out what he knows."

"Yes, I was thinking the same thing."

Hasbee called Anthony Roselli's cell number and Roselli answered. Hasbee quickly learned that Roselli had already received the bad news and was on his way to North Carolina.

Joan Roselli had been escorted to the Durham Detention Center and had called her husband's school and told the receptionist that it was an emergency. Anthony was paged and was told it was his wife. When he answered, she told him that she was arrested for shooting Donald Sprout. He was shocked. He told her to stay calm and he would get there as soon as possible. Anthony rushed to the office and explained to the receptionist that he had a family emergency and had to leave immediately. He then went to classroom 206 where Roanna was taking a math class. He knocked on the door and the teacher stopped the lesson and went to the door.

"Hi Anthony, what's up?"

"Got an emergency and have to take Roanna out of class."

The teacher looked very concerned and said, "Roanna, would you come here, please?"

She got up from her desk and looked quizzically at her father. "Honey, gather your stuff, we have to go. Mom's got a problem."

While walking out of the school to the car, Anthony phoned his dad.

"Dad, I need your help. Are you busy?"

"What's wrong, son. Is Roanna okay?"

"Yes, yes, no, yes, she is with me. I can't get into it now, it's about Joan. Can you pick up Josh and Penny after school today and take them to your house? I would have called Mom but, well, you know, she would have too many questions now. I can't talk now. I just need you to get the kids for me. I will call you as soon as I can. Oh, Josh has a soccer game after school. Dang, just keep him. Don't do the game. Hopefully he won't remember. Oh gosh, Dad, I don't know. You do what you think is best but wait until I get more information before you do anything. I am sorry, I have to go. I will call when I can!"

"No worries, son. I got this. Call me when you can."

They left hurriedly and headed to Durham. Anthony and Joan had always been open with Roanna. Anthony told his daughter what he knew, which wasn't much. She cried for most of the trip.

Anthony had no idea how to find a good criminal attorney, especially in a city and state he wasn't familiar with. He'd heard plenty of commercials on the early morning TV shows and on the radio station he listened to, but that was back in Virginia.

58

Congressman Richard Wilson's speech was cancelled. Wilson told Freeze and Peter Chek that he was shaken and to meet him at his house in an hour. Wilson was quickly apprised of the situation as it had been known to that point.

The congressman arrived to his home before the others and his wife, Dawn, greeted him with a near-life-threatening hug.

"Richard, this is awful. What are we going to do? When will this stop?"

Many questions, not many answers.

"Honey, this guy has been stalking me, not sure why, but he was shot and killed. Peter told me some lady shot him. So, God rest his soul, he won't be troubling me anymore."

"God damn his soul, don't you mean? How do we know he was the only one out there aiming for you?"

"Sid and Peter are coming over in a few minutes. We're going to go over everything and talk about how to proceed. Don't worry, hon, everything will be fine. I would imagine the police will learn everything we need to know."

At this point, all the television stations were at the scene and televising live broadcasts with up to-date news concerning the event. Only one station had been covering the Wilson campaign speaking engagement, so they were the station to first break the news. Wilson and his wife were in front of the television listening to news reports when Freeze and Chek arrived a few minutes apart from each other.

The four of them gathered in Wilson's comfortable living room and Wilson initiated the conversation.

"I want to know everything about what happened today."

Looking lovingly at his wife, Wilson said, "Dawn is scared, and frankly I'm a little shaken. I've been shot once and maybe barely survived today. What do we know other than what the stations are reporting?"

Chek said, "The bastard named Sprout was there behind the bushes, over to the left of the platform. He apparently shot a security man– he died instantly– and then this Sprout guy was shot by some woman. She was obviously apprehended at the scene."

"We need to do something for the family of the security man that was shot. Do we know anything about him?"

Chek answered, "Not yet."

Freeze added, "We'll issue a statement and when Peter's people get us more info, we'll do what's appropriate. You should probably go to the funeral, memorial service, or whatever, if there is one."

Wilson said, "For sure."

Chek continued, "Sprout is the guy who served under you in the Middle East and had a beef with you. You must have really pissed him off. I'll meet with the Staties to see if they think he was acting alone or in coordination with someone else. When I last talked with them, they thought that he was a lone wolf."

Wilson asked, "What do we know about the woman who shot him?"

"Nothing."

Wilson changed the subject, asking where the campaign would go from here. Sid Freeze told Wilson that they needed to have a campaign staff meeting to review the repercussions of the events that had just occurred. Wilson agreed and, with no events scheduled for the next couple of days, Freeze said that he would plan a strategy meeting and gather each campaign group manager together and meet at headquarters in two days.

Wilson's opponent, Mercer Harris, tweeted his concern and hoped everyone was okay. A nice gesture. Wilson told Freeze to tweet him back with his gratitude for his concern.

Wilson wondered out loud what the public would make of all this. Freeze thought that it wouldn't hurt the campaign but wanted to spin the shooter's motivation, whatever it really was, to make Sprout sound like a far-left nut job. Wilson told him to be cautious and not to make any solid statements without proof. He still wanted a clean campaign.

When the campaign staff met two days later, Wilson opened the meeting by saying "Thanks for rearranging your schedules. The event two days ago was frightening. Anyone who was there could have been seriously hurt. That's not what this campaign needs – to risk any of you. So, right here, right now, if any of you want out, put your hand up. The campaign will take care of you until you find other employment."

No hand was raised.

"OK, thank you. I appreciate all of you. Sid, where do we go from here?"

"We've taken a quick poll. We simply asked if the Durham event and the shooting on the Outer Banks made people more inclined, less inclined, or made no difference in whether they would vote for Congressman Wilson. The results, though from a small sample size, were significant. Fifty-six percent said that they were more inclined, eleven percent said less inclined, and the remaining thirty-three percent said no difference. So we didn't lose any ground."

"Sid, you're not suggesting that we hire another shooter, are you?"

Everyone laughed, but not for long. The trauma was still very fresh and real. Freeze continued, "We're moving forward. Our view is that this guy was a crazed left-winger. True or not, we'll put that out there. Richard will attend the memorial service for the security man that was killed. That's scheduled for Saturday. I'll send out the details; if any of you can attend, that would be great. I've published a statement thanking him for protecting the congressman and sacrificing his life. We're way ahead of Harris in all the polls, so we just have to keep up the momentum. Peter, what about security?"

"We will hire four more guards. They will be plainclothes men or women with concealed carry permits. I'll meet with the state police office tomorrow and encourage more protection from them and from the locals. I'm confident that they'll cooperate. They won't want any trouble or embarrassment."

Wilson asked, "What do we know about the lady shooter? Anything new?"

Chek said, "Nothing. The cops aren't talking to me yet. My internet search unearthed a few facts. She's from Virginia. Works at a financial advisory company. Has a daughter that was kidnapped, but escaped and returned home. Her husband is a high school teacher and assistant football coach. That's about it. I haven't figured out the motive for the shooting yet but there had to be a connection."

The meeting got down to the minutia of running the campaign through the full court press time in October.

59

Cody finished wrapping up the night's work at the Bistro and settled in to a few moments at the bar with Willow, now part of his routine.

"Well, big boy, what are we going to do with that real estate bitch? Am I in or out?"

"You're definitely in, Willow. I have to work things out with Phoebe. I don't want to hurt her."

She pulled her dress down over her bra and said, "If you want this, you gotta dump her. Just you and I, Cody. All I want is you. You know that."

"Willow, I want you in the worst way too. I'll make it happen, just give me time."

He gave her a kiss, a pinch on her ample breast, and a thumbs-up and left with a hard-on. Leaning against Kassie in the employee lot was Jayden.

"Well, little lover boy has finally appeared. What do you say, Delaney? Time to pay the piper."

"Your stuff was crap. Watered down at best. I'm not paying top dollar for Pillsbury flour. Now get out of my way." Cody playfully pushed Jayden out of his way to open his driver's side door.

Jayden pulled out a handgun from his back pocket, pointed it at Cody, and said, "I'll bet I could change your mind!"

"Shoot me and go to jail? I don't think you're that stupid, Jayden. You know you sold me cut stuff. I'll pay for the real stuff, not the shit you sold me."

Cody continued to climb into the driver's seat.

"Cody, I'm going to make you pay, one way or another." With that, Jayden flashed the gun at Cody, hid it in his pants, and turned and walked across the parking lot.

Cody didn't sleep well that night and didn't get up until eleven. Phoebe was already dressed for work in a very attractive low-cut dark blue dress.

"My, my, look who's with the living! What's going on, babe?"

"Had a little problem with Jayden last night."

"What happened?"

"He pulled a gun on me. Wants me to pay full price for that crap he sold me last week. You tried it– it was cut with God knows what. Jayden needs to find a better supplier."

"Yeah, that stuff was garbage. Isn't this going to be uncomfortable at the Bistro?"

"You betcha. I'll figure it out. You got a new client?"

"Yeah, a CEO that's been coming for a couple of years. The guy that rents down in Rodanthe. He's a little high-maintenance; I'm on my way there now."

"I take it his place is on the beach."

"Yep. Of course."

"What's he into?"

"Loves fishing. I rented him a boat and first time out he got into a little trouble in the inlet."

"Guy married?"

"Isn't every bigwig?"

"She comes down with him?"

"Naah. He needs to decompress, so he says. You got a lot of questions."

He said half jokingly, "Just wanted to see if he wanted surfing lessons."

"Gotta go, see ya tomorrow a.m."

In her car, Bluetooth on, Phoebe made a call to the talent agency to see if they had a match for Rockford. He'd specified someone who was not a "spring chicken," but the agency didn't have anyone over thirty at the moment. So she called Rockford to see if she could visit him, to see if any other options would be acceptable to him. He had just docked his rental boat and said that he'd be back at the house in half an hour or so. He'd welcome a visit.

When Phoebe arrived, Rockford greeted her holding two glasses of rosé. With eyebrows raised, he questioned, "Is this business or pleasure? Either way, it goes better with wine."

"Thanks, Rocky. Cheers! To answer your question, let's just say a little of both."

"Please come in. Do you have the time to join me out on the deck?"

"Wide open this afternoon, sure."

He escorted her upstairs even though she knew the way. He pulled two deck chairs together, somewhat facing each other, and they sat down with their wine glasses. He was wearing a splint supporting his sprained right shoulder.

"So, tell me, how is my bruised client?"

"As long as I can lift a glass, I'm OK. Seriously, I'm somewhat ambidextrous, so I can function pretty well. I should be able to dump this thing pretty soon. I have an appointment with the doc tomorrow afternoon."

"Does it hurt much?"

"Not with the splint on. The boat ride this morning was good. Had a hard time holding the rod, though. Would you want to go fishing with me and do the physical stuff?"

"Sure, that would be fun. When do you want me aboard?"

"How about tomorrow morning, before my doctor's appointment? Is eight too early?"

"Nope. It's a deal. I can drive you to your appointment afterward, if you like."

"You're on!"

They sat and enjoyed the ocean and the breezes. Phoebe finally got to the female company issue, telling him she'd struck out on the first try.

"Well, Phoebe, I'm enjoying your company a lot right now. Besides, I'm kinda broken, so let's see how it goes." He winked at her and put his hand on her arm. The first nonprofessional touch excited both of them.

Cody decided to do a recon mission to Rodanthe. He hopped into Kassie and headed south. He had just gotten one of his mechanically inclined surfer buddies to give the rustic vehicle a full tune-up and the car sounded much better. But it was still noisier than just about anything else out there on the road. He wasn't sure what he'd be looking for, but he rarely went down to

Rodanthe, so he thought it would be a good idea to scope it out. Rodanthe had very few oceanfront houses on the main drag, Route 12, so checking out all of the oceanfront homes would require turning off many side roads. With just a couple of hours available, he started his search. The houses that he cruised by were nothing like the ones up on Mansion Beach and were more like the buildings in Kill Devil Hills and Nags Head, nearer to his home. They were still large and nice-looking from the outside, but they were not mansions. After going in and out of most of the roads leading to the oceanfront, he didn't uncover any clues and ran out of time to finish his research.

Phoebe had to leave early to get to Rodanthe by eight, so she left a note for her snoozing boyfriend. She wore a bikini that she looked stunning in, with a cover-up. She packed a change of clothing for the ride to Rockford's doctor appointment. She got to Rocky's house ten minutes early and he was all set for the trip. The boat was gassed up and ready to go. Phoebe actually helped Rockford aboard so he didn't risk putting pressure on his shoulder.

"The guys at the store said that they heard there's good fishing south of here, so we head that way."

Phoebe answered, "Aye, aye, captain."

The wind was light and the sound was calm. Rockford left the pier and in fifty yards accelerated to over thirty knots. The calm water meant that the boat cruised flat and smooth, causing little strain on the shoulder. Despite living on the Outer Banks, Phoebe had never fished on a boat. They zoomed about fifteen miles southwest of Rodanthe and Rockford set the boat down. The Pamlico Sound there was an immense body of water. The mainland, still about twenty miles away, was a foggy blur.

"Would the lady like a Bloody Mary and a Danish?"

Phoebe, somewhat astonished, said, "You have Bloody Marys?"

"I wanted to be a good host."

"You get five stars! OK, pour me one, tall and strong. It must be five o'clock somewhere in the world."

"Iran or India."

"Excuse me?"

"It's after five in Iran and India. My company has a distribution division in India. I know the time difference."

They clinked glasses and enjoyed their first sip, pleasantly spicy but not red hot.

"Yum. You can do my Bloody Marys anytime."

"Ever been to Bora Bora?"

Phoebe gasped. "Not on my salary!"

"There's a famous restaurant there named Bloody Mary's. Has a sand floor. Bar stools and tables that look like sawed-off palm tree trunks. When you walk in, there's a display table with all the raw fish, meat, and poultry available for you to choose for your entreé. You point to what you want and they cook it for you. Everybody who's anybody has eaten there."

"Oh, I would love a trip like that. Guess I'm a nobody."

"Don't think so. Hon, you'll get there someday."

As they bobbed around, they did catch and release for a few small fish. Finally, close to when it was time to head back, Phoebe hooked something bigger than a minnow.

"Hey, you got something, honey. Do you know how to bring it in?"

"No, help me! Oh my, I think I might lose it. It is pulling like crazy!"

Rockford wrapped his left arm around her and instructed her on how and when to pull and reel the fish in. She looked over her shoulder and gave him her best smile. She was so happy and excited. It turned out that Phoebe had hooked a nice speckled trout that Rockford guessed was over ten pounds.

"Looks like you got us dinner, if you want to stay."

Phoebe gave him a look of approval. "I think that's the best offer I have tonight. I catch 'em, you cook 'em?"

He laughed "But who cleans it?"

"Not me! I eat 'em - not clean 'em!"

60

Anthony Roselli was escorted into a small room enclosed by concrete blocks painted in faded beige. There was a small table and four folding chairs in the room and nothing else. His wife was brought into the room by a prison guard who said, "You got thirty minutes max." Joan and Anthony hugged each other tightly and both cried.

"Honey, I'm working on getting a lawyer, a good one. Maybe we can get you out of here."

"Anthony, I killed a man. There's no way that they're going to let me out of here. Maybe never." She continued sobbing and mumbled, "I don't deserve to be free."

"How did you know where to find that bastard?"

"He had a beef with Congressman Wilson down here. Hasbee told us. It was speculated that he tried to shoot him before. It was easy to find out when Wilson was making public appearances, so I bagged work a couple of other times thinking I'd find him. I just wanted to confront him. I wanted him to see me face-to-face. I don't know why. I just wanted to . . . I don't know. I had to confront him before I went nuts."

"I get that love. But how did you end up shooting him?"

She told her husband what had happened, how Sprout had tripped and the gun was between them. She instinctively reached for it and he came at her.

"So you fired his gun?"

"Yes."

"Did he do anything threatening to you?"

"He crawled toward me and reached for and grabbed my leg."

"OK. Sounds like maybe it could be self-defense. I'll get a lawyer, the best one I can find."

"But we don't have that kind of money. We can't afford this with me not working."

Joan was shaking her head and the tears just wouldn't stop running down her face. Her eyes were sad and numb-looking.

"We will figure this out. We are a family and we stick together. Don't you ever forget that!"

After changing the subject and settling down a bit, Joan asked about Roanna and if she knew what had happened. He told her that Roanna was there, at the jail, and that Roanna knew the little bit he knew before getting to the detention center. Joan started crying again. He told his wife that their daughter was very upset and maybe he should have handled it some other way, but he didn't know how or what to do. Joan was conflicted. She wanted to see Roanna, but her poor baby had been through so, so much and she didn't want to hurt her.

"Please make sure my baby knows I love her and I would never do anything to hurt her! This all just happened. It just happened. What have I done?"

After thirty minutes, a guard entered the small room and said, "Time's up." Anthony gave his wife a kiss and lengthy hug and said, "Hang in there; I'll get this taken care of." He didn't know how, yet.

Anthony was escorted out to the foyer where Roanna was waiting. "How's Mom?"

"As good as can be expected. She said she loves you. She is so, so sorry, sweetie."

They got into Anthony's car and he checked the location of the Durham Police Department headquarters and headed there. He and Roanna entered the building and asked the receptionist how he could get information about his wife's arrest. The receptionist, a uniformed male, made a few calls and said, "Detective Berwyn will meet you. Please have a seat." Anthony and Roanna waited fifteen minutes and finally a man came through a door and came over to them. He was tall, with slumped shoulders and coal-black, obviously dyed hair, and looked and walked like he was a hundred years old. "Are you asking about the Joan Roselli arrest?"

Anthony stood up and held out his hand. The man did not offer to shake hands. "Yes, I'm her husband, Anthony, and this is our daughter, Roanna. We wanted to find out what happened."

"I'm the detective assigned to the case, Calhoun Berwyn. Come inside to the conference room." He motioned with a big, awkward wave of his arm, never looking anyone in the eyes.

Anthony and Roanna were told that Joan would be charged with voluntary manslaughter and, when the investigation was more complete, perhaps murder. He said, simply, that she'd killed a man by her own admission. He brusquely ended the conversation by saying, "Better get a good lawyer."

Anthony and Roanna left the detective and headed for a motel, one of the less expensive chains in the Durham area. Roanna was visibly shaken. She was scared for her mom but also relieved that that sick bastard who hurt her couldn't and wouldn't find her and hurt her again. She felt guilty for feeling free again.

Anthony had no idea how long he would need motel accommodations. They checked in and settled into their room. Anthony told his daughter that they would go to Walmart or Target to get some toiletries and a change of clothing before deciding what to do. Roanna questioned her father why Sprout was at a function for Congressman Wilson. He had no idea really but, prompted by his daughter's question, decided to call Wilson's campaign headquarters before calling it a day. On the phone, after identifying himself, he was put through to Sid Freeze. Freeze acknowledged that Joan may have saved Wilson's and other's lives and invited Roselli to come in to see what could be done for his wife. Roselli insisted that time was important so Freeze told him to come to the campaign headquarters now. Less than half an hour away, Anthony and Roanna got back in the car and headed to Raleigh. "Honey, shopping will have to wait."

The headquarters, housed in a twelve story office building in downtown Raleigh, had expanded to cover four floors. They took the elevator to the fourth floor where the directory in the lobby indicated the campaign manager's office was located.

Wilson campaign posters were plastered everywhere. Anthony walked up to the reception desk, gave his name, and asked to see Sid Freeze.

"Mr. Freeze is waiting for you."

Sid came out of his office and greeted them, warmly shaking their hands.

While walking and leading the way to his office, Sid continued, "I am so sorry for what has happened. Joan is a hero in our eyes. Tell me what we can do for her and for you."

Pulling a chair out and sitting, Anthony said, "Mr. Freeze, we need a top flight lawyer, and real soon."

"First, please call me Sid. As soon as the shooting occurred, I talked to Congressman Wilson and he directed me to contact a first-class criminal defense lawyer here in Raleigh. Just in case your wife needed one, and I think she does."

"Sid, I'm not sure what we can afford, but I'd like to talk to him, or her, to see what can be done."

"It's a she. Her name is Carrie Woodbridge. She's a senior partner at Dawkins, Woodbridge, and Perch. She is sweet as sugar until she has a fight on her hands, then she's a pit bull. She might come across as a little quirky and out there, but she is gang busters when it comes to her client's defense. The congressman has friends who believe that the campaign owes your wife a debt, so any lawyer fees will be taken care of, if that's alright."

With awe and shock on his face, Anthony couldn't believe what he had just heard.

"That's more than alright. Way more than alright. You have no idea."

Freeze called the lawyer's office and set up an appointment for the next afternoon and gave Roselli the contact information. Freeze stood up, shook Anthony's hand, gave him his campaign card, and said, "Let me know personally what we can do for your wife. It was nice to meet you, Roanna."

61

Anthony and Roanna headed back to the Durham area to their motel but detoured to a Walmart to pick up some essentials, including a couple of changes of clothing. The clerk at the motel, when Roselli asked about additional shopping locations and restaurants, had recommended that they try the Southpoint Mall area just off the interstate. It was almost six o'clock and they were both hungry. Anthony and his daughter negotiated on good comfort food and a quick internet search pointed to Ted's Montana Grill just across the street from the mall. They settled in at their table; Anthony ordered a draft beer and a bison burger with cheese, bacon, grilled onions, mushrooms, and a fried egg, and Roanna ordered a chocolate shake and a burger with cheese and bacon.

"Dad, the lawyer- this is a good thing, right?"

"Yes, honey, considering the circumstances. Mom is going to need the best available. Let's hope this lady is it. We'll see."

Roanna started crying. "This is all my fault. I should have. . . "

"No, honey. You escaped when you had a chance. There's nothing that you did to cause this. He was an evil man. I'm sure that will come out." He gave her a long hug. The server delivered their food and, observing the scene, couldn't help but to have a strange look on her face.

Without her saying a word, Anthony said, "Thanks, everything's cool."

The next day, they had a simple breakfast at the motel and decided to just chill in their room until their appointment with the lawyer, which was scheduled at one. Roanna wanted to research everything and read everything. Anthony was reluctant because he didn't want her to read the articles about the kidnapping. The Rosellis had done a good job of shielding Roanna from the media part of her ordeal, and she was still seeing a therapist for PTSD and the actual trauma. Anthony didn't know what to do or what was the right thing to do, and quite frankly, he was tired. Roanna hadn't been a typical teenager since her kidnapping. She wasn't into her friends and social media and makeup and hanging out, so he relented and let Roanna do what she needed to do. After all, she was part of this family and she was old enough to understand, and maybe, just maybe, it would help her if she could help her mom.

They arrived at the address for Dawkins, Woodbridge, and Perch law firm early. It was housed in its own building near downtown Raleigh. They entered the building and walked up to the receptionist's desk. Anthony told the receptionist that he had an appointment with Carrie Woodbridge.

"Yes, she's expecting you. Let me show you to her office."

Anthony turned to Roanna and said, "Wait here, honey. You can sit over there and read a magazine."

"Dad, I am not sitting out here. I am going in with you."

"Roanna, sweetie, this is important and sensitive stuff that I really don't think you should hear or be part of."

With clenched teeth and a stern look on her face, Roanna said, "Dad, I am the reason Mom is where she is and I am going in!"

"Shhhh, okay, okay. Alright but be quiet in there and let me do the talking. Promise?"

They walked into an office and Carrie's smile went from ear to ear and her eyes seemed to twinkle. Carrie was medium height, with long hair with blond highlights, and dressed in a brightly colored blouse and skirt, not your typical lawyer's suit.

"Hey, good afternoon. My name is Carrie. Carrie Woodbridge. Please make yourself comfortable and have a seat." Carrie's office was equipped with a desk, which was piled high and haphazardly with paper, a desk chair, a love-seat-sized leather sofa, and a plush matching armchair. Anthony and Roanna sat together on the sofa. Carrie, full of energy- like, lots of energy- did not have a seat immediately, but paced back and forth in front of the Rosellis in a thinking posture, clearly lost in her own thoughts.

"I'm Anthony Roselli, and this is my daughter Roanna. We're here. . ."

"Yes, yes, thank you, I've been briefed as to what the police say happened. Give me the background. Why is it that your wife was in Durham? Have you seen her yet– since she was arrested? What does she have to say? Has she ever done anything like this before? I'm sorry, maybe too many questions. Let's get her out of jail. What can you tell me?"

Carrie stopped pacing, flipped off her Crocs. One of her black Crocs actually hit Anthony's leg. "Sorry, I never know where they are going to land. Ya know, why is it we wear shoes inside anyway? I find them so restricting, don't you?" Laughing, she continued, "Oh boy, it is a good thing I didn't have my court room spikes on!! Feel free to get comfortable and take your shoes off. We will be here for a while." The next thing they knew, Carrie was positioning herself on the floor, legs crossed, with her hands resting on her knees and her elbows pointing out. Anthony had a surprised look on his face and Roanna started to giggle. Carrie looked down and realized that her skirt had inched up way too short on her legs. With an "oh well" look and a crooked smile, she pulled her skirt down some and said, "Oops, sorry about that, I seem to need to be comfortable to receive important information, it's the only way I can think."

Roanna looked at her dad and said, "I like her!"

Anthony just didn't know what to say, so he shrugged his shoulders as to say, "Why not." All he could think about was how good it was to hear his daughter giggle.

Anthony tried to answer all of Carrie's questions, going back to Roanna's kidnapping. Despite Anthony's warning, Roanna actually talked and filled Carrie in a lot about her ordeal. Carrie listened and nodded her head and said "um hm" many times. The whole time, Carrie did not have a pen or paper in her hands.

"So, to summarize, Joan, your wife and your mother, was attacked by the dragon, slayed the dragon, because that the dragon attacked you, Roanna. A bad, bad dragon. Sometimes you have to slay the dragon."

Anthony sat there thinking, and Roanna said, "Yup, you pretty much painted the picture right."

"Okay then, we are on the same page." Turning to look at Anthony, she asked, "Do you or Joan own a gun? You know, *bam*." She made a shooting gesture with her hand. Both Roselli's jerked at her loud gunshot noise and pose.

"Um, yes, a handgun we got for protection after Roanna went missing."

"Wonderful! That's good, really good. Did Joan know where it was, you know, in your house?"

"Sure, of course. She and I took classes together and we kept it safe out of our three children's reach." Looking at Roanna, he said, "I don't think they even know that we have a gun?" Roanna just smirked.

"So, she did know how to use it. Good, good."

"Yes. Why is this a good thing?"

"If she intended to blow the bastard- oh, sorry for the lingo- away, she would have packed the gun. Is it still at home?"

"I suppose so. I don't know for sure. I left from the school that I teach at as soon as I heard what happened."

"I need you to find out. Anyone you know who could check right this minute?"

Roanna spoke up. "Dad, granddad has a key."

"Yes, honey, he does, I'll call him."

"Right now, Mr. Roselli. I can wait." She jumped to her feet. She circled the office as if the exercise would do her good. She turned her office phone around on her desk and pointed to it. Anthony used the phone and called his father. The kids were fine and he could get to the house right away. Expressing that it was urgent, he told him where to find the weapon.

"He'll head over right now. He lives fifteen minutes away."

"Okay, we can wait. In the meantime, your wife's preliminary hearing is scheduled for tomorrow. We'll waive the hearing and plead not guilty on self-defense and ask for bail. My office has already received funds to cover bail as long as it's not crazy." She said rhetorically with a smirk on her face, "Can Joan be trusted not to run?"

"Ma'am. We don't have money to run anywhere."

Anthony's father called back and informed them that the gun was in its case in Anthony's nightstand. Woodbridge smiled. "That's what I wanted to hear. Have him take a picture of it and then, right away, a photo of your house with the house number visible. You do have a house number, don't you? You don't live in the sticks, do you? No, no, never mind. I am sure you do not." Handing Anthony her card, she said, "My cell number is on this– have him text it to me. But not while he's driving," she said, tongue in cheek. Anthony relayed the instructions to his father. Carrie told the Rosellis when and where the hearing would take place the next day and for them to be there promptly and that she would meet them there.

The next day, Attorney Woodbridge met Anthony and Roanna at the courthouse. She explained that she'd given notice of her appearance to act as Joan's attorney. She would waive the preliminary hearing and enter a plea of not guilty due to self-defense. She had received the photos from Anthony's father and would show them to the assistant district attorney before the hearing. Getting her out on bail would be the main objective for the day. She chuckled. "A little razzle-dazzle should work. You guys stay here and let me go meet my client."

Once the proceedings started and the charges were read, the judge asked how was the defendant going to plead. Woodbridge stood, took a step toward the bench, waved her left arm toward Joan, and said defiantly, "Clearly not guilty, your honor. It was obviously self-defense. The Rosellis owned a gun; she knew where it was and how to use it. She did not have it. It's still safely snuggled away in her home, probably getting rusty. She came here to confront an evil man who did awful things to her daughter, not to kill him, but to find him and have him arrested. The victim's gun fell on the ground, they both reached for it, and she got it first. She's quick, your honor. This scumbag charged her and she shot him."

The DA objected the facts spoken that were not in evidence. The judge overruled him. When asked if the DA was asking for bail, he responded that the defendant should be remanded until trail.

"Remanded?! *Pulllease*, your honor, for God's sake, she actually saved lives."

"OK, Attorney Woodbridge, what do you recommend?"

"Free on her own recognizance, with an ankle bracelet or a lasso if necessary."

The DA said, "Your honor, that's outrageous. She killed a man."

At that moment, the judge noticed Congressman Wilson's personal attorney, Denny Spate, approach Attorney Woodbridge and whisper to her.

"Attorney Spate, I am not used to seeing you in my courtroom. To what do we owe the honor?"

"Your Honor, it is always a pleasure to be in your courtroom," he said with a smile.

"Indeed she did. One hundred thousand dollars secured." With that, the judge rapped his gavel to end the hearing.

Joan glanced back at her husband, wide-eyed and shocked, clearly thinking that they didn't have $100,000. He mouthed to his wife, "It's OK."

Joan was then escorted by a sheriff back to her cell looking over at her husband as she was led out. Carrie nodded her head to no one in particular and gathered up her briefcase. Walking out she put her arm around Anthony's back and said, "She'll be out before the sun sets. Call my office. Have her come in as soon as I have a couple of hours open."

She looked around and waited for Assistant District Attorney (ADA) Ross Pritchard to leave the courtroom. He was tall and young, one of the newer ADAs. She was surprised that he was assigned to such a big case. She snagged him as he walked by.

"Well, counselor, I thought that was a dirty trick to bring Attorney Spate to the hearing."

"Not my doing, sonny boy. Now, here's the deal: a clear case of self-defense. She had a weapon available and didn't bring it with her."

"Tell it to the jury, Miss Woodbridge."

Carrie then kicked him gently in the leg.

"What the fuck! Why are you kicking me?"

"You only have one leg to stand on. I was doing you a favor and kicking it out from under you. Take this case any further and I'll embarrass you and you'll be mopping the courtroom floors as your second career. No offense to janitors."

He stared at her and left without a word.

62

Cody got up early and told Phoebe he was going to catch a few waves; he was going to try a new spot that he heard should be good. In reality, he was going to head back down to Rodanthe for more recon after having a little morning delight with Willow. He asked her how her new client was doing. She told him that she'd gone out fishing with him to help him since he had an injured shoulder and that she actually caught a fish. Cody told her he was proud of her, gave her a peck on the cheek, and headed south.

Phoebe settled down to her first cup of coffee and checked her Facebook page, her computer on half her lap and Reef on the other half. While sipping her second cup, somebody started banging on their front door, almost breaking it in. Reef went crazy, running to the door, baring his teeth and making a mean growling sound. Phoebe went to the kitchen window where she could see who was at the door. The pounding continued.

"Cody, open the fucking door. This is Jayden. Don't make me break the door down!"

Phoebe went to the door and yelled, "Geez, Jayden, Cody's not here. What do you want?"

"I want the coin the prick owes me. Let me in, I know he's in there."

Phoebe reluctantly opened the door, making no effort to control Reef and gestured for him to come in and take a look. He tried to fend the dog off, but Reef was having none of it. The pit bull jumped up and got Jayden's left arm firmly in his mouth. Jayden struck him hard but to no avail.

"Get your fucking dog off of me or I'll shoot him!" Phoebe called for Reef and said, "Release, Reef." The dog let go but continued to growl.

Jayden hurriedly went from room to room, keeping an eye on Reef, and obviously didn't find Cody. His eyes were wide with anger.

"Where is he, girl?"

"He said he was going to a new spot to find waves."

"Yeah, right. When's he getting back?"

"No idea."

"Maybe I better make myself at home and wait for him."

"Maybe I'll call the cops. They'll find a comfy place for you."

"Shut your smartass mouth, bitch. I'm going. Tell that ball-less jerk I'll be waiting for him. Maybe I'll see if he's at his new girlfriend's." He gave her a knowing wink and left. While he walked to his car, Phoebe yelled, "Shut the fuck up and don't you ever come back here, druggie!"

After Jayden was long gone, Phoebe was unsettled. Her heart was beating and the adrenaline was pumping. She knew why this guy was there and was actually scared. He seemed capable of being violent. Then she started thinking about the last comment about a new girlfriend. Did he say that just to get to her, or did Cody really have a new girl?

She couldn't finish her second cup of coffee, her stomach being upset, so she decided to take a shower and get the day going. She had just finished toweling off when her phone rang.

"Hey Phoebe, got a question for you and don't hesitate to say no. I was thinking that I'd like to go out to a nice restaurant tonight and since I don't have a companion, I was wondering if you would join me. I wouldn't want to ask you to do something unprofessional. Well, maybe I just did."

Pausing to think, she responded, "Well, I don't have a better offer for tonight, so I would really like that. Do you want me to make a reservation?" The thought of a quiet evening would be a lot more pleasant than what just happened at her house.

"If you don't mind; you know the places down here better than I do."

"What time would work for you?"

"How about wine here first and dinner between seven and eight?"

"OK, I'll call you back. I'll have to wait until I can catch one of my contacts, may take me until noon."

"What are you doing this afternoon? I could use an opponent for chess or backgammon or cards."

"I'd be no match at chess. How about I get there around one?"

"Red or white?"

"Today, red. It's already been a doozy of a day."

Phoebe smiled and forgot everything that had happened that morning. She felt a tingle throughout her body. What was going on? Was she falling for this guy? She said to herself, *Just keep it professional. Yeah, right.* As she sat in the bathroom applying makeup, she started humming, looking forward to a real date. If Cody had a new girl, maybe she could have some fun too.

Cody stopped at Willow's apartment as planned and walked in without knocking. He said, "Willow, baby, you here? Are you still sleeping?"

She answered, "In here, if you are Cody."

He entered her bedroom and found Willow lying on her bed completely naked. He got instantly hard. Her body was fantastic, and he wasted no time undressing.

Cody jumped on the bed and Willow giggled.

"There you are. What took you so long?"

"Come here, my love, and kiss me."

"Ah, nothing like morning sex. Are you offering me morning sex, Cody?"

"I'll give you whatever you want, buttercup."

"Ohhh, I see. So, I am in the driver's seat today?"

"You betcha."

"Okay then, I would like your magic hands all over my body, please. And, maybe that hard thing you have there right next to me."

"I am here to serve! Where did you put that oil you like?"

"Second drawer down in the nightstand."

Cody grabbed the bottle and decided it needed to be warmed. He ran to the microwave and yelled, "I'll just be a minute." In his mind he was thinking, literally, just a minute, as he punched the numbers into the microwave.

Cody returned to the bedroom and said, "Okay, I can see this is going to be a nice long process, so tell me, front side first or back?"

With that, Willow smiled and turned over on her stomach and Cody groaned. He loved Willow's body and was really hoping to get started on the front. If he started there, he knew he could not hold out long.

With warm oil on his hands, Cody started from her feet and worked his way up massaging her right leg and then to the left leg. She had such amazingly strong legs. He loved her calves even though it was one part of her body that she did not like. *And those thighs,* he thought, *God she is beautiful.* As Cody inched up the leg to the bottom of her buttocks, she arched her back up a little and moaned softly.

"You really do have magic hands, Cody. You are so stinkin' good at that!"

Cody smiled and said, "Willow, baby, you are beautiful. You have magnificent legs and this nice plump and firm butt and these amazing back muscles. You have such a luscious and wonderful body. I just want to eat you up!" With that, he nipped her lower back and smacked her butt.

"Hey, you."

"Ya, I'm right here." He laid on top of her, rubbing his body against her, the oil helping to make their skin connection silky smooth.

Willow mumbled something low and Cody entered her from behind. They both moaned a sigh of satisfaction at the same time.

"God, I love you, Willow."

"Me too."

Cody continued his love making from behind until he couldn't stand it anymore and exited her and flipped her over. Their eyes locked, and the intensity and passion were so real and obvious between them, even with unspoken words. Cody had truly never thought he could feel like this for anyone. He thought he loved Phoebe, but Willow was different. He ran his right hand around her left eye and down her cheek to her lips.

She took his middle finger into her mouth and sucked on it without breaking eye contact but with a little smirk on her face. Cody smiled and said, "Shall we continue?"

Willow nodded, and Cody rolled on top of her. She intertwined her legs around his and they made slow, sensual, movements together until they both were satisfied and lying on their backs next to each other.

After thoroughly enjoying Willow's body and reluctantly leaving her bedroom, Cody used her shower and headed to Rodanthe. As it turned out, he was only fifteen minutes behind Phoebe. When he got to the town, he resumed his search for any clues. He now knew the new guy used a boat, but he didn't want to ask around just in case somebody could later identify him. He would hang around the few marinas there and just start an idle conversation and see what came up, but that seemed like a needle in a haystack. So back and forth he drove, looking for an expensive car or any other sign. He was finally down to the southern end of the town when he found what he was looking for, though not quite what he'd expected. In the driveway of one of the moderately sized beachfronts was Phoebe's car. This must be the CEO's house, and Phoebe must be there to deliver groceries or some other mundane task. He wanted to observe the house for a while, but his Kassie was easily recognizable, so he decided to park at one of the businesses on the main drag and walk back. He found a sand dune that was far enough away that Phoebe wouldn't see him when she left, but close enough that he could determine that it was her. He waited, no Phoebe. Two o'clock rolled on and he had to get back home to get ready before his shift at the Bistro. Her car had been there at least two hours. Apparently not doing a mundane task. For some reason he was perturbed.

Phoebe was greeted at the door with a glass of red wine and a clink with an audible "Cheers." She said, "Five o'clock already? I love this time zone." They both laughed. Rockford led her out to the deck overlooking the ocean and they pulled up the wooden chairs close to each other. The chairs had wide armrests, perfect for resting a glass in between sips.

"So Miss Phoebe, do we have a destination for tonight?"

"Yes, a nice place in the town of Manteo. It's in an inn right on the water where some large boats dock. The atmosphere is great and so is the food. Our reservation is for eight– is that OK?"

He smiled. "I'm not too busy today, so any time works for me. How long will it take to get there?"

"Thirty-five to forty minutes."

"You up to some competition?"

He brought out a backgammon game that was stored in the house and they played a number of games, splitting the victories. He then challenged her to a game of cornhole. He would be playing left-handed due to his sore right shoulder. Phoebe was very athletic and polished him off in three straight games. After the third win, Rockford wrapped his left arm around her waist, pulled her close, and said, "To the winner go the spoils." They gazed at each other. Phoebe reached up on tippy-toes and kissed him gently, and he returned the kiss with a lot more passion.

"Would I be out of line to invite you in for more of that?"

"I'm right behind you."

They both grabbed their wineglasses, he took her hand, and they went through the sliding glass door. Placing their glasses on the counter, Rocky turned and put Phoebe's hand up to his lips.

"May I?"

Phoebe smiled and nodded yes. Rocky kissed her hand in a very regal gentleman way and looked up into her eyes.

"Do you know how stunning you are?"

"Um, I think you have had too much to drink already."

"I think I know exactly what I am doing at this moment. No slurring of words here. Very clear headed."

"Well, then you need glasses."

"Oh, you women, always unable to see your beauty. Let's see if I can fix that for you."

Rockford took Phoebe into his arms and held her. She was a perfect fit for him. The right height, the right size, not too tall, not too short. Had he died and gone to heaven? He'd had girlfriends and lovers before, but this one, this Phoebe woman, was so different.

Rockford kissed the top of her head and Phoebe turned her face up to look at his. Gosh, he was handsome. So sophisticated and rugged at the same time. Older men always look so distinguished. He did not lack in that area. The way he dressed, the way he spoke, the way he'd treated her in this short time, like a real person, a real lady. Yes, she was happy with him and yes, she was going to do this, whatever "this" was going to be. She deserved some tenderness, some kindness.

Rocky leaned down and kissed Phoebe lightly on the lips and moaned, "You taste so good." He then deepened the kiss, and Phoebe responded as he had hoped and dreamt she would.

As they kissed and nibbled at each other, Rocky paused and said, "Are you okay with this?"

Nodding yes, Phoebe let Rocky take her by the hand and lead her to the bedroom. They entered the bedroom and he said, "Alexa, play Jim Croce." As the music began, he twirled her into a spin with her ending up in his arms, close, and they began to sway and slow-dance to the music.

"I hope this music is okay with you?"

"Mmmm hmmm."

The song ended and he began kissing her from her lips over to her ear and then her neck. Phoebe reached up and began to unbutton his shirt. *Is it the wine or are these buttons ridiculous to undo?* she thought.

Rockford slipped Phoebe's blouse over her shoulders and continued littles kisses down her neck to her collarbone. *Such a sensual spot,* he thought. His left hand wandered up to her right breast and she gasped at the tender touch. Her nipple was perky and hard and that did him in. He picked her up and laid her down on the bed. He kissed her as he undressed her. His hands were everywhere, and Phoebe was relishing in his touch. This was really happening and it was oh so, so nice.

Rocky undressed and laid next to her without being able to take his eyes off her magnificent body. He whispered, "So, so beautiful." With that, Phoebe couldn't take it any longer either and she rolled on top of him, straddled him, and with her body, found his erection and guided him into her. An explosion of feeling and passion had them matching thrust for thrust until both were satisfied and completed.

"What just happened here, Rocky?"

"Girl, you are an unbelievable lover. Shall we do it again?" Before she could answer, he rolled over on top of her. The second time was better than the first, if that could be possible.

After their breathing returned to somewhat normal, Rockford climbed out of bed to retrieve more wine. When he walked back into the bedroom with two full glasses, Phoebe said with full lips, red from lovemaking, "If you're trying to ply me with liquor, it's too late!"

"I'm just enhancing the afterglow." They clinked glasses and sat up in bed and enjoyed the beverage.

"Phoebe, I don't think I want another companion. I can't think of anyone that could outdo you in anything. Especially cornhole."

They both laughed and Phoebe said, "If you hang around a bit longer, I could teach you."

"That's not all we could do together. You are an exceptional lover."

Blushing, Phoebe said, "I bet you say that to all your lady friends."

He took her glass out of her hands and said, "Come here."

They just laid there and snuggled and spooned for a long time. Phoebe thought, *Yes, this is more than just sex, this is real love making.*

Phoebe drove them to dinner with the promise that Rockford would remain sober and drive back. They arrived just before eight and were shown to their window-side table. Twilight had shone an orange glow over the harbor. She ordered the stuffed flounder and he requested the seafood pasta. He added a bottle of chardonnay to match the seafood. The dinners were gourmet quality and neither yearned for dessert.

Rockford drove home. After a silent ride for ten minutes, he asked, "Is it possible that we can continue with this relationship as it's been going?"

"Do you want to keep going?"

"Yes– a no-brainer."

"For how long?"

"I'd say until one of us decides to end it. Phoebe, I'm married but separated. The divorce papers have been filed. I have two adult children, so there's no family issue. I'm not saying that I want or need any kind of commitment; I just want you to know that there won't be any crazed wife coming after either of us."

"OK, let's see where it goes. OK? I can't stay tonight, but we can talk about other nights."

They returned to his house and they both got out of her car. She walked around to the driver's side, kissed him hard, and said, "I'll call you first thing. Will you be on the boat or here?

"Probably a sunrise fishing expedition, but not for long. Text me– I'll keep checking my phone."

63

Cody now knew where his next target was. He knew he was a fisherman, and most fishermen that he knew went out early in the morning. So Cody decided he'd try the Black Pelican in the afternoon, early enough that he could make the pre-shift meeting. He had to be aware of the time it would take for him to get to the Bistro from Rodanthe. Phoebe left while he was still sleeping, so he had ample time to get the drone ready, including charging up the battery. He started to prepare his normal breakfast sandwich when he noticed a note on their second hand dining table. "Be home late– problem with a client. XOXO Phoebs."

He then took Reef out for his morning run, fed him breakfast, and packed a lunch for himself. When he left, he realized that he'd have to return early enough to take Reef out before his shift. Driving down to Rodanthe, he stewed, wondering what was really going on with Phoebe. Yeah, he was cheating on her, mainly because they were rarely together and the sex was becoming less and less frequent. Their careers were tearing them apart. He headed to a spot about half a mile north of the target house and took up position in a hollow in the dune line. He prepared the Black Pelican for flight as usual. Once in the air, he had it hover and then performed some simple practice maneuvers before sending it south toward Rockford's house. When the drone was across the beach from his target house, he could see a man sitting on the deck and there was a woman stretched out on a padded lounge chair. They weren't together or doing anything that was salacious. He took photos anyway. The woman sat up, put on a large wide-brim hat, and took notice of the drone. The man stood up and also watched. Cody decided to bring the drone back; he didn't like being noticed. Meanwhile the lady on the deck said, "Shit."

Rockford gave Phoebe an inquisitive look. "What's the matter?"

"Somebody's been using a drone to spy on people. Just wondering if whoever is flying that drone is spying on us."

"Why would that be a problem? Let them spy. We don't have anything to hide, do we?"

"No, I guess not."

Rockford stood behind Phoebe and kissed her on her neck and placed his hand from his uninjured arm on her breast, and she purred. "Let's go inside and get out of sight. I have a better activity in mind."

Cody brought the drone back and examined the photos. He could make out the man's face but not the woman's. They wore regular bathing suits. He wasn't even sure that he'd photographed Rockford. He really had nothing. He decided to move in case they came looking for him. He had not been careful to disguise where the drone had come from. He packaged up everything and got back into Kassie and drove south beyond the house. He didn't find a place that was suitable for him to hide while launching another attempt, so he pulled over to eat his lunch and decide what to do next. He elected to go home and try again the next day. Curiosity got the best of him and he cruised down the street next to Rockford's house to see if any cars were there. He confirmed that the Black Pelican had pictured the correct house and he easily recognized Phoebe's vehicle in the driveway. Again? Could that possibly have been Phoebs on the deck?

When Cody arrived home, he downloaded the photos onto his computer to get a better view. He still couldn't determine who the girl was, but it easily could have been Phoebe; her face was too shaded by her hat. He did get good shots of the man, and he decided that he would see if he could confirm that this was the client and, if so, what he could find out about him. He only knew, from Phoebe, that he was a CEO at some pharmaceutical company based in Delaware. He went to the internet and googled what he knew. There were a ton of pharmaceutical companies in Delaware. He was running short of time and Reef was making going outside noises, so he cleared his search history and dumped the photos the drone had taken.

The next day, Phoebe left Cody a similar note and Cody became convinced that the girl on the deck was Phoebe. What was going on? He resumed his search after he downloaded the photo of the man's face he'd taken the day before. Most websites had photos of their officers. He finally found a CEO that strongly resembled the deck photo. Pierce Rockford, CEO of Armondson, Inc. Cody read his brief bio. It mentioned that he was married, where he'd received degrees from, how many years he had been with Armondson, and a short list of his professional experience. He then googled Pierce Rockford and didn't uncover anything worthwhile. So the only thing he learned was that this Rockford guy probably had a lot of dough and was married. Good enough.

He headed back down to Rodanthe. When he arrived, he decided it would be best to find a place to set up his equipment that was farther from Rockford's house. He went through the launching process and got the drone in the air, this time flying fairly low over the ocean. He flew past the house and again viewed two people on the deck. The drone flew past the house and neither Phoebe, who was there on the deck again, nor Rockford, noticed it. Cody flew it four or five houses down then hovered the drone and turned back slowly at a higher altitude. The couple was together on the deck, but he couldn't make out what they were doing. The drone snapped away. He returned it to his location and checked out the images on his phone. The man, Rockford, was apparently applying sun tan lotion onto the back of the woman– a topless woman. Phoebe. "That fucking cheating bitch." He packed up and headed home, not sure what to do with his discovery. He had Rockford with a half, or possibly completely, naked woman who was definitely not his wife. But the woman was his live-in girlfriend. Now he really wanted to get this bastard, but what should he do about Phoebe? He couldn't let her know that he knew what was going on. He was pissed at the whole situation and really pissed that Phoebe was off the grid.

He fumed all the way home, and once he got there, he had enough time to download the photos onto his computer. No question that the guy in these photos was Rockford and he was all over the woman. And, that the woman was Phoebe. His Phoebe.

Cody would proceed the same way that had worked twice before. He really wanted to up the ante this time because now Phoebe was in the equation. Was he being emotional or doing good business? He'd go to work, see if he could crash at Willow's, and sleep on it. During his shift, his mind was clearly on other things and his tips reflected it. He didn't make any serious mistakes, but he wasn't his outgoing, charming self. When he had a moment, he stepped behind the bar and whispered into Willow's ear, "I can stay tonight, if I'm welcomed."

Willow gave him a side glance and whispered back, "When are you going to get rid of that real estate bitch?"

"Soon, real soon."

"OK, but you better not be shitting me."

Cody was still distracted, even once at Willow's crib. "What's going on, Cody?"

He told Willow what had happened that day and how he felt cheated on. Willow started laughing almost uncontrollably. "What do you think YOU are doing here with me, big boy? Seriously, looks like it's time to move on. Now, let me take your mind off of all of this."

The next day, back home, Cody reviewed the photos again. He'd go for fifty grand. Surely, it would be easy for the clown to get that. Then he'd split with Phoebe, shack up with Willow, and would have enough dough for the Endless Summer trip. That night he told Willow he had to attend to some business after work and would see her the next day. He composed and printed his note demanding the money, added a couple of photos, and ended with a new burner number and the words "This could stay buried if you are smart" and, of course, his pelican sketch.

He drove down to Rodanthe and parked Kassie in front of a closed gas station and walked to Rockford's house. The lights were out and two cars were in the driveway, a fancy-looking set of wheels and Phoebe's car. He stifled the temptation to piss on her car. He planted the envelope against the front door and got out of there. He would wait for the call.

64

Rockford asked Phoebe if she was up to another fishing trip the next morning and she said she would love it and was looking forward to it. They planned to get up and leave the house by six in the morning. That morning, when Rockford opened the front door, an envelope fell in and onto his foot.

"What's this?" he said.

"Shit, shit, shit."

"Why are you saying 'shit'?"

"Let's just take a look inside first."

Rockford opened the envelope, looked at the photos and the note, and started laughing. He couldn't stop. Phoebe couldn't imagine what was so funny. "What is it?"

"Somebody's trying to blackmail me with some photos. But there's no reason for me to want them hidden. They show me with a beautiful, younger, mostly naked woman. That would be you! I'd brag about what they show, not hide, no offense. So what was with the 'shit'?"

He showed the contents to Phoebe. She didn't respond immediately.

"Come on, lover, what's the matter?"

"There have been two blackmails here in recent months. Both were against clients of mine. My clients! There wasn't any connection between them other than they were my clients."

"What did the cops do? Obviously not catch the blackmailer."

"Neither target wanted any PR, so they refused to get the cops involved. However, I have a friend in the sheriff's office, a detective, so I called him and asked him to sniff around but to keep it on the down low. He didn't turn up anything concrete. He concluded that the photos were taken using a drone."

"Well we saw a drone a couple of times and these photos certainly weren't taken from ground level. What's your friend's name?"

"Clint Heaton."

He got Heaton's cell number and called him. He told Heaton he was Phoebe's client and what had happened so far. Heaton asked if he could come see them and see the evidence. Rockford told Heaton the address and said they would wait for him. Heaton arrived within the hour, introduced himself, and was a little surprised to see Phoebe.

"Miss Razario, you got here quickly!"

"I was very upset that this has happened again."

Rockford handed Heaton the envelope after Heaton put on a pair of gloves. He looked at the note and photos carefully. "Phoebe, do you see any resemblance to the previous notes or photos?"

"Yes, very similar."

"Who handled the envelope and its contents?"

Rockford said, "Just me."

"OK, I'll send these to the lab, check them for prints. We'll need to get you fingerprinted to exclude you. What are you going to do about the note, Mr. Rockford?"

"Nothing. I have nothing to hide and nobody to hide it from."

"Good. Let's see what he does next. I'll canvass the neighborhood to determine if anyone saw anything last night."

Heaton couldn't help but notice the similarity between the woman in the photos and Phoebe. "Who's the babe?"

"Ahh, she's a good friend from where I come from. She's gone home now," Rockford lied.

Heaton smirked. "Looks like a very good friend. Let me know if anything else develops."

Heaton went from door to door asking if anyone saw anything– a drone, a person acting suspiciously, anything. As he expected, he got very little. Rockford told him that the drone had come from the north, so Heaton walked up the beach to see if there was anything that might be a lead. He found nothing. In a resort area, people come and go. There are surfers, beach sitters, partiers, just about anybody. He again had very little to go on.

Heaton was convinced that Phoebe had something to do with the blackmailings, intentionally or by accident. He inspected the photographs with a magnifying glass. The woman with Rockford sure had a close resemblance to Phoebe. A coincidence? Heaton didn't believe in coincidences.

65

Heaton had saved the Bai Molokai Coconut bottle that he'd discovered on the beach when investigating one of the earlier blackmails. He decided to send that in to be printed to see if it matched anything on or in the envelope, if there was anything. He remembered back when he recovered the Bai bottle that Phoebe was curious about the flavor, as if she knew someone that drank Bai. She had told him that the only people who knew information about her clients were the ladies in the office and possibly her boyfriend. Now that he had an official case, it was time to retrace his steps.

He called Phoebe. "Hey Phoebe, Clint here. I need to interview the employees at Sea Dunes. The blackmailing is getting out of hand and I have an official case now. Do your co-workers know what's going on?"

"No, not yet. I better call my boss first, before you visit."

"OK, fine. I'll stop by this afternoon. Will you be there?"

"No, not this afternoon." A wave of anxiety was washing over her. Could it come out that she had her side business?

"OK. Who is your boss? I also want to talk to your boyfriend again. Cody is his name, right? You two are still together?"

"Sharna Curry. And yes to the questions about Cody."

Heaton knew that it would take a couple of days to get the fingerprint results back, but he could start the interviews. He dropped by Sea Dunes Concierge Realty after lunch, flashed his badge, and asked to speak to Sharna. The secretary, Whitney, took him back to Sharna's office and introduced him. Sharna stood up and immediately walked around her desk and shook the detective's hand with great enthusiasm. Sharna was attractive but not beautiful. Heaton right away liked her whole package, especially her bright personality and her short hair with blond highlights. Interviewing Sharna would be a pleasant experience, especially since Heaton was divorced and not dating anyone. He started out by outlining what he knew, including the two previous blackmails. Sharna confessed that Phoebe had not told her about any of this and that she, Sharna, wasn't pleased. Heaton asked her who would have access to client information including where they were staying. She informed him that all of the records were computerized but certain documents were hard-copied and kept in the office file cabinets. She, the secretary, and any of the agents could access any of the data. She added that there were five other agents, besides Phoebe, as well as drivers and handymen employed. Other than those who she specified, no one had access the client information. He questioned if there was any reason to suspect anyone, if anyone was acting in an unusual manner or was living high on the hog beyond what their salaries would allow. Sharna said she had no reason to suspect anyone and everyone was paid well, so risking their job and even incarceration would be hard to understand. Heaton thanked her and concluded with the possibility that he might have to come back to talk to the other agents. Her face lit up and she said, "You may visit anytime you wish, Mr. Detective," and she blew him a kiss.

Heaton got the fingerprint information back in a couple of days. There were prints on the note, other than Rockford's, and they matched the ones on the Bai bottle. Not much of a clue, but something. Finding a match would be his main mission.

Heaton received a call from Rockford. "I called the blackmailer using that phone number he left in the note. I couldn't not call. This is ridiculous. Anyway, he said time was running out and he'd have to go public if I didn't pay within three days. I told him to go for it; that I may even publish the photos myself. He told me not to fuck with him."

"OK, wow, I wish you had waited to call that number. I wanted to be with you. Shame you didn't record the conversation."

"Detective, in my business, I record all of my calls. I'll make you a copy on a thumb drive and get it to you. I'll be up in your area later and can drop it off. Where is your office?"

Heaton was delighted. He excitedly gave Rockford directions to his office.

Heaton called Max Ramsey. After the usual pleasantries, he outlined the blackmail issue. "I'm about to receive a telephone recording between the latest target and presumably the blackmailer. You have the ability to analyze the recording, don't you?"

"Sure. What format will it be on?"

"A thumb drive."

"Good. Overnight it to me and I'll get the geeks on it right away."

Rockford arrived as promised and gave Heaton the drive. Heaton waved him into his office and said, "Ya got a minute?"

Rockford nodded and sat down.

"Would it be possible for us to install a camera on the front and back of the house?"

Rockford hesitated to answer, not what Heaton had anticipated.

"A problem?"

"Well yeah, sort of." He looked at Heaton and then glanced down. "I lied to you about the girl. You see, it was kinda private. She was Phoebe. We've known each other for a while and, well, it just happened. She's the one in the photos. And it isn't my house, it's a vacation rental."

"Any chance Phoebe is in on the scheme?"

"Oh no. We care for each other. No. Not Phoebe."

"OK, what about the cameras?"

"It's okay with me if that is all the approval you need. Sure, go ahead."

So this gave Heaton food for thought, another little piece of information. Phoebe obviously had access to all the information for the three clients. But if she was in on it, why would she get friendly (or intimate) with one of the? The first two had live-in girlfriends, so Phoebe wasn't romantically involved with them. She'd seemed very upset about the blackmails when she consulted with him before, and certainly she wouldn't have disclosed what she knew to him if she was involved. There had to be a connection to Phoebe, but what?

Heaton called FedEx to pick up the thumb drive and overnight it to Ramsey.

He thought about Phoebe's office personnel. They were all women and the voice on the thumb drive was a man. Could be a husband or boyfriend of one of the agents, but why aim at only Phoebe's clients? Did any of them have a beef with Phoebe? He'd go back to see Sharna– not a bad duty, he thought. The next day he drove to Sea Dunes again. He could access the phone conversation between Rockford and the blackmailer on his phone. He walked into the agency and asked to see Sharna.

"Well, I didn't expect to see you so soon. Couldn't stay away from me, I presume?"

"Definitely not easy to stay away, but this is business again, not social. Sorry."

"Come on back to my office."

"Thanks for seeing me again. I was wondering, I have a recording of the blackmailer on my phone and I wanted to play it for you to see if you recognize the voice."

"OK, shoot."

Heaton played the conversation. Sharna asked to hear it again, and he played it again.

"There's something vaguely familiar with the voice, but I can't place it. Did I hear a dog bark in the background?"

"Yes, you're hired– Detective First Class! I'd like to play it to each of your staff, if that would be alright with you."

"Sure, not everybody is here, but you can try with those that are."

Three of the five agents other than Phoebe were in the office. Heaton played the recording to each one and didn't notice any body language that would suggest that any one of them recognized the voice or was involved. He thanked Sharna for permitting him to canvass the office and told her that he might be back to meet the other two agents. She said, "I'll be waiting for you." He really didn't think coming back to see the other two agents would get him anywhere, but it would be really nice to see Sharna again, for sure.

66

Jayden was waiting for Cody in the employee parking lot before their shift. When Cody drove in with Kassie making a racket, Jayden went over to the parked jalopy.

"Well, here's Mister IOU pulling into work. I'm losing my patience with you, Delaney. Time to pay the piper."

"We're done, Jayden. Done! I'm no longer a customer. There are other sources, ya know, in case you haven't figured that out. Get out of my face!"

"Better be careful who you deal with, smart guy. You could end up like Chump Change. Dead from some bad stuff."

"Chump didn't get any bad stuff."

"Oh yeah, what do ya know about what buried the guy?"

"Ahh, nothing really."

"Sounds like you know a lot, Cody. What do you know? Whose stuff was it?"

"Nothing, asshole, nothing. Get the fuck out of my way!"

"Maybe the cops should check into what you do know. No skin off my teeth since you're no longer a customer."

"Maybe the cops would like to know what you do for a side job."

"Delaney, you're not stupid. That shit would blow right back on you, man. Every seller needs buyers."

They both headed into the Bistro agitated. Cody was bummed that he hadn't heard from his latest target. He'd given him three days and the time was up. He decided to get it off his mind at work and make decisions tomorrow. Since his girlfriend, the bitch, Phoebe, was apparently sleeping with clients, he felt free to check with Willow to see if she was interested in an overnight. She answered with just a wink.

Cody got home the next morning and the house was empty as he had expected. He was still muddling over his argument with Jayden and worried that Jayden might actually carry through with his threat. He had to forget that for now and decide what to do with this CEO guy. He needed to turn up the heat somehow. He didn't understand why this guy wasn't responding like the other two attempts. With them he'd gotten quick responses, and quick cash. Why was this guy stone-walling him? He had to be rich. His profile said he was married. He decided to get all the information he could find about Rockford's wife. If he had to, he would actually show up, face-to-face, to let the guy know he meant business. He dug into the internet and pulled up enough data that he thought he'd be taken seriously. The light bulb went on in his head. Instead of showing up with information about the guy's wife, he would try a new tactic– he would call the wife and record the conversation. He was hoping to get something that he could use to scare the guy into paying. Cody dialed the phone.

"Mrs. Rockford, do you know what your husband is up to?"

"Go fuck yourself, whoever you are."

That was a lot more combative in a few words than Cody had envisioned. No sense playing that to Rockford. Damn it, this was getting too complicated and difficult. He decided to show up at the CEO's house, but only if Phoebe's car wasn't there. He would just play it all by ear.

67

Carrie Woodbridge facilitated the payment to a bail bondsman to release Joan. The donations that her practice had received for Joan's defense were staggering and amazed Carrie. When the deputy sheriff went to Joan's cell to tell her that she was free on bond, she collapsed into his arms and broke down sobbing. The deputy didn't know what he should do, so he hugged her, patted her back, and repeated, "It's all right, it's all right."

The Durham police had a quandary as to what to do with Sprout's body. They requested help from the Virginia state police to determine if he had any living relatives. The search produced a person who was indicated as being Sprout's mother, Edna Sprout Michaels, who lived in Petersburg, Virginia. Contact with her confirmed that she was indeed Donald Sprout's mother. She had not seen him since he graduated from high school and showed no emotion when given the news that he was dead. She'd divorced her abusive husband, Sprout's father, when Sprout was two years old. Sprout never really had a dad. She remarried three years ago and moved into her current residence. She expressed no interest in Sprout's final destination but did suggest a military burial. After going through months of bureaucratic crap, the burial was finally arranged.

Anthony Roselli met Joan at the jail and gave her a long embrace. Roanna followed with an equally long, but tearful hug. "Let's take you home and let Carrie do her thing." The trip home was quiet. There were certainly raw emotions in every corner of the car, but each of them kept their thoughts to themselves. Anthony called his dad and told him the good news and that they were on the way home. He asked his dad to bring Josh and Penny home in a couple of hours. His father was delighted about the news and also somewhat eased that he would be relieved of the babysitting duty. He loved his grandkids, but they needed to be at their home with their parents and sister.

Carrie Woodbridge drove to the Durham district attorney's office building, an impressive structure built next to the courthouse. She checked the directory and took the elevator up to the floor where ADA Ross Pritchard's office was located. She entered his office without asking for permission, just saying, "Knock, knock, this is your lucky day."

Pritchard looked up and said, "What now, Carrie?"

Carrie took her shoes off and pulled a wooden chair that was in front of his desk over to the side of the desk, right next to Prichard's chair. "We need to have a nice, friendly chat. Aren't we friends? I really thought we were friends."

"It's what I've always dreamed of, Ms. Woodbridge. What do you want?"

"I want you to drop the frivolous charges against my client! Then we can really be friends." She cocked her head, and her overly broad smile conveyed *wouldn't that be nice?*

"Well, I don't get paid to make friends with defense lawyers. Why would I drop any charges? And what client are you talking about?"

"Well, first of all, my client is a lovely wife and mother. A really beautiful person." Carrie gazed at a painting over his head and said, "Oh, I always love coming into your office and looking at that lovely painting. Such colors! Don't you agree?"

"Yes, Carrie, I bought it so I must like it."

"Well, yes, I suppose you would then. Anyway, I digress. Back to Joan Roselli. How about I give you four reasons for you to drop the charges: One, it was self-defense. Two, she potentially prevented a mass shooting. Three, my client is now a hero to a very popular congressman, soon to be senator. And four, I'll be defending her.

"Any one of these should motivate you to end this now. You've got a loser of a case against my client. You really don't want to be wasting tax payer money by shooting blanks at what would be a trial, especially with the media knocking down the doors. Pritchard, you must have better things to do than mess with this."

"You're pretty cocky, Ms. Woodbridge."

"Oh, please, we're friends now. I really wish you would call me Carrie all the time."

"As I was saying, Ms. Woodbridge, your client killed someone. And you expect me to go to my boss and say, 'Hey boss, this person killed someone, but it's a loser of a case and a PR nightmare, so let's drop it'?"

"Exactly. Why didn't I think of that? If you need to convict my client of something, how about, ummm, standing in a park without a permit or not paying the meter where she parked. We'll plead guilty to something like that."

Carrie stood up, put her shoes back on, and said, "Do yourself a favor and talk to your boss. Tell him Carrie sent you." She turned and walked out and said, "Call me!"

Pritchard knew that all of her points were valid, but would he look like a coward by making those arguments to his boss? Food for thought.

Carrie called Sid Freeze to bring him up to date, per his request. She told Freeze that she thought she would win if it went to trial, but it would take a toll on the Roselli family. Joan was very fragile.

Sid said, "Let me go behind closed doors and see if we can help. Nothing drastic, and we'll say you had nothing to do with it."

"OK, I know nothing." Carrie had changed the tone of her voice and given it a German accent. She giggled to herself thinking of the old show *Hogan's Heroes* and how Sergeant Schultz would say, "I know nothing."

Freeze called Congressman Wilson, who was now leading in the polls by sixteen percentage points, to report the latest on the Roselli case. Sid thought it might help to throw Denny Spate's weight into the mix. Wilson agreed and called Spate. Denny, who had never lost a case that went to trial, told Wilson he'd get right on it. Spate called the Durham County District Attorney's office and made an appointment for the next day on a "very urgent matter."

Denny Spate arrived early. He did not have to introduce himself to the DA's secretary. She told him that the DA, Ralph

Pastore, was finishing a call and would see him in a few minutes. His secretary watched the phone line light and when it went out, she waited to be buzzed. Pastore told her on the intercom to send Spate in.

"Well, Denny, I have a feeling I'm about to be told how to do my job."

"Oh, never, Ralph. I think you know a lot more about being a DA than I do. I just want to talk to you about the Roselli case. Do you know the background?"

"Not the details, that's ADA Pritchard's case."

"Please just indulge me for a few minutes. The victim here, Donald Sprout, has been stalking the congressman for months. We have reason to believe that he attempted to shoot the congressman a few months ago and was successful. The congressman and one of his staff members both took bullets. Both are OK now. Also, there is a warrant out for Sprout's arrest in Virginia for the kidnapping and gruesome abuse of the accused's daughter.

"Sprout was primed and ready to try an assassination attempt again in Durham. As I'm sure you know, he killed a policeman right before Mrs. Roselli distracted him. She did not have a weapon with her despite having one at home. She clearly was not there to assault Sprout, but just to find him to alert the authorities back in Virginia, to get justice for her daughter. Sprout lost control of his gun when he tripped, Mrs. Roselli reached for it and got it before he did, and he clawed at her. She was terrified for her life and instinctively pulled the trigger to defend herself. Ralph, there just isn't a case here. Let's stop inflicting misery on this poor woman. The congressman would deeply appreciate it if you dropped this one."

Pastore didn't say a word. He fumbled with a pen, turned his swivel chair toward the window to his right, stood up, and looked out. "Denny, I represent all those people out there. What would they say if we didn't press charges against a person who killed someone? What would they say? The backlash could cause riots."

"They'd say you had the guts to do the right thing. I do need to forewarn you, the congressman has decided to introduce her at his next rally– a big one in Charlotte. There will be a lot of 'THOSE PEOPLE' who will applaud what she did. Just saying, Ralph."

"I'll talk to Pritchard and my staff about it. No promises, Denny."

68

The Rosellis were trying to resume their former life. Almost impossible, considering everything that had transpired. Anthony had missed a couple of weeks at school and on the football field. The school had substitute teachers, of course, but it would be difficult for Anthony to get his mind back on teaching. His absence on the football field caused some mediocre performances. He was the defensive coordinator and his team leaked a few touchdowns in their first game, an unusual occurrence. Joan had not gone back to full time yet. Her firm, Johnson Travers, was missing her competent performance as administrative assistant. Her boss had talked to Anthony and understood the situation as best as one could. He made sure that Joan knew that they needed her back, but on her own schedule. She promised that she would resume full time soon. Roanna was suffering from as much stress as any teenager could cope with. She started back in school physically, but barely heard a word any of the teachers said. Her math teacher was concerned and sent Roanna to the counselor. After sessions over three days, the counselor asked Anthony to visit her in her office. She told him that Roanna needed intensive therapy. Anthony told her that Roanna was seeing a therapist once a week. The counselor said, "It's not working. She needs something more intensive, or someone different. You could lose her, Anthony!"

Their two younger children appeared to be unaffected by everything that had happened. Whether they were and just not showing it, or weren't, was hard to determine.

Sid Freeze called Anthony and talked about the rally in a week and said that the congressman would very much like Joan to be at the rally, to be introduced. He told Anthony that before they decided, they should consider that such an appearance might put a lot of heat on the Durham DA to drop the charges. Freeze would take care of all of the transportation arrangements and the whole family could come. Anthony asked when he needed to know, and Freeze said ASAP. Anthony agreed to call him back by the next day.

Over dinner, Anthony related his conversation with Freeze. Everyone listened quietly. Joan said, "No."

"Honey, I think you need to think about this. I can't put myself in your shoes. I don't know what you've gone through. But you didn't do a bad thing. You didn't. You need to convince yourself of that. You don't have a bad bone in your body."

"I think it will cause me more trauma, Anthony. And what about the kids?"

"I think you will hear how you actually were a hero. Your instinct was to stop what that animal was about to do. You yelled at a man, an evil man, who had a gun. That took courage. You could have run away from the scene without saying a word. Joan, I think this would be a good thing for you. I think the congressman wants to show his appreciation for possibly saving his life."

Roanna added, "Mom, you'd tell me to do it if it was me. Do it, Mom. Do it for me. I haven't told you yet. I'm so proud of you. I'm so happy that the awful man is dead. I'm not afraid anymore. I love you, Mom. You should do this."

Joan started to cry, and Roanna leaped up and hugged her and started to cry also. Josh and Penny looked at each other and then at their father. They didn't know what to make of all of what was going on. After things settled down, Joan said, "OK, I will agree to go, only because Roanna wants me to."

Anthony called Sid back the next morning and told him that Joan had reluctantly agreed to go and attend the rally. Freeze was delighted. He said that this would be an uplifting experience for the whole family and that he'd make sure that it would be an enjoyable experience. He asked Anthony if he wanted to fly to Charlotte or have a limo pick them up. The flight would be about an hour and a half and the drive would be a little over five hours. The event was scheduled for five on Saturday afternoon. Anthony told him he'd check with Joan and get right back to him. Joan thought the limo would be cool, but the two younger children had never flown before, so that would be an adventure. She told Anthony that either way was fine with her. Anthony called Freeze back and related the nondecision. Freeze thought that flying would be the most efficient method and he told Anthony that his staff would make all the arrangements. He solicited all the pertinent information for each family member. He asked when they could fly, and Anthony said it didn't matter. He would miss another football game coaching, but Joan was more important.

The next day Sid called back with the arrangements. A limo would pick the Rosellis up at their home at two on Friday afternoon and take them to the Norfolk airport. Their flight was scheduled to arrive in Charlotte a little after five, when they'd be picked up again to travel to their hotel, the Embassy Suites. Arrangements were made for the family to be escorted to dine with Congressman Wilson and his wife, Dawn, at the Capital Grille at seven thirty.

A hotel account would be set up to take care of any charges. They would be driven to the rally on Saturday and there would be a reception after the rally that the campaign would be very pleased if they attended.

The flight was without incident and the children especially enjoyed looking out the windows and getting served Coke. They were picked-up and taken to the hotel. Joan and Anthony had stayed in a few nice hotels before, but the kids had not. They looked around the open court area with their eyes wide open. Was this the way Dad and Mom traveled? They unpacked and dressed for dinner. A limo picked them up at seven fifteen and briskly delivered them to the restaurant. Sid Freeze greeted them at the reception desk and escorted them to Wilson's table. This was not the type of restaurant that a family of five typically ate at. The Rosellis had obviously never met the congressman. When Wilson saw Freeze and company approach, he almost leaped out of his chair and said, "The Roselli family, I presume." Anthony and Joan nodded. Wilson gave Joan a gentle hug, gave Anthony a firm handshake, and introduced his wife. Dawn handed each of the children a small gift as they sat down, lovely pink necklaces for the girls and a digital wristwatch for Josh. Wilson was as perfect a host as Dawn was a hostess. They facilitated upbeat conversations that all five Rosellis joined in. Wilson was clearly charismatic, and Dawn could charm the birds out of a tree. Wilson and Dawn ordered Bourbon Manhattans, Joan asked for a glass of chardonnay, and Anthony a scotch and soda. Dawn proposed a toast; "To Joan Roselli, a brave lady without whom we might not be here!" Joan smiled and tears welled up in her eyes.

The conversation continued to make the Rosellis feel very comfortable, and at one moment, Joan turned to Roanna, patted her on the leg, and whispered, "Thank you." They could clearly understand why Wilson was so popular. The server handed out the menus, and Wilson felt it obligatory to say that this was a campaign expense that Sid would take care of. It was important that he introduced the menu in such a fashion. Anthony and Joan almost passed out when they saw the prices. Wilson added, "My intention is that this is to be a happy, memorable evening. Please do not hesitate to order whatever you like. Dawn and I don't get to dine like this often. "I hope to host you all the next time we're in Washington, D.C." Dawn added, "Don't let him forget that invitation!"

The rally the next day was held in a large basketball stadium on a college campus. Every attendee was handed a "Wilson for Senate" button and bumper sticker. The event had been advertised for a month and the campaign had recruited a few celebrities to attract a crowd. The strategy worked; the arena was filling up half an hour before festivities were to start. An emcee began the program by asking all to stand for the playing of the National Anthem. Huge flags located on the rear of the stage artificially waved, being blown by immense fans at their base. When the crowd regained their seats, the emcee introduced the country singer who sat on a stool in the middle of the stage and strummed two of his top ten hits. The crowd went wild. He then sang a song he'd written for the event, extolling the wonders of a future Senator Wilson. He finished with a deeply personal plea to vote for the congressman. He was followed by a popular

NASCAR driver who actually drove his car onto the stage. A flag flew from the car's rear with the words "Wilson for Senate" on it. The crowd rose and applauded for over a minute. He stopped the car, got out, and took the flag off of the car and waved it as he crossed the stage. He didn't say a word, nor did he have to. Finally, Wilson was introduced. His speech, not the usual stump speech, was a folksy summary of the fond experiences he and Dawn had while campaigning across the state. It was personal and mesmerizing. He finished with what happened in Durham. He told how frightened everyone there was when they heard the first gunshot. He told how everyone ran or hit the deck. He related it to experiences he'd had in the Middle East. He then said that one person, a hero, had saved the day. She'd stepped in, confronted a gunman who had just killed a police officer, and took command of the situation. She may have saved numerous lives.

"She is here now. This brave, wonderful lady is here with us. I'd like you to meet her. Joan Roselli, please join me up here."

Joan had not expected this invitation; she thought she was just going to be a guest. Anthony stood up and offered a hand to his wife, but Joan shook her head no. But the crowd didn't let her get away with no. They started chanting, louder and louder, "Joan, Joan, Joan." She finally stood up, overwhelmed, and her husband escorted her up the steps onto the stage. She was crying by now, covering her face with her hands. Wilson walked over to her and gave her a warm, long embrace. The crowd, still on their feet, roared. Wilson stepped away from Joan, took a step back and stretched out his arm signifying that she was the main attraction, not him. She glanced back at him wondering if this was really happening. It was a touching moment. Having a sneaking suspicion that Joan would be uncomfortable addressing the crowd, the emcee whispered to Anthony to go to his wife and walk her off the stage. Joan had regained some composure and waived to the crowd as she walked off. Wilson led the applause.

The rest of the trip was uneventful. Their plane arrived in Norfolk around noon on Sunday and, with one more limo ride, the adventure was over.

Joan and Anthony returned to a normal work schedule. On Tuesday, Joan got a text message to call Carrie Woodbridge. Joan went to the ladies' room and vomited. She knew that she had to call Carrie but was petrified.

She called and the receptionist connected her to the attorney.

"Well, good morning, Joan. I understand that I'm talking to the star of the show! Wowee, I got reports that the audience Saturday loved you. So down to business. The ADA, a dumbass named Pritchard, called me and offered a plea bargain. You'll like it. Plead to disorderly conduct per North Carolina GS. 14-288.4. It's a misdemeanor. No fine, credit for jail time spent, nothing additional, and all other charges dropped. I have to officially ask you to accept the deal, but it's a no-brainer. It would be over. What do you say? Ready to end this nightmare?"

The phone was silent. Joan was dumbfounded and couldn't get any words out.

"Joan, are you still alive?"

"Yes, I can't believe it. Is this real?"

"You betcha. Carrie Woodbridge at your service. What do you say?"

"Yes, of course, I'll take it."

"Okay, we'll take it to the judge."

Joan immediately called Anthony and asked the school secretary to pull him out of class.

"Honey, are you alright?"

"Yes. I just talked to Carrie. They'll drop the charges if I plea to disorderly conduct, no jail time, no fine."

"Oh my God, Joan, that's wonderful. God bless Carrie. God bless Richard and Dawn. You said yes, didn't you?"

"Yes, honey, I did."

"I'll go tell Roanna. She needs some good news."

Anthony went to Roanna's classroom and knocked on the door. He asked her teacher if he could speak with Roanna for a moment.

"Hey, Dad, what's up?"

"They're dropping the charges against Mom. No jail. Mom will explain details tonight."

Roanna put her arms around her dad's neck and gave him a tight hug. Smiling, she returned to her class.

69

Cody spent the night with Willow but was restless and didn't get much sleep. Willow got up around nine and put a pot of coffee on. She sat down next to Cody and said, "What's the matter, big boy?"

"Got some stuff I have to do today. Just been on my mind."

"When are you going to dump that bitch, Phoebe? I'm tired of waiting, Cody. You can have one of us, but not both of us."

"Probably real soon, Willow."

"I heard that from you before. Are you still fucking her?"

"No."

"Better not let me catch you cheating on me. I better not see you with her!"

Just what Cody needed. A drug dealer was up his ass and threatening the cops, his caper was going south, and now Willow was hassling him. He mumbled under his breath, "Could the Endless Summer get any farther away?"

Cody was ready to drive down to Rodanthe but really didn't have a plan of what to say to Rockford. This would be a risky proposition. Rockford could recognize him and be able to identify him to the cops. Was it worth the risk? He decided to hold off until he could somehow disguise himself. He decided to drive north instead to Virginia Beach, where there was a variety of shops, to buy a mask and a pellet gun that resembled a real gun. He would go to Rodanthe the next day so equipped.

That night he strutted up to the bar, leaned over toward Willow, and asked, "Are we on for tonight?"

"No. When you dump that bitch and I verify it, we'll be 'on for the night.' Otherwise, enjoy sleeping alone, if that's what you do."

Jayden caught parts of what she said to Cody. He waited for Cody to head back to one of his tables and went up to Willow and said, "Hon, you know he's still banging Phoebe. He's getting his cake and eating it too. And he's under investigation by the cops. May do some time behind bars." He lied. "How 'bout me, Willow? You wouldn't have any competition with me. I'd be happy to fuck you every night."

"Then start by fucking yourself, Jayden." She walked to the other end of the bar. What Jayden said about Cody made her upset. Very upset.

Clint Heaton had fingerprints and a voice recording, but little else. He was convinced that Phoebe was involved intentionally or accidently, so, with the approval of his captain, he put together a request for a search warrant for Phoebe's apartment. He made three tries to serve the warrant with no success, so he called Phoebe's cell to tell her that he needed to get into the apartment. She was not happy that he had to do that.

"Clint, we're old friends. Do you really think I have anything to do with the blackmailing?"

"No, I don't. But there may be something in your apartment that could help us. Something that could give us a lead. Who knows, maybe your apartment is bugged. Anyway, I have to get in. Sorry."

"Okay, I understand. Sort of. There's a hose hanging on the side wall. There's a key stuck in the top of the hose."

Phoebe didn't realize it, but Heaton was standing outside the unit during the conversation. He easily found the key and let himself in. A dog barked and growled at him, but he had heard it from outside and was equipped with dog biscuits. He handed the dog a couple and Reef became his best friend. There was a laptop sitting on the kitchen table, but it required a password. He checked dresser drawers, kitchen drawers, closets, and finally under the bed. He found a drone. This seemed like the mother lode. He didn't know how to determine if it had been used to commit the crimes but knew an expert that could help. He opened the case and placed the drone on the bed and took a photo of it with his phone. The drone was labeled as a DJI Mavic. He called Josh, his friend with the store in Durham, who was a self-made drone expert. (Josh, as a favor for Clint, had studied a video that Heaton had previously sent him which was taken by a neighbor of one of the blackmailer's targets). Josh had identified the drone most probably as a DJI Mavic. Heaton sent him the new photo and asked him to check the old video to see if they were a match. Josh told him he'd call him back in five. When he returned the call, he pretty much said what he'd thought before– that they were very likely a match, but he couldn't say for sure. Heaton asked if he could tell if there was anything recorded in the camera, if indeed the camera could record things. Josh told him how to view any photos left in memory.

Heaton took the drone as evidence and downloaded the photos as Josh instructed. There were the photos that Rockford had given him from the blackmailer's envelope. The evidence was pretty solid; this drone was clearly the vehicle used. Since Phoebe was on the photos, it was also very likely that her boyfriend was the perpetrator, either with Phoebe's knowledge or behind her back. He decided to drive down to Rodanthe to Rockford's house to ask some more questions. He would corner her boyfriend at work that night.

He was not the only one on his way to Rodanthe. Cody had left earlier with mask and pellet gun in hand. He was ready to confront Rockford to make his threats. He parked Kassie in a parking lot about a ten-minute walk from Rockford's. He got close enough to see that Rockford's and Phoebe's cars were in the drive way. He said, *Fucking bitch*, to himself. He walked back to Kassie and decided to wait an hour and then walk over to the house again. When he did, Phoebe's car was gone and Rockford's was still there. He decided that now was the time.

Heaton arrived about an hour later. Both Rockford's and Phoebe's cars were there by now. He rang the doorbell but nobody answered. He waited and rang the doorbell again. Nothing. He turned the doorknob and it was unlocked. He walked into the hallway that led to the bedrooms, which were on the first elevated floor. He walked up the steps and quietly looked around. Then the shock: two dead bodies flat on the floor. He again yelled if anyone was home. He saw a light in the bathroom and found a man with his head hanging over the toilet. Apparently he had thrown up. It was Rockford.

Heaton stood in full view, with his badge displayed. "Did you call 9 1 1?"

Rockford did not look up but answered, "Yes."

"Good. Don't plan to go anywhere." Heaton called his office and reported the situation and that the emergency number had been called. Crime scene investigators would immediately be on their way. Heaton went back out to the living room to start his preliminary investigation. There was a gun on the floor about five feet from the nearest victim. Both victims were lying face-down and Heaton didn't move either one but did check for pulses. Neither victim had one. Heaton walked around the bodies and focused on the parts of the faces that he could see. He gasped, "Oh my God." He stood there and stared. He'd never investigated a homicide of someone he knew, someone that was a friend. Phoebe was clearly one of the victims, with blood oozing out from under her body. The other, a male, looked very familiar. Could it be Phoebe's boyfriend, whom he had met once? The detective wasn't sure, but he did look familiar.

Heaton went back to check on Rockford, who was now sitting on the bathroom floor.

"Just in case, I'm going to read you your rights. You have the right to remain silent. Anything you say can and will be used against you in a court of law. You have the right to an attorney. If you cannot afford an attorney, one will be provided for you. Do you understand your rights?"

"Yes."

"Okay. What do you know about this?"

"I just got home and found the bodies there."

"Where were you?"

"Over at the marina."

"What were you doing over there?"

"Checking the wind and how choppy the sound was. I was planning on a fishing trip."

"I walked by your car. I noticed it wasn't warm. Did you walk over there?"

"No, I took Phoebe's car. Her car was parked behind mine. This is awful."

"Anybody see you over at the marina?"

"Sure. I went into the store. Am I a suspect?"

"Just getting up to speed. Do you own a gun?"

"Yes."

"So is that your gun on the floor out there?" Heaton pointed to the living room where the bodies were.

"I don't know." Rockford stood up and walked out to the crime scene. He started to bend over as if to pick up the gun.

"Stop, don't touch anything."

Rockford looked at the detective and straightened up. "Oh God, this is awful."

"Is that your gun?" Heaton asked firmly.

"I don't know for sure. It looks like it."

"Would I find your fingerprints on it?"

"Of course, if it's my gun."

"Do you know who the guy is?"

"No idea."

"Have a seat and don't touch anything." Heaton did a cursory check of the room on the second floor. The only thing of interest that he saw was a mask and what appeared to be a pellet gun on the kitchen floor. He thought both items were really odd and must have something to do with what happened. He also found a plastic bag on the floor with two muffins in it. He went back out to where Rockford was sitting and asked him what he knew about the items. He shook his head.

When the crime scene boys arrived, they did their checks and bagged the gun as well as the items in the kitchen. Heaton got a better look at the victims' faces. One clearly was his friend Phoebe. The other he now thought he recognized as her boyfriend. With his gloved hand, he pulled out a wallet from the man's back pants pocket. It was Cody Delaney, who Heaton believed owned the drone and probably was the blackmailer. What was he doing here? Heaton told Rockford that he needed to come with him for questioning. Rockford asked, "Do I need a lawyer?"

"Up to you. Might be a good idea."

Rockford asked to make a couple of calls before they left; Heaton agreed if it didn't take long. Rockford called his personal lawyer up in Delaware and briefly told him the circumstances. The lawyer told him that he didn't handle criminal cases and couldn't do anything in North Carolina. He would make some calls. He asked where the cops were going to take him. Rockford checked with Heaton and relayed the information to the lawyer. The lawyer told him not to say a word and he would get a top-notch guy there as soon as possible.

The lawyer called a friend who told him that the best criminal practice he was aware of was located in Raleigh. He would close the loop and get one of the attorneys to come over to Dare County to meet Rockford as soon as possible. Rockford told Heaton that he wasn't going to say anything further until he talked to a lawyer and would have a lawyer present. Heaton asked when that would be, and Rockford replied that he didn't know but he'd call as soon as he had counsel. Heaton told him to stay in the county but that he had to leave the house, as it was a crime scene. He warned him not to go back home.

70

Later that afternoon, Rockford received a call from a firm identified as Dawkins, Woodbridge, and Perch from Raleigh. He was then connected to an attorney who said her name was Carrie Woodbridge, the same Carrie of Joan Roselli fame.

"Tell me what's going on, Mr. Rockford."

"I rented this house in Rodanthe. Rented it from this lady named Phoebe Razario. I went out to the local marina and came back to the house on Wednesday morning and two people were lying on the floor, apparently shot, maybe with my gun. One of them was Phoebe. I'm afraid I might get charged with the murders. I. . ."

"Whoa, hang on, partner. Nothing more. Do you want me to represent you? Really, who wouldn't?"

"Yes, I've heard you're good."

"That's the rumor I've been spreading! Seriously, we need to meet. Who is the investigator?"

"A detective named Heaton, from Dare County."

"Got it. I'll be over there tomorrow morning. We'll meet at an office of a lawyer I know over there. I'll want you to hire him also– good to have a local. I'll text you the address. Ten o'clock sharp."

Rockford had rented a motel suite in Nags Head, north of Rodanthe. The meeting place was in the town of Kitty Hawk, about ten miles farther north. He arrived at the designated lawyer's firm's building fifteen minutes early. He was nervous. He introduced himself to the receptionist. In a few minutes, a lady, seemingly beaming with happiness, came through the door leading to the offices, stretched out her hand, and said, "You must be Mr. Rockford." He nodded and before he could say anything, she reached down and grabbed his hand and said, "I'm Carrie Woodbridge. You're cute. Come into this legal kingdom." She led him to a conference room and directed,

"Make yourself comfy while I get the boss. But don't sit on the table– they frown on that here."

Carrie returned with a lawyerly looking man in a dark gray pin-striped suit and a navy-blue tie. Carrie introduced him. "Mr. Rockford, this is Graham Michaelson. You are sitting in his conference room, which he has loaned me at no charge. I would like to hire him as second chair. He is the best local criminal attorney for miles around." Michaelson smiled and said, "Obviously my PR people are good!"

Carrie said, "He's not cheap, nor am I for that matter!"

"That's fine, you're hired. Please feel free to call me Pierce."

"Good. Lay out the whole story, every detail. Start by telling us your background and why you're here on the Outer Banks."

Carrie, as was usual for her, kicked off her shoes. Rockford explained what his professional occupation was and what enemies he had, that he was separated from his wife, and how he rented from Sea Dunes Concierge Realty. He continued to expand on this year's vacation. He'd always had Phoebe as his agent. He had gotten a note about female companionship and nobody was available from Phoebe's source. He told them about striking up a relationship with Phoebe and that one thing led to another.

"Phoebe and I were out on the deck. We saw a drone fly by and I didn't think anything of it. But Phoebe said, 'Shit.' She explained that someone was spying on vacationers. I told her I could care less, that I had nothing to hide. The next day, a drone flew by again. We were out on the deck and Phoebe was, let's say, without clothes. She wanted an even tan. Then we found an envelope with photos of Phoebe and me on the deck, the day Phoebe was naked."

"Did you bring that note?"

"No, I called the cops and gave it to them."

Michaelson asked, "What did the note say?"

"Something like, this could go away if I paid a bucket of money."

"And did you just ignore the threat?"

"Well, sort of. I called the number on the note."

Carrie asked, "Did you tell him to shove it up his ass?"

"In essence."

Michaelson said, "Wish you recorded the conversation."

"I did. Let me play it for you."

The two lawyers listened to the recording. The quality was good. They heard the blackmailer threaten to go public with the photos if Rockford didn't pay up in three days and Rockford telling him to go for it, even saying he might publish the pictures himself.

Michaelson said, "We should get this to the cops."

"I already did."

"Okay, anything else noteworthy before the day of the murders?"

"No, not really."

Carrie then directed, "Give us the dump. Everything that happened that day."

"Phoebe stayed overnight. I left early to check the boat she rented for me at the marina in town. She was still sleeping. I took her car because it was parked behind mine. I went into the marina store to buy some bait and ended up talking to some of the locals about the fishing conditions that morning. Got a cup of coffee and a couple of muffins. I took the bait to the boat and made sure everything was ready to go. Met another boater while walking past the piers and he showed me his boat, a nice Boston Whaler. I called Phoebe to make sure she was awake and there was no answer, so I headed back to the house. Walked in and called her, but silence. I found the bodies as soon as the living room was in sight, called 9 1 1, started to cry, and went to the bathroom to vomit. I was there when the detective came in. I don't know how he knew to get there. He asked if I called 9 1 1."

"Do you know who the other victim was?"

"No idea."

Michaelson asked, "Who was the detective?"

Rockford got his wallet out and handed the attorney the detective's card.

"Heaton. He's okay. What did you tell him?"

"Just that I was over at the marina and came in to find the bodies."

"Do you have a gun?"

"Yes. There was a gun on the floor near the victims. It looked like my gun."

Carrie asked, "Did you notice anything else? Anything out of place?"

"No, but the detective found a mask and a pellet gun on the kitchen floor."

The two lawyers looked confused. Carrie asked, "He found what? Were they yours?"

"A mask and a pellet gun. And no, they don't belong to me. I never saw them before."

Michaelson said, "Okay. Here are the rules. First, you don't say anything to anybody unless Miss Woodbridge or I say it's okay. Two, if you remember anything else, tell us immediately. Three, we need to meet with Heaton. Again, not a word unless we say it's okay. Carrie, we'll need a private detective. We have a good one that works for the firm."

Carrie asked, "Is that okay with you, Mr. Rockford?"

"The more, the merrier!"

71

Carrie called the number on Heaton's card and the detective answered. She identified herself and said that she and Michaelson were representing Rockford.

"I need to have him come in for questioning. Like now."

"Okey dokey. I trust that Mr. Michaelson knows where to find you?"

"You bet."

"See you in a few."

She said to Rockford and Michaelson, "Let's pack it up and see what the authorities have to say."

They took Michaelson's Lexus and made the thirty-minute drive to Heaton's office. Not much was said during the trip, both lawyers having their game faces on. When they arrived, Heaton introduced himself to Carrie who said, "Clint, may I call you Clint? You're cute." Heaton wasn't sure what to make of her.

"Graham, Miss Woodbridge, Mr. Rockford, please have a seat in our conference room."

Carrie said, "Where's the bright light that you shine on the interrogatee?" Heaton did not smile.

Their visit with Heaton did not go well. At first, he asked if it was alright to record the meeting. Carrie said, "That would be dandy. You could place my picture on your desk." She got no response from Heaton. Heaton told them that the weapon was indeed registered to Rockford. They hadn't had time to match the bullets to determine if it was the murder weapon, but would have that information in a couple of days. The coroner had removed the bullets from the victims and sent them to the ballistics lab.

Carrie asked, "How do you know it was a double murder? Couldn't it have been a murder–suicide?"

"Miss Woodbridge, we're still investigating. We're checking the entry angles, any powder burns, and so forth. But our preliminary conclusion is a double murder."

"Mr. Rockford, did you know the male victim?"

"No."

"We're almost certain that he was the man trying to blackmail you. Sure you never met him?"

Carrie whispered something in Rockford's ear. He answered, "No, I'm pretty certain I never met him."

"He was Miss Razario's live-in boyfriend. He shows up at your house where you and his girlfriend are shacking up. He must have been pissed. Plus, if he was the blackmailer, he had photos of you and his very much undressed girlfriend. He must have been really pissed." No one said a word. "This is what it looks like to me, Mr. Rockford. You were getting it on with this guy's girlfriend. And, in addition, he tries to blackmail you and you blow him off. He comes to confront you. He gets there and, lo and behold, there's Miss Razario's car in the driveway. Now he's ready to do some damage. The door's unlocked so he comes in and comes at you, like a maniac. You grab your gun to protect yourself. He tells you that you're a sap; Miss Razario was in on the blackmail scheme. He comes at you and you defend yourself and pull the trigger. He goes down. She rushes toward the victim, not you, and instinctively, you shoot again. Sound correct, Mr. Rockford?"

Carrie said, "Pierce, don't say a word. Detective, that's one hundred percent speculation. I haven't heard any evidence to substantiate any of that."

"Well, we have enough for now, Miss Woodbridge. Better book a motel." Heaton then announced that Rockford was under arrest for two counts of second-degree murder and they would be taking him to the magistrate. Rockford now looked panicky, and Carrie hugged him and said not to worry. "They just want to keep you nearby. Is there anyone we should call?"

"Just my lawyer up in Delaware. Have him notify the company. Have him tell them that I'm not guilty and I'll be back. He can also send you some money."

72

Carrie and Graham headed back to his office.

Carrie said, "Looks like I'll be here for a while. Got any suggestions as to where to stay?"

"Our firm owns a couple of condos here on the beach. You're welcome to stay in one as long as you like. We have them for business purposes and to entertain special clients. It's out of season anyway, so not much demand. Will it be just you?"

She winked and giggled. "Yes, got anything in mind?"

"No. You are a catch, but I'm very happily married."

"Let's get your PI in here and get him started."

"I'll have my secretary call him. By the way, her name is Dory. There's nothing she can't do. Kinda a Wonder Woman."

His investigator wasn't available until the next morning, so Graham escorted Carrie out to Dory's office, which he referred to as the "Central Command," and introduced them. He asked Dory to get the key card programmed for one of the condos and to acclimate her to the residence. Dory handed Carrie a form, which was, in essence, a shopping list.

"Just mark whatever you need on this list and we'll send it over. There's everything in the unit that you would otherwise need– bed linens, towels, kitchen utensils, you name it." Carrie marked a number of items and thanked Dory.

Graham came back into Central Command and said to Carrie, "My wife says we're free tonight. Wish to dine with us? No shop talk, though."

"Sure, that sounds dandy."

"Dory, would you get us a table for three at the Atlantic Bistro? Say at seven? Carrie, it's just up from here on the beach road."

Carrie arrived at the restaurant a few minutes early and decided to wait at the bar after telling the receptionist that she was part of the Michaelson party. The bartender, a man, came over to her and asked her what she'd like. She ordered a lemon drop martini and asked about the odd decorations– black linens draped everywhere.

"We had a death in our Bistro family."

"Sorry, what happened?"

"Our most experienced server, nice guy named Cody, murdered down in a town called Rodanthe."

"Oh my. Was he really close to anybody here?"

"Yeah, our head bartender, Willow. She hasn't shown up since it happened. Can't blame her, you know."

Graham and his wife, Amelia, arrived and found Carrie at the bar. After introductions, the hostess escorted them to their table, a cozy booth next to a window with a view of the beach. Carrie opened the conversation. "Well, this is nice. But you'll both have to excuse me– I need to break the 'no shop talk' rule for just a sec. Notice all the black drapery? One of their servers was murdered in Rodanthe. That had to be the guy they found in Rockford's house, don't you think?"

Graham said, "Sounds pretty likely. I'll have our PI start here. By the way, his name is Spencer Midgett. We're scheduled to meet with him tomorrow morning at nine."

The next day, Carrie arrived at Graham's office early. She sat down in front of Dory's desk and said, "Looks like you'll be seeing me here for a while. The condo is spiffy. How long do I have before you kick me out?"

"It's yours until we get a not guilty."

"That's what I like, a positive crystal ball!"

Graham arrived, as did Spencer Midgett. Midgett had local roots. His family dated back for centuries on the Outer Banks. He was smooth, handsome, clean-cut but with a Don Johnson type of beard, very likeable by both men and women, and could talk to anyone. The two lawyers and Midgett went to the conference room and Carrie started the discussion. First, she summarized the crime scene as much as she knew and, then, Rockford's version of the events. She ran through what Detective Heaton had rattled off to Rockford in her presence, highlighting that his speculative version was completely different from Rockford's. Midgett listened without saying a word. Graham said, when Carrie was finished, "Spence, where do we go, in your opinion?"

"OK, so let's assume it's Rockford's firearm. We need to find out whose fingerprints are on it. If it's only his or if it was wiped clean, we've got a problem. If there are someone else's prints on it, the best they've probably got is circumstantial evidence and we have reasonable doubt."

"Miss Woodbridge, do you think he did it?"

"No, he seems sincere, but what do I know?"

"Let's assume our client is innocent. We need to verify his story. I'll canvass the marina down there and talk to the neighbors. I'll see what they know. We need to know if the cops dusted the doorknob and anything else inside that someone else might have touched. By the way, was there a driveway?"

Carrie answered, "Packed sand, no concrete or macadam."

"I'll see if they recorded the tire tracks. What do we know about the vics?"

Carrie said, "Some about her, wild guess about him. Her name is Phoebe Razario. She was an agent with Sea Dunes Concierge Realty. Probably was Rockford's rental agent. Rockford got to know her really well, in the biblical sense." Carrie broadcast a shit-eating smile. "Apparently they developed a relationship that was more than just business. As I mentioned, the cops thought the dead guy was her live-in boyfriend. At least before Rockford stepped in. They also believe he was blackmailing Rockford and had done it previously– all to Razario's clients. Last night, we dined at the Atlantic Bistro, which was draped in black. I was told that a server there had been murdered in Rodanthe. Dum de dum dum. Also, this guy was really close to a female bartender who has been AWOL since the murder."

"What was his name?"

"Don't know. That's for you to find out!"

Spence said, "OK, I'll get started. I'll do the canvass down in Rodanthe, check with the cops to see what they got on prints and go from there. Let's get together in three days and compare notes."

73

Midgett drove down to Rodanthe. He stopped first at the beach house that Rockford had rented. It was decorated with yellow crime scene tape. He walked around to the beach side and then back around to the front. He needed to get a feel for the lay of the land. He took photos from every angle. He noted numerous tire tracks in the sand driveway and snapped shots from every angle. He then canvassed the neighboring house to get any observations that the neighbors might have had. One woman four houses north said she saw a lady go into Rockford's house the morning of the murders and couldn't remember the time or what she looked like. She did not hear any gunshots. He then drove to the nearby marina and talked to the clerk in the marina store and any boaters that he could approach out on the piers. He took notes– lots of them.

Next stop was the county sheriff's office to speak to Detective Clint Heaton. Spence knew him well, and Heaton liked the detective. Midgett often shared information with Heaton, making Heaton's job easier. Spence sat down across Heaton's desk from him and let him know why he was there. Heaton told Midgett that ballistics had confirmed that the bullets came from the weapon found at the scene and that the gun was owned by Rockford. He confirmed that the female victim was Phoebe Razario and the male victim was Cody Delaney, Razario's live-in boyfriend and the apparent blackmailer. He added that there were three sets of prints on the weapon, one of which was Rockford's. The other two he had not identified. Midgett requested a copy of the prints and Heaton told him that he would email what they had to him. He further stated that the mask and pellet gun found at the scene had the male victim's DNA on them. Heaton believed that the shooter was right-handed and had fired at fairly close range. Other than that, he had nothing to disclose.

Spence added nothing to the discussion, but he told Heaton that he would let him know if he uncovered anything significant. He didn't really plan on doing that unless directed by Michaelson.

Carrie and Michaelson had appeared with Rockford in court and, as expected, Rockford was remanded. They explained ahead of time that considering the severity of the alleged crimes and the fact that he was an out-of-state resident, there would be little chance of bail. The lawyers knew that they would have to find a way to create reasonable doubt, but how? They had to find someone who had the opportunity and motivation to commit the crimes to somehow show that Rockford couldn't have done it.

Midgett's problem with getting eyewitnesses was that most of the beach houses were rentals and, since most of them were weekly, people that had been there the morning of the murders were gone. The five houses to the north and to the south were listed for rental by four different real estate companies. So Midgett visited each one, flashed his PI credentials and a big smile, and managed to get the names and telephone numbers for the renter of each nearby house. Ten contacts later, some of which took days to complete, and he learned a few things. The police had not contacted any of them by phone. They did catch three of the renters while they were there, but had not gone the extra mile that he had. Three people, from two houses to the south and the one next to Rockford's house to the north, heard the gunshots. The witnesses all said the pops were close together. One person heard a woman speaking loudly before the shots but no sounds afterward. None of them looked out immediately, and none of them saw anyone coming or going. That was not a good sign for Rockford.

Midgett next visited the Atlantic Bistro, again flashing the credentials and the smile. He met the hostess, Amelia, and asked about Cody– did he have any enemies, anyone who would do this to him? She made him aware of some issues he had with Jayden, a fellow employee, explaining how one night they'd gotten physical and Cody got the worst of it. He learned that this Jayden guy was still an employee but wasn't scheduled that night. She also knew that there was something going on with a bartender named Willow. She suspected that they were more than friends, but she didn't actually know anything to support her suspicions, just observations during work hours. She explained that Cody had a live-in girlfriend named Phoebe and Phoebe occasionally made reservations for clients. She had only met Phoebe once as best as she could remember. Spence asked if Willow was there and Amelia waved toward the bar.

He sat on one of the bar chairs and Willow came over and ask what she could get him. He asked for an IPA on tap. When she returned, he said, "I'm here on business. Got a minute?" He glanced at the otherwise empty bar.

"Sure. Looks like you've got me all to yourself."

"I'm an investigator. I'm investigating the murder of Cody Delaney and his girlfriend. I hear you and Cody were tight. What can you tell me?"

Willow stood there, speechless, and started to tear up. "Not much. Cody was real sweet. I liked him a lot."

"Rumor has it that you more than just liked him."

"I don't know what you mean."

Spence smirked. "Come on, Willow, you know what I mean."

She lied, "We'd sit and have a drink or two after work, but that was it. He had a girlfriend, you know."

"Heard he had a problem with a guy named Jayden, a server here. Know anything about that?"

"Rumor has it that Jayden deals. He and Cody had some real blow outs, I'm not sure about what, but once Jayden beat the shit out of Cody. After that, they just glared at each other. I think Jayden still had a beef with Cody."

"Know how I can find this Jayden?"

"No. I'm sure the Bistro must have his address. I don't know when he's scheduled to work."

"You're a pretty girl– got a boyfriend?"

"Are you applying?"

"No, remember, detectives ask questions."

Spence finished his beer, left a tip, and waved to Willow. There was something strange about her demeanor, but he couldn't put his finger on it. He found Amelia again and asked for information on Jayden. She said that she didn't have any information but gave him the manager's number. Midgett called and asked how he could get in touch with Jayden. The manager hemmed and hawed and thought he couldn't legally give Spence any personnel information. Spence told him he'd get a subpoena for all sorts of records. That threat was enough for Spence to get what he needed. He also got the other employees' addresses.

74

Spence paid a visit to Jayden's address. It was a small house on the west side of the mail road, a so called "beach box." He knocked on the door and a twentyish girl answered, wearing a tight halter top and short, short jeans. She looked at a little spacey.

"Yeah?"

"Jayden here?"

"What's it to you?"

Midgett flashed his ID and said, "Get me Jayden."

She disappeared after slamming the door. Spence waited. In a minute or two, a young guy appeared wearing jeans and looking completely unkempt.

"Can I help you?"

"You Jayden?"

"No, I'm the president of the United States."

Spence showed him his ID and Jayden took it and looked at it closely, then handed it back to Midgett.

"I'll take that as a yes. I got some questions, maybe you can help me."

"Why would I want to help you?"

"Maybe I can keep your ass out of jail. I understand you knew Cody at the Bistro. Understand you knew his girlfriend also, both of whom were murdered."

"Worked with the dude, that was it. Didn't know the girl."

"Not what I hear. Heard you had an ongoing beef with Cody. Got nasty."

"Don't know who told you that. We were cool."

"We both know that's bullshit. Can't help you if you lie to me."

"OK, we had a business misunderstanding once. Cody welched on paying me for, ahh, let's say, services rendered. We settled it."

"By you killing him and his girl?"

"Fuck you, asshole. Why would I do that?"

"You tell me."

The door slammed shut. If Spence had achieved anything, he'd gotten Jayden's fingerprints on his private investigator's ID.

He decided to try Willow's apartment, knowing she was at the Bistro. He knocked and nobody answered. He looked around and didn't see anyone. He tried the door and it was locked. That wasn't a deterrent to the PI; he jimmied the lock and was in. He didn't want to linger, so he took a quick look around, pocketed some souvenirs, and got out.

Next stop, the following morning, was Sea Dunes Concierge Realty. Carrie had informed him that the owner was a lady named Sharna. He entered the office and went up to the desk in the reception room. A name plaque on the desk identified her as Whitney.

"Well, Miss Whitney, I've been on the Outer Banks all my life and never had the pleasure of crossing roads with you. Why is that?"

Whitney turned red and just shrugged her shoulders.

"Surely you're the boss here?"

"Oh no, that would be Miss Curry."

"Yeah, but we know the lady in front knows everything going on. I'm Spence Midgett. I'm investigating the murder of one of your employees."

"That was awful. Terrible. Phoebe was a doll."

"Somebody didn't like her. Any ideas?"

"Oh God, no. Her customers loved her. Everybody here got along. Maybe you better talk to Miss Curry. I'll see if she can see you."

Whitney went to Curry's office, said something, and gestured for Spence to come in. After making introductions, she said, "Please have a seat, and call me Sharna."

"What can you tell me about Miss Razario- who liked her, who didn't?"

"Well, I pretty much told the police everything I know."

"I understand. But I'm working for the person accused of the crime and need to get a feel for what Miss Razario was like."

"She was our most productive agent. Her clients would always request her if they came back and always had good things to say about her. One thing that was odd, something I didn't know much about, but the police told me, was that some of her clients were being blackmailed. Including your client, I understand. Maybe he thought she was shaking him down?"

"Do you think she was shaking him down?"

"No. But it was strange that the blackmail victims were all her clients. But Phoebe made really good money here. Had a boyfriend, always seemed happy."

"She was sleeping with my client."

"What! No, no, no. That can't be true."

"Don't think he'd lie about that. Did she sleep with her other clients?"

"No, she had a- I mean, she had a boyfriend."

"It all happened in the house my client was renting. Think it could have been a murder–suicide?"

"How would I know? I didn't know her boyfriend. How would I know?" Sharna started crying and Spence decided he gone far enough with her.

"If you think of anything, here's my card. My client didn't do it and I need to find out who did."

75

Carrie and Graham met with their jury expert, who Rockford approved hiring. He listened to Carrie outline the case and give a profile of Rockford, his profession, and why he was in North Carolina. He advised that the lawyers look for three things in a juror. First, the understanding that Rockford would not throw away his life on some overnight affair with a girl. Second, that he didn't care about being blackmailed, clearly demonstrating that he could care less if the information of him having an affair got out. Finally, being open-minded enough to consider that a murder-suicide was what happened.

Dare County's courtrooms were located on the second floor of the Justice Center. They were modern and had sophisticated recording equipment. Carrie Woodbridge and Graham Michaelson sat at the table on the right side of the courtroom and their client, Pierce Rockford, was escorted in and led to their table. He looked exhausted and scared. Carrie patted him on the back and said, "We're here to pick the jury that's going to find you not guilty. Just sit here, look the potential jurors in the eye, and look interested. Graham and I have hired a jury consultant who's told us what to look for. Everything will be OK." Rockford appreciated the optimism but didn't share it.

Carrie had Michaelson conduct the voir dire. He was a commanding figure in the courtroom. Tall, distinguished, well spoken, the potential jury members were focused on his every word. He started out with an interesting question. "Please give me a show of hands, who of you would walk into a casino and risk everything– your home, your car, every nickel you have– on a turn of one card? Three people raised their hands, and Michaelson asked them to be excused. Carrie and Graham were going to make a point that Rockford had the world to live for, so why would he throw it away? They wanted jurors who could understand that. The next question was, "If you rented a car and someone stole it, would you physically harm that person?" One person, somewhat with embarrassment, raised his hand. That person was also excused. Michaelson knew that Rockford didn't give a shit about being blackmailed. Then he asked who among them thought that it was possible that someone in addition to Lee Harvey Oswald had shot John F. Kennedy. About half of the hands were raised, and those were the ones Michaelson wanted. Those who had an open mind. At the end of the day the jury was selected. Graham and Carrie were pleased with the final group.

On trial day one, it was time for the Assistant District Attorney, Ann Hamlin, to make her opening statement. Hamlin was a tall, overweight, grumpy-looking person who did not dress for success. She was arrogant and had an attitude that oozed "listen to what I have to say, don't listen to anybody else." The judge asked her if she was ready to proceed and she answered, "Absolutely, your Honor."

She walked toward the jury, notes in hand. This courtroom had no lectern. She held her hand toward Rockford and started by saying, "He looks innocent enough, the defendant, doesn't he? Rich, well heeled, harmless. But no. Not when his lover has been a fake. Not when a woman seduced him and set him up for blackmail. No, this is a successful man, not a man used to finishing in second place. Not a man used to being deceived and tricked. Let's look at what happened. Pierce Rockford rented a cottage in Rodanthe for a few years from Sea Dunes Concierge Realty. The agent he dealt with was Phoebe Razario, the woman we will show, whom he shot. Razario's boyfriend, Cody Delaney, hatched a scheme where he would use a drone and take incriminating photos of Razario's clients to blackmail them. Rockford didn't have a local girlfriend, so how could they blackmail him? So Razario decided to be the seductress herself. Rockford, with his CEO ego, fell for it. He thought he had a special thing with Razario. He was in love. So on the morning of the eleventh, Delaney shows up to shake Rockford down. Mr. Rockford was getting it on with this guy's girlfriend. And, in addition, Delaney tries to blackmail Rockford and he blows him off. Delaney comes to confront him. He gets there and, lo and behold, there's Miss Razario's car in the driveway. Now Delaney's ready to do some damage. The door's unlocked, so he comes in and comes at Rockford like a maniac. Rockford grabs his gun. Delaney tells Rockford that he's a sap; Miss Razario was in on the blackmail scheme. Rockford's hurt and really, really mad. He gets his gun and threatens Delaney with going to the cops. Razario rushes him and *bang,* one dead lady. Delaney, overcome with hate, then comes at Rockford, and he too gets a bullet.

"Ladies and gentlemen, we have the gun, it's his gun. Rockford's fingerprints are on the gun. We have motive. We have no eyewitnesses who can offer a different story. You will not hear any evidence that anyone else was in the house. The man is guilty of two murders. Perhaps Razario and Delaney weren't model citizens. Perhaps they should have been arrested. But they can't be now, they are dead.

"Don't be fooled by the defense lawyers. They will come up with some story. But keep in mind that there's no reasonable doubt here. A scorned man lost it. And there he sits. Thank you."

Hamlin looked at the defendant's table, smirked, and took her seat.

The judge said, "Miss Woodbridge?"

Now it was Carrie Woodbridge's turn. Dressed in her usual bright colors, she leaped up from her table, a picture of boundless energy, and she started. "Wow, that was quite a story! And well performed, I would say. My client must be a real scumbag, don't you think? No, he's not a scumbag, or a murderer. Their evidence is, shall I say, like this feather." She held up a large feather and let it float to the ground.

"Light and fluffy, not much to it. Did she tell you there were other prints on the murder weapon? Do you remember hearing that part? Oh, nobody? Of course my client's prints were on the weapon– he owns the gun. Did she tell you that that there were no powder burns on his hands? You all missed that too. Maybe he asked the two victims to wait a moment for him to put some gloves on so he could shoot them. Or maybe they think he held the gun with his mouth and pulled the trigger with his tongue."

Every member of the jury, the judge, and most of the courtroom chuckled.

"Miss Hamlin said there's no reasonable doubt here. She's right, there isn't. They threw a case together based on nothing. No doubt about that. Their case is as empty as a bowl in a dog pound. The police didn't want to waste their time investigating. They had their man."

Carrie walked away from the jury and then turned around to add, "The wrong man."

ADA Hamlin introduced her first witness, detective Clint Heaton.

Heaton testified how he'd arrived at the scene shortly after the crime had been committed, explaining that he had just found evidence that the male victim was likely blackmailing Rockford. He described what he discovered when he entered the house and that a gun was laying on the floor nearby. He testified that the gun was owned by Mr. Rockford. He also stated that there was no evidence that anyone else had been in the house.

In cross-examination Carrie started by saying, "Good morning, detective. I need you to be more specific on some details. Did you know the victim, Miss Razario- when she was alive, of course?"

"Yes."

"How did that come about?"

"Someone had blackmailed two of her other clients, clients of her real estate firm. She was concerned."

"Other than not being a fan of blackmail, why was she concerned?"

"Because she was the real estate agent for both of them. That seemed like an odd coincidence to her and to me. I think she may have been worried about her job."

"So it turns out that the likely blackmailer was her live-in boyfriend, is that what you determined?"

"We discovered evidence that directly pointed to him."

"Did you uncover any evidence that Miss Razario knew this?"

"Well, no. I had just determined the evidence against her boyfriend and went to the house that was to be the crime scene, so I did not have a chance to confront her."

"In your previous conversations with Miss Razario, did you get any indication that she knew that her boyfriend was the blackmailer, if he indeed was?"

"No."

"Since she wanted to get you involved, isn't that an indication that she didn't know?"

Hamlin said, "Objection, your Honor. Calls for a conclusion."

The judge said, "I'll allow it. Detective, please answer the question."

Heaton said, "I would assume she didn't know."

"OK, what about the weapon that Mr. Rockford owned? Was it the murder weapon?"

"The ballistics report confirmed that it was the murder weapon."

"You testified that Mr. Rockford's prints were on the weapon. Wouldn't that be likely if he owned the gun?"

"Yes, I guess so."

"Were there other prints on the gun?"

"Yes."

"Oh my, someone else held the murder weapon. Whose prints?"

"We haven't been able to determine that."

"Did you try?"

"The prints weren't in our database."

"When you entered the house in question, you testified that Mr. Rockford was in the bathroom vomiting, is that correct?"

"Yes."

"Is that what most of your murderers do when they shot someone?"

"Actually, this is the first case that I am the head detective."

"We're not surprised. So, did my client admit to you that he fired the gun?"

"No."

"Did he say if he was there when the shots were fired?"

"He said he drove over to the marina and came back to find the bodies."

"Did he indicate if he talked to anyone at the marina?"

"Yes."

"And. . .come on, detective, you know what I'll ask next. Did you find anyone who talked to my client?"

"Yes, a few people."

"Well, thank you. Fishing information out of you is harder than surf casting."

The judge said, "Miss Woodbridge, enough."

"Yes, your Honor. So my client produced an alibi, which you verified. Case closed."

"Not exactly. The marina was close by, so Mr. Rockford easily could have gotten back. They don't have any security cameras that are time coded."

"But they do have security cameras?"

"Yes."

"And my client was seen on them?"

"Yes."

"This detective work must be interesting, huh, Detective? Could you tell by anyone's memory or from shadows or anything else when my client was there?"

"No, not really."

"Did you find anything that was purchased at the marina in the house?"

"Yes, a couple of muffins."

"Where did you find them?"

"On the living room floor, in a plastic bag."

"Interesting place to leave the groceries. Is it possible my client dropped it when he was shocked to see the dead bodies?"

"Well, it's possible, but we think. . ."

"You answered my question. Did my client indicate that this was awful?"

"Yes."

"Did my client deny that the weapon was his?"

"No. He said it looked like his gun."

"Did my client admit to knowing the female victim?"

"Yes, it was his new girlfriend."

"Did my client admit to knowing the male victim?"

"No."

"Did my client try to run out of the house?"

"No."

"So, Detective, you have my client's fingerprints on a gun that he happens to own and nothing– nothing else?"

Before he could answer, Carrie said, "No worries, Detective, I think the jury knows the answer."

Hamlin called the coroner, the CSI chief investigator, and Sharna Curry (Phoebe's boss at the realty company). Michaelson did the crosses but didn't labor on any of them. During the final cross of the day, Carrie's phone vibrated. It was a message from Spence Midgett. He said that he had important information and they needed to meet ASAP.

It was the second day of testimony and the prosecution rested. The judge asked, "Miss Woodbridge, are you ready to call witnesses?"

"Your Honor, my witnesses are not available. I would like to move to continue tomorrow."

"Miss Hamlin?"

She said with a sneer, "If it's necessary."

"OK, tomorrow, ten sharp."

ichaelson immediately called Spence to ask what was so important. Midgett simply said, "I've got a 'not guilty' for you."

"We'll be back in my office in half an hour. Meet us there."

Carrie said to Graham, "What's he got?"

"Apparently a bottle of champagne!"

Midgett was waiting for the trio in Michaelson's conference room, feet up on the table, vaping a cloud of smoke.

Carrie said, "You know that stuff is bad for you."

"Clears my mind."

Graham chipped in, "OK, savior of trails, what do you have?"

"Enough for reasonable doubt. In fact, maybe a dismissal of charges."

They had planned on putting Spence on as their first witness, but first they recalled Detective Heaton. He was pleased.

Carrie said, "As I'm sure you know, you are still under oath. One question, exactly: When did the crime occur, as best as could be told?"

"We were lucky to get there quickly. We believe between nine thirty and nine forty in the morning."

"Pretty sure?"

"Yes, pretty sure."

"That's all for the Detective, your Honor. I call Spencer Midgett."

After Spencer was sworn in, Carrie started.

"Mr. Midgett, you are a professional investigator, a private eye, licensed in this county, are you not?"

"Yes."

"Been doing this sleuthing stuff for a while?"

"Yes, eight years."

"And did my client hire you for this case?"

"Well, no, actually Mr. Michaelson did."

"Stand corrected. Per your duties from Mr. Michaelson, you did an independent investigation, is that correct?"

"Yes ma'am."

"Did you talk to any of the people living nearby the house where the bodies were found?"

"Yes."

"What did you learn?"

"Not much. One lady two houses north heard a woman yelling, but that was it. Nobody saw anybody just before or just after the crime was committed, until the detective rolled in."

"The detective, Mr. Heaton, testified that people at the marina remembered seeing my client. Do you have any information as to when that was?"

"Yes. I interviewed a few people who saw him there or talked to him. Also, more significantly, Mr. Rockford's credit card was charged twice at the marina, once for fish bait and then for two muffins and a cup of coffee. The first charge was recorded at nine oh eight and the second charge was recorded at nine fifty-one that morning."

Carrie walked over near the jury. "Again, when were the charges recorded?"

"Nine oh eight and nine fifty-one."

"And did you time how long it would take my client to go from the marina check-out to the house in question?"

"Assuming he left immediately and drove and no traffic slowed him down, five minutes and twenty seconds to the front door of the house."

"Nothing like precision. So, is it correct that the earliest that he could have arrived at the scene was, let me do the math, nine fifty-seven?"

"That's how I calculated it."

"So the only way he could have committed the alleged crimes would be if he went to the marina to buy bait, drove back, did the dirty deed, then calmly went back to the marina to buy the muffins and coffee, and then drove back, is that how you see it?"

"Yes, but he didn't do that. I talked to three people who said he was there the entire time. He never left and came back."

Hamlin said, "Your Honor, objection. Clearly hearsay."

"Sustained."

Carrie said, "No worries, we'll be calling one of them. Now, back to you, Mr. Midgett. What else did you learn during your exhaustive investigation?"

"Two things that are really significant. First, I found security camera footage from a rental house that, in the distance, showed the entrance of the house where the bodies were found."

"Can you show us that footage?"

"You bet." Carrie clicked a couple of buttons on a remote and a TV screen came to life.

"The house is the middle one in the picture. Note that the recording is time-stamped at the bottom. I verified that the timing mechanism was accurate. As you can see, a blond woman walks to the house, climbs the outside steps, and knocks on the door. Someone opens the door, as you can see, a few words are exchanged, and she pushes her way in and the door is shut. She enters at nine twenty-three. The same woman then hurriedly exits the house at nine thirty-six and runs down the steps and runs out of the picture. I was able to blow up a view when she faced the camera, which is what you see now."

"So this woman was in the house during the time that the detective said that the couple was killed?"

"Yes."

"Well, good work, Mr. Midgett. Any idea who she is?"

"Yes. Up on the screen are the photo we just saw and another I took at a different location. You can see a strong resemblance."

"Yes, like me looking at myself in a mirror. OK, save us the suspense, who is your mystery woman?"

"Willow Peters, a bartender at the Atlantic Bistro."

"So why was Miss Peters there?"

"Don't know, but the rumors had it that the male decedent and Peters were in a relationship."

Hamlin said, "Objection, calls for speculation."

"Overruled; he said 'rumors.'"

"So maybe she caught Miss Razario together with Mr. Delaney after Delaney told Peters that his relationship with Razario was over?"

Hamlin said, "Your Honor?"

Carrie said, "Withdrawn. Is there any other evidence that Miss Peters was involved in this crime?"

"Yes. I was able to get Miss Peter's fingerprints. I sent them to the SBI to compare with any of the prints on the murder weapon. They matched."

There was silence in the courtroom, and Carrie stood in front of the witness box to let the words sink in.

"A definite match?"

"Yes."

"Your Honor, I'd like to present the SBI report as defense exhibit two."

"Let me see it. OK, Madame Clerk."

"Mister Midgett, you're pretty good. No further questions."

Carrie called, as promised, a witness from the marina, but the verdict was no longer in question. The closing arguments were quick. Hamlin did her best, but she was sailing into the wind. The judge gave the jury its instructions, detailing the definition of reasonable doubt.

The jury stayed out for two hours and then the forewoman notified the bailiff that a verdict had been reached. The slip handed to the judge recorded a unanimous verdict: not guilty. Upon exiting the courtroom, after hugs from Carrie and handshakes from Michaelson, Carrie sought out Heaton and said, "Better find Miss Peters before the word gets out!"

Epilogue

Willow Peters was arrested for the dual murders of Phoebe Razario and Cody Delaney. In her trial, her lawyer pleaded not guilty due to self-defense. Willow actually testified that she was attacked when she went to the house. She claimed that she just saw a gun lying there, she grabbed it, and shot both Phoebe and Cody. The jury didn't buy it, and she is now serving years in the penitentiary.

Jayden ransacked Phoebe's and Cody's rental house and found their stashes of money. He thought he hit the mother lode. However, he used the money he stole to feed his drug habit and soon overdosed.

Roanna Roselli continued in therapy for her PTSD and depression. She never found happiness in any relationship. She became a political activist supporting sexually abused women. Roanna's dad, Anthony, was hired as a head football coach. He had several very successful seasons with a small school that had never had football success. He retired due to health reasons. Roanna's mom, Joan, went back to work at Johnson Travers and remained in charge of the office for years. Their other two children, Josh and Penny, both graduated from college and had their own families.

Pierce Rockford returned to his CEO position at Armondson, Inc. The attacks on the company had not dissipated and Rockford's life had been severely shaken. He decided that life was too short and retired within three months. He purchased a small house on the North Carolina coast, and a nice fishing boat and never had a long-term girlfriend again.

Senator Richard Curtis Wilson, by his second term, was the nation's leading advocate for victims' rights.

Sharna Curry, owner of Sea Dunes Concierge Realty, and Detective Clint Heaton continue to be happily married. Twelve years older than Clint, didn't make her a cougar.

Carrie Woodbridge returned to her Raleigh law practice and focused on pro bono work, attacking the sex trafficking trade.

Preston Kerrigan continued his pro football career, but his continued unfaithfulness led to an early divorce.

Harrison Shane was convicted of multiple rapes and was sentenced to serve time, perhaps the rest of his life, behind bars.

The murder of Chump Change officially became a cold case.

Kassie, Cody's dilapidated jeep, was purchased by another surfer dude and continued to carry surfboards to the beach. Along with Kassie, the surfer dude adopted Cody's dog, Reef, who faithfully sat on the beach waiting for his new master to come in from his wave-riding.